A BOOK OF

DIFFERENTIAL EQUATIONS

Mathematics Paper - IV

For

B.Sc. Part - I : Semester - II

According to New Revised Syllabus of
Shivaji University, Kolhapur, w.e.f. June 2013

S. R. BHOSALE
M. Sc., M. Phil.
Associate Professor and Head
Department of Mathematics
P. D. V. P. College, Tasgaon, Dist. Sangli
(Ex. Chairman. B. O. S. in Maths
Shivaji University Kolhapur]

Dr. H. T. DINDE
M. Sc. Ph. D.
Associate Professor and Head
Department of Mathematics
K. B. P. College, Islampur, Dist. Sangli
[Chairman. B. O. S. in Maths
Shivaji University Kolhapur]

NIRALI PRAKASHAN
ADVANCEMENT OF KNOWLEDGE

B.Sc. PART - I : SEM. - II : DIFFERENTIAL EQUATIONS (MATHEMATICS PAPER - IV)
Second Edition : January 2016   **ISBN : 978-93-83971-02-2**
©   : **Authors**

Published By :
NIRALI PRAKASHAN
Abhyudaya Pragati, 1312 Shivaji Nagar,
Off J.M. Road, Pune – 411005,
Phone : 25512336/37/39   Fax : (020) 25511379
Email : niralipune@pragationline.com

DISTRIBUTION CENTERS

PUNE
Nirali Prakashan
119, Budhwar Peth, Jogeshwari Mandir Lane,
Pune - 411002, Maharashtra.
Tel : (020) 24452044, 66022708;
Fax : (020) 2445 1538
Email : niralilocal@pragationline.com

Nirali Prakashan
S. No. 28/27, Dhayari,
Near Pari Company, Pune - 411 041,
Tel - (020) 24690204
Email : dhayari@pragationline.com
bookorder@pragationline.com

MUMBAI
Nirali Prakashan
385, S.V.P. Road, Rasdhara Co-op. Hsg. Society, Girgaum, **Mumbai -** 400004,
Maharashtra
Tel : (022) 2385 6339 / 2386 9976, Fax : (022) 2386 9976
Email : niralimumbai@pragationline.com

RETAIL SHOPS

PUNE
Pragati Book Centre
157, Budhwar Peth, Opp. Ratan Talkies,
Pune – 411002, Maharashtra
Tel : 2445 8887 / 6602 2707

Pragati Book Centre
676/B, Budhwar Peth,
Opp. Jogeshwari Mandir,
Pune – 411002, Maharashtra
Tel. : (020) 6601 7784, 2445 2254

PUNE
Pragati Book Centre
Amber Chamber, 28/A, Budhwar Peth,
Appa Balwant Chowk
Pune : 411002, Maharashtra
Tel : (020) 20240335 / 66281669
Email : pbcpune@pragationline.com

Pragati Book Centre
152, Budhwar Peth,
Near Jogeshwari Mandir,
Pune – 411002, Maharashtra
Tel : (020) 6609 2463 / 2445 2254

MUMBAI
Pragati Book Corner
Indira Niwas, 111-A Bhavani Shankar Road,
Dadar (W), **Mumbai** – 400028
Tel : (022) 2422 3525 / 6662 5254
Email : pbcmumbai@pragationline.com

DISTRIBUTION BRANCHES

NAGPUR
Pratibha Book Distributors
Above Maratha Mandir, Shop No. 3, First Floor, Rani Zanshi Square, Sitabuldi,
Nagpur 440012, Maharashtra, Tel : (0712) 254 7129
JALGAON
34, V. V. Golani Market, Navi Peth, Jalgaon 425001, Maharashtra,
Tel : (0257) 222 0395, Mob : 94234 91860
KOLHAPUR
New Mahadvar Road, Kedar Plaza, 1st Floor Opp. IDBI Bank
Kolhapur 416 012, Maharashtra. Mob : 9855046155

www.pragationline.com   info@pragationline.com

PREFACE

We are very pleased to present the first edition of the book : Paper IV, Differential Equations, for B.Sc. Part I, Semester II.

This book is written according to the revised syllabus of Shivaji University, Kolhapur with effect from June 2013.

We have explained all elementary principles and fundamental concepts of mathematics in a simple and lucid language. The worked out examples are very numerous, fully solved and well graded. In exercise also we have included variety of problems.

In this book, we have included the questions and examples asked in the examinations of Shivaji University Kolhapur from April 2011 onwards.

Also, we have included the objective questions with answers and one model question paper which will be benefited to the students.

This book is also useful for the B.Sc. I students of Solapur University also.

We are thankful to Mr. D. K. Furia and Mr. Jignesh Furia, who took the responsibility to publish this book. We are grateful to Mr. M. P. Munde, Mrs. Anagha Kaware and Mrs. Sunita Rajendra Patil for the co-operation they have extended to us. We express thanks to the staff of Nirali Prakashan who availed this book in short time. We are thankful to our colleagues, friends and well-wishers who supported directly or indirectly to publish this book. Finally our families too deserve the special thanks for their support, encouragement and tolerance.

We are also thankful to Mr. Virdhwal Shinde, Mr. Sanjay Bhopale-Patil (Marketing Executive, Kolhapur) and Mr. Ashok Nanavare (Marketing Executive, Sangali) for the promotion of this Book.

We request our colleagues, teaching Mathematics to offer their criticisms and suggestions, for further improvement in the book.

Authors

Prof. S. R. Bhosale and Dr. H. T. Dinde

Syllabus

Unit 1 : Differential Equations of First Order and First Degree   **[10 L]**
1.1 : Introduction
1.2 : Exact differential equations
     1.2.1 Necessary and sufficient condition for exactness
1.3 : Integration factors with Rules
1.4 : Linear Equation $\dfrac{dy}{dx} + Py = Q$

1.5 : Bernoulli's Equation $\dfrac{dy}{dx} + Py = Qy^n$

1.6 : Orthogonal Trajectories
     1.6.1 Definition of trajectory of the given family.
     1.6.2 Definition of orthogonal trajectory.
     1.6.3 Rule for finding the orthogonal trajectory to a given family of curves when its equation is given in (1) Cartesian (2) Polar co-ordinates.
     1.6.4 Examples

Unit 2 : Linear Differential Equations with Constant Coefficients f (D) y = X   **[18 L]**
2.1 : Introduction f (D) y = X
2.2 : General (Complete) Solution of f (D) y = X
2.3 : Solution of f (D) y = 0
2.4 : Solution of Auxiliary equation with real and non-repeated roots
2.5 : Solution of Auxiliary equation with real and repeated roots
2.6 : Solution of Auxiliary equation with imaginary (non-repeated and repeated roots).
2.7 : Solution of (D) y = X, where X is of the form
     2.7.1 e^{ax}, a is constant   2.7.2   sin (ax) and cos (ax)
     2.7.3 x^m, m is positive integer
     2.7.4 e^{ax}, V, V is a function of x
     2.7.5 xV, V is a function of x

Unit 3 : Equations of First Order but not of First Degree   **[6 L]**
3.1 : Equations that can be factorized
     3.1.1 Equations solvable for p
3.2 : Equations that cannot be factorized
     3.2.1 Equations solvable for x.   3.2.2   Equations solvable for y.

Unit 4 : Clairaut's Equation   **[6 L]**
4.1 : Clairaut's form
4.2 : Method of solution
4.3 : Equations reducible to Clairaut's form.
4.4 : Special forms reducible to Clairaut's form.

Contents

DIFFERENTIAL EQUATIONS OF FIRST ORDER AND FIRST DEGREE

1.1 INTRODUCTION

Differential equation is an applicable branch of Mathematics. It has played significant role in fields of Physics, Chemistry, Biology, Economics, Psychology, Sociology and Engineering etc.

1.1.1 (i) Differential Equation

A differential equation is an equation which involves differential coefficients and differentials.

The following are examples of differentials equations :

(i) $\dfrac{dy}{dx} + 3x = 0$

(ii) $\dfrac{dy}{dx} + 3y = 5e^x$

(iii) $\dfrac{d^2y}{dx^2} + \cos x = 0$

(iv) $\dfrac{dy}{dx} = \dfrac{1+x}{1-x}$

(v) $\dfrac{dy}{dx} = \sin(x+y)$

1.1.2 (ii) Types of Differential equations

1. Ordinary Differential Equations.
2. Partial Differential Equations.

1.1.3 (iii) Ordinary Differential Equations

An equation which involves only one independent variable and differential coefficients with respect to it, is called Ordinary Differential Equation.

Above differential equations (i) to (v) are ordinary differential equations.

1.1.4 (iv) Partial Differential Equation

An equation which involves more than one independent variables and partial differential coefficients w.r.t. them, is called partial differential equation.

For example 1. $x\dfrac{\partial z}{\partial x} + y\dfrac{\partial z}{\partial y} = z$

2. $\dfrac{\partial z}{\partial x} + \dfrac{\partial z}{\partial y} = 1$

are partial differential equations with two independent variables x and y and z as dependent variable.

1.1.5 (v) Order of the differential equation

The order of the differential equation is the order of the highest differential coefficients occurring in the differential equation.

For example

1.   The order of the differential equation $\dfrac{dy}{dx} + 3y = x$ is one

2.   The order of the differential equation $\dfrac{d^2y}{dx^2} + 2y = \log x$ is two

1.1.6 (vi) Degree of the differential equation

The degree of the differential equation is the degree of the highest order derivative occurring in it, when the differential coefficients are free from radicals and fractions.

1.   The degree of the differential equation $\dfrac{dy}{dx} + 5x = 0$ is one

2.   The degree of the differential equation

$$\left(\dfrac{dy}{dx}\right)^2 + 2\dfrac{dy}{dx} = x \text{ is two}$$

1.1.7 (vii) Solution of the Differential Equation

The solution of the differential equation is a relation between the variables involved in the differential equation, which satisfies given differential equation.

Types of Solutions :

(a) General Solution : The general solution of the differential equation is that solution in which the number of arbitrary = constants is equal to the order of the differential equation.

The general solution is also known as complete solution or compete integral or complete primitive.

(b) Particular Solution : The particular solution of the differential equation is that solution which is obtained by giving particular values to the arbitrary = constants, in general solution.

(c) Singular Solution : A singular solution of the differential equation is the solution, which does not contain any arbitrary = constants and also it is not obtained from the complete solution by giving particular values to arbitrary = constants.

1.1.8 (viii) Ordinary differential equation of first order and first degree

The standard form of the first order and first degree differential equation is $M \, dx + N \, dy = 0$ ... (1)

Where M and N are constants or functions of x and y only.

The above form (1) also can be written as

$$\frac{dy}{dx} = f(x, y) \qquad \qquad \text{... (2)}$$

or $$\frac{dx}{dy} = g(x, y) \qquad \qquad \text{... (3)}$$

We discuss the following types of the differential equations and methods of solving it.

1. Exact differential equations
2. Linear differential equation
3. Bernoulli's equation.

1.2 EXACT DIFFERENTIAL EQUATION

The equation $M \, dx + N \, dy = 0$ where M, N are functions of x, y is said to be **Exact differential equation.** if $M \, dx + N \, dy = du$ where u is function of x and y such that $\frac{\partial u}{\partial x} \, dx + \frac{\partial u}{\partial y} \, dy = du$

Illustration : 1. Consider the differential equation

$$x \, dy + y \, dx = 0 \qquad \qquad \text{... (1)}$$

We know that

$$d(xy) = \frac{\partial}{\partial x} [xy] \, dx + \frac{\partial}{\partial y} [xy] \, dy$$

$$d(xy) = y \, dx + x \, dy$$

$$d(xy) = x \, dy + y \, dx \qquad \qquad \text{... (2)}$$

Using equation (2) equation (1) becomes

$$d\,(xy) \;=\; 0 \qquad\qquad \text{... (3)}$$

Integrating we get

$$xy \;=\; c \qquad\qquad \text{... (4)}$$

Where c is an arbitrary = constant.

Thus general solution of equation $x\,dy + y\,dx = 0$ is $xy = c$

From equation (2) we say that the differential equation

$$x\,dy + y\,dx \;=\; 0 \qquad \text{is an exact differential equation.}$$

Thus we also define Exact differential equation as follows.

An exact differential equation is one which is derived from its general solution directly by differentiating without any subsequent elimination, multiplication etc.

2.   We have

$$y^2\,dx + 2\,xy\,dy \;=\; d\,(xy^2)$$

Therefore $y^2\,dx + 2xy\,dy = 0$ is an exact differential equation.

3.   As $3\,x^2\,y^2\,dx + 2x^3\,y\,dy \;=\; d\,(x^3\,y^2)$

Hence $3x^2\,y^2\,dx + 2x^3\,y\,dy \;=\; 0$ is an exact differential equation.

4.   As $\dfrac{y\,dx - x\,dy}{y^2} \;=\; d\,(x/y)$

Hence $\dfrac{y\,dx - x\,dy}{y^2} \;=\; 0$ is an exact differential equation.

1.3 NECESSARY AND SUFFICIENT CONDITION FOR EXACTNESS   (April 2012, 2013, Nov. 2012)

Theorem : The necessary and sufficient condition for the differential equation of first order and first degree $M\,dx + N\,dy = 0$ to be exact is that $\dfrac{\partial M}{\partial y} = \dfrac{\partial N}{\partial x}$, where M and N are functions of x and y.

Proof :

I.   Necessary Part :

First we assume that the differential equation $M\,dx + N\,dy = 0$ is exact and Prove that $\dfrac{\partial M}{\partial y} = \dfrac{\partial N}{\partial x}$

Suppose that, the equation

$$M\,dx + N\,dy \;=\; 0 \qquad\qquad \text{... (1) be exact.}$$

Then by definition of exact differential equation

We write $\qquad$ M dx + N dy = du $\qquad$ ... (2)

where u is a function of x and y

and $\qquad$ $du = \dfrac{\partial u}{\partial x}\,dx + \dfrac{\partial u}{\partial y}\,dy$ $\qquad$ ... (3)

From equations (2) and (3) we get

$$M\,dx + N\,dy = \dfrac{\partial u}{\partial x}\,dx + \dfrac{\partial u}{\partial y}\,dy \qquad ... (4)$$

Equating the coefficients of dx and dy.

$$M = \dfrac{\partial u}{\partial x} \qquad\qquad ... (5)$$

$$N = \dfrac{\partial u}{\partial y} \qquad\qquad ... (6)$$

To remaining the unknown function u (x, y) we differentiate equation (5) and (6) partially w. r. t. y and x respectively.

$$\dfrac{\partial M}{\partial y} = \dfrac{\partial^2 u}{\partial y\,\partial x} \qquad\qquad ... (7)$$

and $\qquad$ $\dfrac{\partial N}{\partial x} = \dfrac{\partial^2 u}{\partial x\,\partial y} \qquad\qquad$ ... (8)

Using $\qquad$ $\dfrac{\partial^2 u}{\partial y\,\partial x} = \dfrac{\partial^2 u}{\partial x\,\partial y}$ we get

$$\boxed{\dfrac{\partial^2 M}{\partial y} = \dfrac{\partial N}{\partial x}}$$

which is the necessary condition for exactness.

Sufficiency Part :

> We assume that $\dfrac{\partial M}{\partial y} = \dfrac{\partial N}{\partial x}$
> and prove that M dx + N dy = 0 is an exact differential equation

Let $\qquad$ $\displaystyle\int M\,dx = u$ $\qquad$ ... (1)

where the integral has been performed treating y as constant

differentiating partially w.r.t. x we get

$$M = \dfrac{\partial u}{\partial x} \qquad\qquad ... (2)$$

differentiating partially w.r.t. y

$$\frac{\partial M}{\partial y} = \frac{\partial^2 u}{\partial y\, \partial x} \qquad \qquad \text{... (3)}$$

but $\qquad \frac{\partial M}{\partial y} = \frac{\partial N}{\partial x} \qquad \qquad$ and $\frac{\partial^2 u}{\partial y\, \partial x} = \frac{\partial^2 u}{\partial x\, \partial y}$

Then $\qquad \frac{\partial N}{\partial x} = \frac{\partial^2 u}{\partial x \partial y} \qquad \qquad \text{... (4)}$

$$\frac{\partial N}{\partial x} = \frac{\partial}{\partial x}\left[\frac{\partial u}{\partial y}\right]$$

integrating both sides w. r. t. x, considering y as constant we get

$$N = \frac{\partial u}{\partial y} + \text{function of y}$$

$$N = \frac{\partial u}{\partial y} + f(y) \qquad \qquad \text{... (5)}$$

where f (y) is a function of y only.

We have

$$M\, dx + N\, dy = \frac{\partial u}{\partial x}\, dx + \left[\frac{\partial u}{\partial y} + f(y)\right] dy$$

$$M\, dx + N\, dy = \left[\frac{\partial u}{\partial x}\, dx + \frac{\partial u}{\partial y}\, dy\right] + f(y)\, dy$$

$$M\, dx + N\, dy = du + f(y)\, dy$$

$$M\, dx + N\, dy = du + d\left[\int f(u)\, dy\right]$$

$$M\, dx + N\, dy = d\left[u + \int f(u)\, dy\right]$$

Let $\qquad \qquad v = u + \int f(u)\, du$

$\therefore \qquad \qquad M\, dx + N\, dy = dv \qquad \qquad \text{... (6)}$

It says that M dx + N dy = 0 is an exact differential equation.

Solution of Exact differential equation :

Suppose that the equation M dx + N dy = 0 is exact.

Then $\qquad M\, dx + N\, dy = d\left[u + \int f(y)\, dy\right] \qquad \qquad \text{... (1)}$

integrating both sides, we get

$$u + \int f(u)\, dy = c \qquad \qquad \text{... (2)}$$

but $\qquad u = \int M \, dx \qquad$ ... (3) where y is constant

and $\qquad \int f(y) \, dy = $ Integral of terms in N, not containg x

... (4)

Then equation (4) becomes

$$\int_{y = \text{constant}} M \, dx + \int \begin{bmatrix} \text{terms in N} \\ \text{not containing x} \end{bmatrix} dy = c \qquad ...(5)$$

$\qquad\qquad\qquad\qquad\qquad$ where c is an arbitrary = constant,

This is the solution of an exact differential equation M d + N dy = 0.

Working rule for solving Exact differential equation :

1. Compare the given differential equation with equation

$$M \, dx + N \, dy = 0 \text{ and}$$

calculate the values of M and N

2. Calculate $\dfrac{\partial M}{\partial y}$ and $\dfrac{\partial N}{\partial x}$

3. If $\dfrac{\partial M}{\partial y} = \dfrac{\partial N}{\partial x}$ then we say that given equation is an exact differential equation.

Otherwise we say that it is not exact.

4. Then using following formula, solution is obtained.

$$\int_{y = \text{constant}} M \, dx + \int \begin{bmatrix} \text{Terms in N} \\ \text{not containing x} \end{bmatrix} dy = C$$

SOLVED EXAMPLES

Example 1.1 :

Solve [cos x tan y + cos (x + y)] dx + [sin x sec² y + cos (x + y) dy = 0

Solution : Given differential equation is

[cos x tan y + cos (x + y)] dx + [sin x sec^2 y + cos (x + y) dy = 0 ... (1)

Comparing with

$$M \, dx + N \, dy = 0 \qquad\qquad ... (2)$$

we get, $\qquad\qquad M = \cos x \tan y + \cos (x + y) \qquad ... (3)$

and $$N = \sin x \sec^2 y + \cos (x + y) \qquad \ldots (4)$$

Differentiating equation (3) and (4) respectively we get,

$$\frac{\partial M}{\partial y} = \cos x \cdot [\sec^2 y] - \sin (x + y) \qquad \ldots (5)$$

$$\frac{\partial N}{\partial x} = (\cos x) \sec^2 y - \sin (x + y) \qquad \ldots (6)$$

We have

$$\frac{\partial M}{\partial y} = \frac{\partial N}{\partial x} \qquad \ldots (7)$$

∴ Given differential equation is exact.

The solution is

$$\int_{y = \text{constant}} M \, dx + \int \left[\begin{array}{l} \text{Terms in N,} \\ \text{not containing x} \end{array} \right] dy = \text{Constant} \qquad \ldots (8)$$

i.e. $$\int_{y = \text{constant}} [\cos x \tan y + \cos (x + y)] \, dx + \int 0 \, dy = c$$

$$\tan y \int \cos x \, dx + \int \cos (x + y) \, dx = c$$

$$\tan y \sin x + \sin (x + y) = c$$

∴ $$\sin x \tan y + \sin (x + y) = c \qquad \ldots (9)$$

This is the solution of equation (1).

Example 1.2 : Solve [x² + y²+ 1] dx + 2xy dy = 0   **(April 2013)**

Solution : Given differential equation is

$$[x^2 + y^2 + 1] \, dx + 2xy \, dy = 0 \qquad \ldots (1)$$

Comparing with $$M \, dx + N \, dy = 0 \qquad \ldots (2)$$

$$M = x^2 + y^2 + 1 \quad \ldots (3) \text{ and } \quad N = 2xy \qquad \ldots (4)$$

$$\frac{\partial M}{\partial y} = 2x \qquad \ldots (5) \qquad \bigg| \qquad \therefore \frac{\partial N}{\partial x} = 2x \qquad \ldots (6)$$

From equation (5) and (6), we get $$\frac{\partial M}{\partial y} = \frac{\partial N}{\partial x} \qquad \ldots (7)$$

Therefore equation (1) is Exact.

The solution is

$$\int\limits_{y = constant} M \, dx + \int [\text{Terms in N, not containing } x] \, dy = \text{Constant}$$

$$\int\limits_{y = constant} (x^2 + y^2 + 1) \, dx = c'$$

$$\Rightarrow \qquad \left[\frac{x^3}{3} + 0 + x \right] = c'$$

$$\Rightarrow \qquad x^3 + 3x = 3c'$$

$$\boxed{x^3 + 3x = c} \qquad \qquad \dots (8)$$

This is the solution of equation (1).

Example 1.3 : Solve $(x^2 + y^2) \, dx + 2xy \, dy = 0$ **(April 2012)**

Solution : Given differential equation is

$$(x^2 + y^2) \, dx + 2xy \, dy = 0 \qquad \dots (1)$$

Comparing with $\qquad\qquad M \, dx + N \, dy = 0 \qquad \dots (2)$

$M = x^2 + y^2 \qquad \dots (3)$ and $\quad N = 2xy \qquad \dots (4)$

$\therefore \dfrac{\partial M}{\partial y} = 2 \qquad \dots (5) \qquad \Big| \qquad \therefore \dfrac{\partial N}{\partial x} = 2y \qquad \dots (6)$

From (5) and (6), we get $\dfrac{\partial M}{\partial y} = \dfrac{\partial N}{\partial x} \qquad \dots (7)$

Therefore equation (1) is Exact.

The solution is

$$\int\limits_{y = constant} M \, dx + \int [\text{Terms in N, not containing } x] \, dy = \text{Constant}$$

$$\int\limits_{y = constant} [x^2 + y^2] \, dx = c'$$

$$\Rightarrow \qquad \left[\frac{x^3}{3} + 0 \right] = c'$$

$$\Rightarrow \qquad x^3 = 3c'$$

$$\boxed{x^3 = c} \qquad \qquad \dots (8)$$

This is the solution of equation (1).

Example 1.4 : Solve $(e^y + 1) \cos x \, dx + e^y \sin x \, dy = 0$ **[May 2011]**

Solution : Given differential equation is

$$(e^y + 1) \cos x \, dx + e^y \sin x \, dy = 0 \qquad \qquad \dots (1)$$

Comparing with

$$M \, dx + N \, dy = 0 \qquad \qquad \dots (2)$$

we get

$$M = (e^y + 1) \cos x \qquad \dots (3) \text{ and } \quad N = e^y \sin x \qquad \dots (4)$$

$$\therefore \quad \frac{\partial M}{\partial y} = e^y \cos x \qquad \dots (5) \quad \bigg| \quad \therefore \quad \frac{\partial N}{\partial x} = e^y \cos x \qquad \dots (6)$$

We have

$$\frac{\partial M}{\partial y} = \frac{\partial N}{\partial x} \qquad \qquad \dots (7)$$

$\therefore$ Given differential equation is exact.

The solution is

$$\int_{y = \text{constant}} M \, dx + \int [\text{Terms in N, not containing } x] \, dy = \text{Constant} \dots (8)$$

$$\int_{y = \text{constant}} (e^y + 1) \cos x \, dx = c$$

$$\Rightarrow \qquad (e^y + 1) \int \cos x \, dx = c$$

$$\Rightarrow \qquad (e^y + 1) \sin x = c \qquad \qquad \dots (8)$$

This is the solution of equation (1)

Example 1.5 : Solve $[e^x \cos y - y \cos x] \, dx - [e^x \sin y + \sin x] \, dy = 0$

Solution : Given differential equation is

$$[e^x \cos y - y \cos x] \, dx - [e^x \sin y + \sin x) \, dy = 0 \qquad \dots (1)$$

Comparing with $M \, dx + N \, dy = 0$ \qquad \qquad \dots (2)

$$M = e^x \cos y - y \cos x \dots (3) \qquad \bigg| \qquad N = [e^x \sin y + \sin x] \dots (4)$$

$$\frac{\partial M}{\partial y} = e^x [- \sin y] - 1 \cdot \cos x \quad \bigg| \quad \text{Also} \frac{\partial N}{\partial x} = -[e^x \cdot \sin y + \cos x]$$

$$\qquad \qquad \qquad \qquad \qquad \qquad \qquad \qquad \dots (6)$$

$$\frac{\partial M}{\partial y} = -[e^x \sin y + \cos x] \dots (5)$$

From (5) and (6)

$$\frac{\partial M}{\partial y} = \frac{\partial N}{\partial x} \qquad ... (7)$$

Hence, the given differential equation is exact.

The Solution is

$$\int_{y \,=\, constant} M \, dx + \int \left[\text{Terms from N, free from x}\right] dy = c \qquad ... (8)$$

$$\int_{y \,=\, constant} \left[e^x \cos y - y \cos x\right] dx = c$$

$$\therefore \qquad \cos y \left[e^x\right] - y \left[\sin x\right] = c$$

$$e^x \cos y - y \sin x = c$$

This is the solution of equation (1).

Example 1.6 : Solve [sin x cos y + e²ˣ] dx + [cos x sin y + tan y] dy = 0
(October 2011)

Solution : Given differential equation is

$$[\sin x \cos y + e^{2x}] \, dx + [\cos x \sin y + \tan y] \, dy = 0 \qquad ... (1)$$

Comparing with

$$M \, dx + N \, dy = 0 \qquad ... (2)$$

We get

M = sin x cos y + e²ˣ ... (3)   and   N = cos x sin y + tan y ... (4)

$$\frac{\partial M}{\partial y} = \sin x \left[- \sin y\right] \qquad\qquad \frac{\partial N}{\partial x} = -\sin x \sin y \qquad ... (6)$$

$$\therefore \quad \frac{\partial M}{\partial y} = -\sin x \sin y \qquad ... (5)$$

We have

$$\frac{\partial M}{\partial y} = \frac{\partial N}{\partial x} \qquad ... (7)$$

∴   Given differential equation is exact.

The solution is

$$\int_{y \,=\, constant} M \, dx + \int \left[\text{Terms in N, not containing x}\right] dy = \text{Constant}$$

$$... (8)$$

$$\int (\sin x \cos y + e^{2x}] \, dx + \int \tan y \, dy = c_1$$

y = constant

$$[-\cos x] \cos y + \frac{e^{2x}}{2} + \log (\sec x) = c_1$$

Multiplying by 2

$-2 \cos x \cos y + e^{2x} + 2 \log \sec x = 2c_1 = c$ ... Using $2c_1 = c$ ... (9)

$\therefore \quad e^{2x} + 2 \log \sec x - 2 \cos x \cos y$

This is the solution.

Example 1.7 : Solve (ax + hy + 9) dx + (hx + by + f) dy = 0

Solution : Given differential equation is

$\quad (ax + hy + g) \, dx + (hx + by + f) \, dy = 0$ ... (1)

Comparing with

$$M \, dx + N \, dy = 0 \qquad \qquad ... (2)$$

$M = ax + hy + g$ ... (3)   and $N = hx + by + f$ ... (4)

$\dfrac{\partial M}{\partial y} = h$ ... (5) $\Big| \quad \dfrac{\partial N}{\partial x} = h$ ... (6)

We have

$$\frac{\partial M}{\partial y} = \frac{\partial N}{\partial x} \qquad \qquad ... (7)$$

$\therefore$ hence equation (1) is an exact differential equation.

The general solution is

$$\int M \, dx + \int [\text{terms of N free from x}] \, dy = \text{Constant} \quad ... (8)$$

y = constant

$\therefore \qquad \qquad \int [ax + hy + g] \, dx + \int (by + f) \, dy = c_1$

$$a\left[\frac{x^2}{2}\right] + hy \, x + g \cdot x + \frac{b \cdot y^2}{2} + fy = c_1$$

Multiplying by 2

$$ax^2 + 2hxy + 2gx + by^2 + 2fy = 2c_1$$

Let $\qquad \qquad \qquad \qquad \qquad \qquad 2c_1 = c$

$\qquad ax^2 + 2hxy + by^2 + 2gx + 2fy = c$ ... (9)

Where c is an arbitrary = constant.

Example 1.8 : Solve $(x^2 - ay) dx = (ax - y^2) dy$

Solution : Given differential equation is

$$(x^2 - ay) dx = (ax - y^2) dy \qquad \dots (1)$$

$$(x^2 - ay) dx = (ax - y^2 dy = 0$$

Comparing with

$$M dx + N dy = 0 \qquad \dots (2) \text{ we get}$$

$$M = x^2 - ay \qquad \dots (3) \text{ and} \qquad N = -(ax - y^2) \qquad \dots (4)$$

$$\frac{\partial M}{\partial y} = -a \qquad \dots (5) \qquad \frac{\partial N}{\partial x} = -a \qquad \dots (6)$$

We have

$$\frac{\partial M}{\partial y} = \frac{\partial N}{\partial x} \qquad \dots (7)$$

The given differential equation is exact.

The solution is

$$\int M dx + \int [\text{terms in N, not containing x}] dy = \text{Constant} \dots (8)$$

y = constant

$$\int_{y = \text{constant}} (x^2 - ay) dx + \int -(-y^2) dy = c_1$$

$$\int_{y = \text{constant}} (x^2 - ay) dx + \int y^2 dy = c_1$$

$$\therefore \qquad \frac{x^3}{3} - ay\, x + \frac{y^3}{3} = c_1$$

Multiplying by 3

$$x^3 - 3axy + y^3 = 3c_1$$

Put

$$3c_1 = c$$

$$x^3 - 3axy + y^3 = c \qquad \dots (9)$$

This is the solution.

Example 1.9 : $\sec^2 x \tan y\, dx + \sec^2 y + \tan x\, dy = 0$

Solution : Given differential equation is

$$\sec^2 x + \tan y\, dx + \sec^2 y \tan x\, dy = 0 \qquad \dots (1)$$

Comparing with

$$M dx + N dy = 0 \qquad \dots (2) \text{ we get}$$

$M = \sec^2 x \tan y$ ... (3) and S $N = \sec^2 y \cdot \tan x$ ... (4)

$\dfrac{\partial M}{\partial y} = \sec^2 x \, [\sec^2 y]$ ... (5) $\dfrac{\partial N}{\partial x} = \sec^2 \cdot y \, [\sec^2 x]$ ... (6)

We have

$$\dfrac{\partial M}{\partial y} = \dfrac{\partial N}{\partial x} \qquad \text{... (7)}$$

∴ Given differential equation is exact.

The solution is

$$\int\limits_{y=constant} M \, dx + \int [\text{terms in N, not containing x}] \, dy = \text{Constant}$$

... (8)

$$\int\limits_{y=constant} \sec^2 x \cdot \tan y \, dx + \int 0 \, dy = c$$

$$\tan y \int \sec^2 x \, dx + 0 = c$$

$$\tan y \cdot \tan x + 0 = c$$
$$\tan x \tan y = c \qquad \text{... (9)}$$

This is the solution.

Example 1.10 : Solve $(x^2 - 4xy - 2y^2) \, dx + (y^2 - 4xy - 2x^2) \, dy - 0$

Solution : Given differential equation is

$(x^2 - 4xy - 2y^2) \, dx + (y^2 - 4xy - 2x^2) \, dy = 0$ ... (1)

Comparing with

$$M \, dx + N \, dy = 0 \qquad \text{... (2)}$$

We get,

$M = x^2 - 4xy - 2y^2$ ... (3) and $N = y^2 - 4xy - 2x^2$ ... (4)

$\dfrac{\partial M}{\partial y} = -4x - 4y$ ... (5) $\dfrac{\partial N}{\partial x} = -4y - 4x$ ... (6)

We have

$$\dfrac{\partial M}{\partial y} = \dfrac{\partial N}{\partial x} \qquad \text{... (7)}$$

∴ Given differential equation is exact.

The solution is

$$\int\limits_{y=constant} M \, dx + \int [\text{terms in N, not containing x}] \, dy = \text{Constant ... (8)}$$

$$\int\limits_{y=constant} [x^2 - 4xy - 2y^2] \, dy + \int y^2 \, dy = c_1$$

$$\left[\frac{x^3}{3} - \frac{4x^2}{2} y - 2 y^2 \cdot x\right] + \frac{y^3}{3} = c_1$$

$$\frac{x^3}{3} - 2x^2y - 2y^2x + \frac{y^3}{3} = c_1$$

Multiplying by 3 we get

$$x^3 - 6x^2y - 6xy^2 + y^3 = 3c_1$$

Put

$$3c_1 = c$$

$$x^3 + y^3 - 6x^2y - 6xy^2 = c \qquad \dots (9)$$

This is the solution.

Example 1.11 : Solve

$[2xy + y - \tan y]\, dx + [x^2 - x \tan^2 y + \sec^2 y]\, dy = 0$

Solution : Given differential equation is

$$[2xy + y - \tan y]\, dx + [x^2 - x \tan^2 y + \sec^2 y]\, dy = 0 \qquad \dots (1)$$

Comparing with

$$M\, dx + N\, dy = 0 \qquad \dots (2) \text{ we get}$$

$M = 2xy + y - \tan y \ \dots (3)$ and $\quad N = x^2 - x\tan^2 y + \sec^2 y \dots (4)$

$\dfrac{\partial M}{\partial y} = 2x + 1 - \sec^2 y \qquad\qquad \dfrac{\partial N}{\partial x} = 2x - \tan^2 y \qquad \dots (6)$

$\qquad = 2x - [-1 + \sec^2 y]$

$\dfrac{\partial M}{\partial y} = 2x - \tan^2 y \qquad \dots (5)$

We have

$$\frac{\partial M}{\partial y} = \frac{\partial N}{\partial x} \qquad \dots (7)$$

$\therefore$ The given differential equation is exact.

The solution is

$$\int M\, dx + \int [\text{terms in N, not containing x}]\, dx = \text{Constant} \dots (8)$$

y = constant

$$\int [2xy + y - \tan y]\, dx + \int \sec^2 y\, dy = C$$

y = constant

$$\left[\frac{2x^2}{2} \cdot y + y \cdot x - (\tan y)\, x\right] + \tan y = C$$

$$x^2y + xy - x \tan y + \tan y = C \qquad \dots (9)$$

This is the solution.

Example 1.12 : $(x^2 - 2xy - y^2)\, dx - (x + y)^2\, dy = 0$

Solution : Given differential equation is

$$(x^2 - 2xy - y^2)\, dx - (x + y)^2\, dy = 0 \qquad \dots (1)$$

Comparing with

$$M\ dx + N\ dy\ =\ 0 \qquad \dots (2)$$

we get

$M\ =\ x^2 - 2xy - y^2 \qquad \dots (3)$ and $\qquad N\ =\ -(x+y)^2 \qquad \dots (4)$

$$\dfrac{\partial M}{\partial y}\ =\ -2x - 2y \qquad\qquad N\ =\ -[x^2 + 2xy + y^2]$$

$$\dfrac{\partial M}{\partial y}\ =\ -2\,[x+y] \qquad \dots (5) \qquad \dfrac{\partial N}{\partial x}\ =\ -[2x + 2y] \qquad \dots (6)$$

∴ We have

$$\dfrac{\partial M}{\partial y}\ =\ \dfrac{\partial N}{\partial x} \qquad \dots (7)$$

∴ The given differential equation is exact.

The solution is

$$\int_{y\,=\,constant} M\ dx + \int [\text{terms from N from x}]\ dy\ =\ \text{Constant} \qquad \dots (8)$$

$$\int_{y\,=\,constant} [x^2 - 2xy - y^2]\ dx + \int [-y^2]\ dy\ =\ c_1$$

$$\left[\dfrac{x^3}{3} - 2\dfrac{x^2}{2} \cdot y - y^2 x\right] - \dfrac{y^3}{3}\ =\ c_1$$

$$\left[\dfrac{x^3}{3} - x^2 y - xy^2\right] - \dfrac{y^3}{3}\ =\ c_1$$

Multiplying by 3

$$x^3 - 3x^2 y - 3xy^2 - y^3\ =\ 3c_1$$

Using $\qquad\qquad\qquad\qquad 3c_1\ =\ c$

$$x^3 - 3x^2 y - 3xy^2 - y^3\ =\ c \qquad \dots (9)$$

This is the solution.

EXERCISE 1.1

I. Theory Questions :

1. Define Exact differential equation.

2. State and prove the Necessary and sufficient condition for the differential equation $M\ dx + N\ dy = 0$ to be exact.

3. Explain the solution procedure for exact differential equation $M\ dx + N\ dy = 0$.

II. Solve the following differential equations.

1. $[\sec x + \tan x \tan y - e^x]\,dx + \sec x \sec^2 y\,dy = 0$

2. $y \sin 2x\,dx - (y^2 + \cos^2 x)\,dy = 0$

3. $[x^4 - 2xy^2 + y^2]\,dx - [2x^2y - 4xy^3 + \sin y]\,dy = 0$

4. $(2x - y)\,dx + (x + 2y - 5)\,dy = 0$

5. $(x^2 + 2xy^2)\,dx + (2x^2y + y^2)\,dy = 0$

6. $x\,dx + y\,dy = \dfrac{a^2\,(x\,dy - y\,dx)}{x^2 + y^2}$

7. $(2xy + y - \tan y)\,dx + (x^2 - x\tan^2 y + \sec^2 y)\,dy = 0$

8. $(x^2 + y^2 + e^x)\,dx + 2xy\,dy = 0$

9. $(x^2 - 2xy + 3y^2)\,dx + (4y^3 + 6xy - x^2)\,dy = 0$

10. $\left[y\left(1 + \dfrac{1}{x}\right) + \cos y\right]dx + [x\,(1 - \sin y) + \log x]\,dy = 0$

$$\boxed{\textbf{ANSWRES 1.1}}$$

1. $\sec x + \tan y - e^y = c$

2. $3y \cos 2x + 2y^3 + 3y = c$

3. $\dfrac{x^5}{5} - x^2 y^2 + xy^4 + \cos y = C$

4. $x^2 - xy - y^2 - 5y = c$

5. $x^3 + y^3 + 3x^2 y^2 = c$

6. $x^2y + xy - x\tan y + \tan y = c$

7. $x^2 + y^2 + 2a^2 \tan^{-1}(x/y) = c$

8. $\dfrac{x^3}{3} + xy^2 + e^x = c$

9. $\dfrac{x^3}{3} - x^2 y + 3xy^2 + y^4 = c$

10. $y\,(x + \log x) + x \cos y = c$

1.4 INTEGRATING FACTORS (I. F.)

If an equation of the form M dx + N dy = 0 is not exact, then it can be made exact by multiplying by some function of x and y, such a multiplier is called an **Integrating Factor.**

An equation may have more than one integrating factor.

Integrating Factors by Inspection : Some time integrating factors may be found by inspection, after regrouping the terms of the equation, by considering a particular group of terms, it makes an exact differential. For examples.

	Group of terms	Integrating factor	Exact differentials
1.	(a) $x\,dx + y\,dy$	$\dfrac{1}{x^2 + y^2}$	$\dfrac{x\,dx + y\,dy}{x^2 + y^2} = d\left[\dfrac{1}{2}\log(x^2 + y^2)\right]$
2.	(a) $x\,dy - y\,dx$	$\dfrac{1}{x^2}$	$\dfrac{x\,dx - y\,dy}{x^2} = d\left(\dfrac{y}{x}\right)$
	(b) $x\,dy - y\,dx$	$\dfrac{1}{xy}$	$\dfrac{dy}{y} - \dfrac{dx}{x} = d\left[\log\dfrac{y}{x}\right]$
	(c) $x\,dy - y\,dx$	$\dfrac{1}{x^2 + y^2}$	$\dfrac{x\,dy - y\,dx}{x^2 + y^2} = d\left[\tan^{-1}\dfrac{y}{x}\right]$
	(d) $x\,dy - y\,dx$	$\dfrac{1}{y^2}$	$-\left[\dfrac{y\,dx - x\,dy}{y^2}\right] = d\left[-\dfrac{x}{y}\right]$
3.	(a) $y\,dx - x\,dy$	$\dfrac{1}{x^2}$	$-\left[\dfrac{x\,dy - y\,dx}{x^2}\right] = d\left(-\dfrac{y}{x}\right)$
	(b) $y\,dx - x\,dy$	$\dfrac{1}{xy}$	$\dfrac{dx}{x} - \dfrac{dy}{y} = d\left[\log\dfrac{x}{y}\right]$
	(c) $y\,dx - x\,dy$	$\dfrac{1}{y^2}$	$\dfrac{y\,dx - x\,dy}{y^2} = d\left(\dfrac{x}{y}\right)$
	(d) $y\,dx - x\,dy$	$\dfrac{1}{x^2 + y^2}$	$\dfrac{y\,dx - x\,dy}{x^2 + y^2} = d\left[\tan^{-1}\dfrac{x}{y}\right]$
4.	(a) $x\,dy + y\,dx$	$\dfrac{1}{xy}$	$\dfrac{dy}{y} + \dfrac{dx}{x} = d\,[\log xy]$
	(b) $x\,dy + y\,dx$	1	$x\,dy + y\,dx = d\,(xy)$
	(c) $x\,dy + y\,dx$	$\dfrac{-1}{x^2 y^2}$	$-\left[\dfrac{x\,dy + y\,dx}{x^2 y^2}\right] = d\left[\dfrac{1}{xy}\right]$
5.	(a) $x\,dx - y\,dy$	$\left[\dfrac{1}{x^2 - y^2}\right]$	$\dfrac{x\,dx - y\,dy}{x^2 - y^2} = d\left[\dfrac{1}{2}\log(x^2 - y^2)\right]$
6.	$2xy\,dx - x^2\,dy$	$\dfrac{1}{y^2}$	$\dfrac{2xy\,dx - x^2\,dy}{y^2} = d\left(\dfrac{x^2}{y}\right)$
7.	$2xy\,dy - y^2\,dx$	$\dfrac{1}{x^2}$	$\dfrac{2xy\,dy - y^2\,dx}{x^2} = d\left(\dfrac{y^2}{x}\right)$
8.	$xy^2\,dx - y\,x^2\,dy$	$\dfrac{1}{y^4}$	$\dfrac{xy^2 dx - yx^2\,dy}{y^4} = \dfrac{1}{2}\,d\left(\dfrac{x^2}{y^2}\right)$
9.	$x^2 y\,dy - y^2\,x\,dx$	$\dfrac{1}{x^4}$	$\dfrac{x^2\,y\,dy - y^2\,x\,dx}{x^4} = \dfrac{1}{2}\,d\left(\dfrac{y^2}{x^2}\right)$

If an equation is not exact, then we make it exact by rearranging the terms and using the above formulae, and solve it by directly integrating.

SOLVED EXAMPLES

Example 1.13 : Solve the differential equation $y\,dx - x\,dy = 0$

Solution : Given differential equation is

$$y\,dx - x\,dy = 0 \qquad \ldots (1)$$

We have $\qquad M\,dx + N\,dy = 0 \qquad \ldots (2)$

Comparing we get

$$M = y \qquad \text{and} \qquad N = -x$$

$$\frac{\partial M}{\partial y} = 1 \qquad \text{and} \qquad \frac{\partial N}{\partial x} = -1$$

We observe that $\dfrac{\partial M}{\partial y} \neq \dfrac{\partial N}{\partial x}$

Hence equation (1) is not exact.

We make it exact by multiplying both sides by $\dfrac{1}{xy}$

$$\frac{y\,dx - x\,dy}{xy} = 0$$

$$\therefore \qquad \frac{1}{x}\,dx - \frac{1}{y}\,dy = 0$$

Integrating we get

$$\log x - \log y = \log c$$

$$\log (x/y) = \log c$$

$$\boxed{x/y = c} \qquad \ldots (3)$$

which is the solution of differential equation (1)

Example 1.14 : Solve $(y - 2x^2)\,dx - x\,(1 - xy)\,dy = 0$

Solution : Given differential equation is

$$(y - 2x^2)\,dx - x\,(1 - xy)\,dy = 0 \qquad \ldots (1)$$

$$y\,dx - 2x^2\,dx - x\,dy + x^2\,y\,dy = 0 \qquad \ldots (2)$$

$$[y\,dx - x\,dy] - 2x^2\,dx + x^2\,y\,dy = 0$$

$$[y\,dx - x\,dy] - x^2\,[2\,dx - y\,dy] = 0$$

Dividing by x^2 we get

$$\frac{y\,dx - x\,dy}{x^2} - [2\,dx - y\,dy] = 0 \qquad \ldots (2)$$

$$-\left[\frac{x\,dy - y\,dx}{x^2}\right] - [2\,dx - y\,dy] = 0$$

Changing minus sign we get

$$\therefore \quad \frac{x\,dy - y\,dx}{x^2} + 2\,dx - y\,dy = 0 \qquad \ldots (3)$$

We know that

$$d\left(\frac{y}{x}\right) = \frac{x\,dy - y\,dx}{x^2} \qquad \ldots (4)$$

Equation (3) becomes.

$$d\left(\frac{y}{x}\right) + 2\,dx - y\,dy = 0 \qquad \ldots (5)$$

Integrating

$$\frac{y}{x} + 2x - \frac{y^2}{2} = C \qquad \ldots (6)$$

This is solution.

Example 1.15 : $x\,dy - y\,dx = (x^2 + y^2)\,dx$

Solution : Given differential equation is

$$x\,dy - y\,dx = (x^2 + y^2)\,dx \qquad \ldots (1)$$

dividing throughout by $(x^2 + y^2)$

$$\frac{x\,dy - y\,dx}{x^2 + y^2} = dx \qquad \ldots (2)$$

We have

$$d\left[\tan^{-1}\frac{y}{x}\right] = \frac{1}{1 + y^2/x^2}\, d\left(\frac{y}{x}\right)$$

$$d\left[\tan^{-1}\frac{y}{x}\right] = \frac{1}{\left(\frac{x^2 + y^2}{x^2}\right)}\left[\frac{x\,dy - y\,dx}{x^2}\right]$$

$$d\left[\tan^{-1}\frac{y}{x}\right] = \frac{x\,dy - y\,dx}{x^2 + y^2} \qquad \ldots (3)$$

From equations (2) and (3)

$$d\left[\tan^{-1}\frac{y}{x}\right] = dx$$

Integrating we get

$$\tan^{-1}\left(\frac{y}{x}\right) = x + c \qquad \ldots (4)$$

It is a solution of equation (1)

Example 1.16 : x dx + y dy + (x² + y²) dy = 0

Solution : Given differential equation is

$$x\,dx + y\,dy + (x^2 + y^2)\,dy = 0 \qquad \text{... (1)}$$

Dividing by $(x^2 + y^2)$ we get

$$\frac{x\,dx + y\,dy}{x^2 + y^2} + dy = 0 \qquad \text{... (2)}$$

We know that

$$d\left[\frac{1}{2}\log(x^2 + y^2)\right] = \frac{1}{2}\left[\frac{1}{x^2 + y^2}[2x\,dx + 2y\,dy]\right]$$

$$= \frac{1}{2} \cdot \frac{2\,[x\,dx + y\,dy]}{(x^2 + y^2)}$$

$$d\left[\frac{1}{2}\log(x^2 + y^2)\right] = \frac{x\,dx + y\,dy}{x^2 + y^2} \qquad \text{... (3)}$$

Using equation (3) equation (2) becomes

$$d\left[\frac{1}{2}\log(x^2 + y^2)\right] + dy = 0$$

Integrating we get

$$\frac{1}{2}\log(x^2 + y^2) + y = C \qquad \text{... (4)}$$

This is the solution.

Example 1.17 : Solve x dy − y dx + 2x³ dx = 0

Solution : Given differential equation is

$$x\,dy - y\,dx + 2x^3\,dx = 0 \qquad \text{... (1)}$$

Dividing both sides by x^2

$$\frac{x\,dy - y\,dx}{x^2} + 2x\,dx = 0$$

$$\therefore \qquad d\left(\frac{y}{x}\right) + 2x\,dx = 0$$

Integrating we get

$$\frac{y}{x} + 2\left(\frac{x^2}{2}\right) = C$$

$$\frac{y}{x} + x^2 = C \qquad \text{... (2)}$$

This is the solution of equation (1).

Example 1.18 : Solve x dy − y dx = xy² dx

Solution : Given differential equation is

$$x\,dy - y\,dx = xy^2\,dx \qquad \text{... (1)}$$

$$\therefore \qquad \frac{x\,dy - y\,dx}{y^2} = x\,dx \qquad \ldots (2)$$

$$\therefore \qquad \frac{y\,dx - x\,dy}{y^2} = -x\,dx \qquad \ldots (3)$$

We have

$$d\left(\frac{x}{y}\right) = \frac{y\,dx - x\,dy}{y^2} \qquad \ldots (4)$$

Using equation (4) equation (3) becomes

$$d\left(\frac{x}{y}\right) = -x\,dx$$

Integrating

$$\frac{x}{y} = \frac{-x^2}{2} + C$$

$$\frac{x}{y} + \frac{x^2}{2} = C \qquad \ldots (4)$$

This is the solution of equation (1)

EXERCISE 1.2

I. Theory Question

1. Define Integrating Factor.

II. Method of Inspection

Solve the following differential equations.

1. $(1 + xy)\,y\,dx + (1 - xy)\,x\,dy = 0$

2. $y\,dx - x\,dy + \log x\,dx = 0$

3. $2xy\dfrac{dy}{dx} = y^2 - x$

4. $3x^2 y\,dx - (x^3 + y^3)\,dy = 0$

5. $x\,dy - y\,dx = 9(x^2 + y^2)\,dy$

6. $y(1 + x)\,dx + x(1 - y)\,dy = 0$

7. $(x^2 + y^2 + 1)\,dx - 2xy\,dy = 0$

8. $(xy^2 + y)\,dx - (x^2 y - x)\,dy = 0$

9. $y[2xy + e^x]\,dx - e^x\,dy = 0$

10. $(x^3 + y^3 - 3x)\,dx - 3y^2 x\,dy = 0$

$$\boxed{\textbf{ANSWRES 1.2}}$$

1. $-\dfrac{1}{xy} + \log \dfrac{x}{y} = c$

2. $y + \log x + 1 + cx = 0$

3. $\dfrac{y^2}{2} + \log x = c$

4. $\dfrac{x^3}{y} - y = c$

5. $\tan^{-1}(y/x) = 9y + c$

6. $xy = c^{y-}$

7. $x - \dfrac{1}{x} - \dfrac{y^2}{x} = C$

8. $\log\left(\dfrac{x}{y}\right) - \dfrac{1}{xy} = C$

9. $x^2 y + e^x = cy$

10. $2x^6 + 4x^3 y^3 + 9x^4 = C$

1.5 INTEGRATING FACTORS WITH RULES

Rule 1 : If the equation $M\,dx + N\,dy = 0$ is homogeneous in x and y then $\dfrac{1}{Mx + Ny}$ is an integrating factor of an equation provided that $Mx + Ny \neq 0$.

Proof : Given differential equation is $M\,dx + N\,dy = 0$ ... (1)

where M and N are homogeneous functions of the same degree say n, in variables x and y.

By Euler's Theorem, we have

$$x\dfrac{\partial M}{\partial x} + y\dfrac{\partial M}{\partial y} = n\,M \qquad \qquad \text{... (2)}$$

and

$$x\dfrac{\partial N}{\partial x} + y\dfrac{\partial N}{\partial y} = n\,N \qquad \qquad \text{... (3)}$$

Multiplying equation (1) by $\dfrac{1}{Mx + Ny}$ where $Mx + Ny \neq 0$,

We get

$$\dfrac{M}{Mx + Ny}\,dx + \dfrac{N}{Mx + Ny}\,dy = 0 \qquad \qquad \text{... (4)}$$

It will be exact differential equation if

$$\frac{\partial}{\partial y}\left[\frac{M}{Mx + Ny}\right] = \frac{\partial}{\partial x}\left[\frac{N}{Mx + Ny}\right]$$

Using Quotient rule

i.e.

$$\frac{[Mx + Ny]\frac{\partial M}{\partial y} - M\left[x\frac{\partial M}{\partial y} + \left(N + y\frac{\partial N}{\partial y}\right)\right]}{[Mx + Ny]^2}$$

$$= \frac{[Mx + Ny]\frac{\partial N}{\partial x} - N\left[\left(M + x\frac{\partial M}{\partial x}\right) + y\frac{\partial N}{\partial x}\right]}{[Mx + Ny]^2}$$

i.e.

$$Mx\frac{\partial M}{\partial y} + Ny\frac{\partial M}{\partial y} - Mx\frac{\partial M}{\partial y} - MN - My\frac{\partial N}{\partial y}$$

$$= Mx\frac{\partial N}{\partial x} + Ny\frac{\partial N}{\partial x} - NM - Nx\frac{\partial M}{\partial x} - Ny\frac{\partial N}{\partial x}$$

i.e.

$$Ny\frac{\partial M}{\partial y} - MN - My\frac{\partial N}{\partial y} = Mx\frac{\partial N}{\partial x} - MN - Nx\frac{\partial M}{\partial x}$$

i.e.

$$Ny\frac{\partial M}{\partial y} - M\frac{\partial N}{\partial y} = Mx\frac{\partial N}{\partial x} - Nx\frac{\partial M}{\partial x}$$

$$N\left[y\frac{\partial M}{\partial y}\right] + Nx\frac{\partial M}{\partial x} = Mx\frac{\partial N}{\partial x} + My\frac{\partial N}{\partial y}$$

$$N\left[y\frac{\partial M}{\partial y} - x\frac{\partial M}{\partial x}\right] = M\left[x\frac{\partial N}{\partial x} + y\frac{\partial N}{\partial y}\right] \qquad \ldots (5)$$

Using equations (2) and (3) we get

$$N[n\,M] = M[n\,N]$$
$$n\,MN = n\,MN \qquad \ldots (6)$$

Which is true. Hence $\frac{1}{Mx + Ny}$ where $Mx + Ny \neq 0$ is an integrating factor of homogeneous equation $M\,dx + N\,dy = 0$.

SOLVED EXAMPLES

Example 1.19 : Solve $(3xy^2 - y^3)\,dx - (2x^2y - xy^2)\,dy = 0$

Solution : Given differential equation is

$$(3xy^2 - y^3)\,dx - (2x^2y - xy^2)\,dy = 0 \qquad \ldots (1)$$

Comparing with

$$M\,dx + N\,dy = 0 \qquad \ldots (2)$$

$M = 3xy^2 - y^3$ and $N = -[2x^2y - xy^2]$

$\frac{\partial M}{\partial y} = 6xy - 3y^2$ $\qquad \frac{\partial N}{\partial x} = -[4xy - y^2]$

Here $$\frac{\partial M}{\partial y} \neq \frac{\partial N}{\partial x}$$

∴ equation (1) is not exact, but

1. M and N are homogeneous functions of degree three

2. $$- Mx + Ny = (3xy^2 - y^3) x + \{- (2x^2y - xy^2)\} y$$
$$Mx + Ny = 3x^2 y^2 - xy^3 - 2x^2 y^2 + xy^3$$
$$Mx + Ny = x^2 y^2 \neq 0$$

∴ $$I. F. = \frac{1}{Mx + Ny} = \frac{1}{x^2 y^2}$$

Multiplying equation (1) by I. F.

$$\frac{1}{x^2 y^2} \left[(3xy^2 - y^3) dx - (2x^2y - xy^2) dy\right] = 0$$

$$\left[\frac{3}{x} - \frac{y}{x^2}\right] dx - \frac{2}{y} - \frac{1}{x} dy = 0 \qquad \dots (3)$$

$$M = \frac{3}{x} - \frac{y}{x^2} \qquad \text{and} \qquad N = -\left[\frac{2}{y} - \frac{1}{x}\right] = \frac{-2}{y} + \frac{1}{x}$$

$$\frac{\partial M}{\partial y} = \frac{-1}{x^2} \qquad\qquad\qquad \frac{\partial N}{\partial x} = \frac{-1}{x^2}$$

∴ $$\frac{\partial M}{\partial y} = \frac{\partial N}{\partial x}$$

∴ equation (3) is exact.

Hence, solution is

$$\int_{y = constant} M \, dx + \int [\text{terms of N free from x}] \, dy = \text{Constant}$$

$$\int_{y = constant} \left[\frac{3}{x} - \frac{y}{x^2}\right] dx + \int \frac{-2}{y} dy = C$$

$$3 \log x + y \left(\frac{1}{x}\right) = -2 \log y = C$$

$$3 \log x + \frac{y}{x} - 2 \log y = C \qquad \dots (4)$$

This is the solution.

Example 1.20 : Solve $x^2 y \, dx - (x^3 + y^3) \, dy = 0$

Solution : Given differential equation is

$$x^2y \, dx - (x^3 + y^3) \, dy = 0 \qquad \dots (1)$$

Comparing with

$$M \, dx + N \, dy \; = \; 0 \qquad \qquad \text{... (2)}$$

$M \; = \; x^2 y \qquad$ and $\qquad\qquad\qquad N \; = \; -(x^3 + y^3)$

$\dfrac{\partial M}{\partial y} \; = \; x^2 \qquad\qquad\qquad\qquad\qquad \dfrac{\partial N}{\partial x} \; = \; -3x^2$

Here $\qquad\qquad\qquad\qquad\qquad \dfrac{\partial M}{\partial y} \; \neq \; \dfrac{\partial N}{\partial x}$

$\therefore$ equation (1) is not exact.

1.   M and N are homogeneous functions of third degree

2.
$$xM + yN \; = \; x(x^2 y) + y \, (-(x^3 + y^3)]$$
$$xM + yN \; = \; x^3 y - x^3 y - y^4 \qquad\qquad = -y^4 \neq 0$$

$$\text{I. F.} \; = \; \frac{1}{xM + yN} \; = \; \frac{-1}{y^4}$$

Multiplying equation (1) by I. F. we get

$$\frac{-1}{y^4} \left[x^2 y \, dx - (x^3 + y^3) \, dy \right] \; = \; 0$$

$$\frac{-x^2}{y^3} \, dx + \left(\frac{x^3}{y^4} + \frac{1}{y} \right) dy \; = \; 0 \qquad\qquad \text{... (3)}$$

Here

$M \; = \; \dfrac{-x^2}{y^3} \qquad\qquad$ and $\qquad\qquad N \; = \; \dfrac{x^3}{y^4} + \dfrac{1}{y}$

$\dfrac{\partial M}{\partial y} \; = \; -x^2 \, [-3y^{-4}] \qquad\qquad\qquad \dfrac{\partial N}{\partial x} \; = \; \dfrac{3x^2}{y^4}$

$\dfrac{\partial M}{\partial y} \; = \; \dfrac{3x^2}{y^4}$

Here $\qquad\qquad\qquad\qquad \dfrac{\partial M}{\partial y} \; = \; \dfrac{\partial N}{\partial x}$

$\therefore$ Equation (3) is exact.

Hence, the solution is

$$\int_{y \, = \, constant} M \, dx + \int \left[\text{terms of N free from x} \right] dy \; = \; 0$$

$$\int_{y \, = \, constant} \frac{-x^2}{y^3} \, dx + \int \frac{1}{y} \, dy \; = \; C$$

$\therefore \qquad\qquad\qquad\qquad\qquad \dfrac{-x^3}{3y^3} + \log y \; = \; C \qquad\qquad \text{... (4)}$

This is the solution.

Rule 2 : If the equation $M\,dx + N\,dy = 0$ is of the form $f_1(xy)\,y\,dx + f_2(xy)\,x\,dy = 0$ then $\dfrac{1}{Mx - Ny}$ is an integrating factor of the equation provided that $Mx - Ny \neq 0$.

Proof : The given differential equation is

$$M\,dx + N\,dy = 0 \qquad \qquad \text{... (1)}$$

i.e. $\qquad\qquad f_1(xy)\,y\,dx + f_2(xy)\,x\,dy = 0 \qquad\qquad \text{... (2)}$

Comparing, we have

$M \;=\; f_1(xy)\,y$ ... (3)　and　$\qquad\qquad N = f_2(xy)\,x \qquad\qquad \text{... (4)}$

We have

$$M\,dx + N\,dy = \frac{1}{2}\left[(Mx + Ny)\left[\frac{dx}{x} + \frac{dy}{y}\right] + (Mx - Ny)\left[\frac{dx}{x} - \frac{dy}{y}\right]\right]$$

$$M\,dx + N\,dy = \frac{1}{2}\left[(Mx + Ny)\cdot d(\log xy) + (Mx - Ny)\cdot d(\log x/y)\right]$$

dividing both sides by $Mx - Ny \neq 0$.

$$\frac{M\,dx + N\,dy}{Mx - Ny} = \frac{1}{2}\left[\frac{Mx + Ny}{Mx - Ny}\,d(\log xy) + d\{\log(x/y)\}\right]$$

Using values of M and N for RHS

$$\frac{M\,dx + N\,dy}{Mx - Ny} = \frac{1}{2}\left[\frac{f_1(xy)\,y\cdot x + f_2(xy)\,x\cdot y}{f_1(xy)\,y\cdot x - f_2(xy)\,x\cdot y}\,d(\log xy) + d(\log(x/y))\right]$$

...(5)

here $\dfrac{f_1(xy)\,xy + f_2(xy)\,xy}{f_1(xy)\,xy - f_2(xy)\,xy}$ is a function of xy, say $f(xy)$

$\therefore \qquad \dfrac{M\,dx + N\,dy}{Mx - Ny} = \dfrac{1}{2}\left[f(xy)\,d(\log xy) + d(\log x/y)\right] \qquad \text{... (6)}$

As $\qquad\qquad\qquad\qquad xy = e^{\log xy}$

$\therefore \qquad\qquad\qquad f(xy) = f[e^{\log xy}]$

$\qquad\qquad\qquad\qquad f(xy) = F[\log xy]$ ... Say

equation (6) becomes

$\dfrac{M\,dx + N\,dy}{Mx - Ny} = \dfrac{1}{2}\,F(\log xy)\,d(\log(xy)) + d[\log(x/y)] \qquad\qquad \text{... (7)}$

We observe that, it is an exact differential.

Therefore, $\dfrac{M\,dx + N\,dy}{Mx - Ny} = 0$ is an exact differential equation.

or $\dfrac{M}{Mx - Ny}\,dx + \dfrac{N}{Mx - Ny}\,dy = 0$ is an exact differential equation.

Hence, $\dfrac{1}{Mx - Ny} \neq 0$ is an integrating factor of differential equation $M\,dx + N\,dy = 0$.

SOLVED EXAMPLES

Example 1.21 : $(x^2 y^2 + xy + 1) y \, dx + (x^2 y^2 - xy + 1) x \, dy = 0$

Solution : Given differential equation is

$$(x^2 y^2 + xy + 1) y \, dx + (x^2 y^2 - xy + 1) x \, dy = 0 \qquad \dots (1)$$

It is of the form

$$f_1 (xy) \cdot y \, dx + f_2 (xy) \cdot x \, dy = 0 \qquad \dots (2)$$

i.e. $$M \, dx + N \, dy = 0 \qquad \dots (3)$$

$M = (x^2 y^2 + xy + 1) y$ and $\qquad N = (x^2 y^2 - xy + 1) x$

$M = x^2 y^3 + xy^2 + y \qquad\qquad N = x^3 y^2 - x^2 y + x$

$\dfrac{\partial M}{\partial y} = 2x^2 y^2 + 2xy + 1 \qquad\qquad \dfrac{\partial N}{\partial x} = 3x^2 y^2 - 2xy + 1$

Here $$\dfrac{\partial M}{\partial y} \neq \dfrac{\partial N}{\partial x}$$

$\therefore$ Equation (1) is not exact.

We have

$$Mx - Ny = [x^2 y^2 + xy + 1] yx - [x^2 y^2 - xy + 1] xy$$

$$Mx - Ny = x^3 y^3 + x^2 y^2 + xy - x^3 y^3 + x^2 y^2 - xy$$

$$Mx - Ny = 2x^2 y^2 \neq 0$$

$$\text{I. F.} = \frac{1}{Mx - Ny} = \frac{1}{2x^2 y^2}$$

Multiplying equation (1) by I. F. we get

$$\frac{1}{2x^2 y^2} [x^2 y^2 + xy + 1] y dx + \frac{1}{2x^2 y^2} [x^2 y^2 - xy + 1] x \, dy = 0$$

$$\left[\frac{1}{2} + \frac{1}{2xy} + \frac{1}{2x^2 y^2} \right] y \, dx + \left[\frac{1}{2} - \frac{1}{2xy} + \frac{1}{2x^2 y^2} \right] x \, dy = 0$$

Multiplying by 2

$$\left[y + \frac{1}{x} + \frac{1}{x^2 y} \right] dx + \left[x - \frac{1}{y} + \frac{1}{xy^2} \right] dy = 0 \qquad \dots (4)$$

$M = y + \dfrac{1}{x} + \dfrac{1}{x^2 y} \qquad\qquad N = x - \dfrac{1}{y} + \dfrac{1}{xy^2}$

$\dfrac{\partial M}{\partial y} = 1 - \dfrac{1}{x^2 y^2} \qquad\qquad \dfrac{\partial N}{\partial x} = 1 - \dfrac{1}{x^2 y^2}$

Here, $\dfrac{\partial M}{\partial y} = \dfrac{\partial N}{\partial x}$

$\therefore$ Equation (4) is exact.

Hence, the solution is

$$\int_{y=\text{constant}} M\,dx + \int [\text{terms of N free from x}]\,dy = \text{constant}$$

$$\int_{y=\text{constant}} \left[y + \frac{1}{x} + \frac{1}{x^2 y}\right] dx + \int \left[-\frac{1}{y}\right] dy = C$$

$$yx + \log x + \frac{1}{y}\left(-\frac{1}{x}\right) - \log y = C$$

$$xy + \log x - \frac{1}{xy} - \log y = C$$

$$xy - \frac{1}{xy} + \log\left(\frac{x}{y}\right) = C \qquad \ldots (5)$$

This is the solution.

Example 1.22 : Solve $(xy^2 + 2x^3 y^3)\,dx + (x^2 y - x^3 y^2)\,dy = 0$

Solution : The differential equation is

$$(xy^2 + 2x^2 y^3)\,dx + (x^2 y - x^3 y^2)\,dy = 0 \qquad \ldots (1)$$

Comparing with

$$M\,dx + N\,dy = 0 \qquad \ldots (2)$$

$$M = xy^2 + 2x^3 y^3 \qquad \text{and} \qquad N = x^2 y - x^3 y^2$$

$$\frac{\partial M}{\partial y} = 2xy + 6x^2 y^2 \qquad\qquad \frac{\partial N}{\partial x} = 2xy - 3x^2 y^2$$

Here

$$\frac{\partial M}{\partial y} \neq \frac{\partial N}{\partial x}$$

∴   Equation (1) is not exact.

Equation (1) can be written as

$$[xy + 2x^2 y^2]\, y\, dx + [xy - x^2 y^2]\, x\, dy = 0 \qquad \ldots (2)$$

It is of the form

$$y\, f_1(xy)\, dx + x\, f_2(xy)\, dy = 0 \qquad \ldots (3)$$

We have

$$Mx - Ny = [xy + 2x^2 y^2]\, yx - [xy - x^2 y^2]\, xy$$
$$Mx - Ny = x^2 y^2 + 2x^3 y^3 - x^2 y^2 + x^3 y^3$$
$$Mx - Ny = 3x^3 y^3 \neq 0$$

$$\text{I. F.} = \frac{1}{Mx - Ny} = \frac{1}{3x^3 y^3}$$

Multiplying equation (1) by I. F. we get

$$\frac{1}{3x^3 y^3}\, [xy^2 + 2x^2 y^3]\, dx + \frac{1}{3x^3 y^3}\, [x^2 y - x^3 y^2]\, dy = 0$$

$$\left[\frac{1}{3x^2y} + \frac{2}{3x}\right] dx + \left[\frac{1}{3xy^2} + \frac{1}{3y}\right] dy = 0 \quad \ldots (4)$$

$$M = \frac{1}{3x^2y} + \frac{2}{3x} \qquad \text{and} \qquad N = \frac{1}{3xy^2} - \frac{1}{3y}$$

$$\frac{\partial M}{\partial y} = \frac{1}{3x^2y^2} \qquad\qquad \frac{\partial N}{\partial x} = \frac{-1}{3x^2y^2}$$

Here $\qquad \dfrac{\partial M}{\partial y} = \dfrac{\partial N}{\partial x}$

∴ Equation (4) is exact.

Hence, the solution is

$$\int_{y = \text{constant}} M \, dx + \int [\text{terms of N free from x}] \, dy = \text{constant}$$

$$\int_{y = \text{constant}} \left[\frac{1}{3x^2y} + \frac{2}{3x}\right] dx + \int + -\left(\frac{1}{3y}\right) dy = C_1$$

$$\frac{1}{3y} \int \frac{1}{x^2} dx + \frac{2}{3} \int \frac{1}{x} dx - \frac{1}{3} \int \frac{1}{y} dy = C_1$$

$$\frac{1}{3y} - \left(\frac{1}{x}\right) + \frac{2}{3} \log x - \frac{1}{3} \log y = C_1$$

$$-\frac{1}{3xy} + \frac{2}{3} \log x - \frac{1}{3} \log y = C_1$$

Multiplying by 3

$$-\frac{1}{xy} + 2 \log x - \log y = 3C_1$$

$$-\frac{1}{xy} + \log x^2 - \log y = C$$

$$-\frac{1}{xy} + \log \left(\frac{x^2}{y}\right) = C$$

$$\log \left(\frac{x^2}{y}\right) - \frac{1}{xy} = C \qquad\qquad \ldots (5)$$

This is the solution.

Rule 3 : If in the equation M dx + N dy = 0,

$\dfrac{\dfrac{\partial M}{\partial y} - \dfrac{\partial N}{\partial x}}{N}$ is a function of x only, say f (x) then $e^{\int f(x) \, dx}$, is an integrating factor of the equation,

$$M \, dx + N \, dy = 0$$

Proof : The given differential equation is

$$M \, dx + N \, dy = 0 \qquad\qquad \ldots (1)$$

Multiplying equation (1) by $e^{\int f(x)\,dx}$, we get

$$M \cdot e^{\int f(x)\,dx} \cdot dx + N \cdot e^{\int f(x)\,dx} dy = 0 \qquad \text{...(2)}$$

It will be exact if

$$\frac{\partial}{\partial y}\left[M \cdot e^{\int f(x)\,dx}\right] = \frac{\partial}{\partial x}\left[N \cdot e^{\int f(x)\,dx}\right]$$

or $\qquad e^{\int f(x)\,dx} \cdot \dfrac{\partial M}{\partial y} = \left[e^{\int f(x)\,dx} \cdot f(x)\right] + e^{\int f(x)\,dx} \cdot \dfrac{\partial N}{\partial x}$

Cancelling $e^{\int f(x)\,dx}$ from both sides we get

$$\frac{\partial M}{\partial y} = N \cdot f(x) + \frac{\partial N}{\partial x}$$

i.e. $\qquad \dfrac{\partial M}{\partial y} - \dfrac{\partial N}{\partial x} = N f(x)$

i.e. If $\qquad \dfrac{\dfrac{\partial M}{\partial y} - \dfrac{\partial N}{\partial x}}{N} = f(x) \qquad \text{... (3)}$

Thus if $e^{\int f(x)\,dx}$ is an integrating function of $M\,dx + N\,dy = 0$

then $\qquad \dfrac{\dfrac{\partial M}{\partial y} - \dfrac{\partial N}{\partial x}}{N} = f(x)$

SOLVED EXAMPLES

Example 1.23 : Solve $(x^2 + y^2)\,dx - 2xy\,dy = 0$

Solution : Given differential equation is

$$(x^2 + y^2)\,dx - 2xy\,dy = 0 \qquad \text{... (1)}$$

Comparing with

$$M\,dx + N\,dy = 0 \qquad \text{... (2)}$$

$M = x^2 + y^2 \qquad\qquad$ and $\qquad\qquad N = -2xy$

$\dfrac{\partial M}{\partial y} = 2y \qquad\qquad\qquad\qquad\qquad \dfrac{\partial N}{\partial x} = -2y$

Here $\qquad\qquad \dfrac{\partial M}{\partial y} \neq \dfrac{\partial N}{\partial x} \therefore$ equation (1) is not exact.

We have,

$$\therefore \quad \frac{\left[\dfrac{\partial M}{\partial y} - \dfrac{\partial N}{\partial x}\right]}{N} = \frac{1}{-2xy}[2y + 2y] = \frac{4y}{-2xy} = \frac{-2}{x} = f(x)$$

It is a function of x only.

$$\text{I. F.} = e^{\int f(x)\, dx} = e^{\int \frac{-2}{x} dx}$$

$$\text{I. F.} = e^{-2\log x}$$

$$\text{I. F.} = e^{\log x^{-2}}$$

$$\text{I. F.} = \frac{1}{x^2}$$

Multiplying equation (1) by I. F.

$$\frac{1}{x^2}(x^2 + y^2)\, dx - \frac{1}{x^2} \cdot 2xy\, dy = 0$$

$$\left[1 + \frac{y^2}{x^2}\right] dx - \frac{2y}{x}\, dy = 0$$

$$1\, dx + \frac{y^2}{x^2}\, dx \frac{-2y}{x}\, dy = 0$$

$$dx + \left[\frac{y^2\, dx - 2xy\, dy}{x^2}\right] = 0$$

$$dx - \left[\frac{x\,(2y)\, dy - y^2\, dy}{x^2}\right] = 0$$

$$dx - d\left(\frac{y^2}{x}\right) = 0$$

Integrating

$$x - \frac{y^2}{x} = C$$

$$x^2 - y^2 = xc \qquad \qquad \dots (3)$$

This is the solution.

Example 1.24 : Solve $\left(y + \dfrac{y^3}{3} + \dfrac{x^2}{2}\right) dx + \dfrac{1}{4}(x + xy^2)\, dy = 0$

Solution : The given differential equation is

$$\left(y + \frac{y^3}{3} + \frac{x^2}{2}\right) dx + \frac{1}{4}(x + xy^2)\, dy = 0 \qquad \dots (1)$$

Comparing with $\qquad \qquad M\, dx + N\, dy = 0 \qquad \qquad \dots (2)$

$$M = y + \frac{y^3}{3} + \frac{x^2}{2} \qquad \text{and} \qquad N = \frac{1}{4}(x + xy^2)$$

$$\frac{\partial M}{\partial y} = 1 + \frac{1}{3} \cdot 3y^2 \qquad\qquad \frac{\partial N}{\partial x} = \frac{1}{4}(1 + y^2)$$

$$\frac{\partial M}{\partial y} = 1 + y^2$$

Here $\quad \dfrac{\partial M}{\partial y} \neq \dfrac{\partial N}{\partial x}$

∴   Equation (1) is not exact.

We have

$$\therefore \quad \frac{\left[\dfrac{\partial M}{\partial y} - \dfrac{\partial N}{\partial x}\right]}{N} = \frac{(1 + y^2) - \dfrac{1}{4}(1 + y^2)}{\dfrac{1}{4}(x + xy^2)} = \frac{\dfrac{3}{4}(1 + y^2)}{\dfrac{1}{4}x(1 + y^2)} = \frac{3}{x} = f(x)$$

It is a function of x only.

$$\text{I. F.} = e^{\int f(x)\,dx} = e^{\int \frac{3}{x}\,dx} = e^{3\log x} = e^{\log x^3} = x^3$$

Multiplying equation (1) by x^3, we get

$$x^3 \left[y + \frac{y^3}{3} + \frac{x^2}{2} \right] dx + \frac{x^3}{4} [x + xy^2]\,dy = 0$$

$$\left[x^3 y + \frac{1}{3} x^3 y^3 + \frac{1}{2} x^5 \right] dx + \frac{1}{4} [x^4 + x^4 y^2]\,dy = 0 \qquad\qquad \ldots (3)$$

Here

$$M = x^3 y + \frac{1}{3} x^3 y^3 + \frac{1}{2} x^5 \qquad\qquad N = \frac{1}{4}[x^4 + x^4 y^2]$$

$$\frac{\partial M}{\partial y} = x^3 + \frac{1}{3}(3x^3 y^2) \qquad\qquad \frac{\partial N}{\partial x} = \frac{1}{4}[4x^3 + 4x^3 y^2]$$

$$\frac{\partial M}{\partial y} = x^3 + x^3 y^2 \qquad\qquad \frac{\partial N}{\partial x} = x^3 + x^3 y^2$$

$$\therefore \qquad\qquad \frac{\partial M}{\partial y} = \frac{\partial N}{\partial x}$$

∴   Equation (3) is exact.

Hence, the solution is

$$\int M\,dx + \int [\text{terms in N free from x}]\,dy = \text{constant}$$

y = constant

$$\int \left[x^3\,y + \frac{1}{3} x^2\,y^2 + \frac{1}{2} x^5 \right] dx + \int dy = C$$

Multiply by 12

$$\frac{x^4}{4} + \frac{1}{3}\left(\frac{x^4}{4}\right)y^2 + \frac{1}{2}\frac{x^6}{6} = C$$

$$\Rightarrow \qquad 3x^4 y + x^4 y^2 + x^6 = C$$

Rule 4 : If in the equation M dx + N dy = 0,

$\dfrac{\left[\dfrac{\partial N}{\partial x} - \dfrac{\partial M}{\partial y}\right]}{M}$ is a function of y only, say f (y) then $e^{\int f(y)\,dy}$ is an

integrating factor of the equation M dx + N dy = 0.

Proof : The given differential equation is

$$M\,dx + N\,dy = 0 \qquad\qquad \dots (1)$$

Multiply equation (1) by $e^{\int f(y)\,dy}$

$$M \cdot e^{\int f(y)\,dy}\,dx + N \cdot e^{\int f(y)\,dy}\,dy = 0 \qquad\qquad \dots (2)$$

It will exact if

$$\frac{\partial}{\partial y}\left[M\,e^{\int f(y)\,dy}\right] = \frac{\partial}{\partial x}\left[N \cdot e^{\int f(y)\,dy}\right]$$

$$M\left[e^{\int f(y)\,dy} \cdot f(y)\right] + e^{\int f(y)\,dy}\frac{\partial M}{\partial y} = e^{\int f(y)\,dy}\frac{\partial N}{\partial x}$$

Cancelling $e^{\int f(y)\,dy}$ from both sides, we get

$$M \cdot f(y) + \frac{\partial M}{\partial y} = \frac{\partial N}{\partial x}$$

$$M\,f(y) = \frac{\partial N}{\partial x} - \frac{\partial M}{\partial y}$$

i.e.
$$\frac{\dfrac{\partial N}{\partial x} - \dfrac{\partial M}{\partial y}}{M} = f(y) \qquad\qquad \dots (3)$$

Thus if $e^{\int f(y)\,dy}$ is an integrating factor of M dx + N dy = 0

then $\dfrac{\dfrac{\partial N}{\partial x} - \dfrac{\partial M}{\partial y}}{M} = f(y) \qquad\qquad \dots (4)$

Example 1.25 : $(y^4 + 2y)\,dx + (xy^3 + 2y^4 - 4x)\,dy = 0$

Solution : Given differential equation is

$$(y^4 + 2y)\,dx + (xy^3 + 2y^4 - 4x)\,dy = 0 \qquad\qquad \dots (1)$$

Comparing with

$$M \, dx + N \, dy = 0 \qquad \qquad \dots (2)$$

$M = y^4 + 2y$ and $N = xy^3 + 2y^4 - 4x$

$\dfrac{\partial M}{\partial y} = 4y^3 + 2$ $\dfrac{\partial N}{\partial x} = y^3 - 4$

Here $\dfrac{\partial M}{\partial y} \neq \dfrac{\partial N}{\partial x}$

∴ equation (1) is not exact.

$$\dfrac{\left[\dfrac{\partial N}{\partial x} - \dfrac{\partial M}{\partial y}\right]}{M} = \dfrac{(y^3 - 4) - (4y^3 + 2)}{y^4 + 2y}$$

$$\dfrac{\left[\dfrac{\partial N}{\partial x} - \dfrac{\partial M}{\partial y}\right]}{M} = \dfrac{-3y^3 - 6}{y^4 + 2y}$$

$$\dfrac{\left[\dfrac{\partial N}{\partial x} - \dfrac{\partial M}{\partial y}\right]}{M} = \dfrac{-3\,[y^3 + 2]}{y\,[y^3 + 2]}$$

$$\dfrac{\dfrac{\partial N}{\partial x} - \dfrac{\partial M}{\partial y}}{M} = \dfrac{-3}{y} = f\,(y)$$

It is a function of y only.

I. F. $= e^{\int f\,(y)\,dy} = e^{\int \frac{-2}{y}\,dy} = e^{-3\log y} = e^{\log y^{-3}} = \dfrac{1}{y^3}$

Multiplying equation (1) by I. F.

$$\dfrac{1}{y^3}\,[y^4 + 2y]]\,dy + \dfrac{1}{y^3}\,[xy^3 + 2y^4 - 4x]\,dy = 0$$

$$\left[y + \dfrac{2}{y^2}\right]dy + \left(x + 2y - \dfrac{4x}{y^3}\right)dy = 0 \qquad \dots (3)$$

Here

$M = y + \dfrac{2}{y^2}$ $N = x + 2y - \dfrac{4x}{y^3}$

$\dfrac{\partial M}{\partial y} = 1 - \dfrac{4}{y^3}$ $\dfrac{\partial N}{\partial x} = 1 - \dfrac{4}{y^3}$

$\Rightarrow$ $\dfrac{\partial M}{\partial y} \neq \dfrac{\partial N}{\partial x}$

∴ equation (3) is exact.

Its solution is

$$\int_{y \,=\, \text{constant}} M \, dx + \int [\text{terms in N free from x}] \, dy = \text{Constant}$$

$$\int_{y \,=\, \text{constant}} \left[y + \frac{2}{y^2} \right] dx + \int 2y \, dy = C$$

$$\left(y + \frac{2}{y^2} \right) x + 2 \frac{y^2}{2} = C$$

$$\boxed{xy + \frac{2x}{y^2} + y^2 = C} \qquad \qquad \dots (4)$$

This is the solution.

Example 1.26 : $(xy^3 + y) \, dx + 2 \, (x^2 y^2 + x + y^4) \, dy = 0$

Solution : Given differential equation is

$$(xy^3 + y) \, dx + 2 \, (x^2 y^2 + x + y^4) \, dy = 0 \qquad \dots (1)$$

Comparing with

$$M \, dx + N \, dy = 0 \qquad \dots (2)$$

$$M = xy^3 + y \qquad\quad \text{and} \qquad N = 2 \, (x^2 y^2 + x + y^4)$$

$$\frac{\partial M}{\partial y} = 3xy^2 + 1 \qquad\qquad\qquad \frac{\partial N}{\partial x} = 2 \, [2xy^2 + 1]$$

$$\frac{\partial N}{\partial x} = 4xy^2 + 2$$

Here $\qquad \dfrac{\partial M}{\partial y} \neq \dfrac{\partial N}{\partial x} \qquad \therefore$ equation (1) is not exact

We have

$$\frac{\partial N}{\partial x} - \frac{\partial M}{\partial y} = (4xy^2 + 2) - (3xy^2 + 1)$$

$$\frac{\left[\dfrac{\partial N}{\partial x} - \dfrac{\partial M}{\partial y} \right]}{M} = \frac{1}{(xy^3 + y)} \, [xy^2 + 1]$$

$$\frac{\left[\dfrac{\partial N}{\partial x} - \dfrac{\partial M}{\partial y} \right]}{M} = \frac{(xy^2 + 1)}{y \, (xy^2 + 1)}$$

$$\frac{\left[\dfrac{\partial N}{\partial x} - \dfrac{\partial M}{\partial y} \right]}{M} = \frac{1}{y} = f \, (y)$$

It is a function of y only.

$$\text{I. F.} = e^{\int f \, (y) \, dy} = e^{\int \frac{1}{y} \, dy} = e^{\log y} = y$$

Multiplying equation (1) by I. F.

$$y [xy^3 + y] dx + 2y [x^2 y^2 + x + y^4] dy = 0$$
$$(xy^4 + y^2) dx + (2x^2 y^3 + 2xy + 2y^5) dy = 0$$

Rearranging the terms, we get

$$[xy^4 dx + 2x^2 y^3 dy] + [y^2 dx + 2 xy dy] + 2y^5 dy = 0$$

$$\frac{1}{2} [y^4 \cdot 2x + x^2 \cdot 4y^3] dy + [x \cdot 2y dy + y^2 dx) + 2y^5 dy$$

$$\frac{1}{2} d (y^4 x^2) + d (xy^2) + 2y^5 dy = 0$$

Integrating

$$\frac{1}{2} x^2 y^2 + xy^2 + \frac{y^6}{3} = C$$

$$\Rightarrow \qquad 3x^2 y^2 + 6xy^2 + 2y^6 = C$$

Examples on Rule 5

Example 1.27 : Solve (2y dx + 3x dy) + 2xy (3y dx + 4x dy) = 0

Solution : Given differential equation is

$$(2y dx + 3x dy) + 2xy (3y dx + 4x dy) = 0 \qquad \text{... (1)}$$
$$\therefore \qquad (2y dx + 3x dy) + xy (6y dx + 8x dy) = 0 \qquad \text{... (2)}$$
Let $\qquad [2y + 6xy^2] dx + [3x + 8x^2y] dy = 0 \qquad \text{... (3)}$

Here

$$M = 2y + 6xy^2 \qquad \text{and} \qquad N = 3x + 8x^2y$$
$$\frac{\partial M}{\partial y} = 2 + 12x \qquad\qquad \frac{\partial N}{\partial x} = 3 + 16y$$

Here $\qquad\qquad \dfrac{\partial M}{\partial y} \neq \dfrac{\partial N}{\partial x}$

∴ given equation is not exact.

Let $x^\alpha y^\beta$ be its integrating factor.

Multiplying both sides of equation (3) by $x^\alpha y^\beta$ we get

$$x^\alpha y^\beta [2y + 6xy^2] dx + [3x + 8x^2y] x^\alpha y^\beta dy = 0$$
$$\left[2x^\alpha y^{\beta + 1} + 6x^{\alpha + 1} \cdot y^{\beta + 2}\right] dx + \left[3x^{\alpha + 1} y^\beta + 8x^{\alpha + 2} \cdot y^{\beta + 1}\right] dy = 0 \text{ ... (4)}$$

It will be exact if

$$\frac{\partial M}{\partial y} = \frac{\partial N}{\partial x}$$

i.e. $\quad \dfrac{\partial}{\partial y} \left[2x^\alpha y^{\beta + 1} + 6x^{\alpha + 1} y^{\beta + 2}\right] = \dfrac{\partial}{\partial x} \left[3x^{\alpha + 1} y^\beta + 8x^{\alpha + 2} \cdot y^{\beta + 1}\right] dy$

$$2 (\beta + 1) x^\alpha y^\beta + 6 (\beta + 2) x^{\alpha + 1} y^{\beta + 1} = 3 (\alpha + 1) x^\alpha y^\beta + 8 (\alpha + 2)$$

Equating the coefficient of x, y β and $x^{\alpha + 1}$ $y^{\beta + 1}$

$$2\,(\beta + 1) \;=\; 3\,(\alpha + 1) \quad \text{and}$$
$$2\beta + 2 \;=\; 3\alpha + 3$$
$$3\alpha - 2\beta \;=\; -1 \qquad \dots (5)$$

$$6\,(\beta + 2) \;=\; 8\,(\alpha + 2)$$
$$6\beta + 12 \;=\; 82 + 16$$
$$8\alpha - 6\beta \;=\; -4$$
$$4\alpha - 3\beta \;=\; -2 \qquad \dots (6)$$

Multiplying equation (5) by 3 and equation (6) by 2

$$9\alpha - 6\beta \;=\; -3$$
$$8\alpha - 6\beta \;=\; -4$$

Subtracting we get

$$\boxed{\alpha = 1}$$

Using $\alpha = 1$ equation (5) becomes $\boxed{\beta = 2}$

Thus   I. F. $=\; x^{\alpha}\, y^{\beta} = xy^{2}$

Multiplying equation (3) by xy^{2} we get

$$[2xy^3 + 6\,x^2\,y^4]\,dx + [3x^2\,y^2 + 8x^3\,y^3]\,dy \;=\; 0 \qquad \dots (7)$$

Which must be exact.

It can be written as

Here $M \;=\; 2xy^3 + 6x^2\,y^4$

$$N \;=\; 3x^2\,y^2 + 8x^3\,y^3$$

IM in N terms free from x are absent.

Solution of equation (7) is

$$\int_{y = \text{constant}} M\,dx + \int [\text{terms free from x}]\,dy = C$$

$$\int [2xy^3 + 6x^2\,y^4]\,dx \;=\; C$$

$$2\left(\frac{x^2}{2}\right) y^3 + 6\left(\frac{x^3}{2}\right) y^4 \;=\; C$$

$$x^2\,y^3 + 2x^3\,y^4 \;=\; C \qquad \dots (8)$$

is the general solution of equation (1)

Example 1.28 : $(3x + 2y^2)\, y\, dx + 2x\, (2x + 3y^2)\, dy = 0$

Solution : Given differential equation is

$$(3xy + 2y^3)\,dx + (4x^2 + 6xy^2)\,dy \;=\; 0 \qquad \dots (1)$$

Here

$$M \;=\; 3xy + 2y^3 \qquad \text{and} \qquad N = 4x^2 + 6xy^2$$

$$\frac{\partial M}{\partial y} \;=\; 3x + 6y^2 \qquad \text{and} \qquad \frac{\partial N}{\partial x} \;=\; 8x + 6y^2$$

Here $\dfrac{\partial M}{\partial y} \;\neq\; \dfrac{\partial N}{\partial x}$

$\therefore$ given equation is not exact.

Let $x^{\alpha}\, y^{\beta}$ be it's integrating factor.

Multiplying equation (1) by $x^\alpha y^\beta$ we get

$$x^\alpha y^\beta [3xy + 2y^3] dx + x^\alpha y^\beta [4x^2 + 6xy^2] dy = 0$$

$$[3x^{\alpha+1} \cdot y^{\beta+1} + 2x^\alpha y^{\beta+3}] dx + [4x^{\alpha+2} y^\beta + 6x^{\alpha+1} y^{\beta+2}] dy = 0 \quad \dots (2)$$

It will be exact if

$$\frac{\partial}{\partial y} [3x^{\alpha+1} y^{\beta+1} + 2x^\alpha y^{\beta+2}] = \frac{\partial}{\partial x} [4x^{\alpha+2} y^\beta + 6x^{\alpha+1} y^{\beta+2}]$$

$$3(\beta+1) x^{\alpha+1} y^\beta + 2(\beta+3) x^\alpha y^{\beta+2} = 4(\alpha+2) x^{\alpha+1} y^\beta + (\alpha+1) x^\alpha y^{\beta+2}$$

$$\dots (3)$$

Equating the coefficients of $x^{\alpha+1} \cdot y^\beta$ and $x^\alpha y^{\beta+2}$ we get

$3(\beta+1) = 4(\alpha+2)$ ... (4)	$2(\beta+3) = 6(\alpha+1)$ ... (5)
$3\beta + 3 = 42 + 8$	and $2\beta + 6 = 6\alpha + 6$
$4\alpha - 3\beta = -5$ ... (6)	and $6\alpha - 2\beta = 0$
	$3\alpha - \beta = 0$ ... (7)
	Multiply by 3
	$9\alpha - 3\beta = 0$ ... (8)

Substituting equation (8), from equation (6) we get

$$-5\alpha = -5$$

$$\boxed{\alpha = 1}$$

Using $\alpha = 1$ we get $\beta = 3$

$\therefore$ I. F. $= x^\alpha y^\beta = xy^3$

Multiply equation (1) by xy^3 we get

$$xy^3 [3xy + 2y^3] dx + xy^3 [4x^2 + 6xy^2] dy = 0$$

$$[3x^2 y^4 + 2x y^6] dx + [4x^3 y^3 + 6x^2 y^5] dy = 0 \quad \dots (9)$$

Here $M = 3x^2 y^4 + 2xy^6$

        $N = 4x^3 y^3 + 6x^2 y^5$

In N, the terms free from N are absent.

The solution of equation is

$$\int_{y = \text{constant}} M \, dx + \int \begin{bmatrix} \text{terms in N} \\ \text{free from x} \end{bmatrix} dy = C$$

$$\int_{y = \text{constant}} [3x^2 y^4 + 2xy^6] \, dx + 0 = C$$

$$3\left(\frac{x^3}{3}\right) y^4 + 2\left(\frac{x^2}{2}\right) y^6 = C$$

$$x^3 y^4 + x^2 y^6 = C \quad \dots (10)$$

It is general solution of given differential equation.

EXERCISE 1.3

I. Theory Questions :

1. If the equation M dx + N dy = 0 is homogeneous in x and y then prove that $\dfrac{1}{Mx + Ny}$ is an integrating factor of the equation provided that $Mx + Ny \neq 0$.

2. If an equation M dx + N dy = 0 of the form $f_1(xy) \cdot y\,dx + f_2(xy) \cdot x\,dy = 0$ then prove that $\dfrac{1}{Mx - Ny}$ is an integrating factor of the equation. Provided that $Mx - Ny \neq 0$.

3. If in an equation M dx + N dy = 0 and $\dfrac{\left[\dfrac{\partial M}{\partial y} - \dfrac{\partial N}{\partial x}\right]}{N}$ is the function of x only then prove that $e^{\int f(x)\,dx}$ is an integrating factor of the equation. M dx + N dy = 0

4. If in the equation M dx + N dy = 0, $\dfrac{\left[\dfrac{\partial N}{\partial x} - \dfrac{\partial M}{\partial y}\right]}{M}$ is the function of y only then prove that $e^{\int f(y)\,dy}$ is an integrating factor of the equation M dx + N dy = 0.

II. Solve the following differential equations.

1. $(x^2 - 3xy + 2y^2)\,dx + x(3x - 2y)\,dy = 0$

2. $(xy \sin xy + \cos xy)\,y\,dx + (xy \sin xy - \cos xy) - x\,dy = 0$

3. $y(1 + xy)\,dx + x(1 - xy)\,dy = 0$

4. $(x^3 y^3 + x^2 y^2 + xy + 1)\,y\,dx + (x^3 y^3 - x^2 y^2 - xy + 1)\,x\,dy = 0$

5. $(x^2 + y^2 + 1)\,dx - 2xy\,dy = 0$

6. $(xy^3 + y)\,dx + 2(xy^2 + x + y^4)\,dy = 0$

7. $(y^4 + 2y)\,dx + (xy^3 + 2y^4 - 4x)\,dy = 0$

8. $y(2xy + e^x)\,dx - e^x\,dy = 0$

9. $(y^2 + 2x^2 y)\,dx + (2x^3 - xy)\,dy = 0$

10. $x[4y\,dx + 2x\,dy] + y^3[3y\,dx + 5x\,dy] = 0$

$$\boxed{\textbf{ANSWERS 1.3}}$$

1. $x^2 \log x + 3xy = y^2 + cx^2$
2. $x \sec xy = cy$
3. $-\dfrac{1}{xy} + \log \dfrac{x}{y} = c$
4. $xy - \dfrac{1}{xy} - \log y^2 = c$
5. $x^2 - y^2 - 1 = cx$
6. $3x^2 y^4 + 6xy^3 + 2y^6 = c$
7. $xy + y^2 + \dfrac{2x}{y^2} = c$
8. $x^2 y + e^x = cy$
9. $4\sqrt{xy} - \dfrac{2}{3} \left(\dfrac{y}{x}\right)^{3/2} = C$
10. $x^4 y^2 + x^3 y^5 = c$

1.6　LINEAR DIFFERENTIAL EQUATION

Definition : Linear differential equation :

A differential equation in which the dependent variable and its differential coefficients occur only in the first degree and are not multiplied together, is called Linear Differential Equation.

The standard form of a linear differential equation of the first degree is

$$\frac{dy}{dx} + py = Q$$

where P and Q are the functions of x only or are constants.

Integrating factor of linear equation.

Linear differential equation is

$$\frac{dy}{dx} + Py = Q \qquad \qquad \dots (1)$$

Using $Q = 0$ we get

$$\frac{dy}{dx} + Py = 0 \qquad \qquad \dots (2)$$

$$\therefore \qquad \frac{dy}{y} + P\,dx = 0$$

Integrating w. r. t. x we get

$$\log y + \int P\,dx = \log c$$

$$\log y - \log c = -\int P \, dx$$

$$\log\left(\frac{y}{c}\right) = -\int P \, dx$$

$$\frac{y}{c} = e^{-\int P \, dx}$$

$$y = c \cdot e^{-\int P \, dx} \qquad \ldots (2)$$

$$y \, e^{\int P \, dx} = c \qquad \ldots (3)$$

differentiating w. r. t. x we get

$$y \cdot \left[e^{\int P \, dx} \cdot P \right] + e^{\int P \, dx} \cdot \frac{dy}{dx} = 0$$

$$y \cdot e^{\int P \, dx} \cdot P \, dx + e^{\int P \, dx} \cdot dy = 0$$

$$e^{\int P \, dx} \, [Py \, dx + dy] = 0$$

$$\therefore \qquad e^{\int P \, dx} \left[\frac{dy}{dx} + Py \right] = 0$$

It shows that $\cdot \, e^{\int P \, dx}$ is an integrating factor of the linear differential equation $\frac{dy}{dx} + Py = Q$

Solution of linear differential equation $\frac{dy}{dx} + Py = Q$

The linear differential equation is

$$\frac{dy}{dx} + Py = Q \qquad \ldots (1)$$

where, P and Q are functions of x only or are constants.

Multiplying both sides of equation (1) by integrating factor $e^{\int P \, dx}$, we get

$$e^{\int P \, dx} \left[\frac{dy}{dx} + Py \right] = Q \, e^{\int P \, dx}$$

$$e^{\int P\,dx} \cdot \frac{dy}{dx} + P\, e^{\int P\,dx} \cdot y = Q\, e^{\int P\,dx}$$

$$y\left[e^{\int P\,dx} \cdot P\right] + e^{\int P\,dx} \frac{dy}{dx} = Q\, e^{\int P\,dx} \qquad \ldots (2)$$

We know that

$$\left[\frac{d}{dx}\left[y \cdot e^{\int P\,dx}\right] = y\left[e^{\int P\,dx} \cdot P\right] + e^{\int P\,dx}\frac{dy}{dx}\right] \qquad \ldots (3)$$

Using equation (3) equation (2) becomes

$$\frac{d}{dx}\left[y \cdot e^{\int P\,dx}\right] = Q\, e^{\int P\,dx}$$

integrating both sides w.r.t. x we get

$$y \cdot e^{\int P\,dx} = \int \left[Q\, e^{\int P\,dx}\right] dx + c \qquad \ldots (4)$$

Suppose I. F. $= e^{\int p\,dx}$ then equation (4) can be written as

$$y \cdot [\text{I. F.}] = \int [Q \cdot \text{I. F.}]\, dx + c \qquad \ldots (5)$$

where c is the arbitrary = constant.

This is the solution of the linear differential equation (1).

Procedure for Solving linear equation $\frac{dy}{dx} + py = Q$

1. First express the given differential equation in the form
    $$\frac{dy}{dx} + Py = Q, \qquad \ldots (1)$$
    where P and Q are the functions of x only or constants.

2. Comparing given differential equation with equation (1) calculate P and Q.

3. Find I. F. $= e^{\int P\,dx}$

4. Find the solution by using the formula
    $$y \times \text{I.F.} = \int [Q \times \text{I. F.}]\, dx + c$$

where c is an arbitrary = constant.

Note : Sometimes given differential equation can not be expressed in the form $\frac{dy}{dx} + Py = Q$, then by considering y as independent variable and x as dependent variable, the given differential equation can be expressed in the from $\frac{dx}{dy} + P'x = Q'$

Where P' and Q' functions of y only or constants.

Procedure for solving linear equation $\frac{dx}{dy} + p'y = Q'$ 　　... (4)

1. First express the given differential equation in the form
$$\frac{dx}{dy} + P' x = Q' \qquad \text{... (1)}$$

where P' and Q' are functions of y only or constants.

2. Comparing the given differential equation with equation (1) calculate P' and Q'.

3. Find I. F. $= e^{\int P' \, dy}$

4. Find the solution by using the formula
$$x \times \text{I. F.} = \int [Q' \times \text{I. F.}] \, dy + c$$

where c is an arbitrary = constant.

SOLVED EXAMPLES

Example 1.29 : Solve $\frac{dy}{dx} + \frac{y}{x} = x^2$

Solution : Given differential equation is
$$\frac{dy}{dx} + \frac{y}{x} = x^2 \qquad \text{... (1)}$$

It is a linear differential equation of the form
$$\frac{dy}{dx} + py = Q \qquad \text{... (2)}$$

where $\qquad P = \frac{1}{x}, \qquad Q = x^2$

$$\text{I. F.} = e^{\int P \, dx} = e^{\int \frac{1}{x} dx} = e^{\log x} = x$$

Solution is

$$y \cdot (I. F.) = \int Q \cdot (I. F.) \, dx + c \qquad \dots (3)$$

$$\therefore \qquad y \cdot x = \int x^2 \cdot x \, dx + c$$

$$xy = \int x^3 \, dx + c$$

$$xy = \frac{x^4}{4} + c \qquad \dots (4)$$

It is a solution.

Example 1.30 : Solve : $\dfrac{dy}{dx} + \dfrac{n}{x} \, y = \dfrac{a}{x^n}$ **[May 2011]**

Solution : Given differential equation is

$$\frac{dy}{dx} + \frac{n}{x} \, y = \frac{a}{x^n} \qquad \dots (1)$$

It is a linear differential equation of the form

$$\frac{dy}{dx} + Py = Q \qquad \dots (2)$$

Comparing $\qquad P = \dfrac{n}{x} \quad \text{and} \quad Q = \dfrac{a}{x^n}$

$$I. F. = e^{\int P \, dx}$$

$$I. F. = e^{\int \frac{n}{x} dx} = e^{n \int \frac{1}{x} dx} = e^{n \log x} = e^{\log x^n} = x^n$$

The solution of equation (1) is

$$y (I. F.) = \int [Q \times I. F.] \, dx + c$$

$$y \cdot x^n = \int \left[\frac{a}{x^n} \times x^n \right] dx$$

$$y \cdot x^n = \int a \, dx$$

$$y \cdot x^n = ax + c$$

$$\boxed{x^n \cdot y - ax = c} \qquad \dots (3)$$

This is the solution of equation (1).

Example 1.31 : Solve : $\dfrac{dy}{dx} - y \tan x = e^x$ [May 2011]

Solution : Given differential equation is

$$\frac{dy}{dx} - (\tan x)\, y \; = \; e^x \qquad \text{... (1)}$$

It is a linear differential equation of the form

$$\frac{dy}{dx} + Py \; = \; Q \qquad \text{... (2)}$$

Comparing $P = -\tan x$ and $Q = e^x$

$$\text{I. F.} \; = \; e^{\int p\, dx} \; = \; e^{\int -\tan x\, dx}$$

$$\text{I. F.} \; = \; e^{\int \frac{-\sin x}{\cos x}\, dx}$$

$$\text{I. F.} \; = \; e^{\log(\cos x)}\, dx$$

$$\text{I. F.} \; = \; \cos x \qquad \text{... (3)}$$

The solution of equation (1) is

$$y \cdot (\text{I. F.}) \; = \; \int (Q \times \text{I. F.})\, dx + c$$

$$y \cdot \cos x \; = \; \int e^x \cos x\, dx + c$$

$$y \cdot \cos x \; = \; \frac{e^x}{2}\, [\cos x + \sin x] + c \qquad \text{... (6)}$$

This is the solution of equation (1).

Note :

$$\int e^{ax} \cos(bx + c)\, dx = \frac{e^{ax}}{a^2 + b^2}\, [a\cos(bx + c) + b\sin(bx + c)]$$

Example 1.32 : Solve : $\dfrac{dy}{dx} = y \tan x - 2 \sin x$ [April 2013]

Solution : Given differential equation is

$$\frac{dy}{dx} \; = \; y \tan x - 2 \sin x \qquad \text{... (1)}$$

$$\frac{dy}{dx} - (\tan x)\, y \; = \; -2 \sin x$$

It is a linear differential equation of the form.

$$\frac{dy}{dx} + Py \; = \; Q \qquad \text{... (2)}$$

Where

$$P \; = \; -\tan x$$
$$Q \; = \; -2 \sin x$$

$$\text{I. F.} = e^{\int P \, dx} = e^{\int -\tan x \, dx}$$

$$\text{I. F.} = e^{-\int \tan x \, dx} = e^{\int \frac{-\cos x}{\sin x} dx}$$

$$\text{I. F.} = e^{\log (\cos x)}$$

$$\text{I. F.} = \cos x$$

Solution is

$$y \cdot (\text{I. F.}) = \int [Q \times \text{I. F.}] \, dx + c \qquad \ldots (3)$$

$$y \cdot \cos x = \int -2 \sin x \cdot \cos x \, dx + c$$

$$= \int [-\sin (2x) + c$$

$$y \cos x = \frac{\cos (2x)}{2} + c \qquad \ldots (4)$$

It is a solution.

Example 1.33 : $(1 + x^2) \dfrac{dy}{dx} + 2xy = 4x^2$

Solution : Given differential equation is

$$(1 + x^2) \frac{dy}{dx} + 2xy = 4x^2 \qquad \ldots (1)$$

Dividing both sides by $(1 + x^2)$, we get

$$\frac{dy}{dx} + \frac{2xy}{1 + x^2} = \frac{4x^2}{1 + x^2}$$

$$\frac{dy}{dx} + \left[\frac{2x}{1 + x^2} \right] y = \frac{4x^2}{1 + x^2} \qquad \ldots (2)$$

It is Linear differential equation of the form

$$\frac{dy}{dx} + Py = Q \qquad \ldots (3)$$

where

$$P = \frac{2x}{1 + x^2}$$

$$Q = \frac{4x^2}{1 + x^2}$$

$$\text{I. F.} = e^{\int P \, dx} = e^{\int \frac{2x}{1 + x^2} dx}$$

$$= e^{\log (1 + x^2)} = 1 + x^2$$

The solution is

$$y \cdot (I.\ F.) = \int Q \cdot [I.\ F.]\ dx + c \qquad \dots (4)$$

$$\therefore \qquad y\,(1 + x^2) = \int \frac{4x^2}{1 + x^2} \cdot (1 + x^2)\ dx + c$$

$$y\,(1 + x^2) = \int 4x^2 + c$$

$$y\,(1 + x^2) = 4\frac{x^3}{3} + c \qquad \dots (5)$$

It is the solution of differential equation (1).

Example 1.34 : Solve : $\cos x \dfrac{dy}{dx} + y = \sin x$

Solution : Given differential equation is

$$\cos x \frac{dy}{dx} + y = \sin x \qquad \dots (1)$$

Dividing by cos x throughout, we get

$$\frac{dy}{dx} + \frac{y}{\cos x} = \frac{\sin x}{\cos x}$$

$$\therefore \qquad \frac{dy}{dx} + [\sec x]\, y = \tan x \qquad \dots (2)$$

It is a linear differential equation, of the form

$$\frac{dy}{dx} + Py = Q \qquad \dots (3)$$

where
$$P = \sec x$$
$$Q = \tan x$$

$$I.\ F. = e^{\int P\,dx} = e^{\int \sec x\,dx} = e^{\log\,[\sec x + \tan x]} = \sec x + \tan x$$

Solution is

$$y \cdot (I.\ F.) = \int Q \cdot [I.\ F.]\ dx + c \qquad \dots (4)$$

$$\therefore \qquad y\,(\sec x + \tan x) = \int [\sec x + \tan x]\, \tan x \cdot dx + c$$

$$= \int [\sec x \tan x + \tan^2 x]\ dx + c$$

$$= \int \sec x \tan x\ dx + \int \tan^2 x\ dx$$

$$= \int \sec x \tan x \, dx + \int (\sec^2 x - 1) \, dx + c$$

$$y \, (\sec x + \tan x) = \sec x + \int \sec^2 x \, dx - \int 1 \, dx + c$$

$$y \, (\sec x + \tan x) = \sec x + \tan x - x + c \qquad \qquad \dots (5)$$

It is the solution.

Example 1.35 : Solve : $\dfrac{dy}{dx} = \dfrac{x + 1 + y}{x + 1}$

Solution : Given differential equation is

$$\frac{dy}{dx} = \frac{x + 1 + y}{x + 1} \qquad \qquad \dots (1)$$

$$\frac{dy}{dx} = 1 + \frac{y}{x + 1}$$

$$\frac{dy}{dx} - \frac{1}{x + 1} \cdot y = 1 \qquad \qquad \dots (2)$$

It is a linear differential equation of the form

$$\frac{dy}{dx} + Py = Q \qquad \qquad \dots (2)$$

where

$$P = \frac{-1}{1 + x}, \quad Q = 1$$

$$\text{I. F.} = e^{\int P \, dx}$$

$$\text{I. F.} = e^{\int \frac{-1}{1 + x} \, dx}$$

$$\text{I. F.} = e^{-\log (1 + x)}$$

$$\text{I. F.} = e^{\log (1 + x)^{-1}}$$

$$\text{I. F.} = (1 + x)^{-1}$$

$$\text{I. F.} = \frac{1}{1 + x}$$

Solution is

$$y \cdot (\text{I. F.}) = \int Q \cdot (\text{I. F.}) \, dx + c \qquad \qquad \dots (3)$$

$$y \cdot \frac{1}{x + 1} = \int \frac{1}{x + 1} \, dx + c$$

$$\frac{y}{x + 1} = \log (x + 1) + c \qquad \qquad \dots (4)$$

It is solution.

Example 1.36 : Solve : $x \log x \dfrac{dy}{dx} + y = 2 \log x$

Solution : Given differential equation is

$$x \log x \dfrac{dy}{dx} + y = 2 \log x \qquad \text{... (1)}$$

dividing throughout by x log x, we get

$$\dfrac{dy}{dx} + y \left[\dfrac{1}{x \log x} \right] \cdot y = \dfrac{2 \log x}{x \log x}$$

$$\dfrac{dy}{dx} + \dfrac{1}{x \log x} \cdot y = \dfrac{2}{x} \qquad \text{... (2)}$$

It is a linear differential equation of the form

$$\dfrac{dy}{dx} + Py = Q \qquad \text{... (3)}$$

where $\quad P = \dfrac{1}{x \log x}, \qquad Q = \dfrac{2}{x}$

$$\text{I. F.} = e^{\int P \, dx} = e^{\int \frac{1}{x \log x} \, dx} = e^{\int \frac{\frac{1}{x}}{\log x} \, dx} = e^{\log (\log x)} = \log x$$

Solution is

$$y \cdot \text{I. F.} = \int [Q \times \text{I. F.}] \, dx + c$$

$$y \cdot \log x = \int \dfrac{2}{x} \cdot \log x \, dx + c$$

$$y \log x = 2 \int [\log x] \cdot \dfrac{1}{x} \, dx + c \qquad \text{... (4)}$$

We use

$$\int [f(x)]^n \cdot f'(x) \, dx = \dfrac{f(x)]^{n+1}}{n+1}, \text{ If } n \neq -1$$

$$\therefore \qquad \int [\log x] \cdot \dfrac{1}{x} \, dx = \dfrac{[\log x]^2}{2} \qquad \text{... (5)}$$

Equation (4) becomes

$$y \cdot \log x = 2 \cdot \dfrac{[\log x]^2}{2} + c$$

$$y \log x = [\log x]^2 + c \qquad \text{... (6)}$$

It is a solution.

Example 1.37 : Solve : $\sec x \dfrac{dy}{dx} = y + \sin x$

Solution : Given differential equation is

$$\sec x \frac{dy}{dx} = y + \sin x \qquad \ldots (1)$$

Dividing by sec x, we get

$$\frac{dy}{dx} = \frac{y}{\sec x} + \frac{\sin x}{\sec x}$$

$$\frac{dy}{dx} = y \cos x + \sin x \cos x$$

$$\frac{dy}{dx} - y \cos x = \sin x \cos x \qquad \ldots (2)$$

It is a linear differential equation of the form

$$\frac{dy}{dx} + Py = Q \qquad \ldots (3)$$

where
$$P = -\cos x$$
$$Q = \sin x \cos x$$

$$\text{I. F.} = e^{\displaystyle\int P \, dx} = e^{-\int \cos x \, dx} = e^{-\sin x}$$

Solution is

$$y \cdot (\text{I. F.}) = \int [Q \, \text{I. F.}] \, dx + c \qquad \ldots (4)$$

$$y \cdot e^{-\sin x} = \int [\sin x \cos x] \, e^{-\sin x} \, dx + c$$

$$= \int \sin x \cdot e^{-\sin x} \cdot \cos x \, dx \qquad \ldots (5)$$

Put
$$\sin x = t \qquad \ldots (6)$$
$$\therefore \qquad \cos x \cdot dx = dt \qquad \ldots (7)$$

Equation (5) becomes

$$y \cdot e^{-\sin x} = \int t \cdot e^t \, dt + c$$

Integrating by parts, $\quad y \cdot e^{-\sin x} = t \cdot \left(\dfrac{e^{-t}}{-1}\right) - \int 1 \cdot \left(\dfrac{e^{-t}}{-1}\right) dt + c$

$$= -t \, e^{-t} + \int e^{-t} \, dt + c$$

$$y e^{-\sin x} = -t \, e^{-t} - e^{-t} + c \qquad \ldots (8)$$

put

$$t = \sin x$$

$$y e^{-\sin x} = -\sin x \, e^{-\sin x} - e^{-\sin x} + c$$

Dividing by $e^{-\sin x}$, we get

$$y = -\sin x - 1 + c \, e^{\sin x} \qquad \ldots (9)$$

It is solution.

Example 1.38 : Solve $\cos^2 x \dfrac{dy}{dx} + y = \tan x$

Solution : $\qquad \cos^2 x \dfrac{dy}{dx} + y = \tan x \qquad \ldots (1)$

Dividing throughout by $\cos^2 x \, \pi$ we get

$$\frac{dy}{dx} + \frac{y}{\cos^2 x} = \frac{\tan x}{\cos^2 x}$$

$$\frac{dy}{dx} + [\sec^2 x] \, y = \sec^2 x + \tan x \qquad \ldots (2)$$

It is a linear differential equation of the forms

$$\frac{dy}{dx} + Py = Q \qquad \ldots (3)$$

where $\qquad P = \sec^2 x$

$$Q = \sec^2 x \ \tan x$$

$$\text{I. F.} = e^{\int P \, dx} = e^{\int \sec^2 x \, dx} = e^{\tan x}$$

Solution is

$$y \cdot (\text{I. F.}) = \int Q \cdot (\text{I. F.}) \, dx + c \qquad \ldots (4)$$

$$y \cdot e^{\tan x} = \int e^{\tan x}[\sec^2 x \tan x) \, dx + c \qquad \ldots (5)$$

$$\text{Put } \tan x = t \qquad \ldots (6)$$

$$\sec^2 x \, dx = dt \qquad \ldots (7)$$

Equation (4) becomes

$$y \cdot e^{\tan x} = \int e^t \cdot t \cdot dt + c$$

$$= \int t \cdot e^t \, dt + c$$

Integrating by Parts

$$= [t \cdot e^t] - \int t \cdot e^t \, dt + c$$

$$= t\,e^t - e^t + c$$

$$= e^t\,(t - 1) + c$$

put
$$t = \tan x$$

$$y \cdot e^{\tan x} = e^{\tan x}\,[\tan x - 1] + c$$

Dividing by $e^{\tan x}$ we get

$$y = \tan x - 1 + c\,e^{-\tan x} \qquad \ldots (8)$$

It is a solution.

Example 1.39 : Solve : $\dfrac{dy}{dx} + \dfrac{2x}{x^2 + 1}\,y = \dfrac{1}{(x^2 + 1)^2}$

Given that y = 0, when x = 1.

Solution : Given differential equation is

$$\frac{dy}{dx} + \frac{2x}{x^2 + 1}\,y = \frac{1}{(x^2 + 1)^2} \qquad \ldots (1)$$

It is a linear differential equation of the form

$$\frac{dy}{dx} + Py = Q \qquad \ldots (2)$$

where
$$P = \frac{2x}{x^2 + 1}$$

$$Q = \frac{1}{(x^2 + 1)^2}$$

I. F. $= e^{\int P\,dx} = e^{\int \frac{2x}{x^2 + 1}\,dx} = e^{\log (x^2 + 1)} = x^2 + 1$

Solution is

$$y \cdot (\text{I. F.}) = \int Q \cdot (\text{I. F.})\,dx + c \qquad \ldots (3)$$

$$y \cdot (x^2 + 1) = \int \frac{1}{(x^2 + 1)^2}\,(x^2 + 1)\,dx + c$$

$$= \int \frac{1}{(x^2 + 1)^2}\,dx + c = \int \frac{1}{(1 + x^2)}\,dx + c$$

$$y\,(x^2 + 1) = \tan^{-1} x + c \qquad \ldots (4)$$

Condition is, If $x = 1$ then $y = 0$

∴　Using these values

$$0 = \tan^{-1} 1 + c$$

$$0 = \frac{\pi}{4} + c$$

$$c = -\frac{\pi}{4} \qquad \ldots (5)$$

Equation (4) becomes

$$y (x^2 + 1) = \tan^{-1} x - \frac{\pi}{4} \qquad \ldots (6)$$

It is a solution.

Example 1.40 : Solve : $\dfrac{dy}{dx} + 2y \tan x = \sin x$

Given that y = 0 when x = $\dfrac{\pi}{3}$

Solution : Given differential equation is

$$\frac{dy}{dx} + 2y \tan x = \sin x \qquad \ldots (1)$$

It is a linear differential equation of the form

$$\frac{dy}{dx} + Py = Q \qquad \ldots (2)$$

where
$$P = 2 \tan x$$
$$Q = \sin x$$

$$\text{I. F.} = e^{\int P\, dx} = e^{\int 2 \tan x\, dx}$$

$$= e^{2 \int \tan x\, dx}$$

$$= e^{2 \log (\sec x)}$$

$$= e^{\log \, \sec^2 x}$$

$$\text{I. F.} = \sec^2 x$$

Solution is

$$y \cdot (\text{I. F.}) = \int Q \cdot (\text{I. F.})\, dx + c \qquad \ldots (3)$$

$$y \cdot \sec^2 x = \int \sin x \cdot \sec^2 x\, dx + c$$

$$= \int \sin x \cdot \frac{1}{\cos^2 x}\, dx + c$$

$$= \int \frac{1}{\cos x} \cdot \left[\frac{\sin x}{\cos x} \right] dx + c$$

$$= \int \sec x \cdot \tan x\, dx + c$$

$$y \sec^2 x = \sec x + c$$

Dividing by sec² x, we get

$$y = \frac{1}{\sec^2 x} [\sec x + c]$$

$$y = \frac{1}{\sec x} + \frac{e}{\sec^2 x}$$

$$y = \cos x + c \cos^2 x \qquad \qquad \dots (4)$$

Using condition, if $x = \frac{\pi}{3}$ then $y = 0$

$$0 = \cos \frac{\pi}{3} + c \left[\cos \left(\frac{\pi}{3} \right) \right]^2$$

$$0 = \frac{1}{2} + c \cdot \frac{1}{4}$$

$$0 = 2 + c$$

$$\boxed{c = -2}$$

Equation (4) becomes

$$y = \cos x - 2 \cos^2 x \qquad \qquad \dots (5)$$

It is solution.

EXERCISE 1.4

I.   Theory Questions.

1. Define Linear differential equation and explain the method of solving it.

2. Explain the method of solving the linear differential equation $\frac{dy}{dx} + py = Q$ where P and Q are functions of x.

II. Solve the following differential equations.

1. $\dfrac{dy}{dx} + \dfrac{4x}{1 + x^2} y = \dfrac{1}{(1 + x^2)^3}$

2. $(x^2 - 1) \dfrac{dy}{dx} + 2xy = 1$

3. $(x + y + 1) \dfrac{dy}{dx} = 1$

4. $\dfrac{dy}{dx} + y \tan x = \sec^3 x$

5. $(1 + x^2) \dfrac{dy}{dx} + 2xy = \cos x$

6. $\dfrac{dy}{dx} - y \cot x = \operatorname{cosec} x$

7. $\dfrac{dy}{dx} + \cot xy = \sin x$

8. $(1 + y^2)\, dx + (x - e^{\tan^{-1} y})\, dy = 0$

9. $(1 + x^2)\dfrac{dy}{dx} + y = e^{\tan^{-1} x}$

10. $\dfrac{dy}{dx} + \dfrac{2x}{1 + x^2}\, y = \dfrac{4x^3}{1 + x^2}$ given that $y = 1$ when $x = 0$

ANSWERS 1.4

1. $y (1 + x^2)^2 = \tan^{-1} x + c$

2. $y (x^2 - 1) = x + c$

3. $x = ce^y - y - 2$

4. $y \sec x = c + \tan x + \dfrac{1}{3}\tan^3 x$

5. $y (1 + x^2) \sin x + c$

6. $y = c \sin x - \cos x$

7. $y \sin x = \dfrac{1}{2} x - \dfrac{1}{4}\sin(2x) + c$

8. $x e^{\tan^{-1} y} = \tan^{-1} y + c$

9. $y e^{\tan^{-1} x} = c + \dfrac{1}{2}(e^{\tan^{-1} x})^2$

10. $y (1 + x^2) = x^4 + c$

Equations of the form $\dfrac{dx}{dy} + p_1 x = Q_1$

Procedure (Rule) for finding the orthogonal trajectory to a given family of curves in polar co-ordinates $r = f(\theta)$ or $f(r, \theta) = 0$.

where P_1 and Q_1 are functions of y only

SOLVED EXAMPLES

Example 1.41 : Solve : $(1 + y^2)\, dx = (\tan^{-1} y - x)\, dy$

Solution : Given differential equation is

$$(1 + y^2)\, dx = (\tan^{-1} y - x)\, dy \qquad \qquad \dots (1)$$

$$(1 + y^2)\dfrac{dx}{dy} = \tan^{-1} y \cdot x$$

$$\frac{dx}{dy} = \frac{1}{(1+y^2)}[\tan^{-1}y - x]$$

$$\frac{dx}{dy} = \frac{1}{1+y^2}\tan^{-1}y - \frac{x}{1+y^2}$$

$$\frac{dx}{dy} + \left[\frac{1}{1+y^2}\right]x = \frac{\tan^{-1}y}{1+y^2} \qquad \dots (2)$$

It is linear differential equation of the form

$$\frac{dx}{dy} + P_1 x = Q_1 \qquad \dots (3)$$

where $P_1 = \dfrac{1}{1+y^2}$ and $Q_1 = \dfrac{\tan^{-1}y}{1+y^2}$

$$\text{I. F. } = e^{\int P_1\,dy} = e^{\int \frac{1}{1+y^2}\,dy} = e^{\tan^{-1}y}$$

∴   The solution is

$$x \cdot [\text{I. F.}] = \int [Q_1 \times \text{I. F.}]\,dy + c$$

$$x \cdot e^{\tan^{-1}y} = \int \left[\frac{\tan^{-1}y}{1+y^2}\cdot e^{\tan^{-1}y}\,dy\right] + c \qquad \dots (4)$$

Let

$$t = \tan^{-1}y \qquad \dots (5)$$

$$dt = \frac{1}{1+y^2}\,dy \qquad \dots (6)$$

Equation (4) becomes

$$x \cdot e^{\tan^{-1}y} = \int t \cdot e^t\,dt + c$$

Integrating by parts

$$= t\,e^t - \int t \cdot e^t\,dt + c$$

$$= t\,e^t - e^t + c$$

$$x\,e^{\tan^{-1}y} = e^t[t - 1] + c$$

Using

$$t = \tan^{-1}y \text{ we get}$$

$$x\,e^{\tan^{-1}y} = e^{\tan^{-1}y}[\tan^{-1}y - 1] + c$$

$$x = \tan^{-1}y - 1 + c\,e^{-\tan^{-1}y} \qquad \dots (7)$$

It is the general solution of equation (1).

Example 1.42 : Solve : $(1 + y^2) + (x - e^{\tan^{-1}y})\dfrac{dy}{dx} = 0$

Solution : Given differential equation is

$$(1 + y^2) + (x - e^{\tan^{-1}y})\dfrac{dy}{dx} = 0 \qquad \ldots (1)$$

$$\therefore \qquad (1 + y^2)\dfrac{dx}{dy} + x - e^{\tan^{-1}y} = 0$$

$$\therefore \qquad \dfrac{dx}{dy} + \dfrac{1}{1 + y^2}\, x = \dfrac{e^{\tan^{-1}y}}{1 + y^2} \qquad \ldots (2)$$

It is linear differential equation of the form

$$\dfrac{dx}{dy} + P_1\, x = Q_1 \qquad \ldots (3)$$

where $P_1 = \dfrac{1}{1 + y^2}$ and $Q_1 = \dfrac{e^{\tan^{-1}y}}{1 + y^2}$

$$\text{I. F.} = e^{\int P_1\, dy} = e^{\int \frac{1}{1+y^2}\, dy} = e^{\tan^{-1}y}$$

The solution is

$$x \times \text{I. F.} = \int [Q_1 \times \text{I. F.}]\, dy + c \qquad \ldots (4)$$

$$x\, e^{\tan^{-1}y} = \int \left[\dfrac{e^{\tan^{-1}y}}{1 + y^2} \times e^{\tan^{-1}y}\right] dy + c \qquad \ldots (5)$$

$$\text{Let } \tan^{-1}y = t \quad \ldots (6)$$

$$\therefore \dfrac{1}{1 + y^2}\, dy = dt \quad \ldots (7)$$

$$\therefore \quad \text{Equation (5) becomes}$$

$$x\, e^{\tan^{-1}y} = \int e^t \cdot e^t\, dt + c$$

$$x\, e^{\tan^{-1}y} = \int e^{2t}\, dt + c$$

$$x\, e^{\tan^{-1}y} = \dfrac{e^{2t}}{2} + c$$

$$x\, e^{\tan^{-1}y} = \dfrac{1}{2}\, e^{2\tan^{-1}y} + c$$

$$x = \dfrac{1}{2}\, e^{\tan^{-1}y} + c\, e^{\tan^{-1}y} \qquad \ldots (8)$$

It is the general solution of differential equation (1).

Example 1.43 : Solve : $(4y^3 - x)\dfrac{dy}{dx} = y$

Solution : Given differential equation is

$$(4y^3 - x)\dfrac{dy}{dx} = y \qquad \text{... (1)}$$

$$\therefore \quad \dfrac{dx}{dy} = \dfrac{4y^3 - x}{y}$$

$$\dfrac{dx}{dy} = 4y^2 - \dfrac{x}{y}$$

$$\dfrac{dx}{dy} + \dfrac{1}{y}\, x = 4y^2 \qquad \text{... (2)}$$

It is linear differential equation of the form

$$\dfrac{dx}{dy} + P_1\, x = Q_1 \qquad \text{... (3)}$$

where $P_1 = \dfrac{1}{y}$ and $Q_1 = 4y^2$

$$\text{I. F.} = e^{\int P_1\, dy} = e^{\int \frac{1}{y} dy} = e^{\log y} = y \qquad \text{... (4)}$$

The solution is

$$x \times \text{I. F.} = \int [Q_1 \times \text{I. F.}]\, dy + c \qquad \text{... (5)}$$

$$x \cdot y = \int [4y^2 \times y]\, dy + c$$

$$= \int 4y^3\, dy + c$$

$$= 4 \cdot \left[\dfrac{y^4}{4}\right] + c$$

$$xy = y^4 + c \qquad \text{... (6)}$$

$\therefore \quad y^4 - xy + c = 0$ is the general solution of equation (1).

EXERCISE 1.5

Solve the following differential equations :

1. $(x + 2y^3)\dfrac{dy}{dx} = y$

2. $(2x - 10\, y^3)\dfrac{dy}{dx} + y = 0$

3. $(1 + y^2)\, dx = \left[\sqrt{1 + y^2}\, \sin y - xy\right] dy$

4. $(1 + x^2) \dfrac{dy}{dx} + 2xy - 4x^2 = 0$

5. $(x + y + 1) \dfrac{dy}{dx} = 1$

$$\boxed{\textbf{ANSWERS 1.5}}$$

1. $x - y^2 = cy$
2. $xy^2 = 2y^5 + c$
3. $x\sqrt{1 + y^2} + \cos y = c$
4. $4x^3 = 3y (1 + x^2) + c$
5. $x + y + 2 = ce^y$

1.7 BERNOULLI'S EQUATION

An equation of the form

$$\frac{dy}{dx} + Py = Q y^n \qquad \qquad \text{... (1)}$$

where P and Q are functions of x only or are constants and $n \neq 0$ and $n \neq 1$, is called **Bernoulli's equation.**   **[S. U. Oct. 2011, April 2013]**

Method of Solving Bernoulli's equation.

$$\text{Suppose } \frac{dy}{dx} + Py = Q y^n \qquad \qquad \text{... (1)}$$

is Bernoulli's equation.

where P and Q are functions of x only or constants and $n \neq 0, n \neq 1$.

Dividing both sides of equation (1) by y^n we get

$$\frac{1}{y^n} \left[\frac{dy}{dx} + Py \right] = Q$$

$$y^{-n} \frac{dy}{dx} + Py^{1-n} = Q \qquad \qquad \text{... (2)}$$

$$\text{Let } y^{1-n} = v \qquad \qquad \text{... (3)}$$

Differentiate both sides w.r.t. x we get

$$(1 - n) y^{-n} \frac{dy}{dx} = \frac{dV}{dx}$$

$$y^{-n} \frac{dy}{dx} = \frac{1}{1-n} \frac{dV}{dx} \qquad \qquad \text{... (4)}$$

Using equations (3) and (4), equation (2) becomes

$$\frac{1}{1-n}\frac{dV}{dx} + PV = Q$$

$$\frac{dV}{dx} + (1-n)PV = (1-n)Q \qquad \qquad ...(5)$$

or $$\frac{dV}{dx} + P_1V = Q_1 \qquad \qquad ...(6)$$

where $P_1 = (1-n)P$ and $Q_1 = (1-n)Q$.

This is linear differential equation with v as independent variable and x as dependent variable.

It's

$$I.F. = e^{\int P_1\, dx} = e^{\int (1-n)P_1\, dx}$$

$$I.F. = e^{(1-n)\int P\, dx} \qquad \qquad ...(7)$$

The solution of equation (6) is given as

$$v \times I.F. = \int [Q_1 \times I.F.]\, dx + c$$

$$\therefore \quad v \cdot e^{(1-n)\int P\, dx} = \int \left[(1-n)Q \cdot e^{(1-n)\int P\, dx} \right] dx + c$$

Using $v = y^{1-n}$ we get

$$y^{1-n} \cdot e^{(1-n)\int P\, dx} = (1-n)\int \left[Q \cdot e^{(1-n)\int P\, dx} \right] dx + c \qquad ...(8)$$

which is the solution of Bernoulli's equation (1)

Note : In solving problems we can put $y^{1-n} = v$ or $y^{1-n} = z$ and solve the problem by using above procedure.

SOLVED EXAMPLES

Example 1.44 : Solve : $\sec^2 y \dfrac{dy}{dx} + 2x \tan y = x$ [April 2013]

Solution : Given differential equation is

$$\sec^2 y \frac{dy}{dx} + 2x \tan y = x \qquad \qquad ...(1)$$

Put $$V = \tan y \qquad \qquad ...(2)$$

Differentiating w. r. t. x

$$\frac{dV}{dx} = \sec^2 y \frac{dy}{dx} \qquad \qquad \text{... (3)}$$

Using equations (2) and (3) equation (1) becomes

$$\frac{dV}{dx} + (2x) V = x \qquad \qquad \text{... (4)}$$

It is linear differential equation.

Here $P = 2x$

$$Q = x$$

$\therefore \qquad \qquad$ I. F. $= e^{\int 2x \, dx}$

$\therefore \qquad \qquad$ I. F. $= e^{\int 2\left(\frac{x^2}{2}\right)} = e^{x^2} \qquad \qquad \text{... (5)}$

The solution of equation (4) is

$$V. \, (I. \, F.) = \int (Q \times I. \, F.) \, dx$$

$\therefore \qquad \qquad V \, e^x = \int x e^{x^2} \, dx$

$\therefore \qquad \qquad V \, e^x = \frac{1}{2} \int \left[e^{x^2} \cdot 2x \right] dx$

$\therefore \qquad \qquad V \, e^x = \frac{1}{2} e^{x^2}$

$$\boxed{(\tan y) \, e^x = \frac{1}{2} e^{x^2} + c} \qquad \qquad \text{... (6)}$$

This is solution of equation (1)

Example 1.45 : Solve : $x \dfrac{dy}{dx} + y = x^2 y^2$ **[April 2013]**

Solution : Given differential equation is

$$x \frac{dy}{dx} + y = x^2 y^2 \qquad \qquad \text{... (1)}$$

divide both sides by y^2

$$\frac{x}{y^2} \frac{dy}{dx} + \frac{1}{y} = x^2 \qquad \qquad \text{... (2)}$$

$$\text{Put} \, \frac{1}{y} = V$$

Diff w. r. t. x

$$\frac{-1}{y^2}\frac{dy}{dx} = \frac{dV}{dx}$$

$\therefore$
$$\frac{1}{y^2}\frac{dy}{dx} = \frac{-dV}{dx}$$ ... (4)

Using equation (3) and (4) equation (2) becomes

$$-x\frac{dV}{dx} + V = x^2$$

divide both sides by $(-x)$

$$\frac{dV}{dx} - \frac{1}{x}V = -x$$ ... (5)

It is a linear differential equation of the form

$$\frac{dV}{dx} + PV = Q$$ ... (6)

Comparing $P = \dfrac{-1}{x}$ $Q = -x$

$$\text{I. F. } = e^{\int P\,dx}$$

$$\text{I. F. } = e^{\int \frac{-1}{x}\,dx} = e^{-\log x} = e^{\log x^{-1}} = x^{-1} = \frac{1}{x}$$

Solution of equation (6) is

$$V \cdot (\text{I. F.}) = \int (Q \times \text{I. F.})\,dx + \text{constant}$$

$$V \cdot \frac{1}{x} = \int (-x)\left(\frac{1}{x}\right)dx + c$$

$$\frac{V}{x} = \int (-1)\,dx + c$$

$$\frac{V}{x} = -x + c$$ ... (7)

Put
$$V = \frac{1}{y}$$

$\therefore$
$$\boxed{\frac{1}{xy} + x = c}$$ ... (8)

This is the solution.

Example 1.46 : Solve : $\dfrac{dy}{dx} + xy = x^3 y^3$ [Nov. 2012, April 2013]

Solution : Given differential equation is

$$\frac{dy}{dx} + xy = x^3 y^3 \qquad \qquad \text{... (1)}$$

Dividing throughout by y^3 we get

$$\frac{1}{y^3}\left[\frac{dy}{dx} + xy\right] = x^3$$

$\therefore \qquad\qquad y^{-3}\dfrac{dy}{dx} + xy^{-2} = x^3 \qquad\qquad \text{... (2)}$

Put $\qquad\qquad\qquad\qquad y^{-2} = 2 \qquad\qquad\qquad\qquad \text{... (4)}$

Differentiating

$$-2y^{-3}\frac{dy}{dx} = \frac{dz}{dx}$$

$$y^{-3}\frac{dy}{dx} = \frac{-1}{2}\frac{dz}{dx} \qquad\qquad \text{... (5)}$$

equation (2) becomes

$$\frac{-1}{2}\frac{dz}{dx} + xz = x^3$$

$$\frac{dz}{dx} - 2xz = -2x^3 \qquad\qquad \text{... (6)}$$

It is linear equation in z, of the form

$$\frac{dz}{dx} + Pz = Q \qquad\qquad \text{... (7)}$$

where $\quad P = -2x \quad Q = -2x^3$

$$\text{I. F.} = e^{\int P\,dx} = e^{-\int 2x\,dx} = e^{-2\left(\frac{x^2}{2}\right)dx} = e^{-x^2}$$

Solution is

$$z \cdot (\text{I. F.}) = \int Q \cdot (\text{I. F.})\,dx + c \qquad\qquad \text{... (8)}$$

$$z\,e^{-x^2} = \int -2x^3 \cdot e^{-x^2}\,dx + c$$

$$z\,e^{-x^2} = \int (-2x) \cdot x^2 \cdot e^{-x^2}\,dx + c \qquad\qquad \text{... (9)}$$

Put $\qquad\qquad\qquad\qquad t = -x^2 \qquad\qquad\qquad\qquad \text{... (10)}$

$$dt = -2x\,dx \qquad\qquad \text{... (11)}$$

equation (8) becomes

$$z \cdot e^{-x^2} = \int - t \cdot e^t \, dt + c$$

$$z\, e^{-x^2} = - \int t\, e^t \, dt + c$$

Integrating by parts

$$z\, e^{-x^2} = - \left[t\,(e^t) - \int 1 \cdot e^t \cdot dt + c \right]$$

$$z\, e^{-x^2} = - [t e^t - e^t] + c$$

$$z\, e^{-x^2} = - e^t\, [t - 1] + c$$

$$\therefore \quad z\, e^{-x^2} = - e^{-x^2}\, [-x^2 - 1] + c$$

$$\therefore \quad z = [x^2 + 1] + c e^{\,x2}$$

$$\therefore \quad y^{-2} = (x^2 + 1) + c e^{}\, x^2 \text{ is the solution.}$$

Example 1.47 : Solve : $\dfrac{dy}{dx} + \dfrac{y}{x} = y^2$

Solution : Given differential equation is

$$\frac{dy}{dx} + \frac{y}{x} = y^2 \qquad \qquad \text{... (1)}$$

It is Bernoulli's equation.

Dividing both sides by y^2

$$\frac{1}{y^2} \left[\frac{dy}{dx} + \frac{y}{x} \right] = 1$$

$$y^{-2} \frac{dy}{dx} + \frac{y^{-1}}{x} = 1 \qquad \qquad \text{... (2)}$$

Put $\qquad\qquad\qquad\qquad y^{-1} = -V \qquad\qquad \text{... (3)}$

Differentiating we get

$$-1\,[y^{-2}] \frac{dy}{dx} = \frac{dV}{dx}$$

$$\therefore \qquad - y^{-2} \frac{dy}{dx} = \frac{dV}{dx} \qquad\qquad \text{... (3)}$$

Equation (2) becomes

$$\frac{-dV}{dx} + \frac{V}{x} = 1$$

$$\frac{dV}{dx} - \frac{1}{x}\, V = -1 \qquad\qquad \text{... (4)}$$

It is linear equation in V of the form

$$\frac{dV}{x} + PV = Q \qquad \dots (5)$$

where $P = \dfrac{-1}{x}, \quad Q = -1$

$$I.\, F. = e^{\int P\, dx} = e^{-\int \frac{1}{x} dx} = e^{-\log x} = e^{\log x^{-1}} = x^{-1} = \frac{1}{x}$$

Solution is

$$V \cdot (I.\, F.) = \int Q \cdot (I.\, F.)\, dx + c \qquad \dots (6)$$

$$\therefore \qquad\qquad V \cdot \frac{1}{x} = -\log x + c$$

Put $\qquad\qquad z = y^{-1}$

$$\therefore \qquad\qquad \frac{y^{-1}}{x} = -\log x + c$$

$$\therefore \qquad\qquad \frac{1}{xy} + \log x = c \qquad \dots (7)$$

It is a solution of differential equation (1)

Example 1.48 : $\dfrac{dy}{dx} + y \cos x = y^n \sin 2x$

Solution : Given differential equation is

$$\frac{dy}{dx} + y \cos x = y^n \sin 2x \qquad \dots (1)$$

Dividing throughout by y^n we get

$$\frac{1}{y^n} \frac{dy}{dx} + y \frac{\cos x}{y^n} = \sin 2x$$

$$y^{-n} \frac{dy}{dx} + y^{1-n} \cos x = \sin (2x) \qquad \dots (2)$$

Put $\qquad\qquad y^{1-n} = V \qquad \dots (3)$

Differentiating we get

$$(1-n)\, y^{-n} \frac{dy}{dx} = \frac{dV}{dx} \qquad \dots (4)$$

Equation (2) becomes

$$\frac{1}{(1-n)} \frac{dV}{dx} + V \cos x = \sin (2x)$$

$$\frac{dV}{dx} + (1-n)\, V \cos x = \sin (2x)\, (1-n)$$

It is a linear equation in V of the form

$$\frac{dV}{dx} + PV = Q \qquad \qquad \dots (6)$$

where $\qquad \qquad P = (1 - n) \cos x, \qquad Q = \sin (2x)(1 - n)$

$$\text{I. F.} = e^{\int P \, dx} = e^{\int (1 - n) \cos x \, dx} = e^{(1 - n) \sin x}$$

The solution is

$$(\text{I. F.}) = \int Q \cdot (\text{I. F.}) \, dx + c \qquad \qquad \dots (7)$$

$$V \, e^{(1 - n) \sin x} = \int \sin (2x)(1 - n) \, e^{(1 - n) \sin x} \, dx + c$$

$\therefore$ Put $\qquad \qquad \qquad V = y^{1 - n}$

$$y^{1 - n} \cdot e^{(1 - n) \sin x} = \int 2 \sin x \cos x \cdot (1 - n) \, e^{(1 - n) \sin x} \, dx + c$$

$$y^{1 - n} \cdot e^{(1 - n) \sin x} = 2 \int e^{(1 - n) \sin x} \{(1 - n) \sin x\} [\cos x \, dx] + c \dots (8)$$

Put $\qquad \qquad (1 - n) \sin x = t \qquad \qquad \dots (9)$

Differentiating we get

$$(1 - n) \cos x \, dx = dt$$

$$\cos x \, dx = \frac{1}{(1 - n)} \, dt \qquad \qquad \dots (10)$$

Equation (8) becomes

$$y^{1 - n} \cdot e^{(1 - n) \sin x} = 2 \int e^t \cdot t \cdot \frac{1}{(1 - n)} \, dt + c$$

$$y^{1 - n} \cdot e^{(1 - n) \sin x} = \frac{2}{1 - n} \int t \, e^t \, dt + c$$

$$y^{1 - n} \cdot e^{(1 - n) \sin x} = \frac{2}{1 - n} \cdot [e^t (t - 1)] + c$$

$\therefore \qquad \qquad y^{1 - n} \, e^{(1 - n) \sin x} = \frac{2}{1 - n} [e^{(1 - n) \sin x} \cdot [(1 - n) \sin x - 1)]] + c$

$$y^{1 - n} = \frac{2}{1 - n} [(1 - n) \sin x - 1] + c e^{-(1 - n) \sin x}$$

$$y^{1 - n} = \frac{2}{1 - n} [(1 - n) \sin x - 1] + c e^{(n - 1) \sin x}$$

This is the solution.

Example 1.49 : Solve : $(x + 1)\dfrac{dy}{dx} + 1 = 2e^{-y}$

Given differential equation is

$$(x + 1)\frac{dy}{dx} + 1 = 2e^{-y} \qquad \text{... (1)}$$

$$\frac{dy}{dx} + \frac{1}{x + 1} = \frac{2e^{-y}}{x + 1}$$

Dividing throughout by e^{-y} we get

$$\frac{1}{e^{-y}}\frac{dy}{dx} + \frac{1}{e^{-y}}\left[\frac{1}{x + 1}\right] = \frac{2}{x + 1}$$

$$e^{y}\frac{dy}{dx} + \frac{1}{x + 1}e^{y} = \frac{2}{x + 1} \qquad \text{... (2)}$$

put $\qquad\qquad e^{y} = z \qquad \text{... (3)}$

Differentiating we get

$$e^{y}\frac{dy}{dx} = \frac{dz}{dx} \qquad \text{... (4)}$$

Equation (2) becomes

$$\frac{dz}{dx} + \frac{1}{x + 1}\cdot z = \frac{2}{x + 1} \qquad \text{... (5)}$$

It is linear equation in z of the form

$$\frac{dz}{dx} + Pz = Q \qquad \text{... (6)}$$

where $\quad P = \dfrac{1}{x + 1}, \quad Q = \dfrac{2}{x + 1}$

I. F. $= e^{\int P\,dx} = e^{\int \frac{1}{x + 1}\,dx} = e^{\log(x + 1)} = x + 1$

The solution is

$$z \cdot (\text{I. F.}) = \int Q\,(\text{I. F.})\,dx + c \qquad \text{... (7)}$$

$$z \cdot (x + 1) = \int \frac{2}{(x + 1)}\,(x + 1)\,dx + c$$

$$z\,(x + 1) = \int 2\,dx + c$$

$$z\,(x + 1) = 2x + c$$

$$\text{put } z = e^{y}$$

$$e^{y}\,(x + 1) = 2x + c \qquad \text{... (8)}$$

It is a solution of differential equation (1).

Example 1.50 : $[y \cdot \log x - 1] \, y \, dx = x \, dy$

Solution : Given differential equation is

$$[y \log x - 1] \, y \, dx = x \, dy \qquad \dots (1)$$

$$\therefore \qquad x \frac{dy}{dx} = [y \log x - 1] \, y$$

$$x \frac{dy}{dx} = y^2 \log x - y$$

$$x \frac{dy}{dx} + y = y^2 \log x \qquad \dots (2)$$

$$\frac{dy}{dx} + \frac{1}{x} \, y = y^2 \frac{\log x}{x}$$

Dividing by y^2 we get

$$y^{-2} \frac{dy}{dx} + \frac{1}{x} \, y^{-1} = \frac{\log x}{x} \qquad \dots (3)$$

$$\therefore \quad \text{Put} \qquad\qquad y^{-1} = z \qquad\qquad \dots (4)$$

Differentiating

$$-y^{-2} \frac{dy}{dx} = \frac{dz}{dx}$$

$$y^{-2} \frac{dy}{dx} = \frac{-dz}{dx} \qquad \dots (5)$$

Equation (3) becomes

$$\frac{-dz}{dx} + \frac{1}{x} z = \frac{\log x}{x}$$

$$\frac{dz}{dx} - \frac{1}{x} z = \frac{-\log x}{x} \qquad \dots (6)$$

It is linear equation in z of the form

$$\frac{dz}{dx} + Pz = Q \qquad \dots (7)$$

where $P = \dfrac{-1}{x}$ $Q = \dfrac{-\log x}{x}$

$$\text{I. F.} = e^{\int P \, dx} = e^{\int \frac{-1}{x} dx} = e^{-\log x} = e^{\log x^{-1}} = x^{-1} = \frac{1}{x}$$

Solution is, $z \cdot (\text{I. F.}) = \displaystyle\int Q \cdot (\text{I. F.}) \, dx + c$

$$z \cdot \frac{1}{x} = -\int \frac{\log x}{x} \cdot \frac{1}{x} \, dx + c$$

$$y^{-1} \cdot \frac{1}{x} = \left[\log x \left(-\frac{1}{x^2} \right) \right] dx + c$$

$$y^{-1} \cdot \frac{1}{x} = \left[\log x \left(\frac{1}{x} \right) \right] - \int \frac{1}{x} \left(\frac{1}{x} \right) dx + c$$

$$\frac{1}{xy} = \frac{\log x}{x} + \int \frac{-1}{x^2} dx + c$$

$$\frac{1}{xy} = \frac{\log x}{x} + \frac{1}{x} + c$$

Multiplying by x we get

$$\therefore \qquad \frac{1}{y} = \log x + 1 + cx \qquad \qquad \dots (8)$$

It is solution.

Example 1.51 : Solve : $\dfrac{dy}{dx} + \dfrac{x}{1 - x^2} y = x \sqrt{y}$

Solution : Given differential equation is

$$\frac{dy}{dx} + \frac{x}{1 - x^2} y = x \sqrt{y} \qquad \qquad \dots (1)$$

Dividing throughout by $\sqrt{y}$ we get

$$\frac{1}{\sqrt{y}} \frac{dy}{dx} + \frac{xy}{(1 - x^2) \sqrt{y}} = x$$

$$y^{-1/2} \frac{dy}{dx} + \frac{x}{1 - x^2} y^{1/2} = x \qquad \qquad \dots (2)$$

Put $\qquad \qquad \qquad y^{1/2} = z \qquad \qquad \dots (3)$

Differentiating we get

$$\frac{1}{2} y^{-1/2} \frac{dy}{dx} = \frac{dz}{dx}$$

$$\therefore \qquad \qquad y^{-1/2} \frac{dy}{dx} = 2 \frac{dz}{dx} \qquad \qquad \dots (4)$$

Equation (2) becomes

$$2 \frac{dz}{dx} + \frac{x}{1 - x^2} z = x$$

$$\frac{dz}{dx} + \frac{x}{2(1 - x^2)} z = \frac{x}{2} \qquad \qquad \dots (5)$$

It is linear equation in z of the form

$$\frac{dz}{dx} + Pz = Q \qquad \qquad \dots (6)$$

where $\quad P = \dfrac{x}{2(1-x^2)}, \quad Q = \dfrac{x}{2}$

$$I.\ F. = e^{\int P\,dx} \;=\; e^{\int \frac{x}{2(1-x^2)}\,dx}$$

$$= e^{-\frac{1}{4}\int \frac{-2x}{1-x^2}\,dx}$$

$$= e^{-\frac{1}{4}\cdot\log(1-x^2)}$$

$$= e^{\log(1-x^2)^{-1/4}}$$

$$I.\ F. \;=\; (1-x^2)^{-1/4}$$

The solution is

$$z\cdot(I.\ F.) \;=\; \int Q\cdot(I.\ F.)\,dx + c \qquad\qquad \dots (7)$$

$$z\cdot(1-x^2)^{-1/4} \;=\; \int \frac{x}{2}\,(1-x^2)^{-1/4}\,dx + c$$

Put $\qquad\qquad\qquad z = \sqrt{y}$

$$\sqrt{y}\,(1-x^2)^{-1/4} \;=\; \frac{-1}{4}\int (-2x)\,(1-x^2)^{-1/4}\,dx + c$$

$$\sqrt{y}\,(1-x^2)^{-1/4} \;=\; \frac{-1}{4}\int (1-x^2)^{-1/4}\cdot(-2x)\,dx + c$$

Using formula $\int [f(x)]^n\, f'(x)\,dx = \dfrac{[f(x)]^{n+1}}{n+1}$ If $n \neq -1$

$$\therefore \qquad \sqrt{y}\,(1-x^2)^{-1/4} \;=\; \frac{-1}{4}\,\frac{(1-x^2)^{3/4}}{3/4} + c$$

$$\therefore \qquad \sqrt{y}\,(1-x^2)^{-1/4} \;=\; \frac{-1}{3}\,(1-x^2)^{3/4} + c$$

$$\therefore \qquad \sqrt{y} \;=\; \frac{-1}{3}\,(1-x^2) + c\,(1-x^2)^{1/4} \qquad \dots (8)$$

It is solution.

Example 1.52 : $\dfrac{dy}{dx} + x\sin 2y = x^3 \cos^2 y$

Solution : Given differential equation is

$$\frac{dy}{dx} + x\sin 2y \;=\; x^3\cos^2 y \qquad\qquad \dots (1)$$

Dividing throughout by cos² y we get

$$\frac{1}{\cos^2 y} \frac{dy}{dx} + \frac{1}{\cos^2 y} \cdot x \sin 2y = x^3$$

$$\sec^2 y \frac{dy}{dx} + x \cdot \frac{2 \sin y \cos y}{\cos^2 y} = x^3$$

$$\sec^2 y \frac{dy}{dx} + 2 \frac{\sin y}{\cos y} = x^3$$

$$\sec^2 y \frac{dy}{dx} + 2 x \tan y = x^3 \qquad \dots (2)$$

Put $$\tan y = z \qquad \dots (3)$$

Differentiating we get

$$\sec^2 y \frac{dy}{dx} = \frac{dz}{dx} \qquad \dots (4)$$

Equation (2) becomes

$$\frac{dz}{dx} + 2xz = x^3 \qquad \dots (5)$$

It is a linear equation in z of the form

$$\frac{dz}{dx} + Pz = Q \qquad \dots (6)$$

where $P = 2x$, $Q = x^3$

$$I. F. = e^{\int P \, dx} = e^{\int 2x \, dx} = e^{x^2}$$

The solution is

$$z \cdot (I. F.) = \int Q \cdot (I. F.) \, dx + c \qquad \dots (7)$$

$$z \cdot e^{x^2} = \int x^3 \cdot e^{x^2} \, dx + c$$

Put $$z = \tan y$$

$$\tan y \cdot e^{x^2} = \int x^3 e^{x^2} \, dx + c$$

$$\tan y \cdot e^{x^2} = \frac{1}{2} \int x^2 \cdot e^{x^2} (2x) \, dx + c \qquad \dots (8)$$

Put $$x^2 = t \qquad \dots (9)$$

∴ $$2x \, dx = dt \qquad \dots (10)$$

Equation (8) becomes

$$\tan y \cdot e^{x^2} = \frac{1}{2} \int t \cdot e^t \, dt + c$$

$$\tan y \cdot e^{x^2} = \frac{1}{2} \, e^t \, (t - 1) + c$$

$$\tan y \cdot e^{x^2} = \frac{1}{2} \, e^{x^2} \, (x^2 - 1) + c$$

$$\therefore \qquad \tan y = \frac{1}{2} \, (x^2 - 1) + ce^{-x^2} \qquad \qquad \dots (11)$$

It is a solution.

Example 1.53 : Solve : $\dfrac{dy}{dx} - \dfrac{\tan y}{1 + x} = (1 + x) \, e^x \sec y$

Solution : Given differential equation is

$$\frac{dy}{dx} - \frac{\tan y}{1 + x} = (1 + x) \, e^x \sec y \qquad \qquad \dots (1)$$

Dividing throughout by sec y we get

$$\frac{1}{\sec y} \frac{dy}{dx} - \frac{1}{\sec y} \frac{\tan y}{1 + x} = (1 + x) \, e^x$$

$$\cos y \frac{dy}{dx} - \cos y \cdot \frac{1}{1 + x} \cdot \frac{\sin y}{\cos y} = (1 + x) \, e^x$$

$$\cos y \frac{dy}{dx} - \frac{\sin y}{1 + x} = (1 + x) \, e^x \qquad \qquad \dots (2)$$

Put $\qquad \qquad \sin y = z \qquad \qquad \dots (3)$

Then $\qquad \qquad \cos y \dfrac{dy}{dx} = \dfrac{dz}{dx} \qquad \qquad \dots (4)$

Equation (2) becomes

$$\frac{dz}{dx} - \frac{1}{1 + x} \, z = (1 + x) \, e^x \qquad \qquad \dots (5)$$

It is linear equation in z of the form

$$\frac{dz}{dx} + Pz = Q \qquad \qquad \dots (6)$$

where $\qquad \qquad P = \dfrac{-1}{1 + x}, \qquad \qquad Q = (1 + x) \, e^x$

$$\text{I. F.} = e^{\int P \, dx} = e^{\int \frac{-1}{1 + x} \, dx}$$

$$= e^{-\log (1 + x)}$$

$$= e^{\log (1 + x)^{-1}}$$

$$= (1 + x)^{-1}$$

$$\text{I. F.} = \frac{1}{1 + x}$$

The solution is

$$z \cdot (\text{I. F.}) = \int Q \cdot (\text{I. F.}) \, dx + c \qquad \ldots (7)$$

$$\therefore \qquad z \cdot \frac{1}{1+x} = \int (1+x) \, e^x \cdot \frac{1}{(1+x)} \, dx + c$$

Put

$$z = \sin y$$

$$\therefore \qquad \sin y \cdot \frac{1}{1+x} = \int e^x \, dx + c$$

$$\sin y \cdot \frac{1}{1+x} = e^x + c$$

$$\sin y = (1+x) \, [e^x + c] \qquad \ldots (8)$$

This is solution.

Example 1.54 : Solve : $3 \dfrac{dy}{dx} + \dfrac{2}{x+1} y = \dfrac{x^3}{y^2}$

Solution : Given differential equation is

$$3 \frac{dy}{dx} + \frac{2}{x+1} y = \frac{x^3}{y^2} \qquad \ldots (1)$$

Multiplying throughout by y^2 we get

$$3y^2 \frac{dy}{dx} + \frac{2}{x+1} y^3 = x^3 \qquad \ldots (2)$$

Put

$$y^3 = z \qquad \ldots (3)$$

$$\therefore \qquad 3y^2 \frac{dy}{dz} = \frac{dz}{dx} \qquad \ldots (4)$$

Equation (2) becomes

$$\frac{dz}{dx} + \frac{2z}{x+1} = x^3 \qquad \ldots (5)$$

It is linear equation in z of the form

$$\frac{dz}{dx} + Pz = Q \qquad \ldots (6)$$

where $P = \dfrac{2}{x+1}$, $\qquad Q = x^3$

$$\text{I. F.} = e^{\int P \, dx} = e^{\int \frac{2}{x+1} dx} = e^{2 \int \frac{1}{x+1} dx}$$

$$= e^{2 \log (x+1)}$$

$$= e^{\log (x+1)^2}$$

$$\text{I. F.} = (x+1)^2$$

Solution is

$$z \cdot (\text{I. F.}) = \int Q \cdot (\text{I. F.}) \, dx + c \qquad \ldots (7)$$

$$z \cdot (x + 1)^2 = \int x^2 \cdot (x + 1)^2 \, dx + c$$

Put

$$z = y^3$$

$$y^3 (x + 1)^2 = \int x^3 [x^2 + 2x + 1] \, dx + c$$

$$= \int (x^5 + 2x^4 + x^3) \, dx + c$$

$$y^3 (x + 1)^2 = \frac{x^6}{6} + 2\frac{x^5}{5} + \frac{x^4}{4} + c \qquad \ldots (8)$$

It is a solution.

Example 1.55 : Solve : $\dfrac{dy}{dx} + \dfrac{1}{x} = \dfrac{e^y}{x^2}$

Solution : Given differential equation is

$$\frac{dy}{dx} + \frac{1}{x} = \frac{e^y}{x^2} \qquad \ldots (1)$$

Dividing throughout by e^y we get

$$e^{-y}\frac{dy}{dx} + e^{-y}\frac{1}{x} = \frac{1}{x^2} \qquad \ldots (2)$$

Put

$$e^{-y} = z \qquad \ldots (3)$$

Differentiating we get

$$-e^{-y}\frac{dy}{dx} = \frac{dz}{dx}$$

$$\therefore \qquad e^{-y}\frac{dy}{dx} = \frac{-dz}{dx} \qquad \ldots (4)$$

Equation (2) becomes

$$\frac{-dz}{dx} + z \cdot \frac{1}{x} = \frac{1}{x^2}$$

$$\frac{dz}{dx} - z \cdot \frac{1}{x} = \frac{-1}{x^2} \qquad \ldots (5)$$

It is linear equation in z, of the form

$$\frac{dz}{dx} + Pz = Q \qquad \ldots (6)$$

where $P = \dfrac{-1}{x}$, $Q = \dfrac{-1}{x^2}$

$$\text{I. F.} = e^{\int P\,dx}$$

$$= e^{\int \frac{-1}{x}\,dx} = e^{-\log x} = e^{\log x^{-1}} = x^{-1} = \frac{1}{x}$$

The solution is

$$z \cdot (\text{I. F.}) = \int Q \cdot (\text{I. F.})\,dx + c \qquad \ldots (7)$$

$$z \cdot \frac{1}{x} = \int \left(\frac{-1}{x^2}\right)\frac{1}{x}\,dx + c$$

$$z \cdot \frac{1}{x} = -\int x^{-3}\,dx + c$$

$$z \cdot \frac{1}{x} = -\left[\frac{x^{-2}}{-2}\right] + c$$

$$z \cdot \frac{1}{x} = \frac{1}{2x^2} + c$$

Multiplying by $2x^2$ we get

$$2zx = 1 + 2\,cx^2$$

Put

$$z = e^{-y}$$

$$2\,e^{-y}\,x = 1 + 2cx^2$$

Multiplying by e^y we get

$$\therefore \qquad 2x = e^y + 2c\,e^y\,x^2 \qquad \ldots (8)$$

It is a solution.

EXERCISE 1.6

I. Theory Questions :

1. Define Bernoulli's differential equation and explain the method of solving it.

2. Explain the method of solving the Bernoulli's differential equation $\dfrac{dy}{dx} + Py = Qy^n$ where P and Q are functions of x only.

II. Solve the following differential equations :

1. $2\dfrac{dy}{dx} = \dfrac{y}{x} + \dfrac{y^2}{x^2}$

2. $[y \log x - 1]\, y\, dx = x\, dy$

3. $\dfrac{dy}{dx} - 2y \tan x = y^2 \tan^2 x$

4. $(x^2 y^2 + xy)\, dy = dx$

5. $(1 - x^2)\dfrac{dy}{dx} + xy = xy^2$

6. $\dfrac{dy}{dx} + y = y^2 e^x$

7. $\dfrac{dy}{dx} - y = y^2$

8. $\dfrac{dy}{dx} + \dfrac{y}{x} = \dfrac{y^2}{x^2}$

9. $x\dfrac{dy}{dx} + y = x^2 y^2$

10. $(1 + x^2)\dfrac{dy}{dx} = xy - y^2$

ANSWERS 1.6

1. $\dfrac{1}{xy} + \log x = c$

2. $\dfrac{1}{y} = \log x + 1 + c\,x$

3. $\dfrac{1}{y}\sec^2 x + \dfrac{1}{3}\tan^3 x + c$

4. $x^{-1} = -\,y^2 + 2 + ce^{\frac{-y^2}{2}}$

5. $\dfrac{1}{y} = 1 + c\,(1 - x^2)^{-1/2}$

6. $\dfrac{1}{y} + e^x\,(x - c) = 0$

7. $\dfrac{1}{y} = 1 - x + ce^{-x}$

8. $\dfrac{1}{xy} = \dfrac{1}{2x^2} + c$

9. $y\,(cx - x^2) = 1$

10. $\sqrt{1 + x^2} = y\sin^{-1} x + y\,c$

1.8 ORTHOGONAL TRAJECTORIES

Orthogonal Trajectories :

We study the orthogonal trajectories for the curves which are in Cartesian co-ordinates and polar co-ordinates.

Definition : 1.   Trajectory of the family : A curve which cuts, every member of the family of curves by same definite law, is called the **trajectory** of the family.

2.   Orthogonal Trajectory : A curve which cuts, every member of the family of curves, at **right angles**, is called the **orthogonal** trajectory of the family.

Procedure (Rule) for finding the orthogonal trajectory to a given family of curves in **Cartesian co-ordinates y = f (x).**

Step I : First write the equation of the given family of curves with an arbitrary = constant.

Step II : Differentiate the equation in step I, w. r. t. x and find $\dfrac{dy}{dx}$.

Step III : Replace $\dfrac{dy}{dx}$ by $\dfrac{-dx}{dy}$ in equation obtained in step II.

Step IV : From equations I and III, eliminate the arbitrary = constant and form the New differential equation and call this differential equation as **Equation of orthogonal Trajectories.**

Step V : Lastly Integrating (Solving) the differential equation of step IV, we get the equation of **Orthogonal Trajectories.**

SOLVED EXAMPLES

Example   1.56 : Find the orthogonal trajectories of the family of straight line y = mx.

Solution : The equation of the curve is y = mx   ... (1)

differentiate n w.r.t. x we get

$$\frac{dy}{dx} = m \qquad \qquad ... (2)$$

From equation (1) put $m = \dfrac{y}{x}$

$$\frac{dy}{dx} = \frac{y}{x}$$

Replace $\dfrac{dy}{dx}$ by $\dfrac{-dx}{dy}$

$$\frac{-dx}{dy} = \frac{y}{x}$$

$$-x\,dx = y\,dy$$
$$x\,dx + y\,dy = 0 \qquad \qquad \text{... (3)}$$

This is the differential equation of orthogonal trajectories.

To find orthogonal trajectories :

Integrating equation (3)

$$\int x\,dx + \int y\,dy = c'$$

$$\frac{x^2}{2} + \frac{y^2}{2} = c'$$

$$x^2 + y^2 = 2c'$$

$$\boxed{x^2 + y^2 = c} \qquad \qquad \text{... (4)}$$

This is the equation of the orthogonal trajectories.

Example 1.57 : Find the orthogonal trajectories for the curve $xy = a^2$.

Solution : Equation of the curve is $xy = a^2$ ... (1)

differentiating w. r. t. x we get

$$x\frac{dy}{dx} + y(1) = 0 \qquad \qquad \text{... (2)}$$

replace $\frac{dy}{dx}$ by $\left(-\frac{dx}{dy}\right)$

$$-x\frac{dx}{dy} + y = 0$$

$$-x\,dx + y\,dy = 0$$

$$x\,dx - y\,dy = 0 \qquad \qquad \text{... (3)}$$

This is the differential equation of the orthogonal trajectories.

To find orthogonal trajectories

$$x\,dx - y\,dy = 0$$

Integrating

$$\int x\,dx - \int y\,dy = 0$$

$$\frac{x^2}{2} - \frac{y^2}{2} = C'$$

$$x^2 - y^2 = 2C'$$

$$\boxed{x^2 - y^2 = C}$$

This is the equation of orthogonal trajectories.

Example 1.58 : Find the orthogonal trajectories of the curve $x^3 - 3xy^2 = a$

Solution : Equation of the curve is $x^3 - 3xy^2 = a$ ... (1)

differentiating w.r.t. x we get

$$3x^3 - 3\left[x \cdot 2y \frac{dy}{dx} - y^2 (1)\right] = 0 \qquad \text{... (2)}$$

$$x^2 - 2xy \frac{dy}{dx} - y^2 = 0$$

Replace $\frac{dy}{dx}$ by $\left(-\frac{dx}{dy}\right)$

$$x^2 + 2xy \frac{dx}{dy} - y^2 = 0 \qquad \text{... (3)}$$

This is the differential equation of orthogonal trajectories.

To find orthogonal trajectories

from (4) $[x^2 dy + 2xy dx] - y^2 dy = 0$

$$d[x^2 y] - y^2 dy = 0$$

Integrating we get

$$\int d(x^2 y) - \int y^2 dy = c'$$

$$x^2 y - \frac{y^3}{3} = c'$$

$$3x^2 y - y^3 = 3c'$$

$$y^3 - 3x^2 y = -3c'$$

$$y^3 - 3x^2 y = c \qquad \text{... (4)}$$

This is the equation of the orthogonal trajectories.

Example 1.59 : Find the orthogonal trajectories of the curve $x^2 + 4y^2 = a^2$.

Solution : The equation of the curve is $x^2 + 4y^2 = a^2$ ... (1)

differentiating w.r.t. x we get

$$2x + 8y \frac{dy}{dx} = 0$$

$$x + 4y \frac{dy}{dx} = 0 \qquad \text{... (2)}$$

replace $\frac{dy}{dx}$ by $-\frac{dx}{dy}$

$$x + 4y \left(-\frac{dx}{dy}\right) = 0$$

$$x - 4y \frac{dx}{dy} = 0 \qquad \text{... (3)}$$

This is the differential equation of orthogonal trajectories.

To find orthogonal trajectories

We have
$$x - 4y \frac{dx}{dy} = 0$$

$$x = 4y \frac{dx}{dy}$$

$$\frac{1}{4y} dy = \frac{1}{x} dx$$

Integrating

$$\frac{1}{4} \int \frac{1}{y} dy = \int \frac{1}{x} dx$$

$$\frac{1}{4} \log y = \log x + \log c'$$

$$\log y^{1/4} = \log (xc')$$

$$y^{1/4} = xc'$$

$$y = x^4 c'^4$$

$$\boxed{y = cx^4} \qquad \qquad ... (4)$$

This is the equation of orthogonal trajectories.

Example 1.60 : Find the orthogonal trajectories of the family of curve $\dfrac{x^2}{a^2} + \dfrac{y^2}{b^2 + \lambda} = 1$ where λ being a parameter.

Solution : Equation of the curve is

$$\frac{x^2}{a^2} + \frac{y^2}{b^2 + \lambda} = 1 \qquad \qquad ... (1)$$

Differentiating w.r.t. x. we get

$$\frac{1}{a^2} (2x) + \frac{1}{b^2 + \lambda} \left(2y \frac{dy}{dx}\right) = 0$$

$$\frac{1}{b^2 + \lambda} (2y) \frac{dy}{dx} = -\frac{2x}{a^2} \qquad \qquad ... (2)$$

put
$$\frac{dy}{dx} = -\frac{dx}{dy} \qquad \qquad ... (3)$$

$$-\frac{2y}{b^2 + \lambda} \frac{dx}{dy} = -\frac{2x}{a^2}$$

$$\frac{1}{b^2 + \lambda} = \left(-\frac{2x}{a^2}\right) \left(-\frac{1}{2y} \frac{dy}{dx}\right)$$

$$\frac{1}{b^2 + \lambda} = \frac{x}{a^2 y} \frac{dy}{dx} \qquad \qquad ... (4)$$

Using equation (4) equation (1) becomes

$$\frac{x^2}{a^2} + \left[\frac{x}{a^2 y}\frac{dy}{dx}\right]y^2 = 1 \qquad \dots (5)$$

This is the differential equation of the orthogonal trajectories.

To find the orthogonal trajectories

From equation (5)

$$\left[\frac{x}{a^2 y}\frac{dy}{dx}\right]y^2 = 1 - \frac{x^2}{a^2}$$

$$\frac{xy}{a^2}\frac{dy}{dx} = \left[1 - \frac{x^2}{a^2}\right]$$

$$y\,dy = \frac{a^2}{x}\left[1 - \frac{x^2}{a^2}\right]dx$$

$$y\,dy = a^2\left[\frac{1}{x} - \frac{x}{a^2}\right]dx$$

Integrating

$$\int y\,dy = a^2\left[\int \frac{1}{x}dx - \frac{1}{a^2}\int x\,dx\right]$$

$$\frac{y^2}{2} = a^2\left[\log x - \frac{1}{a^2}\left(\frac{x^2}{2}\right)\right] + c'$$

$$\frac{y^2}{2} = a^2\log x - \frac{x^2}{2} + c'$$

$$\frac{x^2}{2} + \frac{y^2}{2} = a^2\log x + c'$$

$$x^2 + y^2 = 2a^2\log x + 2c'$$

$$x^2 + y^2 = 2a^2 - \log x + c \qquad \dots (6)$$

This is the orthogonal trajectories.

Procedure (Rule) for finding the orthogonal trajectory to a given family of curves in polar co-ordinates r = f (θ) or f (r, θ) = 0.

Step I : First write the equation of the given family of curves in the polar form $r = f(\theta)$ or $f(r, \theta) = 0$.

Step II : Differentiate the equation in step I w. r. t. θ and obtain $\dfrac{dr}{d\theta}$.

Step III : Replace $\dfrac{dr}{d\theta}$ by $\left(-r^2\dfrac{d\theta}{dr}\right)$ in equation obtained in step II.

Step IV : From equations I and III, eliminate the arbitrary = constant and form the new differential equation and call this differential equation as **Equation of Orthogonal trajectories.**

Step V : Lastly Integrating (solving) the differential equation of Step IV, we get the equation of **Orthogonal Trajectories.**

Example 1.61 : Find the orthogonal trajectories for the curve r = a sin (θ).

Solution : Equation of the curve is r = a sin (θ)   ... (1)

Differentiating w. r. t. θ we get

$$\frac{dr}{d\theta} = a \cos \theta \qquad \qquad ... (2)$$

Replace $\frac{dr}{d\theta}$ by $- r^2 \frac{d\theta}{dr}$

$$- r^2 \frac{d\theta}{dr} = a \cos \theta \qquad \qquad ... (3)$$

From (1)   put $a = \dfrac{r}{\sin \theta}$

∴ $$- r^2 \frac{d\theta}{dr} = \frac{r}{\sin \theta} \cos \theta$$

∴ $$- r \frac{d\theta}{dr} = \frac{\cos \theta}{\sin \theta}$$

∴ $$\frac{dr}{r} = \frac{-\sin \theta}{\cos \theta} d\theta \qquad \qquad ... (4)$$

This is the differential equation of Orthogonal trajectories.

To find orthogonal trajectory :

Integrating equation (4)

$$\int \frac{1}{r} \, dr = \int \frac{-\sin \theta}{\cos \theta} \, d\theta \qquad \qquad ... (4)$$

∴ $\log r = \log (\cos \theta) + \log c$

∴ $\log r = \log [c \cos \theta]$

∴ $r = \cos \theta \qquad \qquad ... (5)$

This is the equation of orthogonal trajectory.

Example 1.62 : Find the orthogonal trajectories of the family of cardiodies r = a (1 + cos θ).

Solution : Equation of the cardiode is r = a (1 + cos θ)   ... (1)

Differentiating w. r. t. θ we get

$$\frac{dr}{d\theta} = - a \sin \theta \qquad \qquad ... (2)$$

Replace $\frac{dr}{d\theta}$ by $- r^2 \frac{d\theta}{dr}$

∴ $$- r^2 \frac{d\theta}{dr} = - a \sin \theta \qquad \qquad ... (3)$$

To eliminate a,

from (3)
$$a = \frac{r^2}{\sin \theta} \frac{d\theta}{dr} \qquad \qquad \text{... (4)}$$

from (1)
$$a = \frac{r}{1 + \cos \theta} \qquad \qquad \text{... (5)}$$

Equating equations (4) and (5)

$$\frac{r^2}{\sin \theta} \frac{d\theta}{dr} = \frac{r}{1 + \cos \theta}$$

$$\frac{d\theta}{\sin \theta} \frac{r}{dr} = \frac{1}{1 + \cos \theta}$$

$$\frac{dr}{r} = \frac{1 + \cos \theta}{\sin \theta} d\theta \qquad \qquad \text{... (6)}$$

This is the differential equation of the orthogonal trajectory.

To find orthogonal trajectory

In (6)   put $1 + \cos \theta = 2 \cos^2 (\theta/2)$

and $\sin \theta = 2 \sin \dfrac{\theta}{2} \cos \dfrac{\theta}{2}$

$\therefore$
$$\frac{dr}{r} = \left[\frac{2 \cos^2 (\theta/2)}{2 \sin (\theta/2) \cos (\theta/2)} \right] d\theta$$

$\therefore$
$$\frac{dr}{r} = \cot (\theta/2) \, d\theta$$

Integrating we get

$$\log r = \log \left(\frac{\sin \theta/2}{1/2} \right) + \log c'$$

$$\log r = 2 \log \sin (\theta/2) + \text{loc } c'$$

$$\log r = \log \sin^2(\theta/2) + \log c'$$

$$\log r = \log [c' \sin^2 (\theta/2)]$$

$\therefore$
$$r = c' \sin^2 (\theta/2)$$

Put $\sin^2 \left(\dfrac{\theta}{2} \right) = \dfrac{1 - \cos \theta}{2}$

$\therefore$
$$r = c' \left[\frac{1 - \cos \theta}{2} \right] \qquad \left(\text{Put} \frac{c'}{2} = c \right)$$

$\therefore$
$$r = c [1 - \cos \theta] \qquad \qquad \text{... (7)}$$

This is the equation of orthogonal trajectories for cardiodide (1)

Example 1.63 : Find the orthogonal trajectories for the curve $r^n = a^n \sin(n\theta)$

Solution : Equation of the curve is $r^n = a^n \sin(n\theta)$ ... (1)

Differentiating w. r. t. θ we get

$$n\, r^{n-1} \frac{dr}{d\theta} = a^n \cdot n \cos(n\theta)$$

$$\therefore \qquad \frac{dr}{d\theta} = \frac{a^n}{r^{n-1}} \cos(n\theta) \qquad\qquad ... (2)$$

Replace $\dfrac{dr}{d\theta}$ by $-r^2 \dfrac{d\theta}{dr}$

$$\therefore \qquad -r^2 \frac{d\theta}{dr} = \frac{a^n}{r^{n-1}} \cos(n\theta)$$

$$-r^2 \cdot r^{n-1}\, d\theta = a^n \cos(n\theta)\, dr$$

$$-r^{n+1}\, d\theta = a^n \cdot \cos(n\theta)\, dr$$

From (1) put $\qquad a^n = \dfrac{r^n}{\sin(n\theta)}$

$$\therefore \qquad -r^{n+1}\, d\theta = \frac{r^n}{\sin(n\theta)} \cos(n\theta)\, dr$$

$$\frac{-\sin(n\theta)}{\cos(n\theta)}\, d\theta = \frac{r^n\, dr}{r^{n+1}}$$

$$-\left[\frac{\sin(n\theta)}{\cos(n\theta)}\right] d\theta = \frac{dr}{r} \qquad\qquad ... (3)$$

This is the differential equation of orthogonal trajectories.

To find orthogonal trajectories

Multiply and divide L. H. S. of (3) by n

$$\frac{1}{n}\left[\frac{-n \sin(n\theta)}{\cos(n\theta)}\right] d\theta = \frac{1}{r}\, dr$$

Integrating

$$\frac{1}{n} \int \frac{-n \sin(n\theta)}{\cos(n\theta)}\, d\theta = \int \frac{1}{r}\, dr$$

$$\frac{1}{n} \log \cos(n\theta) = \log r + \log c'$$

$$\frac{1}{n} \log \cos(n\theta) = \log(rc')$$

$$\log \cos(n\theta) = n \log(rc')$$

$$\log \cos(n\theta) = \log(r^n\, c^n)$$

$$\log \cos (n\theta) = \log (r^n \, c^n)$$

$\therefore$
$$\cos (n\theta) = r^n \cdot c^n$$

$\therefore$
$$r^n = \frac{1}{c^n} \cos (n\theta) \quad \Rightarrow r^n = c \, [\cos (n\theta)] \; \dots \; (4)$$

This is the equation of the orthogonal trajectory.

Example 1.64 : Find the orthogonal trajectories for the curve
$$r = \frac{2a}{1 + \cos \theta}.$$

Solution : Equation of the curve is

$$r = \frac{2a}{1 + \cos \theta} \qquad \qquad \dots (1)$$

Differentiating w. r. t. θ we get

$$\frac{dr}{d\theta} = 2a \left[\frac{-1}{(1 + \cos \theta)^2} (- \sin \theta) \right] \qquad \dots (2)$$

Replace $\quad \dfrac{dr}{d\theta}$ by $- r^2 \dfrac{d\theta}{dr}$

$$- r^2 \frac{d\theta}{dr} = + \frac{2a \sin \theta}{(1 + \cos \theta)^2} \qquad \qquad \dots (3)$$

From (1) put $\qquad 2a = r \, (1 + \cos \theta)$

$$- r^2 \frac{d\theta}{dr} = \frac{+ r \, (1 + \cos \theta)}{(1 + \cos \theta)^2} \sin \theta$$

$$- r \frac{d\theta}{dr} = \frac{\sin \theta}{(1 + \cos \theta)}$$

$$- \frac{dr}{r} = \left[\frac{1 + \cos \theta}{\sin \theta} \right] d\theta$$

$$- \frac{dr}{r} = \frac{2 \cos^2 (\theta/2)}{2 \sin (\theta/2) \cos (\theta/2)} \, d\theta$$

$$- \frac{dr}{r} = \cot (\theta/2) \, d\theta$$

$$\frac{dr}{r} = - \cot (\theta/2) \, d\theta \qquad \qquad \dots (4)$$

This is the differential equation of orthogonal trajectory.

To find orthogonal trajectory.

Integrating equation (4)

$$\int \frac{1}{r} \, dr = - \int \cot (\theta/2) \, d\theta$$

$$\log r = -\log \frac{(\sin \theta/2)}{1/2} + \log c$$

$$\log r = -2 \log (\sin \theta/2) + \log c$$

$$\log r = -\log \sin^2 (\theta/2) + \log c$$

$$\log r = \log \left[\frac{c}{\sin^2 (\theta/2)}\right]$$

$$\therefore \qquad r = \frac{c}{\sin^2 (\theta/2)}$$

put $$\qquad \sin^2 (\theta/2) = \frac{1 - \cos \theta}{2}$$

$$\boxed{r = \frac{2c}{1 - \cos \theta}} \qquad \qquad ... (5)$$

This is the equation of orthogonal trajectory.

EXERCISE 1.7

I. 1. Find the orthogonal trajectories for the curve $y^2 = 4ax$ where a is a parameter.

2. Find the orthogonal trajectories for the curve $y = x + ae^x$, where a is a parameter.

3. Find the orthogonal trajectories for the circle $x^2 + y^2 = a^2$ where a is a parameter.

4. Find the orthogonal trajectories of the family of circles $x^2 + y^2 - 29x = 0$ where a is a parameter.

5. Prove that the orthogonal trajectories for the curve $x^p + c \cdot y^p = 1$ where c is a parameter and p is a constant, is $x^2 + y^2 = \frac{2 x^{2-p}}{2 - p} + $ constant.

II. 6. Find the orthogonal trajectories for the curve $r = a \cos \theta$.

7. Find the orthogonal trajectories of the family of cardiodes $r = a (1 - \cos \theta)$.

8. Find the orthogonal trajectories for the curve $r^n = a^n \cos (n\theta)$.

9. Find the orthogonal trajectories for the curve $r = a \sin^2 \theta$.

10. Find the orthogonal trajectories for the curve $r = a\theta$.

ANSWERS 1.7

I.

1. $y^2 + 2x^2 = c$
2. $x = y + 2 - ce^y$
3. $y = cx$
4. $x^2 + y^2 = cx$

II.

1. $r = c \sin \theta$
2. $r = c (1 + \cos \theta)$
3. $r^n = c \sin (n\theta)$
4. $r^2 = c \cos \theta$
5. $r = ce^{-\theta^2/2}$

UNIVERSITY QUESTIONS

April 2013

1. Explain the method of solving the differential equation of the form $\dfrac{dy}{dx} + Py = Qy^n$ where P and Q are functions of x only. Hence solve $x \dfrac{dy}{dx} + y = x^2 y^2$.   **[10 Marks]**

2. Define exact differential equation.
    If M dx + N dy = 0 is an exact differential equation then prove that $\dfrac{\partial M}{\partial y} = \dfrac{\partial N}{\partial x}$.   **[8 Marks]**

3. Solve $(x^2 + y^2 + 1) \, dx + 2xy \, dy = 0$ **[5 Marks]**

4. Solve $\sec^2 y \dfrac{dy}{dx} + 2x \tan y = x^3$ **[5 Marks]**

5. Solve $\dfrac{dy}{dx} = y \tan x - 2 \sin x$ **[4 Marks]**

6. Solve $\dfrac{dy}{dx} + xy = x^3 y^3$ **[4 Marks]**

Nov 2012

1. Prove that, the equation M dx + N dy = 0 is an exact differential equation if and only if $\dfrac{\partial M}{\partial y} = \dfrac{\partial N}{\partial x}$ [8 Marks]

2. Solve $\dfrac{dy}{dx} + xy = x^3 y^3$ [4 Marks]

April 2012

1. Define exact differential equation.
   If M dx + N dy = 0 is an exact differential equation   [8 Marks]
   then prove that $\dfrac{\partial M}{\partial y} = \dfrac{\partial N}{\partial x}$.

2. Solve $(x^2 + y^2) \, dx + 2xy \, dy = 0$.   [4 Marks]

Oct. 2011

1. Define Bernoulli's equation and explain the method of solving it.   [8 Marks]

2. Solve $[\sin x \cos y + e^{2x}] \, dx + [\cos x \sin y + \tan y] \, dy = 0$ [4 Marks]

3. Solve $\dfrac{dy}{dx} + \dfrac{n}{x} \, y = \dfrac{a}{x^n}$ [4 Marks]

May 2011

1. Show how to solve the equation $\dfrac{dy}{dx} + Py = Q$

   where P and Q are functions of x only.   [8 Marks]

2. Solve : $(e^y + 1) \cos x \, dx + e^y \sin x \, dy = 0$ [4 Marks]

3. Solve : $\dfrac{dy}{dx} - y \tan x = e^x$ [4 Marks]

MULTIPLE CHOICE QUESTIONS

Select the correct alternative for the following :

1. If in the differential equation M dx + N dy = 0, $\dfrac{1}{N} \left(\dfrac{\partial M}{\partial y} - \dfrac{\partial N}{\partial x} \right)$ is a function of x then integrating factor (I. F.) = ...

   (a) $e^{-\int f(x) \, dx}$ (b) $e^{\int f(x) \, dx}$

   (c) $\int f(x) \, dx$ (d) $-\int f(x) \, dx$

2. The solution of the differential equation $\dfrac{y\,dx - x\,dy}{y^2} = 0$ is
....

(a) $\dfrac{y}{x} = C$

(b) $\dfrac{x + y}{y} = c$

(c) $\dfrac{x}{y} = C$

(d) $x + y = c$

3. A solution obtained by giving particular values to arbitrary = constants in .... solution is called the particular solution.

(a) General

(b) Complete

(c) Singular

(d) Non-singular

4. The equation M dx + N dy = 0 is said to be exact if

(a) $\dfrac{\partial M}{\partial x} = \dfrac{\partial N}{\partial y}$

(b) $\dfrac{\partial^2 M}{\partial x^2} = \dfrac{\partial^2 N}{\partial y^2}$

(c) $\dfrac{\partial^2 M}{\partial y^2} = \dfrac{\partial^2 N}{\partial x^2}$

(d) $\dfrac{\partial M}{\partial y} = \dfrac{\partial N}{\partial x}$

5. If the equation M dx + N dy = 0 is homogeneous equation in x and y then I. F. = ...

(a) $\dfrac{1}{Mx + Ny}$, provided M dx + N dy ≠ 0

(b) $e^{\int f(x)\,dx}$

(c) $e^{\int f(y)\,dy}$

(d) $\dfrac{1}{Mx - Ny}$, provided M dx − N dy ≠ 0

6. If the differential equation $\dfrac{dy}{dx} + Py = Q$ where P and Q are functions of x only then I. F. = ...

(a) $e^{\int P\,dx}$

(b) $e^{\int Q\,dx}$

(c) $e^{\int Q\,dy}$

(d) $e^{\int P\,dy}$

7. If the differential equation $M\,dx + N\,dy = 0$

   If $\dfrac{1}{M}\left(\dfrac{\partial N}{\partial x} - \dfrac{\partial M}{\partial y}\right)$ is a function of y alone, then I. F. ....

   (a) $\dfrac{1}{Mx + Ny}$ provided $M\,dx + N\,dy \neq 0$

   (b) $e^{\int f(x)\,dx}$

   (c) $e^{\int f(y)\,dy}$

   (d) $\dfrac{1}{Mx - Ny}$ provided $M\,dx - N\,dy \neq 0$

8. The general solution of the differential equation $\dfrac{dx}{dy} + \dfrac{1}{y}\,x = \dfrac{1}{y}$ is ....

   (a) $x = y + c$ (b) $xy = y^2 + c$

   (c) $x = 1 + \dfrac{c}{y}$ (d) $xy = 1 + c$

9. If the differential equation $M\,dx + N\,dy = 0$. If $\dfrac{1}{N}\left(\dfrac{\partial M}{\partial y} - \dfrac{\partial N}{\partial x}\right)$ is a function of x alone then I. F. = ...

   (a) $e^{\int f(x)\,dx}$

   (b) $\dfrac{1}{Mx + Ny}$, provided $M\,dx + N\,dy \neq 0$

   (c) $e^{\int f(y)\,dy}$

   (d) $\dfrac{1}{Mx - Ny}$, provided $M\,dx - N\,dy \neq 0$

10. The general solution of the differential equation $\dfrac{dy}{dx} + \dfrac{y}{x} = \dfrac{1}{x}$ is ....

    (a) $xy = x^2 + c$ (b) $y = 1 + \dfrac{c}{x}$

    (c) $xy = 1 + c$ (d) $y = x + c$

11. If the differential equation $M \, dx + N \, dy = 0$. If $M = y \, f_1(x, y)$ and $N = x \, f_2(x, y)$ then I. F.

   (a) $\dfrac{1}{Mx + Ny}$, provided $M \, dx + N \, dy \neq 0$

   (b) $e^{\int f(x) \, dx}$

   (c) $e^{\int f(y) \, dy}$

   (d) $\dfrac{1}{Mx - Ny}$, provided $M \, dx - N \, dy \neq 0$

12. The degree of the differential equation $\left(\dfrac{d^3y}{dx^3}\right)^2 + \dfrac{d^2y}{dx^2} + \dfrac{dy}{dx} + 5y = 0$ is ....

   (a) 3   (b) 2

   (c) 5   (d) 1

13. An equation which involves only one independent variable and differential coefficients with respect to it, is called .... differential equation.

   (a) Partial   (b) Total

   (c) Ordinary   (d) Simultaneous

14. Which of the following pair is not true.

   (a) $\dfrac{dy}{dx} + Py = Q \leftrightarrow$ linear differential equation

   (b) $\dfrac{dy}{dx} + Py = Qy^n \leftrightarrow$ Bernoulli's differential equation

   (c) $\dfrac{\partial M}{\partial y} = \dfrac{\partial N}{\partial x} \leftrightarrow$ Exact differential equation

   (d) $y = Px + f(D) \leftrightarrow$ Clairaut's equation

ANSWERS

1.	(b)	2.	(c)	3.	(a)	4.	(d)	5.	(a)
6.	(a)	7.	(c)	8.	(c)	9.	(a)	10.	(b)
11.	(d)	12.	(b)	13.	(c)	14.	(c)		

✳ ✳ ✳

LINEAR DIFFERENTIAL EQUATIONS WITH CONSTANT COEFFICIENTS

2.1 INTRODUCTION

In this unit we study the operator D, and linear differential equations with constant coefficients and methods of solving them.

(1) The Operator D :   The symbol D is called the differential operator. It stands for $\dfrac{d}{dx}$. We write

$$D = \frac{d}{dx} \, , D^2 = \frac{d^2}{dx^2} \, , D^3 = \frac{d^3}{dx^3} \, , \ldots\ldots\ldots.D^n = \frac{d^n}{dx^n}$$

Also we write,

$$Dy = \frac{dy}{dx} \, , \quad D^2y = \frac{d^2y}{dx^2} \, , D^3y = \frac{d^3y}{dx^3} \, , \ldots\ldots D^n\, y = \frac{d^ny}{dx^n}$$

Thus,
$$D(x^3) \;=\; \frac{d}{dx}\,(x^3) = 3x^2$$

$$D^2\,(x^3) \;=\; \frac{d^2}{dx^2}\,(x^3) = 6x$$

Properties of Operator C :

1. $\qquad\qquad\qquad (D + a)y \;=\; Dy + ay$

2. $\qquad\qquad\quad D\,(y_1 + y_2) \;=\; Dy_1 + Dy_2$

3. $\qquad\quad (\alpha\, D^m + BD^n)\, y \;=\; \alpha\, D^m y + BD^n\, y$

4. $\qquad\qquad\qquad D^m\,(D^n y) \;=\; D^{m+n}\, y$

(2) The Inverse Operator D^{-1} :

The operator $\dfrac{1}{D}$ or D^{-1} is called the inverse operator of D. It stands for the integration w.r.t. the independent variable.

Thus,

1. $\dfrac{1}{D} f(x) = \int f(x)\,dx$ or $D^{-1} f(x) = dx$

2. $D^{-1}(\sin x) = \int \sin x\,dx = -\cos x$

3. $D^{-2} f(x) = \dfrac{1}{D^2} f(x) = \int \quad dxx$

4. $D^{-2}(x^2) = \dfrac{1}{D^2}(x^2) = \dfrac{1}{D}\left[\int x^2\,dx\right]$

$$= \dfrac{1}{D}\left[\dfrac{x^3}{x}\right] = \dfrac{x^4}{12}$$

5. In general, for positive integer n.

$$D^{-n}[f(x)] = \dfrac{1}{D^n} f(x) = \underset{\text{(n times)}}{\int\int\int} \dots \int [f(x)]\,dx \cdot dx_{\text{for n times}} \dots dx$$

(3) Linear Differential Equation f (D) y = x.

The differential equation which involves the dependent variable and it's derivative in the first degree only is called <u>Linear differential equation.</u>

The general form of the linear differential equation of nth order is

$$\dfrac{d^n y}{dx^n} + P_1 \dfrac{d^{n-1} y}{dx^{n-1}} + P_2 \dfrac{d^{n-2}\cdot y}{dx^{n-2}} + \dots P_{n.y} = x \qquad \dots(1)$$

Where, x is the function of x only or zero and $P_1, P_2, \dots P_n$ are either functions of x or constants.

Using the operator D equation (1) is written as,

$$[D^n + P_1 D^{n-1} + P_2 D^{n-2} + \dots P_n]_y = x \qquad \dots(2)$$

or $\qquad\qquad\qquad\qquad\qquad\qquad\qquad f(D) \cdot y = x \qquad \dots(3)$

Where, $f(D) = [D^n + P_1 D^{n-1} + P_2 D^{n-2} + \dots P_n]$

(4) Linear differential equations with constant coefficients : If in the linear differential equation $[D^n + P_1 D^{n-1} + P_2 D^{n-2} + \dots + P_n]\,y = x$ the coefficients $P_1, P_2 \dots P_n$ are only the constants but not functions of x, then the equation is said to be linear differential equation with constant coefficients.

2.2 GENERAL OR COMLETE SOLUTION OF f(D) Y = 0

Theorem : If $y = y_1$, $y = y_2 = y = y_3$, ... $y = y_n$ are n linearly independent solutions of the linear differential equation $f(D) y = 0$ then $y = c_1y_1 + c_2y_2 + c_3y_3 .... + c_ny_n$ is also the general or complete solution of $f(D) y = 0$ where $c_1, c_2, c_3, ... c_n$ are arbitrary constants.

Proof : The linear differential equation with constant coefficient is

$$f(D) y = 0 \qquad ...(1)$$

$$\therefore \qquad [D^n + P_1D^{n-1} + P_2 D^{n-2}y + ... + P_n] y = 0$$

$$[D^ny + P_1D^{n-1} y + P_2 D^{n-2}y + ... + P_n y] = 0 \qquad ...(2)$$

If $y = y_1$, $y = y_2$, $y = y_3$, ... $y = y_n$ are its solutions then

$$\left. \begin{array}{l} D^ny_1 + P_1D^{n-1} y_1 + P_2 D^{n-2}y_1 + ... + P_ny_1 = 0 \\ D^n y_2 + P_1D^{n-1} y_2 + P_2 D^{n-2} y_2 + ... + P_ny_2 = 0 \\ D^ny_3 + P_2D^{n-1}y_3 + P_2D^{n-2} y_3 + ... + P_ny_3 = 0 \\ \text{--------------------------------------} \\ \text{--------------------------------------} \\ D^ny_n + P_1 D^{n-1} y_n + P_2D^{n-2} y_n + ... + P_ny_n = 0 \end{array} \right\} \qquad ...(3)$$

If $y = c_1y_1 + c_2y_2 + c_3y_3 + ... + c_ny_n$ then

$$[D^ny + P_1D^{n-1}y + P_2D^{n-2}y + ... P_ny]$$

$$= D^n[c_1y_1 + c_2y_2 + c_3y_3 + c_n y_n] + P_1D^{n-1} [c_1y_1 + c_2y_2 + c_3 y_3 + ... c_yy_n]$$

$$+ P_2D^{n-2} (c_1y_1 + c_2y_2 + c_3y_3 + ... c_ny_n) + ... + P_n [c_1y_1 + c_2y_2 + c_3y_3 + ... + c_ny_n]$$

$$= c_1 [D^ny_1 + P_1D^{n-1} y_1 + P_2 D^{n-2}y_1 + ... + P_ny_1] + c_2 [D_ny_2 + P_1 D^{n-1}y_2 + P_2 D^{n-2} y_2 + ... + P_ny_2] + c_3 [D^n y_n + P_1D^{n-1} y_3 + P_2D^{n-2}y_3 + ... + P_ny_3]$$

$$... + c_n [D^ny_n + P_1D^{n-1} y_n + P_2 D^{n-3} y_n + ... + P_ny_n]$$

Using equation (3) it becomes

$$= c_1 (0) + c_2(0) + c_3 (0) + ... + c_n(0)$$

$$[D^ny + P_1D^{n-1}y + P_2D^{n-2}y + .. + P_ny] = 0 \qquad ...(4)$$

Thus, $y = c_1y_1 + c_2y_2 + c_3y_3 + ... + c_ny_n$ satisfies the equation

$$f(D) y = 0$$

As y contains n arbitrary constants, hence it is general or complete solution of $f(D) y = 0$

Auxilliary Equation (A.E.) : Consider the differential equation

$$f(D) y = 0 \qquad ...(1)$$

$$\therefore \qquad (D^n + P_1D^{n-1} + P_2 D^{n-2} + ... + P_n) y = 0 \qquad ... (2)$$

$$D^n y + P_1D^{n-1} y_1 + P_2 D^{n-2} y + ... + P_ny = 0 \qquad ...(3)$$

Let, $y = e^{mx}$ be the solution of equation (3)

Then,
$$Dy = me^{mx},$$
$$D^2y = m^2e^{mx},$$
$$D^3y = m^3 e^{mx}...., \quad D^ny = m^ne^{mx}$$

Using above values equation (3) becomes

$$[m^ne^{mx} + P_1m^{n-1} e^{mx} + P_2 m^{n-2} e^{mx} + ... + P_ne^{mx}] = 0$$

$$[m^n + P_1 m^{n-1} + P_2m^{n-2} + ... P_n] e^{mx} = 0 \qquad ...(4)$$

Cancelling $e^{mx} \neq$ we get

$$[m^n + P_1m^{n-1} + P_2m^{n-2} + ... + P_n] = 0 \qquad ...(5)$$

Thus, e^{mx} will be solution of equation (2).

If m is root of equation (4)

The equation $f(m) = 0$ is called the A. E. for the equation $f(D)y = 0$

Replacing m by D equation (5) becomes

$$f(D) = 0 \qquad ...(6)$$

Thus, equation $f(D) = 0$ is called A. E. for the equation $f(D) y = 0$ which is obtained by equating to zero the symbolic coefficient of y in $f(D) y = 0$.

Thus, we define A. E. as follows :

If the differential equation is

$$[D^n + P_1 D^{n-1} + P_2 D^{n-2} + ... P_n] = 0 \qquad ...(1)$$

then the equation

$$[D^n + P_1 Dn^{-1} + P_2D^{n-2} + ... P_n] = 0 \qquad ...(2)$$

is called the Auxiliary Equation, which is obtained by equating to zero, the symbolic coefficient of y in (1) provided D being algebraic quantity.

Also, we say that $f(D) = 0$ is the A. E. of differential equation $f(D) y = 0$

EXERCISE 2.1

I.   Theory Questions :

1.   Define Linear differential equation with constant coefficient.

2.   Define auxiliary equation w.r.t. $f(D) y = 0$

3.   Prove that, If $y = y_1, y = y_2, y = y_3..... y = y_n$ are n linearly independent solutions of the linear differential equation $f(D) y = 0$ then $y = c_1y_1 + c_2y_2 + c_3y_3 + ... + c_ny_n$ is the general solution of $f(D) y = 0$.

Solution of $f(D) y = 0$, when Auxiliary Equation has different roots.

2.3 SOLUTION OF F (D) y = 0 WHEN A. E. HAS REAL AND NON REPEATED ROOTS

Given differential equation be f (D) y = 0 ...(1)

Suppose its A. E. be f (D) = 0 ...(2)

Let m_1, m_2, m_3 ... m_n be n real and non-repeated roots of A. E. f (D) = 0

Then $y = e^{mx}$, $y = e^{m_2x}$, ... $y = e^{m_3x}$, ... $y = e^{m_nx}$ are the n independent solutions of f (D) y = 0. Hence, the general or complete solution of equation (1) is given by

$$y = c_1 e^{m_1x} + c_2 2e^{m_2x} + c_3 e^{m_3x} + ... + c_n e^{m_nx} \qquad ...(3)$$

Examples on auxiliary equation with real and n on repeated roots :

SOLVED EXAMPLES

Example 2.1 : Solve : $\dfrac{d^2y}{dx^2} - 5\dfrac{dy}{dx} + 6y = 0$

Solution : Given differential equation is

$$\dfrac{d^2y}{dx^2} - 5\dfrac{dy}{dx} + 6y = 0 \qquad ...(1)$$

Using operator $D = \dfrac{d}{dx}$, it can be written as,

$$[D^2 - 5D + 6] y = 0$$

The auxiliary equation

$$[D - 2] [D - 3] = 0$$
$$D - 2 = 0 \quad , \quad D - 3 = 0$$
$$D = 2 \quad , \quad D = 3$$

Let $m_1 = 2$ and $m_2 = 3$

The roots of auxiliary equation are real and non repeated (unequal).

The solution of equation is

$$y = c_1 e^{m_1x} + c_2 e^{m_2x} \qquad ...(3)$$
$$y = c_1 e^{2x} + c_2 e^{3x} \qquad ...(4)$$

Example 2.2 : Solve $\dfrac{d^2y}{dx^2} + 5\dfrac{dy}{dx} + 4y = 0$

Solution : Given differential equation is

$$\dfrac{d^2y}{dx^2} + 5\dfrac{dy}{dx} + 4y = 0 \qquad ...(1)$$

Using operator $D = \dfrac{d}{dx}$ it can be written as

$$[D^2 + 5D + 4]\, y \ = \ 0 \qquad\qquad ...(2)$$

The auxiliary equation is,

$$[D^2 + 5D + 4] \ = \ 0$$
$$[D + 1]\,[D + 4] \ = \ 0$$
$$D + 1 = 0 \ \ \& \ \ D + 4 = 0$$
$$D = -1 \ , \ \ D = -4$$

Say $m_1 = -1$ and $m_2 = -4$

The roots of auxiliary equation are real and non repeated (unequal).

The solution is, $\qquad\qquad\qquad y \ = \ c_1 e^{m_1 x} + c_2\, e^{m_2 x} \qquad ...(3)$

$$y \ = \ c_1 e^{-x} + c_2 e^{-4x} \qquad ...(4)$$

Example 2.3 : Solve : $\dfrac{d^2 y}{dx^2} - 4\,\dfrac{dy}{dx} + y = 0$

Solution : The given differential equation is

$$\frac{d^2 y}{dx^2} - 4\frac{dy}{dx} + y \ = \ 0 \qquad\qquad ...(1)$$

Using the operator $D = \dfrac{d}{dx}$, it can be written as

$$[D^2 - 4D + 1]\, y \ = \ 0 \qquad\qquad ...(2)$$

The auxiliary equation is

$$D^2 - 4D + 1 \ = \ 0 \qquad\qquad ...(3)$$

Comparing with,

$$aD^2 + bD + c \ = \ 0 \qquad\qquad ...(4)$$

We get, $a = 1, b = -4, c = 1$

$$D \ = \ \frac{-b \pm \sqrt{b^2 - 4ac}}{2a}$$

$$D \ = \ \frac{4 \pm \sqrt{16 - 4}}{2}$$

$$D \ = \ \frac{4 \pm \sqrt{12}}{2}$$

$$D \ = \ \frac{4 \pm 2\sqrt{3}}{2}$$

$$D \ = \ 2 \pm \sqrt{3}$$

Let, $D = 2 + \sqrt{3}$ and $D = 2 - \sqrt{3}$

Let $m_1 = 2 + \sqrt{3}$ and $m_2 = 2 - \sqrt{3}$

The roots are auxiliary equation are real and non-repeated (unequal)

The solution is

$$y = c_1 e^{m_1 x} + c_2 e^{m_2 x} \qquad \qquad ...(5)$$

$$y = c_1 e^{[2 + \sqrt{3}]x} + c_2 e^{[2 - \sqrt{3}]x} \qquad \qquad ...(6)$$

Example 2.4 : Solve : $\dfrac{d^3y}{dx^3} - 6\dfrac{d^2y}{dx^2} + 11\dfrac{dy}{dx} - 6y = 0$

Solution : Given differential equation is

$$\dfrac{d^3y}{dx^3} - 6\dfrac{d^2y}{dx^2} + 11\dfrac{dy}{dx} - 6y = 0 \qquad \qquad ...(1)$$

Using the operator $D = \dfrac{d}{dx}$. It can be written as,

$$[D^3 - 6D^2 + 11\,D - 6]\,y = 0 \qquad \qquad ...(2)$$

The auxiliary equation is

$$D^3 - 6D^2 + 11\,D - 6 = 0 \qquad \qquad ...(3)$$

$$D^3 - D^2 - 5D^2 + 5D + 6D - 6 = 0$$

$$D^2\,(D - 1) - 5D\,(D - 1) + 6\,(D - 1) = 0$$

$$(D - 1)\,(D^2 - 5D + 6) = 0$$

$$(D - 1)\,[(D - 2)\,(D - 3)] = 0$$

$$D = 1, D = 2, D = 3$$

Say, $m_1 = 1, m_2 = 2, m_3 = 3$

The roots are auxiliary equation are real and non repeated (unequal).

The solution is,

$$y = c_1 e^{m_1 x} + c_2 e^{m_2 x} + c_3 e^{m_3 x} \qquad \qquad ...(4)$$

$$y = c_1 e^x + c_2 e^{2x} + c_3\,e^{3x} \qquad \qquad ...(5)$$

Example 2.5 : Solve : $2\dfrac{d^3y}{dx^2} - 7\dfrac{d^2y}{dx^2} + 7y\dfrac{dy}{dx} - 2y = 0$

Solution : Given differential equation is

$$2\dfrac{d^3y}{dx^3} - 7\dfrac{d^2y}{dx^2} + 7y\dfrac{dy}{dx} - 2y = 0 \qquad \qquad ...(1)$$

Using the operator $D = \dfrac{d}{dx}$, it can be written as

$$[2D^3 - 7D^2 + 7D - 2]\,y = 0 \qquad \qquad ...(2)$$

The auxiliary equation is

$$2D^3 - 7D^2 + 7D - 2 = 0$$
$$2D^3 - 2D^2 - 5D^2 + 5D + 2D - 2 = 0$$
$$2D^2(D-1) - 5D(D-1) + 2(D-1) = 0$$
$$(D-1)(2D^2 - 5D + 2) = 0$$
$$(D-1) = 0$$
$$D = 1$$
$$2D^2 - 5D + 2 = 0$$
$$a = 2, b = -5, c = 2$$
$$D = \frac{5 \pm \sqrt{25 - 16}}{4}$$
$$D = \frac{5 \pm \sqrt{9}}{4}$$
$$D = \frac{5+3}{4} = 2, D = \frac{5-3}{4} = \frac{1}{2}$$

Say, $m_1 = 1$, $m_2 = 2$, $m_3 = \frac{1}{2}$

The roots of auxiliary roots are real and non-repeated (unequal).

The solution is, $y = c_1 e^{m_1 x} + c_2 e^{m_2 x} + c_3 e^{m_3 x}$ ...(3)

$y = c_1 e^x + c_2 e^{2x} + c_3 e^{x/2}$ ...(4)

Example 2.6 : Solve : $[D^3 + 9D^2 + 23D + 15] y = 0$

Solution : Given differential equation is

$$[D^3 + 9D^2 + 23D + 15] y = 0 \qquad ...(1)$$

The auxiliary equation is

$$D^3 + 9D^2 + 23D + 15 = 0 \qquad ...(2)$$
$$D^3 + D^2 + 8D^2 + 8D + 15D + 15 = 0$$
$$D^2(D+1) + 8D(D+1) + 15(D+1) = 0$$
$$(D+1)(D^2 + 8D + 15) = 0$$
$$(D+1)(D+3)(D+5) = 0$$

$D = -1, D = -3, D = -5$

say $m_1 = -1$, $m_2 = -3$, $m_3 = -5$

The roots of auxiliary equation are real and non-repeated (unequal).

The solution is

$$y = c_1 e^{m_1 x} + c_2 e^{m_2 x} + c_3 e^{m_3 x} \qquad ...(3)$$
$$y = c_1 e^{-x} + c_2 e^{-3x} + c_3 e^{-5x} \qquad ...(4)$$

Example 2.7 : Solve $[D^3 + 6D^2 + 11 D + 6]y = 0$

Solution : Given differential equation is

$$[D^3 + 6D^2 + 11D + 6]y = 0 \qquad \qquad ...(1)$$

The auxiliary equation is

$$D^3 + D^2 + 5D^2 + 5D + 6D + 6 = 0$$

$$D^2 (D + 1) + 5D (D + 1) + 6 (D + 1) = 0$$

$$(D + 1) (D^2 + 5D + 6) = 0$$

$$(D + 1) (D + 2) (D + 3) = 0$$

$$D = -1, D = -2, \ D = -3$$

Say $m_1 = -1, m_2 = -2, m_3 = -3$

The roots are auxiliary equation are real and non-repeated (unequal).

The solution is

$$y = c_1 e^{m_1 x} + c_2 e^{m_2 x} + c_3 e^{m_3 x} \qquad \qquad ...(3)$$

$$y = c_1 e^{-x} + c_2 e^{-2x} + c_3 e^{-3x} \qquad \qquad ...(4)$$

Example 2.8 : Solve : $\dfrac{d^3y}{dx^3} - \dfrac{d^2y}{dx^2} - 12 \dfrac{dy}{dx} = 0$

Solution : Given differential equation is

$$\frac{d^3y}{dx^3} - \frac{d^2y}{dx^2} - 12 \frac{dy}{dx} = 0 \qquad \qquad ...(1)$$

Using the operator $D = \dfrac{d}{dx}$, it can be written as

$$[D^3 - D^2 - 12 D] y = 0$$

The auxiliary equation is

$$D^3 - D^2 - 12 D = 0 \qquad \qquad ...(2)$$

$$D [D^2 - D - 12] = 0$$

$$D [D - 4] [D + 3] = 0$$

$$D = 0, D = 4, D = -3$$

Say $m_1 = 0, m_2 = 4, m_3 = -3$

The solution is

$$y = c_1 e^{m_1 x} + c_2 e^{m_2 x} + c_3 e^{m_3 x} \qquad \qquad ...(3)$$

$$y = c_1 0^x + c_2 e^{4x} + c_2 e^{-3x}$$

$$y = c_1 + c_2 e^{4x} + c_3 e^{-3x} \qquad \qquad ...(4)$$

Example 2.9 : Solve : $\dfrac{d^4y}{dx^4} - 5 \dfrac{d^2y}{dx^2} + 4y = 0$

Solution : The given differential equation is

$$\frac{d^4y}{dx^4} - 5 \frac{d^2y}{dx^2} + 4y = 0 \qquad \qquad ...(1)$$

Using the operator $D = \dfrac{d}{dx}$. It can be written as

$$[D^4 - 5D^2 + 4]\, y \;=\; 0 \qquad\qquad …(2)$$

The auxiliary equation is

$$D^4 - 5D^2 + 4 \;=\; 0$$

$$(D^2 - 1)\,(D^2 - 4) \;=\; 0$$

$$[(D + 1)\,(D - 1)]\,[(D + 2)\,(D - 2)] \;=\; 0$$

$$D = -1,\ D = 1,\ D = -2,\ D = 2$$

Say $m_1 = -1,\ m_2 = 1,\ m_3 = -2,\ m_4 = 2$

The roots are real and non-repeated (unequal).

The solution is

$$y \;=\; c_1 e^{m_1 x} + c_2 e^{m_2 x} + c_3 e^{m_3 x} + c_4 e^{m_4 x} \qquad …(4)$$

$$y \;=\; c_1 e^{-x} + c_1 e^{x} + c_2 e^{-2x} + c_4 e^{2x} \qquad …(5)$$

Example 2.10 : Solve $[D^4 - 5D^3 + 5D^2 + 5D - 6]y = 0$

Solution : The given differential equation is

$$[D^4 - 5D^3 + 5D^2 + 5D - 6]y \;=\; 0 \qquad …(1)$$

The auxiliary equation is

$$D^4 - 5D^3 + 5D^2 + 5D - 6 \;=\; 0 \qquad …(2)$$

$$D^4 + D^3 - 6D^3 - 6D^2 + 11D^2 + 11D - 6D - 6 \;=\; 0$$

$$D^3\,(D + 1) - 6D^2\,(D + 1) + 11D\,(D + 1) - 6\,(D + 1) \;=\; 0$$

$$(D + 1)\,(D^3 - 6D^2 + 11D - 6) \;=\; 0$$

$(D + 1) = 0$	$D^3 - 6D^2 + 11D - 6 \;=\; 0$
$D = -1$	$D^3 - D^2 - 5D^2 + 5D + 6D - 6 \;=\; 0$

$$D^2\,(D - 1) - 5D\,(D - 1) + 6\,(D - 1) = 0$$

$$(D - 1)\,(D^2 - 5D + 6) \;=\; 0$$

$$(D - 1)\,(D - 2)\,(D - 3) \;=\; 0$$

$$D = 1,\ D = 2,\ D = 3$$

Say, $m_1 = -1,\ m_2 = 1,\ m_3 = 2,\ m_4 = 3$

The solution is

$$y \;=\; c_1 e^{m_1 x} + c_2 e^{m_2 x} + c_3 e^{m_3 x} + c_4 e^{m_4 x} \qquad …(3)$$

$$y \;=\; c_1 e^{-x} + c_2 e^{x} + c_3 e^{2x} + c_4 e^{3x} \qquad …(4)$$

EXERCISE 2.2

I. Theory Questions

1. Explain the method of solving the differential equation, $f(D) = 0$ when the auxiliary equation has real and non-repeated roots.

II. Problems :

Solve the following differential equations :

1. $\dfrac{d^2y}{dx^2} - 3\dfrac{dy}{dx} - 4y = 0$

2. $[D^2 + 3D + 2]\, y = 0$

3. $[D^2 + 2D - 1]y = 0$

4. $\dfrac{d^2y}{dx^2} - 7\dfrac{dy}{dx} - 44y = 0$

5. $\dfrac{d^3y}{dx^3} - 9\dfrac{d^2y}{dx^2} + 23\dfrac{dy}{dx} - 15\, y = 0$

6. $[D^3 - 7D - 6]y = 0$

7. $[D^3 - 4D^2 + D + 6]y = 0$

8. $[D^3 - 9D^2 + 26D - 24]y = 0$

9. $\dfrac{d^4y}{dx^4} - 10\dfrac{d^2y}{dx^2} + 9y = 0$

10. $[D^4 - 10D^3 + 35\,D^2 - 50\,D + 24]\, y = 0$

ANSWERS 2.2

II.

1. $y = c_1 e^{4x} + c_2 e^{-x}$

2. $y = c_1 e^{-x} + c_2 e^{-2x}$

3. $y = c_1 e^{[-1+\sqrt{2}]x} + c_2 e^{[-1-\sqrt{2}]x}$

4. $y = c_1 e^{11x} + c_2 e^{-4x}$

5. $y = c_1 e^x + c_2 e^{3x} + c_3 e^{5x}$

6. $y = c_1 e^{-x} + c_2 e^{-2x} + c_3 e^{3x}$

7. $y = c_1 e^{-x} + c_2 e^{2x} + c_3 e^{3x}$

8. $y = c_1 e^{2x} + c_2 e^{3x} + c_3 e^{4x}$

9. $y = c_1 e^{-x} + c_2 e^x + c_3 e^{-3x} + c_4 e^{3x}$

10. $y = c_1 e^x + c_2 e^{2x} + c_3 e^{3x} + c_4 e^{4x}$

2.4 SOLUTION OF F (D) y = 0 WHEN A. E. HAS REAL AND REPEATED (EQUAL) ROOTS

Given differential equation be $f(D) y = 0$ ...(1)

Suppose it's A. E. be $f(D) = 0$ ...(2)

Let, $m_1, m_2, m_3, ... m_n$ be its real roots in which m_1 roots is repeated twice there fore $m_1 = m_2$

Then, the solution is written as

$$y = c_1 e^{m_1 x} + c_2 e^{m_1 x} + c_3 e^{m_3 x} + ... + c_n e^{m_n x}$$

$$y = (c_1 + c_2) e^{m_1 x} + c_3 e^{m_3 x} + ... + c_n e^{m_n x}$$

Let $\qquad c_1 + c_2 = A$

$$y = A e^{m_1 x} + c_3 e^{m_3 x} + ... + c_n e^{m_n x} \qquad ... (3)$$

This solution contains $(n - 1)$ arbitrary constants which is not general solution. Therefore we use the following procedure to find the general solution.

Consider the equation $(D - m_1)^2 y = 0$ ...(4)

which is 2nd order whose A. E. $(D - m_1)^2 = 0$ ...(5)

has both the roots equal.

$\therefore \qquad (D - m_1)(D - m_1) y = 0$ ...(6)

Let, $\qquad (D - m_1) y = u$ ...(7)

Using equation (7) equation (6) becomes

$$(D - m_1) u = 0$$

$\therefore \qquad \dfrac{du}{dx} - m_1 u = 0$

$$\dfrac{du}{u} - m_1 dx = 0$$

Integrating, $\qquad \log u = m_1 x + \log c$

$$\log u - \log c = m_1 x$$

$$\log \dfrac{u}{c} = m_1 x$$

$$\dfrac{u}{c} = e^{m_1 x}$$

$$u = c e^{m_1 x} \qquad ...(8)$$

Again substituting value of u we write

$$(D - m_1) y = c e^{m_1 x}$$

It can be written as

$$\frac{dy}{dx} - m_1 y = ce^{m_1 x} \qquad \qquad ...(9)$$

It is linear differential equation of first order.

$$\text{I.F.} = e^{\int m_1 dx} = e^{-m_1 x}$$

The solution is

$$y.e^{-m_1 x} = \int ce^{m_1 x} \cdot c^{-m_1 x} \, dx + c_1$$

$$ye^{-m_1 x} = \int c \, dx + c_1$$

$$ye^{-m_1 x} = cx + c_1$$

$$y = (cx + c_1) e^{m_1 x}$$

Replacing c. by c_2, $y = (c_1 + c_2 x) e^{m_1 x} \qquad \qquad ...(10)$

Where, c_1 and c_2 are arbitrary constants. This is the general solution of equation. $f(D) y = 0$ when A. E. has real and twice repeated roots.

Remarks :

1. If three roots of A. E. $f(D) = 0$ are repeated say $m_1 = m_2 = m_3$ then the complete solution is $y = (c_1 + c_2 x + c_3 x^2)e^{m_1 x}$

2. If k roots of A. E. $f(D) = 0$ are repeated. say $m_1 = m_2 = m_3 = ... $ k times then the complete solution is
    $y = [c_1 + c_2 x + c_3 x^2 + c_4 x^3 + ... + c_k x^{k-1}] e^{m_1 x}$

3. If two roots of A. E. are equal and others are different then complete solution is $y = (c_1 + c_2 x) e^{m_1 x} + c_3 e^{m_3 x} + ... + c_n e^{m_n x}$

SOLVED EXAMPLES

Example 2.11 : Solve $[D^3 + 2D^2 + D] y = 0$

Solution : Given differential equation is

$$[D^3 + 2D^2 + D] y = 0 \qquad \qquad ...(1)$$

Auxiliary equation is

$$[D^3 + 2D^2 + D] = 0 \qquad \qquad ...(2)$$

$$D[D^2 + 2D + 1] = 0$$

$$D[D + 1]^2 = 0$$

$D = 0, D = -1, D = -1$

one root $D = 0$ is real.

Other two roots are real and equal.

Let, $m_1 = 0, m_2 = m_3 = -1$.

The solution is

$$y = c_1 e^{m_1 x} + [c_2 + c_3 x] e^{m_2 x}$$
$$y = c_1 e^{0x} + [c_2 + c_3 x] e^{-x}$$
$$y = c_1 + [c_2 + c_3 x] e^{-x} \qquad ...(3)$$

This is the solution of equation (1)

Example 2.12 : Solve $[D^4 + 2D^3 + D^2] y = 0$

Solution : Given differential equation is

$$[D^4 + 2D^3 + D^2] y = 0 \qquad ...(1)$$

Auxiliary equation is

$$[D^4 + 2D^3 + D^2] = 0 \qquad ...(2)$$
$$D^2 [D^2 + 2D + 1] = 0$$
$$D^2 [D + 1]^2 = 0$$
$$D^2 = 0, [D + 1]^2$$
$$D = 0, D = 0, D = -1, D = -1$$

Let, $m_1 = m_2 = 0, m_3 = m_4 = -1$

The roots are real and equal in pairs

The solution is

$$y = (c_1 + c_2 x) e^{m_1 x} + (c_3 + c_4 x) e^{m_3 x}$$
$$y = (c_1 + c_2 x) e^6 + (c_3 + c_4 x) e^{-x}$$
$$y = (c_1 + c_2 x) + (c_3 + c_4 x) e^{-x} \qquad ...(3)$$

This is the solution of equation (1)

Example 2.13 : Solve : $\dfrac{d^2 y}{dx^2} - 2 \dfrac{dy}{dx} + y = 0$

Solution : Given differential equation is

$$\dfrac{d^2 y}{dx^2} - 2 \dfrac{dy}{dx} + y = 0 \qquad ...(1)$$

Using the operator $D = \dfrac{d}{dx}$, it can be written as

$$[D^2 - 2D + 1] y = 0 \qquad ...(2)$$

The A. E. is

$$[D^2 - 2D + 1] = 0$$
$$[D - 1]^2 = 0$$
$$D = 1, 1$$

The roots are real and equal (repeated)

The solution is

$$y = [c_1 + c_2 x] e^{m_1 x} \qquad ...(3)$$
$$y = [c_1 + c_2 x] e^x \qquad ...(4)$$

Example 2.14 : Solve : $\dfrac{d^3y}{dx^3} + 3\dfrac{d^2y}{dx^2} + 3\dfrac{dy}{dx} + y = 0$

Solution : Given differential equation is

$$\dfrac{d^3y}{dx^3} + 3\dfrac{d^2y}{dx^2} + 3\dfrac{dy}{dx} + y = 0 \qquad \ldots(1)$$

Using the operator $D = \dfrac{d}{dx}$, it can be written as

$$[D^3 + 3D^2 + 3D + 1]\, y = 0 \qquad \ldots(2)$$

The Auxiliary equation is

$$D^3 + 3D^2 + 3D + 1 = 0 \qquad \ldots(3)$$

$$[D + 1]^3 = 0$$

$D + 1 = 0, D + 1 = 0, D + 1 = 0$

$D = -1, \quad D = -1, \quad D = -1$

Let, $m_1 = m_2 = m_3 = -1$

The roots of A. E. are real and equal (repeated).

The Solution is

$$y = [c_1 + c_2\, x + c_3\, x^2]\, e^{m_1 x} \qquad \ldots(4)$$

$$y = [c_1 + c_2 x + c_3\, x^2]\, e^{-x} \qquad \ldots(5)$$

Example 2.15 : Solve $[D^3 - 3D^2 + 4]\, y = 0$

Solution : Given differential equation is

$$[D^3 - 3D^2 + 4]\, y = 0 \qquad \ldots(1)$$

The A. E. is

$$[D^3 - 3D^2 + 4] = 0 \qquad \ldots(2)$$

$$[D^3 + D^2] - 4D^2 + 4 = 0$$

$$D^2\, [D + 1] - 4\, [D^2 - 1] = 0$$

$$D^2\, [D + 1] - 4\, [D + 1]\, [D - 1] = 0$$

$$[D + 1]\, [D^2 - 4\, (D - 1)] = 0$$

$$[D + 1]\, [D^2 - 4D + 4] = 0$$

$$[D + 1]\, [D - 2]^2 = 0$$

$$[D + 1]\, [D - 2]\, [D - 2] = 0$$

$$D = -1, 2, 2$$

Let, $m_1 = -1, m_2 = m_3 = 2$

The A. E. has real roots one pair of roots is equal.

The solution is

$$y = c_1\, e^{m_1 x} + [c_2 + c_3\, x]e^{m_2 x} \qquad \ldots(3)$$

$$y = c_1\, e^{-x} + [c_2 + c_3\, x]\, e^{2x} \qquad \ldots(4)$$

Example 2.16 : Solve : $\dfrac{d^3y}{dx^3} - 5\dfrac{d^2y}{dx^2} + 8\dfrac{dy}{dx} - 4y = 0$

Solution : Given differential equation is

$$\frac{d^3y}{dx^3} - 5\frac{d^2y}{dx^2} + 8\frac{dy}{dx} - 4y = 0 \qquad \qquad \text{...(1)}$$

Using the operator $D = \dfrac{d}{dx}$. It can be written as

$$[D^3 - 5D^2 + 8D - 4]\, y = 0 \qquad \qquad \text{...(2)}$$

The A. E. is

$$[D^3 - 5D^2 + 8D - 4] = 0 \qquad \qquad \text{...(3)}$$
$$[D^3 - D^2] - 4D^2 + 4D + [4D - 4] = 0$$
$$D^2\,(D - 1) - 4D\,(D - 1) + 4\,(D - 1) = 0$$
$$(D - 1)\,[\,D^2 - 4D + 4\,] = 0$$
$$[D - 1]\,[D - 2]^2 = 0$$

$D = 1, D = 2, 2$

Let, $m_1 = 1, m_2 = m_3 = 2$

The roots of A. E. are real and one pair of roots is equal.

The solution is,

$$y = c_1 e^{m_1 x}\,[c_2 + c_3 x]\, e^{m_2 x} \qquad \qquad \text{...(4)}$$
$$y = c_1\, e^x + [c_2 + c_3 x]\, e^{2x} \qquad \qquad \text{...(5)}$$

Example 2.17 : Solve $[(D - 2)^3 (D + 4)]y = 0$

Solution : Given differential equation is

$$[(D - 2)^3\,(D+ 4)]\, y = 0 \qquad \qquad \text{...(1)}$$

The A. E. is

$$(D - 2)^3\,(D + 4) = 0 \qquad \qquad \text{...(2)}$$
$$(D - 2)^3 = 0 \qquad (D + 4) = 0$$

$D = 2, 2, 2, D = - 4$.

Let, $m_1 = m_2 = m_3 = 2$ and $m_4 = - 4$

The roots are real in which 3 roots are equal.

The solution is

$$y = [c_1 + c_2 x + c_3\, x^2]\, e^{m_1 x} + c_4\, e^{m_4 x} \qquad \qquad \text{...(3)}$$
$$y = [c_1 + c_2 x + c_3 x^2]\, e^{2x} + c_4\, e^{- 4x} \qquad \qquad \text{...(4)}$$

Example 2.18 : Solve : $[D^3 - 6D^2 + 12\,D - 8]\, y = 0$

Solution : The given differential equation is

$$[D^3 - 6D^2 + 12\,D - 8]\, y = 0 \qquad \qquad \text{...(1)}$$

The A. E. is

$$[D^3 - 6D^2 + 12\,D - 8] = 0 \qquad \ldots(2)$$
$$[D^3 - 2D^2] - 4D^2 + 8D + [4D - 8] = 0$$
$$D^2\,[D - 2] - 4D\,[D - 2] + 4\,[D - 2] = 0$$
$$[D - 2]\,(D^2 - 4D + 4) = 0$$
$$(D - 2)\,(D - 2)^2 = 0$$
$$(D - 2)^3 = 0$$
$$D = 2, 2, 2$$

Let, $m_1 = m_2 = m_3 = 2$

The solution is

$$y = [c_1 + c_2 x + c_3\,x^2]\,e^{m_1 x} \qquad \ldots(3)$$
$$y = [c_1 + c_2\,x + c_3\,x^2]\,e^{2x} \qquad \ldots(4)$$

Example 2.19 : Solve : $\dfrac{d^4 y}{dx^4} - 6\,\dfrac{d^2 y}{dx^2} + 9y = 0$

Solution : The given differential equation is,

$$\frac{d^4 y}{dx^4} - 6\frac{d^2 y}{dx^2} + 9y = 0 \qquad \ldots(1)$$

Using the operator $D = \dfrac{d}{dx}$. It can be written as

$$[D^4 - 6D^2 + 9]\,y = 0 \qquad \ldots(2)$$

The A. E. is

$$[D^4 - 6D^2 + 9] = 0 \qquad \ldots(3)$$
$$[D^2 - 3]^2 = 0$$
$$[D^2 - 3]\,[D^2 - 3] = 0$$
$$D^2 - 3 = 0 \quad , \quad D^2 - 3 = 0$$
$$D^2 = 3, \qquad D^2 = 3$$
$$D = \pm\sqrt{3}, \qquad D = \pm\sqrt{3}$$
$$D = -\sqrt{3}, \sqrt{3}, -\sqrt{3}, \sqrt{3}$$
$$D = -\sqrt{3}, -\sqrt{3}, \sqrt{3}, \sqrt{3}$$

Let, $m_1 = m_2 = -\sqrt{3}$, $m_3 = m_4 = \sqrt{3}$

The roots are real and equal in two pairs.

The solution is,

$$y = [c_1 + c_2\,x]\,e^{m_1 x} + [c_3 + c_4\,x]\,e^{m_3 x} \qquad \ldots(4)$$
$$y = [c_1 + c_2\,x]\,e^{-\sqrt{3}x} + [c_3 + c_4\,x]\,e^{\sqrt{3}x} \qquad \ldots(5)$$

Example 2.20 : Solve : $[D^4 - D^3 - 9D^2 - 11D - 4]\, y = 0$

Solution : The given differential equation is

$$[D^4 - D^3 - 9D^2 - 11D - 4]\, y \;=\; 0 \qquad \dots(1)$$

The A. E. is

$$[D^4 - D^3 - 9D^2 - 11D - 4] \;=\; 0 \qquad \dots(2)$$

$$D^4 - 4D^3 + 3D^3 - 12\,D^2 + 3D^2 - 12D + D - 4 \;=\; 0$$

$$D^3\,(D - 4) + 3D^2\,(D - 4) + 3D\,(D - 4) + 1\,(D - 4) \;=\; 0$$

$$(D - 4)\,[D^3 + 3D^2 + 3D + 1] \;=\; 0$$

$$(D - 4)\,(D + 1)^3 \;=\; 0$$

$$D \;=\; 4$$

$D = -1, -1, -1$

Let, $m_1 = 4$, $m_2 = m_3 = m_4 = -1$

The roots are real and 3 roots are equal.

The solution is

$$y \;=\; c_1 e^{m_1 x} + [c_2 + c_3\, x + c_4 x^2] e^{m_2 x} \qquad \dots(3)$$

$$y \;=\; c_1\, e^{4x} + [c_2 + c_3\, x + c_4\, x^2]\, e^{-x} \qquad \dots(4)$$

Example 2.21 : Solve $[D^4 - 6D^3 + 13\,D^2 - 12\,D + 4]\, y = 0$

Solution : The given differential equation is

$$[D^4 - 6D^3 + 13\,D^2 - 12D + 4]\, y \;=\; 0 \qquad \dots(1)$$

The A. E. is

$$[D^4 - 6D^3 + 13\,D^2 - 12\,D + 4] \;=\; 0 \qquad \dots(2)$$

$$D^4 - D^3 - 5D^3 + 5D^2 + 8D^2 - 8D - 4D + 4 \;=\; 0$$

$$D^3\,(D - 1) - 5D^2\,(D - 1) + 8D\,(D - 1) - 4\,(D - 1) \;=\; 0$$

$$(D - 1)\,[D^3 - 5D^2 + 8D - 4] \;=\; 0$$

$$(D - 1)\,[D^3 - D^2 - 4D^2 + 4D + 4D - 4] \;=\; 0$$

$$(D - 1)\,[D^2\,(D - 1) - 4D\,(D - 1) + 4\,(D - 1)] \;=\; 0$$

$$(D - 1)\,(D - 1)[D^2 - 4D + 4] \;=\; 0$$

$$(D - 1)\,(D - 1)\,(D - 2)^2 \;=\; 0$$

$$(D - 1)^2\,(D - 2)^2 \;=\; 0$$

$D = 1, 1, 2, 2.$

Let, $m_1 = m_2 = 1$, $m_3 = m_4 = 2$.

The roots of A. E. are equal in two pairs.

The solution is

$$y \;=\; [c_1 + c_2\, x]\, e^{m_1 x} + [c_3 + c_4 x]\, e^{m_3 x} \qquad \dots(3)$$

$$y \;=\; [c_1 + c_2\, x]\, e^{x} + [c_3 + c_4\, x]\, e^{2x} \qquad \dots(4)$$

EXERCISE 2.3

I. Theory Questions :

1. Explain the method of solving the differential equation $f(D) y = 0$ when the auxiliary equation has two equal roots.

2. Show that the solution of $(D - m)^2 y = 0$ is $y = 0$ is
$y = (c_1 + c_2 x)\, e^{mx}$ where c_1 and c_2 are arbitrary constants.

II. Problems :

Solve the following differential equations.

1. $\dfrac{d^2 y}{dx^2} - 2 \dfrac{dy}{dx} + y = 0$

2. $\dfrac{d^3 y}{dx^3} - 2 \dfrac{d^2 y}{dx^2} = 4 \dfrac{dy}{dx} + 8y = 0$

3. $\dfrac{d^3 y}{dx^3} - 4 \dfrac{d^2 y}{dx^2} + 5 \dfrac{dy}{dx} - 2y = 0$

4. $[D^3 - 4D^2 + 5D - 2]y = 0$

5. $[D^3 - 3D - 2]y = 0$

6. $[D^4 + 2D^3 + D^2]\, y = 0$

7. $[D^4 - 2D^3 - 3D^2 + 4D + 4] = 0$

ANSWERS 2.3

1. $y = (c_1 + c_2 x)e^x$

2. $y = (c_1 + c_2 x)\, e^{2x} + c_3\, e^{-2s}$

3. $y\, (c_1 + c_2 x)\, e^x + c_3 e^{2x}$

4. $y = [c_1 + c_2 x]\, e^x + c_3\, e^{2x}$

5. $y\, [c_1 + c_2 x]e^{-x} + c_3\, e^{2x}$

6. $y\, [c_1 + c_2 x] + [c_3 + c_4\, x]\, e^{-x}$

7. $y\, [c_1 + c_2 x]\, e^{2x} + [c_3 + c_4\, x]e^{-x}$

2.5 SOLUTION OF F (D) y = 0 WHEN A. E. HAS IMAGINARY (COMPLEX) ROOTS

Suppose the differential equation be $f(D) = y = 0$ ...(1)

Let it's A. E. be $f(D) = 0$ ...(2)

Suppose that A. E. has a pair of imaginary roots say
$\alpha + i\beta$ and $\alpha - i\beta$

Let $m_1 = \alpha + i\beta$ and $m_2 = \alpha - i\beta$ where, α is real part and β is imaginary part.

The complete solution is

$$y = c_1 e^{m_1 x} + c_2 e^{m_2 x}$$
$$y = c_1 e^{(\alpha + i\beta)x} + c_2 e^{(\alpha - i\beta)x}$$
$$y = c_1 e^{\alpha x} e^{i\beta x} + c_2 e^{\alpha x} e^{-i\beta x}$$
$$y = c_1 e^{\alpha x} [\cos \beta x + i \sin \beta x] + c_2 e^{\alpha x} [\cos \beta x - i \sin \beta x]$$
$$y = e^{\alpha x} [c_1 \cos \beta x + c_2 \cos \beta x] + i e^{\alpha}x [c_1 \sin \beta x - c_2 \sin \beta x]$$
$$y = e^{\alpha x} (c_1 + c_2) \cos \beta x + i e^{\alpha x} (c_1 - c_2) \sin \beta x$$

Put, $c_1 + c_2 = $ A and $i (c_1 - c_2) = \beta$ then

$$y = e^{\alpha x} A \cos \beta x + e^{\alpha x} \beta \sin \beta x$$
$$y = e^{\alpha x} [A \cos \beta x + \beta \sin \beta x] \qquad \qquad ...(3)$$

Replacing A by c_1 and B by c_2 we write

$$y = e^{\alpha x} [c_1 \cos \beta x + c_2 \sin \beta x] \qquad \qquad ...(4)$$

Where, c_1 and c_2 are arbitrary constants.

Equation (4) is the solution of $f(D) y = 0$ when the roots of A. E. are imaginary.

Remarks 1 : (i) If the A. E. $f(D) = 0$ has a pair of imaginary roots $\alpha \pm i\beta$ which is repeated twice then the general (complete) solution of equation $f(D) y = 0$ is given by

$$y = e^{\alpha x} [(c_1 + c_2 x) \cos \beta x + (c_3 + c_4 x) \sin \beta x]$$

Remarks 2 : If the A. E. $f(D) = 0$ has a pair of imaginary roots $\alpha \pm i\beta$ which is repeated three times then the general (complete) solution of equation $f(D) = 0$ is given by

$$y = e^{\alpha x} [(c_1 + c_2 x + c_3 x^2) \cos \beta x + (c_4 + c_5 x + c_6 x^2) \sin \beta x]$$

Remarks 3 : If the A. E. $f(D) = 0$ has one pair of imaginary roots and other roots are real and other roots are real and districts then the general solution is given by

$$y = e^{\alpha x} [c_1 \cos \beta x + c_2 \sin \beta x] + c_3 e^{m_3 x} + c_4 e^{m_4 x} + ... + c_n e^{m_n x}$$

SOLVED EXAMPLES

Example 2.22 : Solve : $[D^2 + 1]^2 [D^2 + D + 1]y = 0$

Solution : Given differential equation is

$$[D^2 + 1]^2 [D^2 + D + 1] = 0 \qquad \qquad ...(1)$$

The auxiliary equation is

$$[D^2 + 1]^2 [D^2 + D + 1] = 0 \qquad \qquad ...(2)$$
$$[D^2 + 1]^2 = 0 \qquad [D^2 + D + 1] = 0$$

$$D^2 + 1 = 0 \ \& \ D^2 + 1 = 0, \qquad\qquad D^2 + D + 1 = 0$$

$$D^2 = -1 \qquad\qquad D = \frac{-1 \pm \sqrt{1-4}}{2}$$

$$D^2 = i^2 \qquad\qquad D = \frac{-1 \pm \sqrt{-3}}{2}$$

$$D = \pm i$$

$$\boxed{D = 0 \pm i} \ , \boxed{D = 0 \pm i} \ \text{and} \ \boxed{D = \frac{-1 \pm i\sqrt{3}}{2}}$$

There are six complex roots.

Here, one pair of imaginary roots is repeated twice and other pair is repeated once.

Let, $D = 0 \pm i = \alpha \pm i\beta \Rightarrow \alpha = 0, \beta = 1$

Let, $D = \dfrac{-1 \pm i\sqrt{3}}{2} = \alpha_1 \pm i\beta$, where $\alpha_1 = -1, \beta_1 = \dfrac{\sqrt{3}}{2}$

The solution is

$y = e^{\alpha x} [(c_1 + c_2 x) \cos \beta x + (c_3 + c_4 x) \sin \beta x] + e^{\alpha_1 x} [c_5 \cos \beta_1 x + c_6 \sin \beta_1 x]$

$y = e^{0x} [(c_1 + c_2 x) \cos x + (c_3 + c_4 x) \sin \beta x]$

$$+ e^{-x} \left[c_5 \cos \left(\frac{\sqrt{3}}{2} x \right) \right] + c_6 \sin \left(\frac{\sqrt{3}}{2} x \right)$$

$$y = [c_1 + c_2 x] \cos x + [c_3 + c_4 x] \sin \beta x + e^{-x} \left[c_5 \cos \frac{\sqrt{3}}{2} x + c_6 \sin \frac{\sqrt{3}}{2} x \right]$$

This is the solution of equation (1).

Example 2.23 : Solve : $(D^2 + 1) y = 0$

Solution : Given differential equation is

$$(D^2 + 1) y = 0 \qquad\qquad ...(1)$$

The A. E. is

$$D^2 + 1 = 0 \qquad\qquad ...(2)$$
$$D^2 = -1$$
$$D^2 = i^2$$
$$D = \pm i$$
$$D = 0 \pm i \qquad\qquad ...(3)$$

Comparing with $\qquad D = \alpha \pm i\beta \qquad\qquad$ ...(4) we get

$\alpha = 0, \beta = 1$

The roots of A. E. are imaginary.

The solution is

$$y = e^{\alpha x} [c_1 \cos \beta x + c_2 \sin \beta x] \qquad\qquad ...(4)$$
$$y = e^{0x} [c_1 \cos x + c_2 \sin x]$$
$$y = c_1 \cos x + c_2 \sin x \qquad\qquad ...(5)$$

Example 2.24 : Solve $[D^2 - 2D + 5] y = 0$ **given that** $y = 0$ **and** $\dfrac{dy}{dx} = 4$ **when x = 0.** **(April 2012)**

Solution : The given differential equation is

$$[D^2 - 2D + 5] y = 0 \qquad \qquad ...(1)$$

The A. E. is

$$[D^2 - 2D + 5] = 0 \qquad \qquad ...(2)$$
$$D^2 - 2D + 1 + 4 = 0$$
$$D^2 - 2D + 1 = -4$$
$$D^2 - 2D + 1 = 4i^2$$
$$(D - 1)^2 = 4i^2$$

Taking square root we get,

$$D - 1 = \pm 2i$$
$$D = 1 \pm 2i \qquad \qquad ...(3)$$

Here, $\alpha = 1$ and $\beta = 2$

The roots of A. E. are imaginary

The solution is

$$y = e^{\alpha x} [c_1 \cos \beta x + c_2 \sin \beta x] \qquad ...(4)$$
$$y = e^x [c_1 \cos 2x + c_2 \sin 2x] \qquad ...(5)$$

Differentiate w.r.t. x

$$\frac{dy}{dx} = e^x [-2c_1 \sin (2x) + 2 c_2 \cos (2x)] + [c_1 \cos (2x) + c_2 \sin (2x)]e^x \quad ...(6)$$

Using condition, when x = 0 then y = 0 and $\dfrac{dy}{dx} = 4$

From (5) we get $\boxed{c_1 = 0}$

From (6) we get

$$4 = 2c_2 + c_1$$
$$4 = 2c_2$$
$$\Rightarrow \qquad \qquad c_2 = 2$$

Using values of c_1 and c_2 equation (5) becomes

$$y = e^x [0 + 2 \sin (2x)]$$
$$\therefore \qquad \qquad y = 2e^x \sin (2x) \text{ is solution}$$

Example 2.25 : Solve $\dfrac{d^2y}{dx^2} - 2 \dfrac{dy}{dx} + 10 y = 0$

Solution : The given differential equation is

$$\frac{d^2y}{dx^2} - 2\frac{dy}{dx} + 10y = 0 \qquad \qquad ...(1)$$

Using the operator it can be written as
$$[D^2 - 2D + 10]y = 0 \qquad \qquad ...(2)$$
The A. E. is
$$D^2 - 2D + 10 = 0 \qquad \qquad ...(3)$$
$$[D^2 - 2D + 1] + 9 = 0$$
$$D^2 - 2D + 1 = -9$$
$$D^2 - 2D + 1 = 9i^2$$
$$(D - 2)^2 = 9i^2$$
Taking square root of both sides
$$(D - 1) = \pm 3i$$
$$D = 1 \pm 3i$$
here $\alpha = 1$ and $\beta = 3$
The roots of A. E. are imaginary.
The solution is
$$y = e^{\alpha x} [c_1 \cos \beta x + c_2 \sin \beta x] \qquad ...(4)$$
$$y = e^x [c_1 \cos 3x + c_2 \sin 3x] \qquad ...(5)$$

Example 2.26 : Solve : $(D^2 - 4D + 13)y = 0$

Solution : The given differential equation is
$$[D^2 - 4D + 13]y = 0 \qquad \qquad ...(1)$$
The A. E. is
$$D^2 - 4D + 13 = 0 \qquad \qquad ...(2)$$
$$[D^2 - 4D + 4] + 9 = 0$$
$$[D^2 - 4D + 4] = -9i^2$$
Taking square root of both sides
$$D - 2 = \pm 3i$$
$$D = 2 \pm 3i$$
Here, $\alpha = 2$ and $\beta = 3$
The roots of A. E. are imaginary.
The solution is
$$y = e^{\alpha x} [c_1 \cos \beta x + c_2 \sin \beta x] \qquad ...(3)$$
$$y = e^{2x} [c_1 \cos 3x + c_2 \sin 3x] \qquad ...(4)$$

Example 2.27 : Solve : $(D^3 + 9D) y = 0$

Solution : Given differential equation is
$$(D_3 + 9D) y = 0 \qquad \qquad ...(1)$$
The A. E. is
$$D^3 + 9D = 0 \qquad \qquad ...(2)$$
$$D (D^2 + 9) = 0$$
$$D = 0 \text{ and } \quad D^2 + 9 = 0$$

$$\text{Let } m_1 = 0 \qquad\qquad D = 9i^2$$
$$D = \pm 3i$$
$$D = 0 \pm 3i$$
$$\text{here } \alpha = 0 \ , \ \ \beta = 3$$

Here, the roots of A. E. are real and imaginary.

The solution is

$$y = c_1 e^{m1x} + e^{\alpha x} [c_2 \cos \beta x + c_3 \sin \beta x] \qquad ...(3)$$
$$y = c_1 e^{0x} + e^{0x} [c_2 \cos 3x + c_3 \sin 3x] \qquad ...(4)$$
$$y = c_1 + c_2 \cos (3x) + c_3 \sin (3x) \qquad ...(5)$$

Example 2.28 : Solve $[D^2 - 2D + 5]^2 y = 0$

Solution : The given differential equation is

$$[D^2 - 2D + 5]^2 y = 0 \qquad ...(1)$$

The A. E. is

$$[D^2 - 2D + 5]^2 = 0 \qquad ...(2)$$
$$D^2 - 2D + 5 = 0, \qquad\qquad \text{twice}$$
$$D^2 - 2D + 1 = -4$$
$$D^2 - 2D + 1 = 4i^2$$
$$(D - 1)^2 = 4i^2$$

Taking square-root of both sides

$$D - 1 = \pm 2i$$
$$D = 1 \pm 2i, \qquad\qquad \text{twice}$$

here $\alpha = 1$, and $\beta = 2$

The pair of imaginary roots are A. E. is repeated.

The solution is

$$y = e^{\alpha x} [(c_1 + c_2 x) \cos \beta x + (c_3 + c_4 x) \sin \beta x] \ ...(3)$$
$$y = e^x [(c_1 + c_2 x) \cos 2x + (c_3 + c_4 x) \sin 2x] \qquad ...(4)$$

Example 2.29 : Solve : $\dfrac{d^4y}{dx^4} + 8 \dfrac{d^2y}{dx^2} + 16y = 0.$

Solution : Given differential equation is

$$\frac{d^4y}{dx^4} + 8 \frac{d^2y}{dx^2} + 16y = 0 \qquad ...(1)$$

Using the operator $D = \dfrac{d}{dx}$ it can be written as

$$[D^4 + 8D^2 + 16]y = 0 \qquad ...(2)$$

The A. E. is

$$D^4 + 8D^2 + 16 = 0 \qquad ...(3)$$
$$(D^2 + 4)^2 = 0$$
$$(D^2 + 4)(D^2 + 4) = 0$$

$$D^2 = -4 \text{ and } D^2 = -4$$
$$D^2 = 4i^2 \text{ and } D^2 = 4i^2$$
$$D = \pm 2i \text{ and } D = \pm 2i, \qquad \text{twice}$$

here $\alpha = 0$, $\beta = 2$

The roots of A.E. are equal and imaginary.

The solution is

$$y = e^{\alpha x}[(c_1 + c_2 x) \cos \beta x + (c_3 + c_4 x) \sin \beta x] \quad ...(4)$$
$$y = e^{0x}[(c_1 + c_2 x) \cos 2x + (c_3 + c_4 x) \sin 2x]$$
$$y = (c_1 + c_2 x) \cos 2x + (c_3 + c_4 x) \sin 2x$$

Example 2.30 : Solve $\dfrac{d^4y}{dx^4} + 13 \dfrac{d^2y}{dx^2} + 36 y = 0$

Solution : Given differential equation is

$$\frac{d^4y}{dx^4} + 13 \frac{d^2y}{dx^2} + 36 y = 0 \qquad ...(1)$$

Using the operator $D = \dfrac{d}{dx}$ it can be written as

$$[D^4 + 13D^2 + 36]y = 0 \qquad ...(2)$$

The A. E. is

$$D^4 + 13D^2 + 36 = 0 \qquad ...(3)$$
$$(D^2 + 4)(D^2 + 9) = 0$$

$$D^2 + 4 = 0 \qquad \text{and } D^2 + 9 = 0$$
$$D^2 = -4 \qquad \text{and} \qquad D^2 = -9$$
$$D^2 = 4i^2 \qquad \text{and} \qquad D = 9i^2$$
$$D = \pm 2i \qquad \text{and} \qquad D = \pm 3i$$
$$D = 0 \pm 2i \quad \text{and} \qquad D = 0 + 3i$$

Let $\alpha_1 = 0$, $\beta_1 = 2$ and Let $\alpha_2 = 0$, $\beta_2 = 3$

The roots of A. E. are imaginary.

The solution is

$$y = e^{\alpha_1 x}[c_1 \cos \beta_1 x + c_2 \sin \beta_1 x] + e^{\alpha_2 x}[c_3 \cos \beta_2 + c_4 \sin \beta_2 x]$$
$$y = e^{0x}[c_1 \cos 2x + c_2 \sin 2x] + e^{0x}[c_3 \cos 3x + c_4 \sin 3x] \quad ...(4)$$
$$y = c_1 \cos 2x + c_2 \sin 2x + c_3 \cos 3x + c_4 \sin 3x \qquad ...(5)$$

Example 2.31 : Solve : $(D^4 - 16)y = 0$

Solution : The given differential equation is

$$[D^4 - 16]y = 0 \qquad ...(1)$$

The A. E. is

$$D^4 - 16 = 0 \qquad ...(2)$$
$$(D^2 - 4)(D^2 + 4) = 0$$

$$D^2 - 4 = 0 \qquad \text{and} \quad D^2 + 4 = 0$$

$$D^2 = 4 \qquad \text{and} \qquad D^2 = -4$$

$$D \pm 2 \quad \text{and} \qquad D^2 = 4i^2$$

Let $m_1 = 2$ $\qquad\qquad D = \pm 2i$

$\quad m_2 = -2$ $\qquad\qquad D = 0 \pm 2i$

Let $\qquad\qquad\qquad\qquad \alpha = 0, \beta = 2$

Here roots of A. E. are real and imaginary.

The solution is

$$y = c_1 e^{m_1 x} + c_2 e^{m_2 x} + e^{\alpha x}[c_3 \cos \beta x + c_4 \sin \beta x]$$

$$y = c_1 e^{2x} + c_2 e^{-2x} + e^{0x}[c_3 \cos 2x + c_4 \sin 2x]$$

$$y = c_1 e^{2x} + c_2 e^{-2x} + c_3 \cos (2x) + c_4 \sin (2x)$$

Example 2.32 : Solve $\dfrac{d^4y}{dx^4} + m^4 y = 0$

Solution : The given differential equation is

$$\frac{d^4y}{dx^4} + m^4y = 0 \qquad\qquad ...(1)$$

Using the operator $D = \dfrac{d}{dx}$ it can be written as

$$(D^4 + m^4)y = 0 \qquad\qquad ...(2)$$

The A. E. is

$$D^4 + m^4 = 0$$

$$[D^4 + 2m^2 D^2 + m^4] - 2m^2 D^2 = 0$$

$$(D^2 + m^2)^2 - \left(\sqrt{2}\, mD\right)^2 = 0$$

$$[D^2 + m^2 + \sqrt{2}\, mD][D^2 + m^2 - \sqrt{2}\, mD] = 0$$

$D^2 + \sqrt{2}\, mD + m^2 = 0 \quad$ and $\qquad D^2 - \sqrt{2}\, mD + m^2 = 0$

$$D = \frac{-\sqrt{2}m \pm \sqrt{2m^2 - 4m^2}}{2} \qquad\qquad D = \frac{\sqrt{2}\, m \pm \sqrt{2m^2 - 4m^2}}{2}$$

$$D = \frac{-\sqrt{2}\, m \pm \sqrt{-2m^2}}{2} \qquad\qquad D = \frac{\sqrt{2}\, m \pm \sqrt{-2m^2}}{2}$$

$$D = \frac{-\sqrt{2}\, m \pm \sqrt{2m^2 i^2}}{2} \qquad\qquad D = \frac{\sqrt{2}\, m \pm \sqrt{2\, m^2\, i^2}}{2}$$

$$D = -\frac{m}{\sqrt{2}} \pm i\frac{m}{\sqrt{2}} \qquad\qquad D = \frac{m}{\sqrt{2}} \pm \frac{im}{\sqrt{2}}$$

Here, $\alpha_1 = -\dfrac{m}{\sqrt{2}}$ Here $\alpha_2 = \dfrac{m}{\sqrt{2}}$

$\beta_1 = \dfrac{m}{\sqrt{2}}$ $\beta_2 = \dfrac{m}{\sqrt{2}}$

The roots of A. E. are imaginary.

The solution is

$y = e^{\alpha_1 x}[c_1 \cos \beta_1 x + c_2 \sin \beta_1 x] + e^{\alpha_2 x}[c_3 \cos \beta_2 x + c_4 \sin \beta_2 x]$

$y = e^{\frac{-mx}{\sqrt{2}}}\left[c_1 \cos \dfrac{mx}{\sqrt{2}} + c_2 \sin \dfrac{mx}{\sqrt{2}}\right] + e^{\frac{mx}{\sqrt{2}}}\left[c_3 \cos \dfrac{mx}{\sqrt{2}} + c_4 \sin \dfrac{mx}{\sqrt{2}}\right]$

EXERCISE 2.4

I. Theory Questions :

1. Explain the method of solving the differential equation f (D) y = 0 when the auxiliary equation has one pair of imaginary roots.

II. Problems :

Solve the following differential equations :

1. $\dfrac{d^2y}{dx^2} + 25y = 0$

2. $\dfrac{d^3y}{dx^3} + y = 0$

3. $(D^2 + 1)^3\, y = 0$

4. $(D^4 + 16)y = 0$

5. $\dfrac{d^4y}{dx^4} + 18\dfrac{d^2y}{dx^2} + 81y = 0$

6. $\dfrac{d^4y}{dx^4} - 4\dfrac{d^3y}{dx^3} + 8\dfrac{d^2y}{dx^2} - 8\dfrac{dy}{dx} + 4y = 0$

7. $\dfrac{d^4y}{dx^4} - y = 0$

8. $\dfrac{d^4y}{dx^4} + 8\dfrac{d^2y}{dx^2} + 16y = 0$

9. $(D^2 + 4)\, y = 0$

10. $[D^4 + 8D^2 + 16]\, y = 0$

$$\boxed{\textbf{ANSWERS 2.4}}$$

1.　$y = c_1 \cos 5x + c_2 \sin 5x$

2.　$y = c_1 e^{-x} + e^{x/2}\left[c_2 \cos\left(\dfrac{\sqrt{3}x}{2}\right) + c_3 \sin\left(\dfrac{\sqrt{3}}{2}\right)x\right]$

3.　$y = (c_1 + c_2 x + c_3 x^2) \cos x (c_4 + c_5 x + c_6 x^2] \sin x$

4.　$y = e^{-\sqrt{2}x}[c_1 \cos(\sqrt{2}x) + c_2 \sin(\sqrt{2}x)] + e^{\sqrt{2}x}[c_3 \cos(\sqrt{2}x) + c_4 \sin(\sqrt{2}x)]$

5.　$y = (c_1 + c_2 x) \cos(3x) + (c_3 + c_4 x) \sin(3x)$

6.　$y = e^x[(c_1 + c_2 x) \cos x + (c_3 + c_4 x) \sin x]$

7.　$y = c_1 e^x + c_2 e^{-x} + \left[c_3 \cos\left(\dfrac{\sqrt{3}}{2}x\right) + c_4 \sin\left(\dfrac{\sqrt{3}}{2}x\right)\right]$

8.　$y = (c_1 + c_2 x) \cos(2x) + (c_3 + c_4 x) \sin(2x)$

9.　$y = c_1 \cos(2x) + c_2 \sin(2x)$

10.　$y = (c_1 + c_2 x) \cos(2x) + (c_3 + c_4 x) \sin(2x)$

2.6 GENERAL OR COMPLETE SOLUTION OF F (D) y = X

The general solution of f (D) y = x consist of two parts.

1.　Complementary function (C. F.)

The first part y = Y which is the general solution of f (D) y = 0, is known as **complementary function. (C. F.)**

2.　Particular Integral (P. I.)

The second part y = u which contains no arbitrary constants and which is the only particular solution of f (D) y = X is known as **Particular Integral** (P. I.)

3.　General or Complete Solution of f (D) y = X.

The sun of the complementary function and particular Integral is known as **General** or Complete solution of f (D) y = X.

Thus, $\boxed{y = \text{C. F.} + \text{P. I}}$ is general solution of f (D) y = X.

4.   The operator $\dfrac{1}{f(D)}$

$\dfrac{1}{f(D)} X$ is the function of x, which is free from arbitrary constants, and which when operated upon by $f(D)$ gives X.

i.e. $f(D) \dfrac{1}{f(D)} X = X$

Thus $f(D)$ and $\dfrac{1}{f(D)}$ are inverse operators.

The operators $f(D)$ and $\dfrac{1}{f(D)}$ when act on any function, then they cancel each other and there remains only given function.

Theorem on Solution of $f(D) y = X$

Theorem 1 :

If $y = Y$ be the complete solution of the equation $f(D) y = 0$

and $y = u$ be the particular solution of the equation $f(D) y = X$ where X is the function of x.

then the complete solution of equation $f(D) y = X$ is $y = Y + u$

Proof : The linear differential equation with constant coefficients be

$$f(D) y = X \qquad \qquad \text{... (1)}$$

where X is a function of x

Let $f(D) = D^n + P_1 D^{n-1} + P_2 D^{n-2} + \ldots + P_n$

Equation (1) becomes

$$[D^n + P_1 D^{n-1} + P_2 D^{n-2} + \quad P_n] y = X \qquad \text{... (2)}$$

Consider the equation $f(D) y = 0$ $\qquad \qquad \qquad \text{... (3)}$

Let $y = y_1, y = y_2, y = y_3, \ldots.. y = y_n$ be the solutions of equation (3)

Therefore $f(D) y_1 = 0$, $f(D) y_2 = 0$, $f(D) y_3 = 0$, $\ldots f(D) y_n = 0$

Then $Y = c_1 y_1 + c_2 y_2 + c_3 y_3 + \ldots + c_n y_n$ $\qquad \qquad \text{... (4)}$

where $c_1, c_2, c_3 \ldots c_n$ are arbitrary constants, is also solution of equation (3). Therefore we have

$$f(D) Y = 0 \qquad \qquad \text{... (5)}$$

Let $y = u$ be the solution of $f(D) y = X$

$\therefore$ $f(D) u = X$ $\qquad \qquad \text{... (6)}$

If $y = Y + u$ then

L.H.S. of (1) $=$ $f(D) [Y + u) = f(D) Y + f(D) u$

$\qquad \qquad \qquad \qquad$ Using equations (5) and (6)

$$f(D)[Y + u) = 0 + X$$

$$\boxed{f(D)[y + u] = X}$$

$$= \text{RHS of (1)}$$

Therefore $y = Y + u$ is a solution of $f(D)y = X$

It contains n arbitrary constants.

Hence $y = Y + u$ is the **complete** solution of $f(D)y = X$.

$$\boxed{\text{Theorems on operator } \frac{1}{f(D)}}$$

Theorem 2 : $\frac{1}{f(D)} X$ is the particular integral of the equation $f(D) y = X$.

Proof : The given equation is $f(D) y = X$ ... (1)

put $\qquad\qquad\qquad\qquad y = \frac{1}{f(D)} X$ then

LHS of (1) = $\qquad f(D) y = f(D) \cdot \left[\frac{1}{f(D)} X\right] = X = \text{R.H.S. of (1)}$

Thus $\qquad\qquad\qquad\qquad y = \frac{1}{f(D)} X$ satisfies equation (1)

Hence $\qquad\qquad\qquad\qquad y = \frac{1}{f(D)} X$ is the solution of equation (1).

It contains no arbitrary constants.

Hence $y = \frac{1}{f(D)} X$ is particular Integral of the equation $f(D) y = X$.

Note (1) The particular Integral (P.I.) does not contain any arbitrary constant.

Theorem 3 : If X is a function of x

then $\frac{1}{D-a} X = e^{ax} \int X e^{-ax} dx$ where, a is constant **[S. U. Oct. 2011]**

Proof :

Let $\qquad\qquad\qquad\qquad y = \frac{1}{D-a} X$ ... (1)

Operating by $(D - a)$ on both sides

$$(D - a) y = (D - a)\left[\frac{1}{(D-a)} X\right]$$

$$(D - a) y = X$$

$$\frac{dy}{dx} - ay = X \qquad\qquad\qquad ... (2)$$

Which is linear differential equation

It's   I. F. $= e^{\int a\,dx} = e^{-ax}$ ... (3)

It's solution is

$$y \cdot (\text{I.F.}) = \int X \cdot (\text{I.F.}) \cdot dx$$

$$y \cdot e^{-ax} = \int X\,e^{-ax} \cdot dx$$

Multiplying both sides by e^{ax} we get

$$\boxed{y = e^{ax} \int X\,e^{-ax}\,dx}$$

Using value of y we write

$$\boxed{\frac{1}{D-a}X = e^{ax} \int X\,e^{-ax}\,dx}$$ ... (4)

Remark (1)

We do not add a constant of integration after Finding particular integral (P.I.) of the given function, by any method.

Remark (2)   **[S. U. Oct. 2011]**

If we put $a = 0$ in $\dfrac{1}{D-a}X = e^{ax} \int X\,e^{-ax}\,dx$

then $\dfrac{1}{D}X = e^{ox} \int X\,e^{-ox}\,dx$

$$\boxed{\frac{1}{D}X = \int X\,dx}$$

Remark (3) we use

$$(D - \alpha)(D - \beta)\,y = (D - \beta)(D - \alpha)\,y$$

Theorem 4 :

If X is a function of x then $\dfrac{1}{D+a}X = e^{-ax} \int X\,e^{ax}\,dx$ **[S. U. May 2011]**

Proof : Let $y = \dfrac{1}{D+a}X$ ... (1)

Operating $(D + a)$ on both sides

$$(D + a)\,y = (D + a)\left[\frac{1}{(D+a)}X\right]$$

$$(D + a)\,y = X$$

$$\therefore \qquad \frac{dy}{dx} + ay = X \qquad \qquad \dots (2)$$

Which is linear differential equation.

It's $\qquad \qquad \text{I.F.} = e^{\int a\,dx} = e^{ax} \qquad \qquad \dots (3)$

It's solution is

$$y \cdot (\text{I. F.}) = \int X \cdot (\text{I. F.})\,dx$$

$$y\,e^{ax} = \int X\,e^{ax}\,dx$$

Multiplying both sides by e^{-ax} we get

$$y = e^{-ax} \int X\,e^{ax}\,dx$$

Using value of y we write

$$\boxed{\frac{1}{D+a} X = e^{-ax} \int X\,e^{ax}\,dx} \qquad \qquad \dots (4)$$

Remark 1 : The above theorems can be used to evaluate P. I. in any problem but generally they are used for the problems in which X is of the form tan (ax), cot (ax) . sec (ax) . cosec (ax) etc.

Illustration 1 : $\quad \dfrac{1}{D+2} e^x = e^{-2x} \displaystyle\int e^x \cdot e^{2x}\,dx \qquad$ **[S. U. May 2011]**

$$= e^{-2x} \int e^{3x}\,dx$$

$$= e^{-2x} \left[\frac{e^{3x}}{3}\right] = \frac{1}{3} e^{-2x+3x}$$

$$\boxed{\frac{1}{D+2} e^x = \frac{1}{3} e^x}$$

General Methods of finding the Particular Integral of $f(D) y = X$ where X is a function of x

Let $\qquad \qquad f(D) y = X \qquad \dots (1)$ where X is a function of x be the linear differential equation with constant coefficients.

Suppose $\qquad f(D) = \left[D^n + P_1 D^{n-1} + P_2 D^{n-2} + \dots + P_n\right]$

Then $\qquad \qquad \text{P. I.} = \dfrac{1}{f(D)} X \qquad \qquad \dots (2)$

For finding P. I. the following methods are useful.

Method I : Method of factors

Suppose f (D) is factorised as

$$f(D) = (D - m_1)(D - m_2)(D - m_3) \ldots (D - m_{n-1})(D - m_n) \quad \ldots (1)$$

$$P.I. = \frac{1}{f(D)} X \qquad \ldots (2)$$

$$P.I. = \frac{1}{(D - m_1)(D - m_2)(D - m_3) - (D - m_{n-1})(D - m_n)} X$$

$$P.I. = \frac{1}{(D - m_1)(D - m_2)(D - m_3) - (D - m_{n-1})} \left[\frac{1}{D - m_n} X \right] \ldots (3)$$

First we evaluate $\dfrac{1}{[D - m_n]} X$ by using formula

$$\frac{1}{D - a} X = e^{ax} \int x e^{-ax} dx$$

Therefore, $\dfrac{1}{[D - m_n]} X = e^{m_n x} \int X e e^{-m_n x} dx = X_1$ say $\qquad \ldots (4)$

Using equation (4) equation (3) becomes

$$P.I. = \frac{1}{(D - m_1)(D - m_2)(D - m_3) .. (D - m_{n-1})} X_1$$

$$P.I. = \frac{1}{(D - m_1)(D - m_2)(D - m_3) .. (D - m - 2)} \left[\frac{1}{D - m_{n-1}} X_1 \right] \ldots (5)$$

Let $\dfrac{1}{[D - m_{n-1}]} X_1 = e^{m_{n-1}} \int X_1 e^{-m_{n-1}x} dx = X_2$ say $\qquad \ldots (6)$

$$P.I. = \frac{1}{(D - m_1)(D - m_2)(D - m_3) .. (D - m_{n-2})} X_2 \qquad \ldots (7)$$

Continuing the same procedure upto last factor, we can obtain P.I.

SOLVED EXAMPLES

Example 2.33 : Find P.I. of [D² + 3D + 2] y = x

Solution :

$$P.I. = \frac{1}{D^2 + 3D + 2} X = \frac{1}{(D + 2)(D + 1)} X$$

$$P.I. = \frac{1}{D + 2} \left[\frac{1}{D + 1} X \right]$$

Using formula $\dfrac{1}{D + a} X = e^{-ax} \int X e^{ax} dx$

$$P.I. = \frac{1}{D + 2} \left[e^{-x} \int x e^x dx \right]$$

$$\text{P. I.} = \frac{1}{D+2}\left[e^{-x}\left\{x\,e^x - \int 1\cdot e^x\,dx\right\}\right]$$

$$\text{P. I.} = \frac{1}{D+2}\left[e^{-x}\{xe^x - e^x\}\right]$$

$$\text{P. I.} = \frac{1}{D+2}[x - e^0]$$

$$\text{P. I.} = \frac{1}{D+2}[x - 1]$$

Again using above formula

$$\text{P. I.} = e^{-2x}\int (x-1)\,e^{2x}\,dx$$

$$\text{P. I.} = e^{-2x}\left[(x-1)\frac{e^{2x}}{2} - \int 1\cdot\frac{e^{2x}}{2}\,dx\right]$$

$$\text{P. I.} = e^{-2x}\left[(x-1)\frac{e^{2x}}{2} - \frac{e^{2x}}{4}\right]$$

$$\text{P. I.} = e^{-2x}(x-1)\frac{e^{2x}}{2} - e^{-2x}\frac{e^{2x}}{4}$$

$$\text{P. I.} = \left(\frac{x-1}{2}\right) - \frac{1}{4} = \frac{2(x-1)-1}{4}$$

$$\text{P. I.} = \frac{2x-2-1}{4}$$

$$\text{P. I.} = \left(\frac{2x-3}{4}\right)$$

Method 2 : Method of Partial fractions

Suppose $\quad f(D) = [D^n + P_1 D^{n-1} + P_2 D^{n-2} + \ldots + P_n]$

by factorizing

$$f(D) = (D-m_1)(D-m_2)(D-m_3)\ldots(D-m_n)$$

$$\frac{1}{f(D)} = \frac{1}{(D-m_1)(D-m_2)(D-m_3)\ldots(D-m_n)}$$

by partial fractions we write

$$\frac{1}{f(D)} = \frac{A_1}{D-m_1} + \frac{A_2}{D-m_2} + \frac{A_3}{D-m_3} + \ldots + \frac{A_n}{D-m_n}$$

$$\text{P. I.} = \frac{1}{f(D)}\, X, \text{becomes}$$

$$\text{P. I.} = \left[\frac{A_1}{D-m_1} + \frac{A_2}{D-m_2} + \frac{A_3}{D-m_3} + \ldots + \frac{A_n}{D-m_n}\right] X$$

$$P. I. = A_1 \frac{1}{D - m_1} X + A_2 \frac{1}{D - m_2} X + A_3 \frac{1}{D - m_3} X + ... +$$

$$A_n \frac{1}{D - m_3} X$$

by using formula $\boxed{\dfrac{1}{D - a} X = e^{ax} \int X e^{-ax} \, dx}$ we get

$$P.I. = A_1 e^{m_1 x} \int X e^{-m_1 x} \, dx + A_2 e^{m_2 x} \int X e^{-m_2 x} \, dx + A_3 e^{m_3 x} \int X e^{-m_3 x}$$

$$+ ... + A_n e^{m_n x} \int X e^{-m_n x} \, dx$$

Example 2.34 : Find P.I. of $[D^2 - 3D + 2] = e^{2x}$

Solution : $P. I. = \dfrac{1}{D^2 - 3D + 2} e^{2x} = \dfrac{1}{(D - 1)(D - 2)} e^{2x}$

by partial fraction

$$P. I. = \left[\frac{1}{D - 2} - \frac{1}{D - 1} \right] e^{2x}$$

$$P. I. = \frac{1}{D - 2} e^{2x} - \frac{1}{D - 1} e^{2x}$$

$$P. I. = e^{2x} \int e^{2x} e^{-2x} \, dx - e^x \int e^{2x} e^{-x} \, dx$$

$$P. I. = e^{2x} \int 1 \, dx - e^x \int e^x \, dx$$

$$P. I. = e^{2x} \cdot x - {}^+e^x \cdot e^x$$
$$P. I. = xe^{2x} - e^{2x} = e^{2x} (x - 1)$$

Remark (1) $\qquad \dfrac{1}{D} [e^{ax}] = \dfrac{e^{ax}}{a}$

(2) $\qquad \dfrac{1}{D} \sin(3x) = \int \sin(3x) dx = \dfrac{-\cos(3x)}{3}$

Example 2.35 : Evaluate $\dfrac{1}{D^2} (x^2)$

Solution : $\qquad \dfrac{1}{D^2} (x^2) = \dfrac{1}{D} \cdot \dfrac{1}{D} (x^2)$

$$= \frac{1}{D} \left[\int x^2 \, dx \right]$$

$$= \frac{1}{D} \left[\frac{x^3}{3} \right]$$

$$= \int \frac{x^3}{3} \, dx$$

$$\frac{1}{D^2} (x^2) = \frac{x^4}{12}$$

Example 2.36 : Evaluate $\dfrac{1}{D + 3} \cos x$

Solution : $\dfrac{1}{D + 3} \cos x = e^{-3x} \displaystyle\int \cos x \cdot e^{3x} \, dx$ ... (1)

We use the formula

$$\int e^{ax} \cos (bx) \, dx = \frac{e^{ax}}{a^2 + b^2} [a \cos (bx) + b \sin (bx)]$$

$\therefore$ $\displaystyle\int e^{3x} \cos x \, dx = \dfrac{e^{3x}}{3^2 + 1^2} [3 \cos x + 1 \sin x]$

$$\int e^{3x} \cos x \, dx = \frac{e^{3x}}{10} [3 \cos x + \sin x] \qquad \text{... (2)}$$

Using equation (2) equation (1) becomes

$$\frac{1}{D + 3} \cos x = e^{-3x} \left[\frac{e^{3x}}{3} (3 \cos x + \sin x) \right]$$

$$\frac{1}{D + 3} \cos x = \frac{1}{3} [3 \cos x + \sin x]$$

Example 2.37 : Evaluate $\dfrac{1}{(D - 1)(D + 2)} e^{3x}$

OR

Find P. I. of $(D - 1)(D + 2) y = e^{3x}$

Solution : Given differential equation is

$$(D + 1)(D + 2) y = e^{3x} \qquad \text{... (1)}$$

$$\text{P. I.} = \frac{1}{(D + 1)(D + 2)} e^{3x}$$

$$\text{P. I.} = \frac{1}{(D + 1)} \left[\frac{1}{D + 2} e^{3x} \right]$$

$$\text{P. I.} = \frac{1}{(D + 1)} \left[e^{-2x} \int e^{3x} \cdot e^{2x} \, dx \right]$$

$$\text{P. I.} = \frac{1}{D + 1} \left[e^{-2x} \int e^{5x} \, dx \right]$$

$$\text{P. I.} = \frac{1}{D + 1} \left[e^{-2x} \cdot \frac{e^{5x}}{5} \right]$$

$$\text{P. I.} = \frac{1}{D+1}\left[\frac{e^{3x}}{5}\right]$$

$$\text{P. I.} = \frac{1}{5}\left[\frac{1}{D+1}\, e^{3x}\right]$$

$$\text{P. I.} = \frac{1}{5}\left[e^{-x}\int e^{3x}\cdot e^{x}\, dx\right]$$

$$\text{P. I.} = \frac{1}{5}\left[e^{-x}\int e^{4x}\, dx\right]$$

$$\text{P. I.} = \frac{1}{5}\left[e^{-x}\cdot\frac{e^{4x}}{4}\right]$$

$$\boxed{\text{P.I.} = \frac{1}{20}\, e^{3x}} \qquad\qquad \dots (2)$$

OR

$$\frac{1}{(D+1)(D+2)}\, e^{3x} = \frac{1}{20}\, e^{3x} \qquad\qquad \dots (3)$$

Example 2.38 : Evaluate $\dfrac{1}{D+2}\cos x$

OR

Find the P. I. of $(D+2)\, y = \cos x$

Solution : Given differential equation is

$$(D+2)\, y = \cos x \qquad\qquad \dots (1)$$
$$\Rightarrow \qquad\qquad f(D)\, y = X \qquad\qquad \dots (2)$$

where
$$f(D) = D+2$$
$$X = \cos x$$

$$\text{P. I.} = \frac{1}{f(D)}\, X = \frac{1}{D+2}\cos x$$

$$\text{P. I.} = \frac{1}{f(D)}\, X = e^{-2x}\int \cos x\, e^{2x}\, dx$$

$$\text{P. I.} = e^{-2x}\int e^{2x}\cos x\, dx \qquad\qquad \dots (3)$$

Using the formula,

$$\int e^{ax}\cos bx\, dx = \frac{e^{ax}}{a^2+b^2}[a\cos bx + b\sin bx]$$

$$\therefore \qquad \int e^{2x}\cos x\, dx = \frac{e^{2x}}{4+1}[2\cos x + 1\sin x]$$

$$\int e^{2x}\cos x\, dx = \frac{e^{2x}}{5}[2\cos x + \sin x] \qquad\qquad \dots (3)$$

Using equation (3) equation (2) becomes

$$\text{P. I. } = e^{-2x}\left[\frac{e^{2x}}{5}(2\cos x + \sin x)\right]$$

$$\text{P. I. } = \frac{1}{5}[2\cos x + \sin x] \qquad \ldots (4)$$

Also we say that

$$\frac{1}{D+2}\cos x = \frac{1}{5}[2\cos x + \sin x] \qquad \ldots (5)$$

Example 2.39 : Solve $(D^2 - 5D + 6)\,y = e^{4x}$

Solution : Given differential equation is

$$[D^2 - 5D + 6]\,y = e^{4x} \qquad \ldots (1)$$

$$f(D)\,y = X$$

where

$$f(D) = D^2 - 5D + 6$$

$$X = e^{4x}$$

To find C. F.

A. E. is $D^2 - 5D + 6 = 0$

$$(D-2)(D-3) = 0$$

$$D = 2, 3$$

Let

$$m_1 = 2, \qquad m_2 = 3$$

$$\text{C. F. } = c_1 e^{m_1 x} + c_2 e^{m_2 x}$$

$$\text{C. F. } = c_1 e^{2x} + c_2 e^{3x} \qquad \ldots (2)$$

To find P. I.

$$\text{P. I. } = \frac{1}{f(D)}\,e^{4x}$$

$$\text{P. I. } = \frac{1}{D^2 - 5D + 6}\,e^{4x}$$

$$\text{P. I. } = \frac{1}{(D-2)(D-3)}\,e^{4x}$$

$$\text{P. I. } = \frac{1}{D-2}\left[\frac{1}{D-3}\,e^{4x}\right]$$

$$\text{P. I. } = \frac{1}{D-2}\left[e^{3x}\int e^{4x}\cdot e^{-3x}\,dx\right]$$

$$\text{P. I. } = \frac{1}{D-2}\left[e^{3x}\int e^{x}\,dx\right]$$

$$\text{P. I. } = \frac{1}{D-2}[e^{3x}\,e^{x}\,dx]$$

$$\text{P. I. } = \frac{1}{D-2}[e^{4x}]$$

$$\text{P. I.} = e^{2x} \int e^{4x} \, e^{-2x} \, dx$$

$$\text{P. I.} = e^{2x} \int e^{2x} \, dx$$

$$\text{P. I.} = e^{2x} \left[\frac{e^{2x}}{2} \right]$$

$$\text{P. I.} = \frac{e^{4x}}{2} \qquad \qquad \dots (3)$$

The general solution is

$$y = \text{C. F.} + \text{P. I.}$$

$$y = c_1 e^{2x} + c_2 e^{3x} + \frac{1}{2} e^{4x} \qquad \qquad \dots (4)$$

Example 2.40 : Solve $\dfrac{d^2y}{dx^2} + \dfrac{dy}{dx} - 2y = 2x$

Solution : Given differential equation is

$$\frac{d^2y}{dx^2} + \frac{dy}{dx} - 2y = 2x \qquad \qquad \dots (1)$$

$$\therefore \qquad [D^2 + D - 2] \, y = 2x \qquad \qquad \dots (2)$$

$$f(D) \, y = X \Rightarrow$$

$$f(D) = D^2 + D - 2$$

$$X = 2x$$

To find C. F.

$$\text{A. E. is } f(D) = 0$$

$$D^2 + D - 2 = 0$$

$$(D + 2)(D - 1) = 0$$

$$D = -2, D = 1$$

Let

$$m_1 = -2, \; m_2 = 1$$

$$\text{C. F.} = C_1 e^{m_1 x} + C_2 e^{m_2 x}$$

$$\text{C. F.} = C_1 e^{-2x} + C_2 e^{-x}$$

To find P. I.

$$\text{P. I.} = \frac{1}{f(D)} X = \frac{1}{(D + 2)(D - 1)} [2x]$$

$$\text{P.I.} = \frac{1}{(D + 2)} \left[\frac{1}{D - 1} 2x \right]$$

$$\text{P. I.} = \frac{1}{D + 2} \left[e^x \int 2x \cdot e^{-x} \, dx \right]$$

$$\text{P. I.} = \frac{1}{D + 2} \, 2e^x \left[- xe^{-x} - \int \frac{1 e^{-x} \, dx}{(-1)} \right]$$

$$\text{P. I.} = \frac{1}{D+2} 2e^x \left[-xe^{-x} - e^{-x} \right]$$

$$\text{P. I.} = \frac{1}{D+2} \cdot 2 \left[-x - 1 \right]$$

$$\text{P. I.} = \frac{1}{D+2} \left[-2(x+1) \right]$$

$$\text{P. I.} = e^{-2x} \int -2(x+1) \cdot e^{2x} \, dx$$

$$\text{P. I.} = 2e^{-2x} \left[\int (x+1) e^{2x} \, dx \right]$$

$$\text{P. I.} = -2e^{-2x} \left[(x+1) \cdot \frac{e^{2x}}{2} - \int 1 \cdot \frac{e^{2x}}{2} \, dx \right]$$

$$\text{P. I.} = -2e^{-2x} \left[(x+1) \frac{e^{2x}}{2} - \frac{e^{2x}}{4} \right]$$

$$\text{P. I.} = -2 \left[\frac{x+1}{2} - \frac{1}{4} \right] = -(x+1) + \frac{1}{2} = -x - 1 + \frac{1}{2}$$

$$\text{P. I.} = -x - \frac{1}{2}$$

The general solution is $y = \text{C. F.} + \text{P. I.}$

$$y = \left[c_1 e^{-2x} + c_2 e^{-x} \right] - x - \frac{1}{2}$$

Example 2.41 : Solve : $\dfrac{d^2y}{dx^2} - 5\dfrac{dy}{dx} + 4y = 3 - 2x$

Solution : Given differential equation is

$$\frac{d^2y}{dx^2} - 5\frac{dy}{dx} + 4y = 3 - 2x \qquad \dots (1)$$

$\therefore \qquad [D^2 - 5D + 4] y = 3 - 2x \qquad \dots (2)$

i.e. $\qquad\qquad f(D) y = X \qquad\qquad\qquad \dots (3)$

$$f(D) = D^2 - 5D + 4$$
$$X = 3 - 2x$$

To find C. F.

$$\text{A. E. is } f(D) = 0$$
$$D^2 - 5D + 4 = 0$$
$$(D-1)(D-4) = 0$$
$$D = 1, 4$$

Let $\qquad\qquad m_1 = 1 \text{ and } m_2 = 4$

$$\text{C. F.} = c_1 e^{m_1 x} + c_2 e^{m_2 x}$$

$$\text{C. F.} = c_1 e^x + c_2 e^{4x} \qquad \dots (4)$$

To Find P. I.

$$\text{P. I.} = \frac{1}{f(D)} X = \frac{1}{(D-1)(D-4)}[3-2x]$$

$$\text{P. I.} = \frac{1}{D-1}\left[\frac{1}{D-4}(3-2x)\right]$$

$$\text{P. I.} = \frac{1}{D-1}\left[e^{4x}\int(3-2x)e^{-4x}\,dx\right]$$

$$\text{P. I.} = \frac{1}{D-1}\left[e^{4x}\left\{(3-2x)\frac{e^{-4x}}{(-4)} - \int(-2)\frac{e^{-4x}}{(-4)}\,dx\right\}\right]$$

$$\text{P. I.} = \frac{1}{D-1}\left[e^{4x}\left\{-\frac{(3-2x)}{4}e^{-4x} - \frac{2}{4}\left(\frac{e^{-4x}}{-4}\right)\right\}\right]$$

$$\text{P. I.} = \frac{1}{D-1}\left[\frac{-(3-2x)}{4} + \frac{1}{8}\right]$$

$$\text{P. I.} = \frac{1}{D-1}\left[\frac{-2(3-2x)+1}{8}\right]$$

$$\text{P. I.} = \frac{1}{D-1}\left[\frac{-6+4x+1}{8}\right]$$

$$\text{P. I.} = \frac{1}{D-1}\left[\frac{4x-5}{8}\right]$$

$$\text{P. I.} = e^x\int\left(\frac{4x-5}{8}\right)e^{-x}\,dx$$

$$= \frac{e^x}{8}\left[(4x-5)\frac{e^{-x}}{(-1)} - \int 4\frac{e^{-x}}{(-1)}\,dx\right]$$

$$\text{P. I.} = \frac{e^x}{8}\left[-(4x-5)e^{-x} + 4\left(\frac{e^{-x}}{-1}\right)\right]$$

$$\text{P. I.} = \frac{1}{8}[-(4x-5)-4] = \frac{1}{8}[-4x+5-4] = \frac{1}{8}[-4x+1]$$

$$\text{P. I.} = \frac{-1}{2}x + \frac{1}{8}$$

The general solution is

$$y = \text{C. F.} + \text{P. I.}$$

$$y = [c_1 e^x + c_2 e^{4x}] - \frac{1}{2}x + \frac{1}{8}$$

Example 2.42 : Solve : $(D^2 + a^2)\, y = \sec ax$

Solution : The given differential equation is

$$(D^2 + a^2)\, y = \sec ax \qquad\qquad \ldots (1)$$

i.e.
$$f(D)\, y = X$$

where
$$f(D) = D^2 + a^2$$

$$X = \sec ax$$

To find C. F.

$$\text{A. E. is } D^2 + a^2 = 0$$

$$D^2 = -a^2 = a^2 i$$

$$D = \pm ai = 0 \pm i a$$

$$\therefore \qquad \alpha = 0; \ \beta = a$$

$$\text{C. F.} = e^{ax}[c_1 \cos Bx + c_2 \sin Bx]$$

$$\text{C. F.} = e^{ox}[c_1 \cos ax + c_2 \sin ax]$$

$$\text{C. F.} = c_1 \cos ax + c_2 \sin ax \qquad\qquad \dots (2)$$

To find P. I.

$$\text{P. I.} = \frac{1}{f(D)} X$$

$$\text{P. I.} = \frac{1}{D^2 + a^2} \sec ax$$

$$\text{P. I.} = \frac{1}{(D + ia)(D - ia)} \sec ax$$

$$\text{P. I.} = \frac{1}{2ia}\left[\frac{1}{D - ia} - \frac{1}{D + ia}\right] \sec ax$$

$$\dots \text{(by partial fractions)}$$

$$\text{P. I.} = \frac{1}{2ia}\left[\frac{1}{D - ia} \sec ax - \frac{1}{D + ia} \sec ax\right]$$

$$\text{P. I.} = \frac{1}{2ia}\left[e^{iax}\int \sec ax \cdot e^{-iax}\,dx - e^{-iax}\int \sec ax\, e^{iax}\,dx\right]$$

$$\text{put} \qquad e^{-iax} = \cos ax - i \sin ax$$

$$\text{and} \qquad e^{iax} = \cos ax + i \sin ax$$

$$\text{P. I.} = \frac{1}{2ia}\left[e^{iax}\int \sec ax \{\cos ax - i \sin ax\}\,dx - e^{iax}\int \sec x \{\cos ax + i \sin ax\}\,dx\right]$$

$$\text{P. I.} = \frac{1}{2ia}\left[e^{iax}\int[1 - i \tan x]\,dx - e^{-iax}[1 + i \tan x]\,dx\right]$$

$$\text{P. I.} = \frac{1}{2ia}\left[e^{iax}\left\{x - \frac{i}{a}\log \sec ax\right\} - e^{-iax}\left\{x + \frac{i}{a}\log \sec ax\right\}\right]$$

$$\text{P. I.} = \frac{1}{2ia}\left[x\{e^{iax} - e^{-iax}\}\frac{-i}{a}\log \sec ax \{e^{iax} + e^{-iax}\}\right]$$

$$\text{P. I.} = \frac{x}{a}\left[\frac{e^{iax} - e^{-iax}}{2i}\right] - \frac{1}{a^2}\log \sec ax\left[\frac{e^{iax} + e^{-iax}}{2}\right]$$

$$\text{P. I.} = \frac{x}{a} \sin ax - \frac{1}{a^2}\log \sec ax \cdot \cos ax$$

P. I. $= \dfrac{x}{a} \sin ax - \dfrac{1}{a^2} \cos ax \cdot \log \sec ax$ ... (3)

The general solution is $y = $ C. F. + P. I.

$\therefore \quad y = c_1 \cos ax + c_2 \sin ax + \dfrac{x}{2} \sin ax - \dfrac{1}{a^2} \cos ax \log \sec ax$

Example 2.43 : Solve $\dfrac{d^2y}{dx^2} + y = \operatorname{cosec} x$

Solution : Given differential equation is

$$\dfrac{d^2y}{dx^2} + y = \operatorname{cosec} x \qquad \text{... (1)}$$

$\therefore \qquad\qquad (D^2 + 1)\, y = \operatorname{cosec} x \qquad \text{... (2)}$

i.e. $\qquad\qquad\qquad f(D)\, y = X$

where $\qquad\qquad\qquad f(D) = D^2 + 1$

$\qquad\qquad\qquad\qquad X = \operatorname{cosec} x$

To find C. F.

$\qquad\qquad$ A. E. is $D^2 + 1 = 0$

$\qquad\qquad\qquad\qquad D^2 = -1$

$\qquad\qquad\qquad\qquad D^2 = i^2$

$\qquad\qquad\qquad\qquad D = \pm i = 0 \pm i = \alpha \pm i\beta$

$\qquad\qquad\qquad\qquad \alpha = 0, \qquad \beta = 1$

$\qquad\qquad\qquad$ C. F. $= e^{ax}\,[c_1 \cos \beta x + c_2 \sin Bx]$

$\qquad\qquad\qquad$ C. F. $= e^{0x}\,[c_1 \cos x + c_2 \sin x]$

$\qquad\qquad\qquad$ C. F. $= c_1 \cos x + c_2 \sin x \qquad \text{... (3)}$

To find P. I.

$$\text{P. I.} = \dfrac{1}{f(D)} X = \dfrac{1}{D^2 + 1} \operatorname{cosec} x$$

$$\text{P. I.} = \dfrac{1}{(D + i)(D - i)} \operatorname{cosec} x$$

$$\text{P. I.} = \dfrac{1}{2i}\left[\dfrac{1}{D - i} - \dfrac{1}{D + i}\right] \operatorname{cosec} x \text{... (partial fractions)}$$

$$\text{P. I.} = \dfrac{1}{2i}\left[\dfrac{1}{D - i} \cdot \operatorname{cosec} x - \dfrac{1}{D + i} \operatorname{cosec} x\right]$$

$$\text{P. I.} = \dfrac{1}{2i}\left[e^{ix} \int \operatorname{cosec} x \cdot e^{-ix}\, dx - e^{-ix} \int \operatorname{cosec} x\, e^{ix}\, dx\right]$$

$\qquad\qquad$ put $\qquad e^{-ix} = \cos x - i \sin x$

$\qquad\qquad$ and $\qquad\quad e^{ix} = \cos x + i \sin x$

$$P.\ I. = \frac{1}{2i}\left[e^{ix}\int \cosec\ x\ \{\cos x - i \sin x\}\ dx - e^{ix}\int \cosec\ x\ \{\cos x + i \sin x\}\ dx\right]$$

$$P.\ I. = \frac{1}{2i}\left[e^{ix}\int(\cot x - i)\ dx - e^{-ix}\int(\cot x + i)\ dx\right]$$

$$P.\ I. = \frac{1}{2i}\left[e^{ix}(\log \sin x - ix) - e^{ix}(\log \sin x + ix)\right]$$

$$P.\ I. = \frac{1}{2i}\left[\log \sin x\ (e^{ix} - e^{-ix}) - ix\ (e^{ix} + e^{-ix})\right]$$

$$P.\ I. = \log \sin x\left[\frac{e^{ix} - e^{-ix}}{2i}\right] - x\left[\frac{e^{ix} + e^{-ix}}{2}\right]$$

$$P.\ I. = \log \sin x \cdot \sin x - x \cdot \cos x$$

$$P.\ I. = \sin x \cdot \log \sin x - x \cos x \qquad \dots (4)$$

The general solution is y = C. F. + P. I.

$$\therefore \quad y = [c_1 \cos x + c_2 \sin x] + \sin x \log \sin x - x \cos x$$

EXERCISE 2.5

I. Theory Questions

1. If y = Y be the complete solution of f (D) y = 0 and y = u be the particular solution of f (D) y = X then prove that y = Y + u is the complete (general) solution of the equation f (D) y = X.

2. Define (i) Complementary function

     (ii) Particular Integral

     (iii) General solution of f (D) y = X.

3. If X is a function of x then

     Prove that $\dfrac{1}{D - a}\ X = e^{ax}\int Xe^{-ax}\ dx$

     where, a is constant

     Hence deduce $= \dfrac{1}{D}X = \int X\ dx$

4. Prove that

     $$\frac{1}{D + a}\ X = e^{-ax}\int X\ e^{ax}\ dx$$

     where, X is a function of x
     and a is constant

II. Evaluate the following :

1. $\dfrac{1}{D-2} \sin x$

2. $\dfrac{1}{(D-2)(D-3)} e^x$

3. $\dfrac{1}{D+3} x^2$

III. Find the P. I. of $(D-2)(D-3) y = e^{6x}$

2. Find the P. I. of $(D-4) y = x$

IV. Solve the following differential equations.

1. $(D^2 - 4) y = 1 + x$

2. $\dfrac{d^2y}{dx^2} - 3\dfrac{dy}{dx} + 2y = e^{2x}$

3. $\dfrac{d^2y}{dx^2} - 2\dfrac{dy}{dx} - 3y = x + 5$

4. $(D^2 + 1) y = \sec x$

5. $(D^2 + a^2) y = \operatorname{cosec}(ax)$

ANSWERS 2.5

II. Evaluate the following :

1. $\dfrac{-1}{5} [2 \sin x + \cos x]$

2. $\dfrac{1}{2} e^x$

3. $\dfrac{x^3}{3} - \dfrac{2x}{9} + \dfrac{2}{27}$

III. 1. $\dfrac{1}{12} e^{6x}$

2. $\dfrac{-x}{4} - \dfrac{1}{16}$

IV. Solve the following differential equations.

1. $y = c_1 e^{2x} + c_2 e^{-2x} - \left(\dfrac{1+x}{4}\right)$

2. $y = c_1 e^x + c_2 e^{2x} + x e^{2x}$

3. $y = c_1 e^{3x} + c_2 e^{-x} - \dfrac{1}{9}(3x + 13)$

4. $y = c_1 \cos x + c_2 \sin x + \dfrac{x}{2} \sin x - \cos x \log \sec x$

5. $y = c_1 \cos ax + c_2 \sin ax + \dfrac{1}{a^2} \sin ax \log \sin ax - \dfrac{x}{a} \cos ax$

2.7 SPECIAL METHODS FOR FINDING PARTICULAR INTEGRALS

The general methods for finding Particular Integrals are longer methods.

In Practice, there are special methods for finding particular integrals, which are short.

We discuss some special methods, when X in f (D) y = X, takes following forms.

1. $X = e^{ax}$, where a is constant
2. $X = \sin(ax)$ or $X = \cos(ax)$
3. $X = x^m$ where m is a positive integer.
4. $X = e^{ax} \cdot V$ where V is a function of x
5. $X = x. V$ where V is a function of x

2.7.1 Particular Integral (P.I.) when $X = e^{ax}$ where a is any constant

Theorem 1   **[S. U. April 2012]**

If f (D) y = X where $X = e^{ax}$ and a is constant

then P. I. $= \dfrac{1}{f(D)} e^{ax} = \dfrac{1}{f(a)} e^{ax}$ where $f(a) \neq 0$.

Proof : We have f (D) y = X   ... (1) and $X = e^{ax}$ ... (2)

By successive differentiation we have

$$D[e^{ax}] = a\,e^{ax} \qquad\qquad ... (3)$$
$$D^2[e^{ax}] = D[D\,e^{ax}] = D[a \cdot e^{ax}] = a^2\,e^{ax}$$

Similarly,

$$D^3[e^{ax}] = a^3\,e^{ax}$$
$$D^4[e^{ax}] = a^4\,e^{ax}$$

Continuing in this way

$$D^n[e^{ax}] = a^n \cdot e^{ax}$$

Let $f(D) = [D^n + P_1 D^{n-1} + P_2 D^{n-2} + ... + P_{n-1} D + P_n]$ ... (4)

$f(D)\,e^{ax} = [D^n + P_1 D^{n-1} + P_2 D^{n-2} + ... + P_{n-1} D + P_n]\,e^{ax}$

$f(D)\,e^{ax} = D^n e^{ax} + P_1 D^{n-1} e^{ax} + P_2 D^{n-2} \cdot e^{ax} + ... + P_{n-1} D e^{ax}$
$\qquad\qquad + P_n e^{ax}$

$f(D)\,e^{ax} = a^n e^{ax} + P_1 a^{n-1} e^{ax} + P_2 a^{n-2} e^{ax} + ... + P_{n-1} a e^{ax}$
$\qquad\qquad + P_n e^{ax}$

$\qquad\qquad = [a^n + P_1 a^{n-1} + P_2 a^{n-2} + ... + P_{n-1} a + P_n]\,e^{ax}$

$f(D)\,e^{ax} = f(a)\,e^{ax}$ ... (5)

where, $f(a) = [a^n + P_1 a^{n-1} + P_2 a^{n-2} + ... + P_{n-1} a + P_n]$

Operating on both sides by $\dfrac{1}{f(D)}$, we get

$$\dfrac{1}{f(D)} \cdot f(D)\, e^{ax} = \dfrac{1}{f(D)} \cdot f(a) \cdot e^{ax}$$

$\therefore$
$$e^{ax} = \dfrac{1}{f(D)} \cdot f(a) \cdot e^{ax}$$

$$e^{ax} = f(a) \cdot \left[\dfrac{1}{f(D)}\, e^{ax}\right] \qquad [\because f(a) \text{ is constant}]$$

Dividing both sides by $f(a) \neq 0$

$$\dfrac{1}{f(a)}\, e^{ax} = \dfrac{1}{f(D)}\, e^{ax}$$

Hence
$$\boxed{\dfrac{1}{f(D)}\, e^{ax} = \dfrac{1}{f(a)}\, e^{ax}}$$

Remember :

To evaluate $\dfrac{1}{f(D)}\, e^{ax}$, put $D = a$ If $f(a) \neq 0$

Particular Case : Suppose $f(D)\, y = X$ where $X = e^{ax}$ and $f(a) = 0$
then

$$\text{P. I.} = \dfrac{1}{f(D)}\, e^{ax} = \dfrac{1}{f(0)}\, e^{ax} = \dfrac{1}{0}\, e^{ax} = \infty$$

here if $f(a) = 0$ then P. I. can not be exist.
and we can not apply above result.
If $f(a) = 0$ then $(D - a)$ must be the factor of $f(D)$.
Suppose $(D - a)$ factor is repeated r times then we write.

$$f(D) = (D - a)^{r}\, \phi(0) \qquad\qquad \text{where } \phi(a) \neq 0$$

We discuss the another theorem for finding the P. I. when $f(a) = 0$.

Theorem 2

If
$$f(D) = (D - a)^{r}\, \phi(D) \text{ where } \phi(a) \neq 0$$

then
$$\dfrac{1}{f(D)}\, e^{ax} = \dfrac{1}{\phi(a)} \cdot \dfrac{x^{r} \cdot e^{ax}}{r!} \qquad\qquad \text{where } r > 0$$

Proof : Let
$$f(D)\, y = X \qquad\qquad \text{where } X = e^{ax} \ \ldots (1)$$

If $f(a) = 0$ then a is a root of $f(D) = 0$
Then $(D - a)$ must be factor of $f(D) = 0$
If factor $(D - a)$ is repeated r times then we write.
$$f(D) = (D - a)^{r}\, \phi(D) \qquad\qquad\qquad \ldots (2)$$
$$\text{where } \phi(a) \neq 0$$

$$\frac{1}{f(D)} e^{ax} = \frac{1}{(D-a)^r \phi(D)} e^{ax}$$

$$\frac{1}{f(D)} e^{ax} = \frac{1}{(D-a)^r} \left[\frac{1}{\phi(D)} e^{ax} \right]$$

$$\frac{1}{f(D)} e^{ax} = \frac{1}{(D-a)^r} \left[\frac{1}{\phi(a)} e^{ax} \right] \qquad ... \text{ where } \phi(a) \neq 0$$

$$\frac{1}{f(D)} e^{ax} = \frac{1}{\phi(a)} \left[\frac{1}{(D-a)^r} e^{ax} \right]$$

$$\frac{1}{f(D)} e^{ax} = \frac{1}{\phi(a)(D-a)^{r-1}(D-a)} e^{ax}$$

$$\frac{1}{f(D)} e^{ax} = \frac{1}{\phi(a)(D-a)^{r-1}} \left[\frac{1}{(D-a)} e^{ax} \right]$$

$$\frac{1}{f(D)} e^{ax} = \frac{1}{\phi(a)(D-a)^{r-1}} \cdot e^{ax} \int e^{ax} \cdot e^{-ax} \, dx$$

$$\frac{1}{f(D)} e^{ax} = \frac{1}{\phi(a)(D-a)^{r-1}} e^{ax} \int 1 \, dx$$

$$= \frac{1}{\phi(a)(D-a)^{r-1}} e^{ax} \cdot x$$

$$\frac{1}{f(D)} e^{ax} = \frac{1}{\phi(a)(D-a)^{r-2}} \left[\frac{1}{D-a} x e^{ax} \right]$$

$$\frac{1}{f(D)} e^{ax} = \frac{1}{\phi(a)(D-a)^{r-2}} \cdot e^{ax} \int x \, e^{ax} \cdot e^{-ax} \, dx$$

$$\frac{1}{f(D)} e^{ax} = \frac{1}{\phi(a)(D-a)^{r-2}} e^{ax} \int x \, dx$$

$$\frac{1}{f(D)} e^{ax} = \frac{1}{\phi(a)(D-a)^{r-2}} e^{ax} \cdot \frac{x^2}{2}$$

$$\frac{1}{f(D)} e^{ax} = \frac{1}{\phi(a)(D-a)^{r-3}} \left[\frac{1}{(D-a)} \left(\frac{x^2 e^{ax}}{2} \right) \right]$$

$$\frac{1}{f(D)} e^{ax} = \frac{1}{\phi(a)(D-a)^{r-3}} \left[e^{ax} \int \frac{x^2 \cdot e^{ax}}{2} \cdot e^{-ax} \, dx \right]$$

$$\frac{1}{f(D)} e^{ax} = \frac{1}{\phi(a)(D-a)^{r-3}} e^x \int \frac{1}{2} x^2 \, dx$$

$$\frac{1}{f(D)} e^{ax} = \frac{1}{\phi(a)(D-a)^{r-3}} e^{ax} \cdot \left(\frac{x^3}{6} \right)$$

$$\frac{1}{f(D)} e^{ax} = \frac{1}{\phi(a) \cdot (D-a)^{r-3}} \frac{x^3 e^{ax}}{3!}$$

Applying the process r times we get

$$\boxed{\frac{1}{f(D)} e^{ax} = \frac{x^r \cdot e^{ax}}{\phi(a) \, r!}}$$

Thus $\boxed{\dfrac{1}{(D-1)^r \, \phi(D)} e^{ax} = \dfrac{x^r \, e^{ax}}{\phi(a) \cdot r!}}$ ... (A)

Theorem 3

If $f(D) = (D-a) \, \phi(D)$ and $\phi(a) \neq 0$

then $\dfrac{1}{f(D)} e^{ax} = \dfrac{x \, e^{ax}}{\phi(a)}$

Proof : Let $f(D) \, y = x$ .... (1) where $X = e^{ax}$

If $f(a) = 0$ then $(D-a)$ must be a factor of $f(D) = 0$

Then we write

$$f(D) = (D-a) \, \phi(D) \qquad \text{... (2) where } \phi(a) \neq 0$$

$$\frac{1}{f(D)} e^{ax} = \frac{1}{(D-a) \, \phi(D)} e^{ax}$$

$$\frac{1}{f(D)} e^{ax} = \frac{1}{(D-a)} \left[\frac{1}{\phi(D)} e^{ax} \right]$$

Using $D = a$

$$\frac{1}{f(D)} e^{ax} = \frac{1}{(D-a)} \left[\frac{1}{\phi(a)} e^{ax} \right]$$

$$\frac{1}{f(D)} e^{ax} = \frac{1}{\phi(a)} \left[\frac{1}{D-a} e^{ax} \right]$$

$$\frac{1}{f(D)} e^{ax} = \frac{1}{\phi(a)} \left[e^{ax} \int e^{ax} \cdot e^{-ax} \, dx \right]$$

$$\frac{1}{f(D)} e^{ax} = \frac{1}{\phi(a)} \left[e^{ax} \int 1 \, dx \right]$$

$$\frac{1}{f(D)} e^{ax} = \frac{1}{\phi(a)} [e^{ax} \cdot x]$$

$$\boxed{\frac{1}{f(D)} e^{ax} = \frac{x e^{ax}}{\phi(a)} \text{ where } \phi(a) \neq 0}$$

Theorem 4

If $f(D) = (D-a)^2 \, \phi(D)$ and $\phi(a) \neq 0$

then $\dfrac{1}{f(D)} e^{ax} = \dfrac{x^2}{2!} \dfrac{e^{ax}}{\phi(a)}$

Proof : If $f(D) \, y = X$ ... (1)   where $X = e^{ax}$

If $f(a) = 0$ then $(D-a)$ must be factor of $f(D) = 0$

Suppose $(D-a)$ is repeated twice, then we write

$$f(D) = (D-a)^2 \phi(D) \quad \dots (2) \qquad \text{where } \phi(a) \neq 0$$

$$\frac{1}{f(D)} e^{ax} = \frac{1}{(D-a)^2 \phi(D)} e^{ax}$$

$$= \frac{1}{(D-a)^2} \left[\frac{1}{\phi(D)} e^{ax} \right]$$

Using D = a

$$= \frac{1}{(D-a)^2} \left[\frac{1}{\phi(a)} e^{ax} \right]$$

$$= \frac{1}{\phi(a)} \left[\frac{1}{(D-a)^2} e^{ax} \right]$$

$$= \frac{1}{\phi(a)} \cdot \frac{1}{(D-a)} \left[\frac{1}{D-a} e^{ax} \right]$$

but $\dfrac{1}{D-a} e^{ax} = x\, e^{ax}$

$$= \frac{1}{\phi(a)} \cdot \frac{1}{D-a} [x e^{ax}]$$

$$= \frac{1}{\phi(a)} \cdot \left[e^{ax} \int (x\, e^{ax})\, e^{-ax}\, dx \right]$$

$$= \frac{1}{\phi(a)} \left[e^{ax} \int x\, dx \right]$$

$$= \frac{1}{\phi(a)} \cdot e^{ax} \cdot \frac{x^2}{2}$$

$$\boxed{\frac{1}{f(D)} e^{ax} = \frac{x^2}{2!} \frac{e^{ax}}{\phi(a)} \text{ where } \phi(a) \neq 0}$$

Formulae

I. 1. $\dfrac{1}{(D-a)^n} e^{ax} = \dfrac{x^n}{n!} e^{ax}$

2. $\dfrac{1}{(D-a)^3} e^{ax} = \dfrac{x^3}{3!} e^{ax}$

3. $\dfrac{1}{(D-a)^2} e^{ax} = \dfrac{x^2}{2!} e^{ax}$

4. $\dfrac{1}{(D-a)} e^{ax} = x e^{ax}$

II. 5. $\dfrac{1}{(D+a)^n} e^{-ax} = \dfrac{x^n}{n!} e^{-ax}$

6. $\dfrac{1}{(D+a)^3} e^{-ax} = \dfrac{x^3}{3!} e^{-ax}$

7. $\dfrac{1}{(D+a)^2} e^{-ax} = \dfrac{x^2}{2!} e^{-ax}$

8. $\dfrac{1}{(D+a)} e^{-ax} = x e^{-ax}$

SOLVED EXAMPLES

Example 2.44 : Evaluate : $\dfrac{1}{(D-1)^2\,(D^2+4)}\ e^x$

Solution :

$$\dfrac{1}{(D-1)^2\,(D^2+4)}\ e^x = \dfrac{1}{(D-1)^2}\left[\dfrac{1}{D^2+4}\,e^x\right] \qquad \text{put } D = 1$$

$$= \dfrac{1}{(D-1)^2}\left[\dfrac{1}{5}\,e^x\right] = \dfrac{1}{5}\left[\dfrac{1}{(D-1)^2}\,e^x\right]$$

$$\text{If } D = 1 \text{ then } (D-1)^2 = 0$$

$$= \dfrac{1}{5}\left[\dfrac{x^2\,e^x}{2!}\right]$$

$$\dfrac{1}{(D-1)^2\,(D^2+4)}\ e^x = \dfrac{x^2\,e^x}{10}$$

Example 2.45 : Evaluate $\dfrac{1}{(D-2)\,(D+2)}\ e^{2x}$

Solution : $\dfrac{1}{(D-2)\,(D+2)}\ e^{2x} = \dfrac{1}{(D-2)}\left[\dfrac{1}{D+2}\,e^{2x}\right]$

$$\text{put } D = 2$$

$$\dfrac{1}{(D-2)\,(D+2)}\ e^{2x} = \dfrac{1}{D-2}\left[\dfrac{e^{2x}}{4}\right] = \dfrac{1}{4}\left[\dfrac{1}{D-2}\,e^{2x}\right]$$

$$\text{If we put } D = 2 \text{ then } D-2 = 0$$

$$\dfrac{1}{(D-2)\,(D+2)}\ e^{2x} = \dfrac{1}{4}\left[x\cdot e^{2x}\right]$$

Example 2.46 : Solve $\dfrac{d^2y}{dx^2} - 5\dfrac{dy}{dx} + 6y = 2e^{3x}$ **(April 2013)**

Solution : Given differential equation is

$$\dfrac{d^2y}{dx^2} - 5\dfrac{dy}{dx} + 6y = 2e^{3x} \qquad\qquad \text{... (1)}$$

$$\therefore \qquad [D^2 - 5D + 6]\,y = 2e^{3x} \qquad\qquad \text{... (2)}$$

$$\text{i.e.} \qquad f(D)\,y = X \qquad\qquad \text{... (3)}$$

$$\text{where} \qquad f(D) = D^2 - 5D + 6$$

$$X = 2e^{3x}$$

To find C. F.

The A. E. is $\qquad D^2 - 5D + 6 = 0$

$$(D-2)\,(D-3) = 0$$

$$D = 2, 3$$

Let $\qquad m_1 = 2, \; m_2 = 3$

$$\text{C. F.} = c_1 \, e^{m_1 x} + c_2 e^{m_2 x}$$

$$\text{C. F.} = c_1 \, e^{2x} + c_2 \, e^{3x} \qquad \qquad \dots (4)$$

To find P. I.

$$\text{P. I.} = \frac{1}{f(D)} \, X = \frac{1}{D^2 - 5D + 6} \, [2e^{3x}]$$

$$\frac{1}{f(D)} \, X = \frac{1}{(D-2)(D-3)} \cdot 2e^{3x}$$

$$\frac{1}{f(D)} \, X = \frac{1}{(D-3)} \left[\frac{1}{D-2} \cdot 2e^{3x} \right]$$

$$\text{put } D = 3$$

$$\frac{1}{f(D)} \, X = \frac{1}{(D-3)} \, [2e^{3x}]$$

If we put $D = 3$ then $D - 3 = 0 \Rightarrow f(a) = 0$

$$\frac{1}{f(D)} = \frac{x}{1!} \, [2e^{3x}]$$

$\therefore \qquad\qquad \text{P. I.} = 2xe^{3x}$

The general solution is

$$y = \text{C. F.} + \text{P. I.}$$

$$y = c_1 \, e^{2x} + c_2 e^{3x} + 2xe^{3x} \qquad \qquad \dots (5)$$

Example 2.47 : Solve $\left[\dfrac{d^2y}{dx^2} + 4\dfrac{dy}{dx} + 4y \right] = 2 \cosh (2x)$ **(S. U. May 2011)**

Solution : The given differential equation is

$$\frac{d^2y}{dx^2} + 4\frac{dy}{dx} + 4y = 2 \cosh (2x) \qquad \dots (1)$$

$$[D^2 + 4D + 4] = 2 \cosh (2x) \qquad \dots (2)$$

i.e. $\qquad\qquad\qquad f(D) \, y = X \qquad \dots (3)$

where $\qquad\qquad\qquad f(D) = D^2 + 4D + 4$

$$X = 2 \cosh (2x)$$

To find C. F.

A. E. is $\qquad\qquad D^2 + 4D + 4 = 0 \qquad \dots (4)$

$$(D + 2)^2 = 0$$

$$D = -2, D = -2$$

Let $\qquad\qquad\qquad m_1 = m_2 = -2$

The roots are real and equal.

$$\text{C. F.} = (c_1 + c_2 \, x) \, e^{m_1 x}$$

$$\text{C. F.} = (c_1 + c_2 \, x) \, e^{-2x} \qquad \dots (5)$$

To find P. I.

$$\text{P. I.} = \frac{1}{f(D)} X$$

$$\text{P. I.} = \frac{1}{(D^2 + 4D + 4)} 2 \cosh(2x)$$

put $\qquad \cosh(2x) = \dfrac{e^{2x} + e^{-2x}}{2}$

$$\text{P. I.} = \frac{1}{(D+2)^2} \cdot 2 \left[\frac{e^{2x} + e^{-2x}}{2} \right]$$

$$\text{P. I.} = \frac{1}{(D+2)^2} e^{2x} + \frac{1}{(D+2)^2} e^{-2x}$$

$$\text{P. I.} = \frac{1}{(2+2)^2} e^{2x} + \frac{x^2}{2!} e^{-2x} = \frac{e^{2x}}{16} + \frac{x^2}{2} e^{-2x} \quad \dots (6)$$

The solution of equation (1) is

$$y = \text{C. F.} + \text{P. I.}$$

$$y = (c_1 + c_2 x) e^{-2x} + \frac{e^{2x}}{16} + \frac{x^2}{2} e^{-2x} \qquad \dots (7)$$

Example 2.48 : Solve $\dfrac{d^2y}{dx^2} - \dfrac{2dy}{dx} + 5y = e^{-x}$

Solution : Given differential equation is

$$\frac{d^2y}{dx^2} - \frac{2dy}{dx} + 5y = e^{-x} \qquad \dots (1)$$

$\therefore \qquad\qquad [D^2 - 2D + 5] y = e^{-x} \qquad\qquad \dots (2)$

i. e. $\qquad\qquad f(D) y = X$

$$\text{where } f(D) = D^2 = 2D + 5$$
$$X = e^{-x}$$

To find C. F.

Auxilliary equation (A. E.) is

$$D^2 - 2D + 5 = 0$$

$$D = \frac{2 \pm \sqrt{4 - 20}}{2}$$

$$D = \frac{2 \pm \sqrt{-16}}{2} = \frac{2 \pm 4i}{2} = 1 \pm 2i$$

$$D = 1 \pm 2i = \alpha \pm i\beta$$

$\therefore \qquad\qquad \alpha = 1 \qquad\qquad \beta = 2$

Here roots are complex

$$\text{C. F.} = e^{\alpha x} [c_1 \cos Bx + c_2 \sin Bx]$$

$$\text{C. F.} = e^x [c_1 \cos 2x + c_2 \sin 2x] \qquad \dots (3)$$

To find P. I.

$$\text{P. I.} = \frac{1}{f(D)} \times = \frac{1}{D^2 - 2D + 5} e^{-x}$$

put $D = -1$

$$= \frac{1}{(-1)^2 - 2(-1) + 5} e^{-x}$$

$$= \frac{1}{1 + 2 + 5} e^{-x}$$

$$\text{P. I.} = \frac{e^{-x}}{8} \qquad \qquad \dots (4)$$

The general solution is

$$y = \text{C. F.} + \text{P. I.}$$

$$y = e^x [c_1 \cos 2x + c_2 \sin 2x] + \frac{e^{-x}}{8} \qquad \dots (5)$$

Example 2.49 : Solve $\left[\dfrac{d^3y}{dx^3} + 3\dfrac{d^2y}{dx^2} + \dfrac{3dy}{dx} + y\right] = e^{-x} + e^{2x}$

Solution : The given differential equation is

$$\frac{d^3y}{dx^3} + 3\frac{d^2y}{dx^2} + 3\frac{dy}{dx} + y = e^{-x} + e^{2x} \qquad \dots (1)$$

$$[D^3 + 3D^2 + 3D + 1] y = e^{-x} + e^{2x} \qquad \dots (2)$$

i.e. $\qquad\qquad\qquad f(D) y = X \qquad \dots (3)$

where $\qquad\qquad\quad f(D) = D^3 + 3D^2 + 3D + 1$

$$X = e^{-x} + e^{2x}$$

To find C. F.

A. E. is $D^3 + 3D^2 + 3D + 1 = 0$

$$(D + 1)^3 = 0$$

$$D = -1, -1, -1$$

Let $\qquad\qquad\qquad m_1 = m_2 = m_3 = -1$

Here roots are real and equal

$$\text{C. F.} = [c_1 + c_2 x + c_3 x^2] e^{-x} \qquad \dots (4)$$

To find P. I.

$$\text{P. I.} = \frac{1}{f(D)} X = \frac{1}{(D+1)^3} [e^{-x} + e^{-2x}]$$

$$\text{P. I.} = \frac{1}{(D+1)^3} e^{-x} + \frac{1}{(D+1)^3} e^{2x}$$

put $D = 2$

$$\text{P. I.} = \frac{1}{(D+1)^3} e^{-x} + \frac{1}{27} e^{2x}$$

If we put $D = -1$ then $(D + 1) = 0$

$$\text{P. I.} = \frac{x^3}{3!} e^{-x} + \frac{1}{27} e^{2x}$$

$$\text{P. I.} = \frac{x^3}{6} e^{-x} + \frac{1}{27} e^{2x} \qquad \text{... (5)}$$

The general solution is

$$y = \text{C. F.} + \text{P. I.}$$

$$y = [c_1 + c_2 + c_3 x^2] e^{-x} + \frac{x^3}{6} e^{-x} + \frac{1}{27} e^{2x} \qquad \text{... (6)}$$

Example 2.50 : Solve $\dfrac{d^2y}{dx^2} - 3\dfrac{dy}{dx} + 2y = e^x$

Solution : The given differential equation is

$$\frac{d^2y}{dx^2} - 3\frac{dy}{dx} + 2y = e^x \qquad \text{... (1)}$$

$\therefore$
$$[D^2 - 3D + 2] y = e^x \qquad \text{... (2)}$$

i.e.
$$f(D) y = X$$

$$\text{where } f(D) = D^2 - 3D + 2$$
$$X = e^x$$

To find C. F.

A. E. is
$$D^2 - 3D + 2 = 0$$
$$(D - 1)(D - 2) = 0$$
$$D = 1, 2$$

Let $m_1 = 1$, $m_2 = 2$

$$\text{C. F.} = c_1 e^{m_1 x} + c_2 e^{m_2 x}$$
$$\text{C. F.} = c_1 e^x + c_2 e^{2x} \qquad \text{... (3)}$$

To find P. I.

$$\text{P. I.} = \frac{1}{f(D)} X = \frac{1}{D^2 - 3D + 2} \cdot e^x$$

$$\text{P. I.} = \frac{1}{(D - 1)(D - 2)} e^x$$

$$\text{P. I.} = \frac{1}{D - 1} \left[\frac{1}{D - 2} e^x \right]$$

$$\text{put } D = 1$$

$$\text{P. I.} = \frac{1}{D - 1} \left[\frac{e^x}{-1} \right]$$

$$\text{P. I.} = -\frac{1}{D - 1} [e^x]$$

If we put $D = 1$ then $D - 1 = 0$

$$\text{P. I.} = \frac{x}{1!} \, e^x$$

$$\text{P. I.} = -x \, e^x \qquad \qquad \text{... (4)}$$

The general solution is

$$y = \text{C. F.} + \text{P. I.}$$

$$y = c_1 e^x + c_2 e^{2x} - x e^x \qquad \qquad \text{... (5)}$$

Example 2.51 : Solve : $[D^3 - 2D^2 - 4D + 8] \, y = e^{2x}$

Solution : The given differential equation is

$$[D^3 - 2D^2 - 4D + 8] \, y = e^{2x} \qquad \qquad \text{... (1)}$$

i.e.
$$f(D) \, y = X \qquad \qquad \text{... (2)}$$

where
$$f(D) = D^3 - 2D^2 - 4D + 8$$
$$X = e^{2x}$$

To find C. F.

A. E. is
$$D^3 - 2D^2 - 4D + 8 = 0$$
$$D^2 (D - 2) - 4(D - 2) = 0$$
$$(D - 2)(D^2 - 4) = 0$$
$$(D - 2)(D - 2)(D + 2) = 0$$
$$(D - 2)^2 (D + 2) = 0$$
$$(D - 2)^2 = 0 \qquad \text{and } D + 2 = 0$$

$$\therefore \qquad\qquad D = 2, 2 \qquad\qquad \text{and } D = -2$$

Let
$$m_1 = m_2 = 2 \qquad\qquad m_3 = -2$$
$$\text{C. F.} = (c_1 + c_2 \, x) \, e^{m_1 x} + c_3 \, e^{m_3 x}$$
$$\text{C. F.} = (c_1 + c_2 x) \, e^{2x} + c_3 \, e^{-2x} \qquad \qquad \text{... (3)}$$

To find P. I.

$$\text{P. I.} = \frac{1}{f(D)} \, X = \frac{1}{D^3 - 2D^2 - 4D + 8} \, e^{2x}$$

$$\text{P. I.} = \frac{1}{(D - 2)^2 (D + 2)} \, e^{2x}$$

$$\text{P. I.} = \frac{1}{(D - 2)^2} \left[\frac{1}{D + 2} \, e^{2x} \right]$$

Using $D = 2$

$$\text{P. I.} = \frac{1}{(D - 2)^2} \left[\frac{1}{4} \, e^{2x} \right]$$

If we put $D = 2$ then $(D - 2) = 0$

$$\text{P. I.} = \frac{x^2}{2!} \left[\frac{1}{4} \, e^{2x} \right]$$

$$\text{P. I.} = \frac{x^2}{8} \, e^{2x}$$

The general solution is

$$y = C. F. + P. I.$$

$$y = [c_1 + c_2 x] e^{2x} + c_2 e^{-2x} + \frac{x^2}{e} e^{2x} \qquad \dots (4)$$

EXERCISE 2.6

I. Theory Questions

1. If $f(D) y = X$ where $X = e^{ax}$ and a is constant

    Prove that $\dfrac{1}{f(D)} e^{ax} = \dfrac{1}{f(a)} e^{ax}$ where $f(a) \neq 0$ **[S. U. April 2012]**

    OR

2. Obtain the particular integral of $f(D) y = e^{ax}$
    when $f(a) \neq 0$

3. If $f(D) y = X$ where $X = e^{ax}$ and $f(a) = 0$
    then prove that

    $$\frac{1}{f(D)} e^{ax} = \frac{1}{\phi(a)} \cdot \frac{x^r \cdot e^{ax}}{r!}$$

    where $f(D) = (D - a)^r \phi(D)$, and $\phi(a) \neq 0$

4. Prove that, $\dfrac{1}{f(D)} e^{ax} = \dfrac{x e^{ax}}{\phi(a)}$

    where $f(D) = (D - a) \phi(D)$ and $\phi(a) \neq 0$

5. Prove that $\dfrac{1}{f(D)} e^{ax} = \dfrac{x^2}{2!} \dfrac{1}{\phi(a)} e^{ax}$

    where $f(D) = (D - a)^2 \phi(D)$, and $\phi(a) \neq 0$

II. Solve the following differential equations.

1. $[D^2 - 5D + 6] y = e^{2x}$

2. $\dfrac{d^2y}{dx^2} + \dfrac{dy}{dx} + y = e^{-x}$

3. $\dfrac{d^2y}{dx^2} - 2\dfrac{dy}{dx} + y = e^{-x}$

4. $\dfrac{d^2y}{dx^2} - 2\dfrac{dy}{dx} + y = e^{x+1}$

5. $[D^3 - 4D^2 + 5D - 2] y = e^x$

6. $(D^2 - 4D + 3) y = e^{3x}$

7. $[D^2 - 3D + 2] y = \cosh x$ Use $\cosh x = \dfrac{e^x + e^{-x}}{2}$

8. $[D^3 - 3D^2 + 4D - 2] y = e^x$

9. $[D^2 + 4D + 4] y = e^{2x} - e^{-2x}$

10. $\dfrac{d^3y}{dx^3} - y = (e^x + 1)^2$

$$\boxed{\textbf{ANSWERS 2.6}}$$

1. $y = c_1 e^{2x} + c_2 e^{3x} - xe^{2x}$

2. $y = e^{-x/2}\left[c_1 \cos \dfrac{\sqrt{3}}{2} x + c_2 \sin \dfrac{\sqrt{3}}{2} x\right] + e^{-x}$

3. $y = [c_1 + c_2 x] e^x + \dfrac{x^2 e^x}{2}$

4. $y = [c_1 + c_2 x] e^x + \dfrac{x^2 e^x}{2} + 1$

5. $y = (c_1 + c_2 x) e^x + c_3 e^{2x} - \dfrac{x^2}{2} e^x$

6. $y = c_1 e^x + c_2 e^{3x} + \dfrac{1}{2} xe^{3x}$

7. $y = c_1 e^x + c_2 e^{2x} - \dfrac{x}{2} e^x + \dfrac{1}{12} e^{-x}$

8. $y = c_1 e^x + e^x [c_1 \cos x + c_3 \sin x] + xe^x$

9. $y = (c_1 + c_2 x) e^{-2x} + \dfrac{e^{2x}}{16} - \dfrac{x^2}{2} e^{-2x}$

10. $y = c_1 e^x + \left[c_2 \cos \dfrac{\sqrt{3}}{2} x + c_3 \sin \dfrac{\sqrt{3}}{2} x\right] e^{-x} + \dfrac{e^{2x}}{7} + \dfrac{2e^x}{3} - 1$

2.7.2 Particular Integrals

when $X = \sin (ax)$ and $X = \cos (ax)$

First we prove two theorems

Theorem 1   **[S. U. Nov. 2012, April 2013]**

$$\dfrac{1}{f(D)^2} \sin (ax) = \dfrac{1}{f(-a)^2} \sin (ax) \qquad \text{where } f(-a^2) \neq 0$$

Proof :

By successive differentiation we have

$$D [\sin ax] = a \cos ax \qquad \qquad \dots (1)$$

$$D^2 \cdot [\sin ax] = -a^2 \sin ax = (-a^2)^1 \sin ax \qquad \dots (2)$$

$$D^3 [\sin ax] = -a^3 \cos ax \qquad \dots (3)$$

$$D^4 [\sin ax] = a^4 \sin ax = (-a^2)^2 \sin ax \qquad \dots (4)$$

$$D^5 [\sin ax] = a^5 \cos ax \qquad \dots (5)$$

$$D^6 [\sin ax] = -a^6 \sin ax = (-a^2)^3 \sin ax \qquad \dots (6)$$

Continuing in this way, we have

$$D^{2n} [\sin ax] = (- a^2)^n \sin ax$$
$$[D^2]^n \sin (ax) = (- a^2)^n \sin ax \qquad \qquad ... (7)$$

From above results, we can write

$$f (D^2) \sin ax = f (- a^2) \sin ax \qquad \qquad ... (8)$$

Operating on both sides by $\dfrac{1}{f (D^2)}$, we get

$$\frac{1}{f (D^2)} \cdot f (D^2) \sin ax = \frac{1}{f (D^2)} f (- a^2) \sin ax$$

$$\Rightarrow \qquad \qquad \sin (ax) = f (- a^2) \cdot \frac{1}{f (D^2)} \sin (ax)$$

Dividing both sides by $f (- a)^2$

$$\frac{1}{f (- a)^2} \sin (ax) = \frac{1}{f (D)^2} \sin (ax)$$

$$\boxed{\therefore \; \frac{1}{f (D^2)} \sin (ax) = \frac{1}{f (- a^2)} \sin (ax) \quad \text{where } f (- a^2) \neq 0}$$

Theorem 2

$$\frac{1}{f (D)^2} \cos (ax) = \frac{1}{f (- a)^2} \cos (ax) \text{ where } f (- a^2) \neq 0$$

[S. U. Oct. 2011, April 2013]

Proof : By successive differentiation, we have

$$D [\cos ax] = - a \sin ax \qquad \qquad ... (1)$$
$$D^2 [\cos ax] = - a^2 \cos ax = (- a^2) \cos ax \qquad ... (2)$$
$$D^3 [\cos ax] = a^3 \sin ax \qquad \qquad ... (3)$$
$$D^4 [\cos ax] = a^4 \cos ax = (- a^2)^2 \cos ax \qquad ... (4)$$
$$D^5 [\cos ax] = - a^5 \cdot \sin ax \qquad \qquad ... (5)$$
$$D^6 [\cos ax] = - a^6 \cos ax = (- a^2)^3 \cos ax \qquad ... (6)$$

- -
- -

Continuing in this way we have

$$D^{2n} [\cos ax] = (- a^2)^n \cos ax$$
$$[D^2]^n \cos ax = (- a^2)^n \cos ax \qquad \qquad ... (7)$$

From above results we can write

$$f (D^2) \cos ax = f (- a^2) \cos ax \qquad \qquad ... (8)$$

Operating on both sides by $\dfrac{1}{f (D^2)}$, we get

$$\frac{1}{f (D^2)} f (D^2) \cos ax = \frac{1}{f (D^2)} f (- a^2) \cos ax$$

$$\Rightarrow \qquad \cos(ax) = f(-a^2)\frac{1}{f(D^2)}\cos(ax)$$

Dividing both sides by $f(-a^2)$

$$\frac{1}{f(-a^2)}\cos(ax) = \frac{1}{f(D^2)}\cos(ax)$$

$$\boxed{\therefore \; \frac{1}{f(D^2)}\cos(ax) = \frac{1}{f(-a^2)}\cos(ax) \quad \text{where } f(-a^2) \neq 0}$$

Remember

1.   To evaluate

$$\frac{1}{f(D^2)}\sin(ax) \text{ or } \frac{1}{f(D^2)}\cos(ax) \text{ put } D^2 = -a^2 \text{ if } f(-a^2) \neq 0$$

2.   For finding the P. I. of $\dfrac{1}{f(D)}\sin(ax)$ or $\dfrac{1}{f(D)}\cos(ax)$

put
$$D^2 = -a^2$$
$$D^3 = D^2 \cdot D = -a^2 D$$
$$D^4 = (D^2)^2 = (-a^2)^2 = a^4$$
$$D^5 = D^4 \cdot D = a^4 D$$
$$D^6 = D^2 D^2 D^2 = (-a^2)(-a^2)(-a^2) = -a^6$$

and so on ultimately $f(D)$ becomes linear in D and solve it by using known formulae.

Illustrations : Suppose $\dfrac{1}{f(D)}\cos(ax) = \dfrac{1}{D+A}\cos(ax)$

Then

$$\frac{1}{D+a}\cos(ax) = \frac{(D-A)}{(D+A)(D-A)}\cos(ax)$$

$$\frac{1}{D+a}\cos(ax) = \frac{D-A}{D^2-A^2}\cos(ax)$$

$$\text{put } \boxed{D^2 = -a^2}$$

$$= \frac{D-A}{-a^2-A^2}\cos(ax)$$

$$\frac{1}{D+a}\cos(ax) = \frac{-1}{a^2+A^2}[D-A]\cos(ax)$$

$$\frac{1}{D+a}\cos(ax) = \frac{-1}{a^2+A^2}[D\cos(ax) - A \cdot \cos(ax)]$$

$$\text{Using } D = \frac{d}{dx}$$

$$\frac{1}{D+a} \cos(ax) = \frac{-1}{a^2 + A^2}\left[\frac{d}{dx}[\cos(ax)] - A\cos(ax)\right]$$

$$\frac{1}{D+A} \cos(ax) = \frac{-1}{a^2 + A^2}[-a\sin(ax) - A\cos(ax)]$$

3. $\quad \dfrac{1}{f(D^2)} \sin(ax+b) = \dfrac{1}{f(-a^2)} \sin(ax+b)$ where $f(-a^2) \neq 0$

4. $\quad \dfrac{1}{f(D^2)} \cos(ax+b) = \dfrac{1}{f(-a^2)} \cos(ax+b)$ where $f(-a^2) \neq 0$

5. **Particular Case If $f(-a)^2 = 0$ then above theorem fails**

Thus If $f(-a)^2 = 0$ then $\dfrac{1}{f(D^2)} \sin(ax) = \dfrac{1}{f(-a)^2} \sin(ax) = \dfrac{1}{0}$

$\sin ax = \infty$

or $\qquad \dfrac{1}{f(D^2)} \cos(ax) = \dfrac{1}{f(-a^2)} \cos(ax) = \dfrac{1}{0} \cos(ax) = \infty$

In this way. We can not apply above Theorem

1. If $f(-a)^2 = 0$ then $D^2 + a^2$ is a factor of $f(D^2)$

We consider $f(D^2) = (D^2 + a^2)\, \phi(D^2)$ where $\phi(-a^2) \neq 0$

Then for example

(i) $\quad \dfrac{1}{f(D^2)} \sin(ax) = \dfrac{1}{(D^2 + a^2)\,\phi(D^2)} \sin(ax) = \dfrac{1 \sin(ax)}{(D^2 + a^2)\,\phi(-a^2)}$

OR

(ii) $\quad \dfrac{1}{f(D^2)} \cos(ax) = \dfrac{1}{(D^2 + a^2)\,\phi(D^2)} \cos(ax) = \dfrac{1 \cos(ax)}{(D^2 + a^2)\,\phi(-a^2)}$

Hence for solving $\dfrac{1}{D^2 + a^2} \sin ax$ or $\dfrac{1}{D^2 + a^2} \cos(ax)$

we prove following theorems

Theorem 3

(i) $\qquad \dfrac{1}{D^2 + a^2} \cos(ax) = \dfrac{x}{2a} \sin(ax)$

(ii) $\qquad \dfrac{1}{D^2 + a^2} \sin(ax) = \dfrac{-x}{2a} \cos(ax)$

Proof : We know that $e^{iax} = \cos ax + i\sin ax$

$$\frac{1}{D^2 + a^2}[\cos ax + i\sin ax] = \frac{1}{[D^2 + a^2]} e^{iax}$$

$$\frac{1}{D^2 + a^2}[\cos ax + i\sin ax] = \frac{1}{[D^2 - i^2 a^2]} e^{iax}$$

$$\frac{1}{D^2 + a^2}[\cos ax + i\sin ax] = \frac{1}{(D + ia)(D - ia)} e^{iax}$$

$$\frac{1}{D^2 + a^2} [\cos ax + i \sin ax] = \frac{1}{[D + ia]} \left[\frac{1}{D - ia} e^{iax} \right]$$

$$[\text{If } D = ia \text{ then } (D - ia) = 0]$$

$$\frac{1}{D^2 + a^2} [\cos ax + i \sin ax] = \frac{1}{[D + ia]} \cdot xe^{iax}$$

$$\text{put } D = ia$$

$$= \frac{1}{2ia} xe^{iax}$$

$$= \text{Multiply and divide by } i$$

$$\frac{1}{D^2 + a^2} [\cos ax + i \sin ax] = \frac{ix \, e^{iax}}{2i^2a}$$

$$\therefore \quad \frac{1}{D^2 + a^2} [\cos ax + i \sin ax] = \frac{ix}{-2a} [\cos ax + i \sin ax]$$

$$\frac{1}{D^2 + a^2} [\cos ax + i \sin ax] = \frac{x}{-2a} [-i \cos ax + i^2 \sin ax]$$

$$\frac{1}{D^2 + a^2} [\cos ax + i \sin ax] = \frac{x}{2a} [i \cos ax + \sin ax]$$

$$\frac{1}{D^2 + a^2} [\cos ax] + i \frac{1}{D^2 + a^2} [\sin ax] = \frac{x}{2a} [\sin ax + i \cos ax]$$

Equating real and imaginary parts

$$\boxed{\frac{1}{D^2 + a^2} \cos (ax) = \frac{x}{2a} \sin (ax)}$$

and

$$\boxed{\frac{1}{D^2 + a^2} \sin (ax) = \frac{-x}{2a} \cos (ax)}$$

Remark 1

If in $f(D^2)$ the factor $D^2 + a^2$ is repeated twice

then $\quad\quad f(D^2) = (D^2 + a^2)^2 \, \phi(D^2)$ where $\phi(D^2) \neq 0$ and $f(D^2) = 0$

In this case we have the following formulae.

(i) $\quad\quad \dfrac{1}{[D^2 + a^2]^2} \cos (ax) = \dfrac{-x^2}{2!} \cdot \dfrac{1}{4a^2} \cos (ax)$

(ii) $\quad\quad \dfrac{1}{[D^2 + a^2]^2} \sin (ax) = \dfrac{-x^2}{2!} \cdot \dfrac{1}{4a^2} \sin (ax)$

Remark 2

If the factor $(D^2 + a^2)$ is repeated r times in $f(D)$ then

$$\frac{1}{[D^2 + a^2]^r} [\cos ax + i \sin ax] = \frac{(-1)^r (i)^r x^r}{2^r \cdot a^r \cdot r!} [\cos ax + i \sin ax] \quad\quad \dots \text{(A)}$$

Therefore $\dfrac{1}{[D^2 + a^2]^r} \cos(ax)$ = Real Part of (A)

and $\dfrac{1}{[D^2 + a^2]^r} \sin(ax)$ = Imaginary part of (A)

Remark 3

1. $\dfrac{1}{D^2 + 4} \cos(2x) = \dfrac{x}{4} \sin(2x)$

2. $\dfrac{1}{D^2 + 9} \sin(3x) = \dfrac{-x}{6} \cos(3x)$

3. $\dfrac{1}{(D^2 + 4)^2} \cos(2x) = \dfrac{-x^2}{2!} \times \dfrac{1}{4 \times 4} \cos(2x) = \dfrac{-x^2}{32} \cos(2x)$

4. $\dfrac{1}{(D^2 + 9)^2} \sin(3x) = \dfrac{-x^2}{2!} \times \dfrac{1}{4 \times 9} \sin(3x) = \dfrac{-x^2}{72} \sin(3x)$

SOLVED EXAMPLES

Example 2.52 : Solve : $[D^2 - 5D + 6] y = \cos(3x)$ **[S. U. April 2013]**

Solution : Given differential equation is

$$[D^2 - 5D + 6] y = \cos(3x) \qquad \ldots (1)$$

i.e. $f(D) y = X \qquad \ldots (2)$

where $f(D) = D^2 - 5D + 6$

$X = \cos(3x)$

To Find C. F.

A. E. is $[D^2 - 5D + 6] = 0 \qquad \ldots (3)$

$(D - 2)(D - 3) = 0$

$D = 2, D = 3$

Let $m_1 = 2, m_2 = 3$

The roots are real and unequal.

C. F. $= c_1 e^{m_1 x} + c_2 e^{m_2 x}$

C. F. $= c_1 e^{2x} + c_2 e^{3x} \qquad \ldots (4)$

To Find P. I.

$$\text{P. I.} = \dfrac{1}{f(D)} X = \dfrac{1}{D^2 - 5D + 6} \cos(3x)$$

Put $D^2 = -a^2 = -9$

$$\text{P. I.} = \dfrac{1}{9 - 5D + 6} \cos(3x)$$

$$\text{P. I.} = \dfrac{1}{(-5D + 15)} \cos(3x) = \dfrac{1}{-5(D - 3)} \cos(3x)$$

$$\text{P. I.} = \frac{1}{-5(D-3)}\frac{(D+3)}{(D+2)}\cos(3x)$$

$$\text{P. I.} = \frac{(D+3)}{-5(D^2-9)}\cos(3x)$$

Put $D^2 = -9$

$$\text{P. I.} = \frac{(D+3)\cos(3x)}{-5(-18)}$$

$$\text{P. I.} = \frac{1}{90}[D(\cos(3x)) + 3\cos(3x)]$$

$$\text{P. I.} = \frac{1}{90}[-3\sin(3x) + 3\cos(3x)]$$

$$\text{P. I.} = \frac{-3}{90}[\sin(3x) - \cos(3x)]$$

$$\text{P. I.} = \frac{-1}{30}[\sin(3x) - \cos(3x)] \qquad \dots (5)$$

The solution is $y = \text{C. F.} + \text{P. I.}$

$$y = [c_1 e^{2x} + c_2 e^{3x}] - \frac{1}{30}[\sin(3x) - \cos(3x)] \quad \dots (6)$$

Example 2.53 : Solve $\dfrac{d^2y}{dx^2} + 4y = \cos(3x)$ **[S. U. April 2013]**

Solution : Given differential equation is

$$\frac{d^2y}{dx^2} + 4y = \cos(3x) \qquad \dots (1)$$

$\therefore$ $[D^2 + 4]y = \cos(3x)$ $\dots (2)$

i.e. $f(D)y = X$ $\dots (3)$

where $f(D) = D^2 + 4$

$X = \cos(3x)$

To Find C. F.

A. E. is $D^2 + 4 = 0$ $\dots (4)$

$$D^2 = -4$$

$$D^2 = 4i^2$$

$$D = \pm 2i$$

$$D = 0 \pm 2i = \alpha \pm i\beta$$

where $\alpha = 0$, $\beta = 2$

The roots are imaginary.

$$\text{C. F.} = e^{\alpha x}[c_1 \cos\beta x + c_2 \sin\beta x]$$

$$\text{C. F.} = e^{0x}[c_1 \cos(2x) + c_2 \sin(2x)]$$

$$\text{C. F.} = [c_1 \cos(2x) + c_2 \sin(2x)] \qquad \dots (5)$$

To Find P. I.

$$\text{P. I.} = \frac{1}{f(D)} X = \frac{1}{D^2 + 4} \cos(3x)$$

$$\text{Put } D^2 = -a^2 = -9$$

$$\text{P. I.} = \frac{1}{-9 + 4} \cos(3x)$$

$$\text{P. I.} = \frac{-1}{5} \cos(3x) \qquad \qquad \dots (6)$$

The solution of equation (1) is

$$y = \text{C. F.} + \text{P. I.}$$

$$y = c_1 \cos(2x) + c_2 \sin(2x) - \frac{1}{5} \cos(3x) \dots (7)$$

Example 2.54 : Solve $\dfrac{d^2y}{dx^2} - 4y = \cos(2x)$ $\qquad$ **[S. U. April 2012]**

Solution : Given differential equation is

$$\frac{d^2y}{dx^2} - 4y = \cos(2x) \qquad \qquad \dots (1)$$

$$[D^2 - 4] y = \cos(2x) \qquad \qquad \dots (2)$$

i.e. $\qquad \qquad f(D) y = X$

$$\text{where } f(D) = D^2 - 4$$

$$X = \cos(2x)$$

To Find C. F.

$$\text{A. E. is } [D^2 - 4] = 0$$

$$[D - 2][D + 2] = 0$$

$$D = 2 \qquad \text{or} \qquad D = -2$$

Let $\qquad \qquad m_1 = -2 \quad \text{and} \quad m_2 = 2$

The roots are real and unequal

$$\text{C. F.} = c_1 e^{m_1 x} + c_2 e^{m_2 x}$$

$$\text{C. F.} = c_1 e^{-2x} + c_2 e^{2x} \qquad \qquad \dots (4)$$

To Find P. I.

$$\text{P. I.} = \frac{1}{f(D)} X$$

$$\text{P. I.} = \frac{1}{D^2 - 4} \cos(2x)$$

$$\text{put } D^2 = -a^2 = -4$$

$$\text{P. I.} = \frac{1}{-4 - 4} \cos(2x)$$

$$\text{P. I.} = \frac{-1}{8} \cos(2x) \qquad \qquad \dots (5)$$

The solution of equation (1) is

$$y = C.F. + P.I.$$

$$y = c_1 e^{-2x} + c\, 2e^{2x} - \frac{1}{8} \cos(2x) \qquad \dots (6)$$

Example 2.55 : Solve $[D^2 - 1]\, y = \cos(2x)$ **[S. U. Oct. 2011]**

Solution : Given differential equation is

$$[D^2 - 1]\, y = \cos(2x) \qquad \dots (1)$$

i.e. $\qquad\qquad f(D)\, y = X \qquad\qquad \dots (2)$

$$\text{where } f(D) = [D^2 - 1]$$
$$X = \cos(2x)$$

To Find C. F.

$$\text{A. E. is } D^2 - 1 = 0$$
$$(D - 1)(D + 1) = 0$$
$$D = 1, D = -1$$

Let $\qquad\qquad m_1 = -1 \text{ and } m_2 = 1$

The roots are real and unequal

$$C.F. = c_1 e^{m_1 x} + c_2 e^{m_2 x}$$
$$C.F. = c_1 e^{-x} + c_2 e^{x} \qquad \dots (4)$$

To Find P. I.

$$P.I. = \frac{1}{f(D)} X$$

$$P.I. = \frac{1}{D^2 - 1} \cos(2x)$$

$$\text{put } D^2 = -4$$

$$P.I. = \frac{1}{-4 - 1} \cos(2x)$$

$$P.I. = \frac{-1}{5} \cos(2x) \qquad \dots (5)$$

The solution of equation (1) is

$$y = C.F. + P.I.$$

$$y = c_1 e^{-x} + c_2 e^{x} - \frac{1}{5} \cos(2x) \qquad \dots (6)$$

Example 2.56 : Solve : $[D^2 + 3D - 4]\, y = \sin(2x)$

Solution : The give differential equation is

$$[D^2 + 3D - 4]\, y = \sin(2x) \qquad \dots (1)$$

$\therefore \qquad\qquad f(D)\, y = X \qquad\qquad \dots (2)$

$$\text{where } f(D) = D^2 + 3D - 4$$
$$X = \sin 2x$$

To Find C. F.

The A. E. is $D^2 + 3D - 4 = 0$ ... (3)

$$(D - 1)(D + 4) = 0$$

$$D = 1, -4$$

Let $m_1 = 1$ $m_2 = -4$

The roots are real and unequal.

$$\text{C. F.} = c_1 e^{m_1 x} + c_2 e^{m_2 x}$$

$$\text{C. F.} = c_1 e^x + c_2 e^{-4x} \quad \text{... (4)}$$

To find P. I.

$$\text{P. I.} = \frac{1}{f(D)} X = \frac{1}{D^2 + 3D - 4} \sin(2x)$$

put $D^2 = -a^2 = -4$

$$\text{P. I.} = \frac{1}{-4 + 3D - 4} \sin(2x) = \frac{1}{3D - 8} \sin(2x)$$

$$\text{P. I.} = \frac{(3D + 8)}{(3D - 8)(3D + 8)} \sin(2x)$$

$$\text{P. I.} = \frac{3D + 8}{9D^2 - 64} \sin 2x$$

$$\text{putting } D^2 = -4$$

$$\text{P. I.} = \frac{3D + 8}{-36 - 64} \sin 2x$$

$$\text{P. I.} = \frac{-1}{100} [3D(\sin 2x) + 8\sin(2x)]$$

$$\text{P. I.} = \frac{-1}{100} [6\cos(2x) + 8\sin(2x)] \quad \text{... (5)}$$

$$\text{P. I.} = \frac{-3}{50} \cos(2x) - \frac{2}{25} \sin(2x) \quad \text{... (6)}$$

The general solution is

$$y = \text{C. F.} + \text{P. I.}$$

$$y = c_1 e^x + c_2 e^{-4x} - \frac{3}{50} \cos(2x) - \frac{2}{25} \sin(2x) \text{... (7)}$$

Example 2.57 : Solve $(D^2 + 1)(D^2 + 9) y = \cos(2x + 3)$

Solution : The given differentiable equation is

$$(D^2 + 1)(D^2 + 9) y = \cos(2x + 3) \quad \text{... (1)}$$

$\therefore$ $f(D) y = X$ ... (2)

where $f(D) = (D^2 + 1)(D^2 + 9)$

$$X = \cos(2x + 3)$$

To find C. F.

The A. E. is $(D^2 + 1)(D^2 + 9) = 0$ ... (3)

$$D^2 + 1 = 0 \qquad\qquad D^2 + 9 = 0$$

$$D^2 = -1 = i^2 \qquad\qquad \text{and } D^2 = -9 = 9i^2$$

$$D = \pm i \qquad\qquad D = \pm 3i$$

$$D = 0 \pm i\,0 \text{ and} \qquad\qquad D = 0 \pm 3i$$

The roots are complex in pairs.

C. F. $= [c_1 \cos x + c_2 \sin x] + [c_3 \cos 3x + c_4 \sin 3x]$ ... (4)

To find P. I.

$$P. I. = \frac{1}{f(D)} X = \frac{1}{(D^2 + 1)(D^2 + 9)} \cos(2x + 3)$$

$$\text{putting } D^2 = -a^2 = -4$$

$$= \frac{1}{[-4 + 1][-4 + 9]} \cos(2x + 3)$$

$$P. I. = \frac{-1}{15} \cos(2x + 3) \qquad\qquad \text{... (5)}$$

The general solution is

$$y = C. F. + P. I.$$

$$y = [c_1 \cos x + c_2 \sin x] + [c_3 \cos 3x + c_4 \sin 3x] \quad \text{... (6)}$$

Example 2.58 : Solve : $(D^3 - 3D^2 + 4D - 2)\, y = e^x + \cos x$

Solution : Given differential equation is

$$[D^3 - 3D^2 + 4D - 2]\, y = e^x + \cos x \qquad\qquad \text{... (1)}$$

$\therefore \qquad\qquad f(D)\, y = X$ ... (2)

$$\text{where } f(D) = D^3 - 3D^2 + 4D - 2$$

$$X = e^x + \cos x$$

To Find C. F.

The A. E. is $D^3 - 3D^2 + 4D - 2 = 0$ ... (3)

$$D^3 - D^2 - 2D^2 + 2D + 2D - 2 = 0$$

$$D^2(D - 1) - 2D(D - 1) + 2(D - 1) = 0$$

$$(D - 1)(D^2 - 2D + 2) = 0$$

$$D - 1 = 0 \quad D^2 - 2D + 2 = 0$$

$$D = 1, \qquad D = \frac{2 \pm \sqrt{-4}}{2} = \frac{2 \pm \sqrt{4i^2}}{2} = \frac{2 \pm 2i}{2} = 1 \pm i$$

$$C. F. = c_1 e^x + e^x [c_2 \cos x + c_3 \sin x] \quad \text{... (4)}$$

To Find P. I.

$$P. I. = \frac{1}{f(D)} X = \frac{1}{D^3 - 3D^2 + 4D - 2} [e^x + \cos x]$$

$$P. I. = \frac{1}{(D - 1)(D^2 - 2D + 2)} [e^x + \cos x]$$

$$P. I. = \frac{1}{[D - 1][D^2 - 2D + 2]} e^x + \frac{1}{[D - 1][D^2 - 2D + 2]} \cos x$$

$$P. I. = \frac{1}{[D - 1]}\left[\frac{1}{D^2 - 2D + 2}\right] e^x + \frac{1}{[D - 1]}\left[\frac{1}{D^2 - 2D + 2}\right] \cos x$$

$$\text{put } D = 1 \qquad\qquad\qquad \text{put } D^2 = -1$$

$$P. I. = \frac{1}{[D - 1]} e^x \qquad\qquad + \frac{1}{(D - 1)}\left[\frac{1}{1 - 2D}\right] \cos x$$

$$D = 1 \Rightarrow D - 1 = 0$$

$$P. I. = x e^x \qquad\qquad\qquad + \frac{1}{[3D - 2D^2 - 1]} \cos x$$

$$\text{put } D^2 = -1$$

$$P. I. = x e^x + \frac{1}{[3D + 1]} \cos x$$

$$P. I. = x e^x + \frac{[3D - 1]}{[3D + 1][3D - 1]} \cos x$$

$$P. I. = x e^x + \frac{[3D - 1]}{9D^2 - 1} \cos x$$

$$\text{put } D^2 = -1$$

$$P. I. = x e^x - \frac{1}{10} [3D - 1] \cos x$$

$$P. I. = x e^x - \frac{1}{10} [3D(\cos x) - \cos x]$$

$$P. I. = x e^x - \frac{1}{10} [3(-\sin x) - \cos x]$$

$$P. I. = x e^x + \frac{1}{10} [3 \sin x + \cos x] \qquad\qquad ... (5)$$

The general solution is y = C. F. + P. I.

$$y = c_1 e^x + e^x [c_2 \cos x + c_3 \sin x] + xe^x + \frac{1}{10} [3 \sin x + \cos x] \quad ... (6)$$

Example 2.59 : Solve $\dfrac{d^2y}{dx^2} + 4y = \cos 3x + \sin 3x$

Solution : Given differential equation is

$$\frac{d^2y}{dx^2} + 4y = \cos 3x + \sin 3x \qquad\qquad ... (1)$$

$\therefore$ $\qquad$ $(D^2 + 4) y = \cos 3x + \sin 3x$ $\qquad$ ... (2)

$\therefore$ $\qquad$ $f(D) y = X$ $\qquad$ ... (3)

$$\text{where } f(D) = D^2 + y$$
$$X = \cos 3x + \sin 3x$$

To Find C. F.

The A. E. is $\qquad D^2 + 4 = 0$ $\qquad$ ... (4)

$$D^2 = -4 = 4i^2$$
$$D = \pm 2i = 0 \pm 2i = \alpha \pm i\,\beta$$

$\therefore$ $\qquad\qquad \alpha = 0, \; \beta = 2$

The roots are imaginary

$$\text{C. F.} = e^{ax}[c_1 \cos Bx + c_2 \sin Bx]$$
$$\text{C. F.} = e^{0x}[c_1 \cos 2x + c_2 \sin 2x]$$
$$\text{C. F.} = c_1 \cos 2x + c_2 \sin 2x \qquad \text{... (5)}$$

To Find P. I.

$$\text{P. I.} = \frac{1}{f(D)} X = \frac{1}{D^2 + 4}[\cos 3x + \sin 3x]$$

$$\text{P. I.} = \frac{1}{D^2 + 4} \cos 3x + \frac{1}{D^2 + 4} \sin 3x$$

$$\text{put } D^2 = -a^2 = -3^2 = -9$$

$$\text{P. I.} = \frac{1}{-9 + 4} \cos 3x + \frac{1}{-9 + 4} \sin 3x$$

$$\text{P. I.} = \frac{-1}{5} \cos 3x - \frac{1}{5} \sin 3x$$

$$\text{P. I.} = \frac{-1}{5}[\cos 3x + \sin 3x] \qquad \text{... (6)}$$

The general solution is

$$y = \text{C. F.} + \text{P. I.}$$

$$y = c_1 \cos 2x + c_2 \sin 2x - \frac{1}{5}[\cos 3x + \sin 3x] \quad \text{... (7)}$$

Example 2.60 : Solve : $(D^2 + 4) y = \sin (2x)$

Solution : Given differential equation is

$\qquad\qquad (D^2 + 4) y = \sin 2x$ $\qquad$ ... (1)

$\therefore$ $\qquad\qquad f(D) y = X$ $\qquad$ ... (2)

$$\text{where } f(D) = D^2 + 4$$
$$X = \sin 2x$$

To Find C. F.

The A. E. is $\qquad D^2 + 4 = 0$ $\qquad$ ... (3)

$$D^2 = -4 = 4i^2$$
$$D = \pm 2i = 0 \pm 2i$$
$$\alpha = 0, \; \beta = 2$$

$$C. F. = e^{\alpha x} [c_1 \cos Bx + c_2 \sin Bx]$$
$$C. F. = e^{0x} [c_1 \cos 2x + c_2 \sin 2x]$$
$$C. F. = c_1 \cos 2x + c_2 \sin 2x \qquad \text{... (4)}$$

To Find P. I.

$$P. I. = \frac{1}{f(D)} X = \frac{1}{D^2 + 4} \sin 2x$$

Here
$$f(D^2) = D^2 + 4$$

$\therefore$
$$f(-a^2) = (-a^2) + 4$$

$$\text{put } a = 2$$

$$f(-a^2) = -4 + 4 = 0$$

$\therefore$ We use formula

$$\frac{1}{D^2 + a^2} \sin(ax) = \frac{-x}{2a} \cos(ax)$$

$\therefore$
$$P. I. = \frac{-x}{4} \cos 2x \qquad \text{... (5)}$$

The general solution is
$$y = C. F. + P. I.$$

$$y = c_1 \cos 2x + c_2 \sin 2x - \frac{x}{4} \cos 2x \quad \text{... (6)}$$

Example 2.61 : Solve $(D^2 + 4)^2 y = \cos 2x$

Solution : The given differential equation is
$$(D^2 + 4)^2 y = \cos 2x \qquad \text{... (1)}$$

$\therefore$
$$f(D) y = X \qquad \text{... (2)}$$

$$\text{where } f(D) = (D^2 + 4)^2$$
$$X = \cos 2x$$

To Find C. F.

The A. E. is
$$(D^2 + 4)^2 = 0 \qquad \text{... (3)}$$

$$(D^2 + 4)(D^2 + 4) = 0$$

$$D^2 = -4 = 4i^2$$

$$D = \pm 2i = 0 \pm 2i, \text{ also } D = 0 \pm 2i$$

Here
$$\alpha = 0, \ \beta = 2$$

The pair of imaginary roots is repeated.

$\therefore$
$$C. F. = e^{\alpha x} [(c_1 + c_2 x) \cos \beta x + (c_3 + c_4 x) \sin Bx]$$
$$C. F. = e^{0x} [(c_1 + c_2 x) \cos 2x + (c_3 + c_4 x) \sin 2x]$$
$$C. F. = [c_1 + c_2 x] \cos 2x + [c_3 + c_4 x] \sin 2x \qquad \text{... (4)}$$

To Find P. I.

$$P. I. = \frac{1}{f(D)} X = \frac{1}{(D^2 + 4)^2} \cos(2x)$$

$$P. I. = \frac{1}{[D^2 + 2^2]^2} \cos 2x$$

here a = 2

$\therefore$ $f(D^2) = D^2 + 4$

$f(-a^2) = -a^2 + 4 = -4 + 4 = 0$

$\Rightarrow$ $f(-2^2) = 0$

We use the formula

$$\frac{1}{(D^2 + a^2)^2} \cos ax = \frac{-x^2}{2!} \cdot \frac{1}{4a^2} \cos ax$$

$\therefore$ $$\frac{1}{(D^2 + 4)^2} \cos 2x = \frac{-x^2}{2} \times \frac{1}{16} \cos 2x$$

$\therefore$ $$P. I. = \frac{-x^2}{32} \cos 2x \qquad \qquad ... (5)$$

The general solution is

$$y = C. F. + P. I.$$

$$y = [c_1 + c_2 x] \cos 2x + [c_3 + c_4 x] \sin 2x - \frac{x^2}{32} \cos 2x ... (6)$$

Example 2.62 : Solve $(D^2 + 4)^2 (D - 2)^2 y = \cos^2 x$

Solution : Given differential equation is

$$(D^2 + 4)^2 (D - 2)^2 y = \cos^2 x \qquad \qquad ... (1)$$

$\therefore$ $$f(D) y = X \qquad \qquad ... (2)$$

where $f(D) = (D^2 + 4^2)(D - 2)^2$

$X = \cos^2 x$

To Find C. F.

The A. E. is

$$(D^2 + 4^2)(D - 2)^2 = 0 \qquad \qquad ... (3)$$

$\therefore$ $(D - 2)^2 = 0$ and $(D^2 + 4)^2 = 0$

$D = 2, 2$ and $D^2 + 4 = 0$

$D^2 = -4 = 4i^2$

$D = \pm 2i, \pm 2i$

C. F. $= [c_1 + c_2 x] e^{2x} + e^{0x} [(c_3 + c_4 x) \cos 2x + (c_5 + c_6) \sin 2x]$

C. F. $= [c_1 + c_2 x] e^{2x} + [(c_3 + c_4 x) \cos 2x + (c_5 + c_6 x) \sin 2x]$ ... (4)

To Find P. I.

P. I. $= \dfrac{1}{f(D)} X = \dfrac{1}{(D^2 + 4^2)(D-2)^2} \cos^2 x \qquad$ put $\cos^2 x = \dfrac{1}{2}[1 + \cos 2x]$

P. I. $= \dfrac{1}{(D^2 + 4)^2(D-2)^2} \dfrac{1}{2}[1 + \cos 2x]$

P. I. $= \dfrac{1}{2 \cdot (D^2 + 4^2)(D-2)^2}(1) + \dfrac{1}{2(D^2 + 4)^2(D-2)^2}\cos(2x)$

P. I. $= \dfrac{1}{2(D^2 + 4)^2(D-2)^2}e^{0x} + \dfrac{1}{2(D^2 + 4)^2}$

$\qquad \left[\dfrac{1}{D^2 - 4D + 4}\cos(2x)\right]$

P. I. $= \dfrac{1}{128} + \dfrac{1}{2(D^2 + 4)^2}\left[-\dfrac{1}{4D}\right]\cos(2x)$

P. I. $= \dfrac{1}{128} + \dfrac{1}{2(D^2 + 4)^2}\left(\dfrac{-1}{4}\right)\left[\dfrac{\sin(2x)}{2}\right]$

P. I. $= \dfrac{1}{128} - \dfrac{1}{16} \cdot \dfrac{1}{(D^2 + 4)^2}\sin(2x)$

If we put $D^2 = -4$ then $(D^2 + 4)^2 = 0$

$\therefore$ Use formula $\dfrac{1}{(D^2 + a^2)^2}\sin(2x) = \dfrac{-x^2\sin(ax)}{2! \cdot 4a^2}$

P. I. $= \dfrac{1}{128} - \dfrac{1}{16}\left[\dfrac{-x^2}{2(4)(4)}\sin(2x)\right]$

P. I. $= \dfrac{1}{128} + \dfrac{x^2\sin(2x)}{512} \qquad\qquad\qquad$ ... (5)

The general solution is

$\qquad y = C.F. + P.I.$

$\qquad y = [c_1 + c_2 x]e^{2x} + [(c_3 + c_4 x)\cos(2x) + (c_5 + c_6 x)\sin(2x)]$

$\qquad + \dfrac{1}{128} + \dfrac{x^2}{512}\sin(2x) \qquad\qquad$ ... (6)

EXERCISE 2.7

I.   Theory Questions

1.   Prove that $\dfrac{1}{f(D^2)}\sin(ax) = \dfrac{1}{f(-a^2)}\sin ax \qquad$ where $f(-a^2) \neq 0$

[S. U. Nov. 2012, April 2013]

2.   Prove that $\dfrac{1}{f(D^2)}\cos(ax) = \dfrac{1}{f(-a^2)}\cos(ax) \qquad$ where $f(-a^2) \neq 0$

[S. U. Oct. 2011, April 2013]

3.　Prove that $\dfrac{1}{D^2 + a^2} \cos(ax) = \dfrac{x}{2a} \sin(ax)$

4.　Prove that $\dfrac{1}{D^2 + a^2} \sin(ax) = \dfrac{-x}{2a} \cos(ax)$

II.　Problems

Solve the following differential equations.

1.　$\dfrac{d^2y}{dx^2} - 2\dfrac{dy}{dx} + y = \cos 3x$　　　　　2.　$\dfrac{d^2y}{dx^2} + 9y = \cos 3x$

3.　$(D^2 + 4)\, y = \sin 5x$　　　　　　　　　4.　$(D^2 + D + 1)\, y = \sin 2x$

5.　$(D^4 + 2D^3 - 3D^2)\, y = 4 \sin x$　　　　6.　$[D^3 - 3D + 2]\, y = \cos x$

7.　$\dfrac{d^2y}{dx^2} + y = \cos 2x$

8.　$D^2(D^2 + 1)\, y = \sin 3x$

9.　$\dfrac{d^2y}{dx^2} + 4y = e^x + \sin 2x$

10.　$(D^2 + 9)\, y = \sin 2x \cos x$

ANSWERS 2.7

1.　$y = e^x(c_1 + c_2 x) - \dfrac{1}{50}\,[3 \sin 3x + 4 \cos 3x]$

2.　$y = [c_1 \cos 3x + c_2 \sin 3x] + \dfrac{x}{6} \sin 3x$

3.　$y = c_1 \cos 2x + c_2 \sin 2x - \dfrac{\sin 5x}{2!}$

4.　$y = \left[c_1 \cos \dfrac{\sqrt{3}}{2} x + c_2 \sin \dfrac{\sqrt{3}}{2} x\right] e^{-x/2} - \dfrac{2}{13} \cos(2x) - \dfrac{3}{13} \sin(2x)$

5.　$y = (c_1 + c_2 x) + c_3 e^x + c_4 e^{-3x} + \dfrac{2}{5}\,[\cos x + 2 \sin x]$

6.　$y = c_1 e^x + c_2 e^{2x} - \dfrac{1}{130}\,[9 \sin 3x + 7 \cos 3x]$

7.　$y = c_1 \cos x + c_2 \sin x - \dfrac{1}{3} \cos 2x$

8.　$y = [c_1 + c_2 x] + [c_3 \cos x + c_4 \sin x] + \dfrac{1}{72} \sin 3x$

9.　$y = c_1 \cos 2x + c_2 \sin 2x + \dfrac{e^x}{5} - \dfrac{\sin 3x}{5}$

10.　$y = c_1 \cos 3x + c_2 \sin 3x - \dfrac{1}{2} x \cos 3x + \dfrac{1}{15} \sin x$

2.7.3 Particular Integral when X is of the form X^m where m is A Positive Integer

Let $f(D) y = X$ where $X = x^m$ and m being positive integer.

then procedure for finding

$$P.\ I.\ =\ \frac{1}{f(D)}\ x^m \text{ is as follows :}$$

1. First take out the lowest degree term from $f(D)$ to make the first term unity.

   Then the remaining factor will be of the form

   $$[1 + \phi(D)] \text{ or } [1 - \phi(D)]$$

   $$P.\ I.\ =\frac{1}{[1 + \phi(D)]}\ x^m \text{ or } P.\ I.\ =\frac{1}{[1 - \phi(D)]}\ x^m$$

2. Take this factor in the numerator.

   $$P.\ I.\ = [1 + \phi(D)]^{-1}\ x^m \text{ or } P.\ I.\ = [1 - \phi(D)]^{-1}\ x^m$$

3. Expand above by using Binomial Theorem.

   For this purpose use following formulae

   $$(1 + D)^{-1}\ =\ 1 - D + D^2 - D^3 + \ldots..$$
   $$(1 - D)^{-1}\ =\ 1 + D + D^2 + D^3 + \ldots.$$
   $$(1 + D)^{-2}\ =\ 1 - 2D + 3D^2 - 4D^3 + \ldots.$$
   $$(1 - D)^{-2}\ =\ 1 + 2D + 3D^2 + 4D^3 + \ldots.$$

This expression is carried out upto the term D^m.

4. Then operating each term of the expansion on x^m, the P.I. can be obtained.

SOLVED EXAMPLES

Example 2.63. : Solve $2\dfrac{d^2y}{dx^2} + 5\dfrac{dy}{dx} + 2y = x$

Solution : The given differential equation is

$$2\frac{d^2y}{dx^2} + 5\frac{dy}{dx} + 2y\ =\ x \qquad\qquad\qquad ...(1)$$

$$\therefore \qquad\qquad [2D^2 + 5D + 2]\ y\ =\ x \qquad\qquad\qquad ...(2)$$

We have $\qquad\qquad f(D)\ y\ =\ x \qquad\qquad$ Where $f(D) = 2D^2 + 5D + 2$

$$X = x$$

To find C. F.

The A. E. is $\qquad 2D^2 + 5D + 2\ =\ 0$

$$2D^2 + 4D + D + 2\ =\ 0$$

$$2D\ [D + 2] + 1\ [D + 2]\ =\ 0$$

$$[D + 2]\ [2D + 1]\ =\ 0$$

$$D = -2 \text{ and } D = -\frac{1}{2}$$

Let, $m_1 = -2$ and $m_2 = -\frac{1}{2}$

Here, roots are real and unequal.
$$\text{C. F.} = c_1 e^{m_1 x} + c_2 e^{-x/2} \qquad \qquad ...(3)$$

To find P. I.

$$\text{P.I.} = \frac{1}{f(D)} X$$

$$= \frac{1}{2D^2 + 5D + 2} X$$

$$= \frac{1}{2\left[\left(D^2 + \frac{5}{2}D\right) + 1\right]} X$$

$$= \frac{1}{2\left[1 + \left(\frac{5}{2}D + D^2\right)\right]} X$$

$$= \frac{1}{2}\left[1 + \left(\frac{5}{2}D + D^2\right)\right]^{-1} X$$

$$\text{P. I.} = \frac{1}{2}\left[1 - \left(\frac{5}{2}D + D^2\right) + \left(\frac{5}{2}D + D^2\right)^2 ...\right]$$

$$= \frac{1}{2}\left[1 - \frac{5}{2}D - D^2 + \left\{\frac{25}{4}D^2 - 5D^3 + D^4\right\} ...\right] x$$

$$= \frac{1}{2}\left[x - \frac{5}{2}D(x) - D^2(x) + \frac{25}{4}D^2(x) - 5D^3(x) + D^4(x)...\right]$$

$$= \frac{1}{2}\left[x - \frac{5}{2}(1) - 0\right]$$

$$= \frac{1}{2}x - \frac{5}{4} \qquad \qquad ...(4)$$

The general solution is
$$y = \text{C. F.} + \text{P. I.}$$

$$y = c_1 e^{-2x} + c_2 e^{-x/2} + \frac{1}{2}x - \frac{5}{4} \qquad \qquad ...(5)$$

Example 2.64 : Solve $\dfrac{d^2y}{dx^2} + \dfrac{dy}{dx} - 6y = x$ **[S. U. Oct. 2011, Nov. 2012]**

Solution : Given differential equation is

$$\frac{d^2y}{dx^2} + \frac{dy}{dx} - 6y = x \qquad \qquad ...(1)$$

$$[D^2 + D - 6] y = x \qquad \qquad ...(2)$$

i.e. $\qquad \qquad f(D) y = x \qquad \qquad ...(3)$

Where $\qquad f(D) = D^2 + D - 6$
$$X = x$$

To find C. F.

A. E. is $\qquad D^2 + D - 6 = 0 \qquad\qquad ...(4)$
$$(D + 3)(D - 2) = 0$$
$$D = -3 \ , \ D = 2$$

Let, $m_1 = -3$, $m_2 = 2$

The roots are real and unequal.

$$C. F. = c_1 e^{m_1 x} + c_2 e^{m_2 x}$$
$$C. F. = c_1 e^{-3x} + c_2 e^{2x} \qquad\qquad ...(5)$$

To find P. I. $\qquad P. I. = \dfrac{1}{f(D)} X = \dfrac{1}{D^2 + D - 6} (x)$

$$P. I. = \dfrac{1}{-6\left[\dfrac{D^2 + D}{-6} + 1\right]} x$$

$$P. I. = \dfrac{-1}{6}\left[1 - \left(\dfrac{D^2 + D}{6}\right)\right]^{-1} \cdot x$$

$$= \dfrac{-1}{6}\left[1 + \dfrac{D^2 + D}{6} + ...\right] x$$

$$= \dfrac{-1}{6}\left[x + \dfrac{1}{6} D^2(x) + \dfrac{1}{6} D(x) + ...\right]$$

$$= \dfrac{-1}{6}\left[x + 0 + \dfrac{1}{6}\right]$$

$$P. I. = \dfrac{-1}{6}\left(\dfrac{6x + 1}{6}\right)$$

$$P. I. = \dfrac{-1}{36}(6x + 1) \qquad\qquad ...(6)$$

The solution of equation (1) is
$$y = C. F. + P. I.$$
$$y = c_1 e^{-3x} + c_2 e^{2x} - \dfrac{1}{36}(6x + 1) \qquad ...(7)$$

Example 2.65 : Solve $\dfrac{d^3y}{dx^3} - 3\dfrac{dy}{dx} + 2y = x$ 　　　　　　[S. U. April 2013]

Solution : Given differential equation is

$$\dfrac{d^3y}{dx^3} - 3\dfrac{dy}{dx} + 2y = x \qquad\qquad ...(1)$$

$\therefore \qquad [D^3 - 3D + 2]y = x \qquad\qquad ...(2)$

i.e. $\qquad f(D) = x \qquad\qquad$ where, $\quad f(D) = D^3 - 3D + 2$
$$X = x$$

To find c.f.

The A. E. is
$$D^3 - 3D + 2 = 0$$
$$D^3 - D^2 + D^2 - D - 2D + 2 = 0$$
$$D^2 (D - 1) + D (D - 1) - 2 (D - 1) = 0$$
$$(D - 1) (D^2 + D - 2) = 0$$
$$(D - 1) (D - 1) (D + 2) = 0$$
$$(D - 1)^2 (D + 2) = 0$$

$$D = 1, 1, - 2$$

Let, $m_1 = m_2 = 1, m_3 = - 2$

The roots are real

$$C. F. = (c_1 + c_2 x) e^{m_1 x} + c_3 e^{m_3 x}$$
$$C. F. = (c_1 + c_2 x) e^x + c_3 e^{-2x} \qquad ...(3)$$

To find P. I.

$$P. I. = \frac{1}{f(D)} X = \frac{1}{D^3 - 3D + 2} \cdot x$$

$$= \frac{1}{2 \left[1 + \dfrac{D^3 - 3D}{2} + 1 \right]} x$$

$$= \frac{1}{2 \left[1 + \left(\dfrac{D^3 - 3D}{2} \right) \right]} x$$

$$= \frac{1}{2} \left[1 + \left(\frac{D^3 - 3D}{2} \right) \right]^{-1} x$$

$$= \frac{1}{2} \left[1 - \left(\frac{D^3 - 3D}{2} \right) + ... \right] x$$

$$= \frac{1}{2} \left[x - \frac{1}{2} D^3 (x) + \frac{3}{2} D (x) + ... \right]$$

$$= \frac{1}{2} \left[x - 0 + \frac{3}{2} (1) \right]$$

$$P. I. = \frac{x}{2} + \frac{3}{4} \qquad ..(4)$$

The general solution is

$$y = C. F. + P. I.$$

$$y = (c_1 + c_2 x) e^x c_3 e^{-2x} + \frac{x}{2} + \frac{3}{4} \qquad ...(5)$$

Example 2.66 : Solve : $\dfrac{d^2y}{dx^2} - 4\dfrac{dy}{dx} + 4y = x^2$

Solution : Given differential equation is

$$\frac{d^2y}{dx^2} - 4\frac{dy}{dx} + 4y = x^2 \qquad \qquad ..(1)$$

$\therefore \qquad\qquad [D^2 - 4D + 4]\, y = 0 \qquad\qquad ...(2)$

i.e. $\qquad\qquad\qquad f(D)\, y = X \qquad\qquad$ where, $f(D) = D^2 - 4D + 4$

$$X = x^2$$

To find E. F.

The A. E. is $\qquad D^2 - 4D + 4 = 0$

$$(D - 2)^2 = 0$$

$$D = 2, 2$$

Let, $m_1 = m_2 = 2$

Here, roots are real and equal.

$$C.\,F. = (c_1 + c_2 x)e^{m_1 x}$$

$$C.\,F. = (c_1 + c_2 x)e^{2x} \qquad\qquad ...(3)$$

To find P. I. $\quad P.\,I. = \dfrac{1}{f(D)}\, X = \dfrac{1}{(D-2)^2}\, x^2$

$$P.I. = \frac{1}{\left[-2\left(\dfrac{-D}{2}+1\right)\right]^2}\, x^2$$

$$= \frac{1}{4\left(1-\dfrac{D}{2}\right)^2}\, x^2$$

$$= \frac{1}{4}\left(1-\frac{D}{2}\right)^{-2}\, x^2$$

$$= \frac{1}{4}\left[1 + 2\left(\frac{D}{2}\right) + 3\left(\frac{D}{2}\right)^2 + ...\right] x^2$$

$$= \frac{1}{4}\left[1 + D + \frac{3}{4}D^2 + ...\right] x^2$$

$$= \frac{1}{4}\left[x^2 + D(x^2) + \frac{3}{4}D^2(x^2)...\right]$$

$$= \frac{1}{4}\left[x^2 + 2x + \frac{3}{4}(2)\right]$$

$$= \frac{1}{4}\left[x^2 + 2x + \frac{3}{2}\right]$$

$$P.I. = \frac{1}{8}\,[2x^2 + 4x + 3] \qquad\qquad ...(4)$$

The general solution is

$$y = C.F. + P.I.$$

$$y = (c_1 + c_2 x)e^x + \frac{1}{8}[2x^2 + 4x + 3] \qquad ...(5)$$

EXERCISE 2.8

I. Theory questions :

1. Explain the method of finding P. I. $= \frac{1}{f(D)} x^m$ where m is the positive integer.

II. Solve the following differential equations :

1. $[D^3 + 3D^2 + 2D] y = 0$
2. $[D^3 - D^2 - 6D] y = x^2 + 1$
3. $[D^4 - 2D^3 + D^2] y = x^3$
4. $[D^2 - 13D + 12]y = x$
5. $[D^2 - 5D + 6] y = x$

ANSWERS 2.8

II. Solve the following differential equations :

1. $y = c_1 + c_2 e^{-x} + c_3 e^{-2x} + \frac{1}{2}[2x^3 - 9x^2 + 21x]$

2. $y = c_1 + c_2 e^{3x} + c_3 e^{-2x} - \frac{1}{6}\left[\frac{x^3}{3} - \frac{x^2}{6} + \frac{25x}{18}\right]$

3. $y = c_1 + c_2 x + (c_3 + c_4 x) e^x + \frac{x^5}{20} + \frac{x^6}{2} + 3x^3 + 12x^2$

4. $y = c_1 e^x + c_2 e^{12x} + \frac{x}{12} + \frac{13}{144}$

5. $y = c_1 e^{2x} + c_2 e^{3x} + \frac{1}{6}x + \frac{5}{36}$

2.7.4 Particular integral when X is of the form e^{ax} V is a function of x

Theorem 11 :

If $f(D) y = X$ where , $X = e^{ax} V$ and V is a function of x then $\frac{1}{f(D)} e^{ax}$

$V = e^{ax}\left[\frac{1}{f(D+a)}\right]V.$ **[S. U. April 2012, Nov. 2012, April 2013]**

Proof : Let V_1 be the function of x.

By successive differentiation we get,

$$D [e^{ax} V_1] = e^{ax} \cdot DV_1 + V_1 [ae^{ax}] = e^{ax} [D + a] V_1 \qquad \text{...(1)}$$

Again

$$D^2 [e^{ax} \cdot V_1] = D [D (e^{ax} V_1)]$$
$$= D [e^{ax} (D + a) V_1]$$
$$= e^{ax} \cdot D [(D + a) V_1] + (D + a) V_1 [ae^{ax}]$$
$$D^2 [e^{ax} V_1] = e^{ax} (D + a) V_1 [D + a]$$
$$D^2 [e^{ax} V_1] = e^{ax} [D + a]^2 V_1 \qquad \text{...(2)}$$

Similarly,

$$D^3 [e^{ax} V_1] = e^{ax} [D + a]^3 V_1 \qquad \text{...(3)}$$

Continuing in this way we get,

$$D^n [e^{ax} V_1] = e^{ax} [D + a]^n V_1 \qquad \text{...(4)}$$

It can be written as

$$f (D) e^{ax} V_1 = e^{ax} f (D + a) V_1 \qquad \text{...(5)}$$

Let, $f (D + a) V_1 = V$ ...(6)

Therefore, $V_1 = \dfrac{1}{f (D + a)} V$ ...(7)

Using value of V_1 equation (5) becomes

$$f (D) e^{ax} \left[\frac{1}{f (D + a)} V \right] = e^{ax} f (D + a) \left[\frac{1}{f (D + a)} V \right]$$

$$f (D) e^{ax} \left[\frac{1}{f (D + a)} V \right] = e^{ax} V$$

operating on both sides by $\dfrac{1}{f(D)}$ we get,

$$\frac{1}{f (D)} \cdot f (D) e^{ax} \left[\frac{1}{f (D + a)} V \right] = \frac{1}{f (D)} [e^{ax} V]$$

$$e^{ax} \frac{1}{f (D + a)} V = \frac{1}{f (D)} e^{ax} V$$

Changing the sides

$$\frac{1}{f (D)} e^{ax} V = e^{ax} \cdot \frac{1}{f (D + a)} V \qquad \text{...(8)}$$

Remarks :

1. From above theorem, for finding P. I. of e^{ax} V first take e^{ax} outside and replace D by D + a in f (D).

2. V is a function of x means V takes the forms as sin (ax + b), cos (ax + b). log x, x^m etc.

Illustration :

1. $\dfrac{1}{D^2 + 4D + 5} e^{3x} \cos x = e^{3x} \cdot \dfrac{1}{[(D + 3)^2 + 4(D + 3) + 5]} \cos x$

$$= e^{3x} \dfrac{1}{[D^2 + 6D + 9 + 4D + 12 + 5]} \cos x$$

$\dfrac{1}{D^2 + 4D + 5} e^{3x} \cos x = e^{3x} \dfrac{1}{[D^2 + 10D + 26]} \cos x$

2. $\dfrac{1}{D^2 + 2D + 3} e^{x} \log x = e^{x} \dfrac{1}{[D + 1]^2 + 2[D + 1] + 3} \log x$

$\dfrac{1}{D^2 + 2D + 3} e^{x} \log x = e^{x} \dfrac{1}{[(D^2 + 2D + 1) + 2D + 2 + 3]} \log x$

$\dfrac{1}{D^2 + 2D + 3} e^{x} \log x = e^{x} \dfrac{1}{[D^2 + 4D + 6]} \log x$

$\dfrac{1}{D^2 + 2D + 3} e^{x} \log x = e^{x} \dfrac{1}{[D^2 + 4D + 6]} \log x$

SOLVED EXAMPLES

Example 2.67 : Solve $[D^2 - 4D + 4] y = x^2 e^{2x}$ **[S. U. April 2013]**

Solution : Given differential equation is

$$[D^2 - 4D + 4] y = x^2 e^{2x} \qquad \qquad \dots(1)$$

i.e. $\qquad \qquad f(D) y = X \qquad \qquad \dots(2)$

$$\text{where, } f(D) = [D^2 - 4D + 4]$$
$$X = x^2 e^{2x}$$

To find C. F.

A. E. is $\qquad [D^2 - 4D + 4] = 0 \qquad \qquad \dots(3)$

$$[D - 2]^2 = 0$$

$$D - 2 = 0 \text{ and } (D - 2) = 0$$

$$D = 2 \qquad D = 2$$

Let, $m_1 = m_2 = 2$

The roots are real and equal.

$$\text{C. F.} = (c_1 + c_2 x) e^{m_1 x}$$

$$\text{C. F.} = (c_1 + c_2 x) e^{2x} \qquad \qquad \dots(4)$$

To find P.I.

$$\text{P. I.} = \dfrac{1}{f(D)} X$$

$$= \dfrac{1}{D^2 - 4D + 4} \cdot x^2 e^{2x} \qquad \text{Here, } a = 2, v = x^2$$

Using formula, $\dfrac{1}{f(D)} e^{ax} V = e^{ax} \left[\dfrac{1}{f(D + a)} \right] V \qquad \qquad \dots(5)$

$$\text{P.I.} = e^{2x}\left[\frac{1}{(D+2)^2 - 4(D+2) + 4}\right] x^2$$

$$= e^{2x}\left[\frac{1}{(D^2 + 4D + 4) - 4D - 8 + 4}\right] x^2$$

$$= e^{2x}\left[\frac{1}{D^2}\right](x^2)$$

$$= e^{2x}\frac{1}{D}\left(\frac{x^3}{3}\right)$$

$$= e^{2x}\left(\frac{x^4}{4 \times 3}\right)$$

$$= \frac{x^4}{12} e^{2x} \qquad \qquad ...(6)$$

The solution of equation (1) is

$$y = \text{C. F.} + \text{P. I.}$$

$$y = (c_1 + c_2 x) e^{2x} + \frac{x^4}{12} e^{2x} \qquad \qquad ...(7)$$

Example 2.68 : Solve : $[D^2 + 4] y = xe^{2x}$

Solution : Given differential equation is

$$[D^2 + 4] y = xe^{2x} \qquad \qquad ...(1)$$

$$f(D) y = x \qquad \qquad ...(2)$$

$$\text{where, } f(D) = D^2 + 4$$

$$X = xe^{2x}$$

To find C. F.

The A. E. is $D^2 + 4 = 0$ ...(3)

$$D^2 = -4$$

$$D^2 = 4i^2$$

$$D = \pm 2i = 0 \pm 2i = \alpha \pm i\beta$$

$\alpha = 0, \beta = 2$

The roots are imaginary.

$$\text{C. F.} = e^{\alpha x}[c_1 \cos \beta x + c_2 \sin \beta x]$$

$$= e^{0x}[c_1 \cos 2x + c_2 \sin 2x]$$

$$= c_1 \cos 2x + c_2 \sin 2x \qquad \qquad ...(4)$$

To find P. I.

$$\text{P. I.} = \frac{1}{f(D)} X = \frac{1}{D^2 + 4} xe^{2x}$$

$$\text{Using formula} \left[\frac{1}{f(D)} e^{ax}V = e^{ax}\frac{1}{f(D+a)} V\right]$$

$$\text{P. I.} = e^{2x} \left[\frac{1}{(D+2)^2 + 4} \, (x) \right]$$

$$= e^{2x} \frac{1}{D^2 + 4D + 8} \, x$$

$$= e^{2x} \frac{1}{8 \left[\left(\dfrac{D^2 + 4D}{8} \right) + 1 \right]} \, x$$

$$= e^{2x} \frac{1}{8} \left[1 + \frac{D^2 + 4D}{8} \right]^{-1} x$$

$$= \frac{1}{8} \, e^{2x} \left[1 - \frac{D^2 + 4D}{8} + \dots \right] x$$

$$= \frac{1}{8} \, e^{2x} \left[1 - \frac{D^2}{8} - \frac{1}{2} D + \dots \right] x$$

$$= \frac{1}{8} \, e^{2x} \left[x - \frac{1}{8} D^2 \, (x) - \frac{1}{2} D \, (x) \dots \right]$$

$$\text{P. I.} = \frac{1}{8} \, e^{2x} \left[x - 0 - \frac{1}{2} \right] = \frac{1}{16} \cdot e^{2x} \, [2x - 1] \qquad \dots(5)$$

The general solution is y = C.F. + P. I.

$$y = c_1 \cos 2x + c_2 \sin 2x + \frac{1}{16} \, e^{2x} \, (2x - 1) \quad \dots(6)$$

Example 2.69 : Solve $(D^2 - 2D + 1) \, y = x^3 \, e^{3x}$

Solution : Given differential equation is

$$[D^2 - 2D + 1] \, y = x^3 \, e^{3x} \qquad \dots(1)$$

$$f \, (D) = D^2 - 2D + 1$$

$$X = x^3 e^{3x}$$

To find c.f.

The A. E. is $\quad D^2 - 2D + 1 = 0 \qquad \dots(2)$

$$(D - 1)^2 = 0$$

$$D = 1, 1 \qquad\qquad \text{Let } m_1 = m_2 = 1$$

The roots are real and equal.

$$\text{C. F.} = (c_1 + c_2 \, x) \, e^{m_1 x}$$

$$\text{C. F.} = [c_1 + c_2 x] \, e^x \qquad \dots(3)$$

To find P. I.

$$\text{P. I.} = \frac{1}{f(D)} X = \frac{1}{D^2 - 2D + 1} \, x^3 \, e^{3x}$$

$$\text{P.I.} = \frac{1}{(D-1)^2} x^3 e^{3x}$$

$$= e^{3x} \frac{1}{[(D+3)-1]^2} x^3 = e^{3x} \frac{1}{[D+2]^2} x^3$$

$$= e^{3x} \frac{1}{\left[2\left(\frac{D}{2}+1\right)\right]^2} x^3$$

$$= \frac{e^{3x}}{4} \left[1+\frac{D}{2}\right]^{-2} (x^3)$$

$$= \frac{e^{3x}}{4} \left[1 - 2\frac{D}{2} + 3\left(\frac{D}{2}\right)^2 - 4\left(\frac{D}{2}\right)^3 + \dots\right] x^3$$

$$= \frac{e^{3x}}{4} \left[1 - D + \frac{3}{4}D^2 - \frac{4}{8}D^3 + \dots\right] x^3$$

$$= \frac{e^{3x}}{4} \left[x^3 - D(x^3) + \frac{3}{4}D^2(x^3) - \frac{1}{2}D^3(x^3)\right]$$

$$= \frac{e^{3x}}{4} \left[x^3 - 3x^2 + \frac{3}{4}(6x) - \frac{1}{2}(6)\right]$$

$$= \frac{e^{3x}}{4} \left[x^3 - 3x^2 + \frac{9}{2}x - 3\right]$$

$$= \frac{e^{3x}}{8} [2x^3 - 6x^2 + 9x - 6] \qquad \dots(4)$$

The general solution is y = C. F. + P. I.

$$y = [c_1 + c_2 x] e^x + \frac{e^{3x}}{8} [2x^3 - 6x^2 + 9x - 6] \qquad \dots(5)$$

Example 2.70 : Solve : $\dfrac{d^2y}{dx^2} - y = e^x \cos x$

Solution : Given differential equation is

$$\frac{d^2y}{dx^2} - y = e^x \cos x \qquad \dots(1)$$

$$[D^2 - 1] y = e^x \cos x \qquad \dots(2)$$

∴ $f(D) y = x$

⇒ $f(D) = D^2 - 1$

          $X = e^x \cos x$

To find C. F.

The A. E. is $D^2 - 1 = 0$ ...(3)

          $D^2 = 1$

          $D = \pm 1$

Let $m_1 = 1$, $m_2 = -1$

The roots are real and unequal.

$$\text{C. F.} = c_1 e^{m_1 x} + c_2 e^{m_2 x}$$

$$\text{C. F.} = c_1 e^x + c_2 e^{-x} \qquad \qquad ...(4)$$

To find P. I.

$$\text{P. I.} = \frac{1}{f(D)} X = \frac{1}{D^2 - 1} e^x \cos x$$

$$= e^x \frac{1}{[(D + 1)^2 - 1]} \cos x$$

$$= e^x \frac{1}{[D^2 + 2D + 1] - 1} \cos x$$

$$= e^x \frac{1}{[D^2 + 2D]} \cos x \qquad \qquad \text{put } D^2 = -1$$

$$= e^x \frac{1}{[-1 + 2D]} \cos x$$

$$= e^x \frac{[2D + 1]}{[2D - 1][2D + 1]} \cos x$$

$$= e^x \frac{[2D + 1]}{[4D^2 - 1]} \cos x \qquad \qquad \text{put } D^2 = -1$$

$$= e^x \frac{[2D + 1]}{-5} \cos x$$

$$= -\frac{e^x}{5} [2D (\cos x) + \cos x]$$

$$= \frac{-e^x}{5} [-2 \sin x - \cos x]$$

$$\text{P. I.} = \frac{e^x}{5} [2 \sin x + \cos x] \qquad \qquad ...(5)$$

The general solution is $y = \text{C. F.} + \text{P. I.}$

$$y = c_1 e^x + c_2 e^{-x} + \frac{e^x}{5} [2 \sin x + \cos x] \qquad ...(6)$$

Example 2.71 : Solve : $\left[\dfrac{d^3 y}{dx^3} - \dfrac{d^2 y}{dx^2} + 3 \dfrac{dy}{dx} + 5y \right] = e^x \cos 3x.$

Solution : Given differential equation is

$$\left[\frac{d^3 y}{dx^3} - \frac{d^2 y}{dx^2} + 3 \frac{dy}{dx} + 5y \right] = e^x \cos 3x \qquad ...(1)$$

$$[D^3 - D^2 + 3D + 5] y = e^x \cos 3x \qquad ...(2)$$

$$F(D) = D^3 - D^2 + 3D - 5$$

$$X = e^x \cos 3x$$

To find C. F.

The A. E. is $\qquad$ $D^3 - D^2 + 3D + 5 = 0$ $\qquad$ ...(3)

$$D^3 + D^2 - 2D^2 - 2D + 5D + 5 = 0$$

$$D^2(D + 1) - 2D(D + 1) + 5(D + 1) = 0$$

$$(D + 1)(D^2 - 2D + 5) = 0$$

$D = -1$	$D^2 - 2D + 5 = 0$
	$D = \dfrac{2 \pm \sqrt{4 - 20}}{2}$
	$= \dfrac{2 \pm \sqrt{-16}}{2}$
	$= \dfrac{2 \pm \sqrt{16i^2}}{2}$
	$= \dfrac{2 \pm 4i}{2} = 1 \pm 2i$

$\alpha = 1, \beta = 2$

The roots are imaginary and real

$\qquad$ C. F. $= c_1 e^{-x} + e^x [c_2 \cos 2x + c_3 \sin 2x]$ $\qquad$ ...(4)

To find P. I.

$$\text{P. I.} = \frac{1}{f(D)} x = \frac{1}{D^3 - D^2 + 3D + 5} [e^x \cos 3x]$$

$$\text{P. I.} = \frac{1}{[D + 1][D^2 - 2D + 5]} e^x \cos 3x$$

$$\text{P. I.} = e^x \frac{1}{[(D + 1) + 1][(D + 1)^2 - 2(D + 1) + 5]} \cos 3x$$

$$= e^x \frac{1}{[D + 2][D^2 + 4]} \cos 3x$$

$$\text{put } D^2 = -a^2 - 3^2 = -9$$

$$= e^x \frac{1}{(D + 2)(-5)} \cos 3x$$

$$\text{P.I.} = \frac{[-e^x]}{5} \frac{(D - 2)}{(D + 2)(D - 2)} \cos 3x$$

$$= \frac{-e^x}{5} \frac{D - 2}{D^2 - 4} \cos(3x)$$

$$= -\frac{e^x}{5} \frac{D - 2}{-13} \cos(3x)$$

$$= \frac{e^x}{65} [D(\cos 3x) - 2\cos 3x]$$

$$= \frac{e^x}{65} [-3\sin 3x - 2\cos 3x]$$

$$= \frac{-e^x}{65} [3 \sin x + 2 \cos x] \qquad \qquad ...(5)$$

The general solution is $y = $ C. F. + P. I.

$$y = c_1 e^{-x} + e^x [c_2 \cos 2x + c_3 \sin 2x] - \frac{e^x}{65} [3 \sin x + 2 \cos x] \quad ...(6)$$

Example 2.72 : Solve : $\dfrac{d^2y}{dx^2} - 2\dfrac{dy}{dx} + y = e^{2x} \sin 2x$

Solution : Given differential equation is

$$\frac{d^2y}{dx^2} - 2\frac{dy}{dx} + y = e^{2x} \sin 2x \qquad \qquad ...(1)$$

$$[D^2 - 2D + 1] y = e^{2x} \sin 2x \qquad \qquad ...(2)$$

$\therefore$ $\qquad \qquad f (D) y = x \qquad \qquad$ where, $f (D) = D^2 - 2D + 1$

$$X = e^{2x} \sin 2x$$

To find c. f.

The A. E. is $\qquad D^2 - 2D + 1 = 0 \qquad \qquad ...(3)$

$$(D - 1)^2 = 0$$

$$D = 1, 1 \qquad \qquad \text{Let, } m_1 = m_2 = 1$$

The roots are real and equal.

$$\text{C. F.} = [c_1 + c_2 x] e^{m_1 x}$$

$$\text{C. F.} = [c_1 + c_2 x] e^x \qquad \qquad ...(4)$$

To find P. I.

$$\text{P.I.} = \frac{1}{f (D)} X = \frac{1}{D^2 - 2D + 1} e^{2x} \sin (2x)$$

$$= \frac{1}{(D - 1)^2} e^{2x} \sin 2x$$

$$= e^{2x} \frac{1}{[D + 1]^2} \sin (2x)$$

$$= \frac{e}{(D^2 + 2D + 1)} \sin (2x) \qquad \text{put } D^2 = -4$$

$$= e^{2x} \frac{1}{[(D + 2) - 1]^2} \sin 2x \qquad \text{put } D^2 = -4$$

$$= e^{2x} \frac{1}{[2D - 3]} \sin 2x$$

$$= e^{2x} \frac{(2D + 3)}{(2D - 3) (2D + 3)} \sin 2x$$

$$= e^{2x} \frac{(2D + 3) \sin 2x}{4D^2 - 9} \qquad \text{put } D^2 = -4$$

$$= e^{2x} \frac{(2D + 3)}{-25} \sin 2x$$

$$\text{P.I.} = -\frac{e^{2x}}{25} [2D (\sin 2x) + 3 \sin 2x]$$

$$= -\frac{e^{2x}}{25} [4 \cos 2x + 3 \sin 2x] \qquad \ldots(5)$$

The general solution is $y = \text{C. F.} + \text{P. I.} = (c_1 + c_2 x) e^x - \frac{e^{2x}}{25} [4 \cos 2x + 3 \sin 2x]$

$$\ldots (6)$$

EXERCISE 2.9

I.   Theory questions :

1. If $f(D) y = x$ where $x = e^{ax} V$ and V is a function of x then prove that   **[Nov. 2012, April 2012, April 2013]**

    $$\frac{1}{f(D)} e^{ax}. V = e^{ax} \left[\frac{1}{f(D + a)} \right] V$$

2. Obtain the particular integral of $f(D) y = e^{ax} V$ where V is the function of x.

II. Problems : Solve the following differential equations :

1. $\dfrac{d^2y}{dx^2} - 2\dfrac{dy}{dx} + y = x^2 e^x$

2. $\dfrac{d^2y}{dx^2} = e^x \cos x$

3. $[D^2 - 4D + 3] y = e^{2x} \sin 3x$

4. $[D^3 - 3D^2 + 3D - 1] y = (x + 1) e^x$

5. $\dfrac{d^2y}{dx^2} + 3\dfrac{dy}{dx} + 2y = xe^{3x}$

6. $[D^2 + 2] y = x^2 e^{3x}$

7. $\dfrac{d^2y}{dx^2} - 2\dfrac{dy}{dx} + y = x^2 e^{3x}$

8. $[D^3 - 3D - 2] y = x^3 e^{-x}$

9. $[D^2 - 4D + 4] y = x^2 e^{2x}$

10. $[D^4 + 2D^2 + 1] y = \cos x$

$$\boxed{\textbf{ANSWERS 2.9}}$$

II. Problems : Solve the following differential equations :

1. $y = (c_1 + c_2 x)\, e^x + \dfrac{1}{2}\, e^x\, x^4$

2. $y = [c_1 + c_2 x] + \dfrac{1}{2}\, e^x \sin x$

3. $y = c_1 e^x + c_2 e^{3x} - \dfrac{1}{10}\, e^{2x} \sin 3x$

4. $y = [c_1 + c_2 x + c_3 x^2]\, e^x + \dfrac{1}{24}\, [x^4 + 6x^3]\, e^x$

5. $y = c_1 e^{-x} + c_2 e^{-2x} + \dfrac{e^{3x}}{400}\, (20x - 9)$

6. $y = c_1 \cos \sqrt{2}\, x + c_2 \sin \sqrt{2}\, x + \left[x^2 - \dfrac{12x}{11} + \dfrac{50}{121} \right] \dfrac{e^{2x}}{11}$

7. $y = (c_1 + c_2\, x)\, e^x + \dfrac{e^{3x}}{8}\, (2x^2 - 4x + 3)$

8. $y = c_1 e^{2x}\, [c_2 + c_3 x]\, e^{-x} - \left[\dfrac{x^5}{60} + \dfrac{x^4}{36} + \dfrac{x^3}{27} + \dfrac{x^2}{27} \right] e^{-x}$

9. $y\, (c_1 + c_2\, x)\, e^{2x} + \dfrac{1}{12}\, x^4\, e^{2x}$

10. $y = [c_1 + c_2 x] \cos x + [c_3 + c_4\, x] \sin x - \dfrac{1}{8}\, x^2 \cos x$

2.7.5 Particular Integral When x is of the form xV where V is a function of x

Theorem 1 : If $f(D)\, y = X$, where $X = xV$ and v is a function of x

then P. I. $= \dfrac{1}{f(D)}\, xV = \left\{ x \cdot \dfrac{1}{f(D)}\, V - \dfrac{f'(D)}{[f(D)]^2}\, V \right\}$

Proof : Let $\qquad\qquad f(D)\, y \;=\; X$ ...(1)

Where $X = x\, V$ and V is a function of x

Suppose, V_1 be the function of x.

By successive differentiation, we have

$$D\, (x\, V_1) \;=\; x \cdot D\, V_1 + V_1 \cdot 1 \qquad\qquad \text{...(2)}$$

We have $\qquad D^2\, (x\, V_1) \;=\; D\, [D\, (x\, V_1)]$

$$\qquad\qquad\qquad\;\; = D\, [x \cdot D\, V_1] + D\, (V_1)$$

$$\qquad\qquad\qquad\;\; = [x \cdot D^2 V_1 + D V_1] + D V_1$$

$$D^2\, (x\, V_1) \;=\; x\, D^2 V_1 + 2\, D V_1 \qquad\qquad \text{...(3)}$$

Also,

$$D^3 (x V_1) = D [D^2 (x V_1)]$$
$$= D [x \cdot D^2 V_1 + 2 D V_1]$$
$$= D [x \cdot D^2 V_1] + 2D^2 V_1$$
$$= [x \cdot D^3 V_1 + D^2 V_1] + 2D^2 V_1$$
$$D^3 [x V_1] = x \cdot D^3 V_1 + 3D^2 V_1 \qquad \qquad ...(4)$$

$$.................$$

$$..............$$

Continuing in this way

$$D^n (x V_1) = x \cdot D^n y_1 + n D^{n-1} y_1 \qquad \qquad ...(5)$$

Using,

$$n \cdot D^{n-1} = \frac{d}{dD} (D^n) \qquad \qquad ...(6)$$

$$D^n (xV_1) = x D^n y_1 + \frac{d}{dD} (D^n) y_1 \qquad \qquad ...(7)$$

Hence, we write it as

$$f (D) (x V_1) = x \cdot f (D) y_1 + f' (D) y_1 \qquad \qquad ...(8)$$

Put

$$f (D) V_1 = V$$

$$\therefore \qquad V_1 = \frac{1}{f (D)} V \qquad \qquad ...(9)$$

Using equation (9) equation (8) becomes

$$f (D) \left[x \cdot \frac{1}{f(D) V} \right] = x f (D) \frac{1}{f (D)} V + f' (D) \frac{1}{f (D)} V$$

$$f (D) \left[x \cdot \frac{1}{f (D)} V \right] = xV + f' (D) \frac{1}{f (D)} V$$

$$xV = f (D) \left[x \frac{1}{f (D)} V \right] - f' (D) \frac{1}{f (D)} V$$

Operating on both sides by $\frac{1}{f (D)}$ we get

$$\frac{1}{f (D)} xV = \frac{1}{f(D)} f (D) \left[x \cdot \frac{1}{f (D)} V \right] - \frac{1}{f (D)} \left[f' (D) \cdot \frac{1}{f (D)} V \right]$$

$$= x \cdot \frac{1}{f (D)} V - \frac{1}{f (D)} \cdot f' (D) \left[\frac{1}{f (D)} V \right]$$

$$\frac{1}{f (D)} xV = \left[x - \frac{1}{f(D)} f' (D) \right] \frac{1}{f (D)} V \qquad \qquad ...(10)$$

$$\frac{1}{f(D)} xV = \left[x \cdot \frac{1}{f (D)} V - \frac{1}{f (D)^2} f' (D) V \right] \qquad \qquad ...(11)$$

SOLVED EXAMPLES

Example 2.73 : Solve $[D^2 + 1]$ y = x sin (2x).   [S. U. April 2013]

Solution : Given differential equation is

$$[D^2 + 1] \, y = x \sin (2x) \qquad \ldots(1)$$

i.e.
$$f(D) \, y = X \qquad \ldots(2)$$

Where,
$$f(D) = D^2 + 1$$
$$X = x \sin (2x)$$

To find C. F.

A. E. is
$$D^2 + 1 = 0 \qquad \ldots(3)$$

∴
$$D^2 = -1$$
$$D^2 = i^2$$
$$D = \pm i = 0 \pm i$$

Let, $D = \alpha + i\beta = 0 \pm i$,   where $\alpha = 0, \beta = 1$

The roots are imaginary.

$$C. F. = e^{\alpha x} [c_1 \cos \beta x + c_2 \sin \beta x]$$
$$= e^{0x} [c_1 \cos x + c_2 \sin x]$$
$$= [c_1 \cos x + c_2 \sin x] \qquad \ldots(4)$$

To find P. I.

$$P. I. = \frac{1}{f(D)} \, X$$

$$P. I. = \frac{1}{D^2 + 1} [x \cdot \sin (2x)]$$

Using the formula,

$$\frac{1}{f(D)} \, xV = \left[x \cdot \frac{1}{f(D)} V - \frac{f'(D)}{[f(D)]^2} \cdot V \right] \qquad \ldots(5)$$

We get,
$$P. I. = x \cdot \frac{1}{D^2 + 1} \sin (2x) - \frac{2D}{(D^2 + 1)^2} \sin (2x)$$

Put, $D^2 = -a^2 = -4$

$$P. I. = x \left(\frac{1}{-3} \right) \sin (2x) - \frac{2D}{9} \sin (2x)$$

$$= \frac{-1}{3} x \sin (2x) - \frac{2}{9} D (\sin 2x)$$

$$= \frac{-1}{3} x \sin (2x) - \frac{4}{9} \cos (2x) \qquad \ldots(6)$$

The solution of equation (1) is

$$y = C. F. + P. I.$$

$$y = c_1 \cos x + c_2 \sin x - \frac{1}{3} x \sin (2x) - \frac{4}{9} \cos (2x) \quad \ldots(7)$$

Example 2.74 : Solve $\dfrac{d^2y}{dx^2} + 4y = x \sin x$

Solution : Given differential equation is

$$\frac{d^2y}{dx^2} + 4y = x \sin x \qquad \qquad ...(1)$$

$\therefore \qquad \qquad (D^2 + 4)\, y = x \sin x \qquad \qquad ...(2)$

$\therefore \qquad \qquad \qquad f(D)\, y = X \qquad \qquad \text{where } f(D) = D^2 + 4$

$$X = x \sin x$$

To find C. F.

The A. E. is $\qquad D^2 + 4 = 0$

$$D^2 = -4 = 4i^2$$

$$D = \pm 2i = 0 + 2i$$

$\therefore \quad \alpha = 0,\ \beta = 2$

The roots are complex

$$C.F. = e^{\alpha x} [c_1 \cos \beta x + c_2 \sin \beta x]$$

$$C.F. = e^{0x} [c_1 \cos 2x + c_2 \sin 2x]$$

$$C.F. = c_1 \cos 2x + c_2 \sin 2x \qquad \qquad ...(3)$$

To find P. I.

$$P.\,I. = \frac{1}{f(D)}\, X = \frac{1}{D^2 + 4}\, (x \sin x)$$

Using $\qquad \dfrac{1}{f(D)}\, [xV] = x \dfrac{1}{f(D)}\, V - \dfrac{f'(D)}{[f(D)]^2}\, V \qquad$ we get

$$P.\,I. = x \cdot \frac{1}{D^2 + 4}\, \sin x - \frac{2D}{(D^2 + 4)}\, \sin x$$

Put $D^2 = -a^2 = -1$

$$P.\,I. = x \cdot \frac{1}{3}\, \sin x - \frac{2D}{9}\, \sin x$$

$$P.I. = \frac{1}{3}\, x \sin x - \frac{2}{9}\, \cos x$$

$$P.\,I. = \frac{1}{9}\, [3x \sin x - 2 \cos x] \qquad \qquad ...(4)$$

The general solution is

$$y = C.\,F. + P.\,I.$$

$$y = c_1 \cos 2x + c_2 \sin 2x + \frac{1}{9}\, [3x \sin x - 2 \cos x] \qquad ...(5)$$

Example 2.75 : Solve : $[D^2 - 1]y = x \cos x$

Solution : Given differential equation is

$$(D^2 - 1)\, y = x \cos x \qquad \qquad ...(1)$$

$$f(D)\, y = X \qquad \qquad ...(2)$$

where, $f(D) = D^2 - 1$

$X = x \cos x$

To find C. F.

The A. E. is $D^2 - 1 = 0$

$D^2 = 1$

$D = \pm 1$

Let $m_1 = 1$ and $m_2 = -1$

The roots are real and unequal.

$$C. F. = c_1 e^{m_1 x} + c_2 e^{m_2 x}$$

$$C. F. = c_1 e^x + c_2 e^{-x} \qquad \qquad ...(3)$$

To find P. I.

$$P. I. = \frac{1}{f(D)} X = \frac{1}{D^2 - 1} x \cos x$$

By using formula $\frac{1}{f(D)} xV = x \frac{1}{f(D)} V - f'(D) \frac{1}{[f(D)]^2} V$

$$P. I. = x \cdot \frac{1}{D^2 - 1} \cos x - \frac{2D}{(D^2 - 1)} \cos x$$

Put $D^2 = -a^2 = -1$

$$P. I. = \frac{x \cos x}{(-2)} - \frac{2D}{4} \cos x$$

$$P. I. = \frac{-x}{2} \cos x - \frac{1}{2} D [\cos x]$$

$$= \frac{-x}{2} \cos x - \frac{1}{2} (-\sin x)$$

$$= \frac{-x}{2} \cos x + \frac{1}{2} \sin x$$

$$= \frac{1}{2} (\sin x - x \cos x) \qquad \qquad ...(4)$$

The general solution is

$$y = C. F. + P. I.$$

$$y = c_1 e^{-x} + c_2 e^{-x} + \frac{1}{2} [\sin x - x \cos x] \; ...(5)$$

Example 2.76 : Solve : $[D^2 + 2D + 1] y = x \cos x$

Solution : Given differential equation is

$$[D^2 + 2D + 1] y = x \cos x \qquad \qquad ...(1)$$

$$f(D) y = X \qquad \qquad ...(2)$$

Where $f(D) = D^2 + 2D + 1$

$X = x \cos x$

To find C. F.

The A. E. is $D^2 + 2D + 1 = 0$

$$(D + 1)^2 = 0$$

$$D = -1, -1$$

Let, $m_1 = m_2 = -1$

The roots are real and equal.

$$C. F. = (c_1 + c_2 x)\, e^{m_1 x}$$

$$C. F. = (c_1 + c_2 x) e^{-x} \qquad \qquad ...(3)$$

To find P. I.

$$P. I. = \frac{1}{f(D)} x = \frac{1}{(D + 1)^2} x \cos x$$

$$= \frac{1}{D^2 + 2D + 1} x \cos x$$

Using the formula, $\dfrac{1}{f(D)} x V = x \dfrac{1}{f(D)} V - \dfrac{f'(D)}{[f(D)]^2} V$

$$P.I. = x \frac{1}{2D} \cos x - \frac{(2D + 2)}{(2D)^2} \cos x$$

$$= \frac{x}{2} \left[\frac{1}{D} \cos x \right] - \frac{2(D + 1)}{4D^2} \cos x$$

$$= \frac{x}{2} (-\sin x) - \frac{1}{2} (D + 1) \cdot \frac{1}{D^2} \cos x$$

$$= \frac{x}{2} (-\sin x) - \frac{1}{2} (D + 1) (-\cos x)$$

$$= \frac{x}{2} (-\sin x) - \frac{1}{2} D (-\cos x) + \frac{1}{2} \cos x$$

$$= -\frac{x}{2} \sin x + \frac{1}{2} D (\cos x) + \frac{1}{2} \cos x$$

$$= -\frac{x}{2} \sin x - \frac{1}{2} \sin x + \frac{1}{2} \cos x$$

$$= -\frac{1}{2} [x \sin x + \sin x - \cos x] \qquad ...(4)$$

The general solution is

$$y = C. F. + P. I.$$

$$y = [c_1 + c_2 x] e^{-x} - \frac{1}{2} [x \sin x + \sin x - \cos x]$$

Example 2.77 : Solve : $\dfrac{d^2y}{dx^2} - 2\dfrac{dy}{dx} + y = xe^x \sin x.$

Solution : The given differential equation is

$$\frac{d^2y}{dx^2} - 2\frac{dy}{dx} + y = xe^x \sin x \qquad ...(1)$$

$$[D^2 - 2D + 1]\, y = xe^x \sin x \qquad ...(2)$$

$\therefore$ $\qquad$ $f(D) y = x$ $\qquad$ where, $f(D) = D^2 - 2D + 1$

$$X = x e^x \sin x$$

To find C. F.

The A. E. is $\qquad D^2 - 2D + 1 = 0$

$$[D - 1]^2 = 0$$

$$D = 1, 1 \qquad\qquad \text{Let } m_1 = m_2 = 1$$

The roots are real and equal.

$$\text{C. F.} = [c_1 + c_2 x] e^{m_1 x}$$

$$\text{C. F.} = [c_1 + c_2 x] e^x \qquad\qquad ...(3)$$

To find P. I.

$$\text{P. I.} = \frac{1}{f(D)} x = \frac{1}{(D-1)^2} x e^x \sin x$$

Using formula $\left[\dfrac{1}{f(D)} e^{ax} V = e^{ax} \dfrac{1}{f(D+a)} V\right]$

$$\text{P. I.} = e^x \left[\frac{1}{\{(D+1)-1\}^2} (x \sin x)\right]$$

$$\text{P. I.} = e^x \frac{1}{D^2} [x \sin x]$$

Using formula, $\dfrac{1}{f(D)} x V = x \cdot \dfrac{1}{f(D)} V - \dfrac{f'(D)}{[f(D)]^2} V$

$$\text{P. I.} = e^x \left[x \cdot \frac{1}{D^2} \sin x - \frac{2D}{D^4} \sin x\right]$$

$$= e^x \left[x \cdot (-\sin x) - 2 \cdot \frac{1}{D^3} \sin x\right]$$

$$= e^x [-x \sin x - 2 (\cos x)]$$

$$= e^x [-x \sin x - 2 \cos x]$$

$$= -e^x [x \sin x + 2 \cos x] \qquad\qquad ...(5)$$

The general solution is $\quad y = \text{C. F.} + \text{P. I.}$

$$y = [c_1 + c_2 x] e^x - e^x [x \sin x + 2 \cos x] \ ...(6)$$

Example 2.78 : Solve : $\dfrac{d^2y}{dx^2} - 4y = x \cos 2x$

Solution : Given differential equation is

$$\frac{d^2y}{dx^2} - 4y = x \cos 2x \qquad\qquad ...(1)$$

$$[D^2 - 4] y = x \cos 2x \qquad\qquad ...(2)$$

i.e. $\qquad\qquad f(D) y = x$

$$\text{where } f(D) = D^2 - 4$$

$$X = x \cos 2x$$

To find C. F.

The A. E. is $\qquad$ $D^2 - 4 = 0$

$$D^2 = 4$$

$$D = \pm 2 \qquad\qquad \text{Let } m_1 = 2, m_2 = -2$$

The roots are real and unequal.

$$\text{C. F.} = c_1 e^{m_1 x} + c_2 e^{m_2 x}$$

$$\text{C. F.} = c_1 e^{2x} + c_2 e^{-2x} \qquad\qquad ...(3)$$

To find P. I. $\qquad$ $\text{P.I.} = \dfrac{1}{f(D)} x$

$$\text{P. I.} = \dfrac{1}{D^2 - 4} x \cos(2x)$$

$$\text{P. I.} = x \cdot \dfrac{1}{D^2 - 4} \cos 2x - \dfrac{2D}{(D^2 - 4)^2} \cos 2x$$

$$\text{Using formula} \left[\dfrac{1}{f(D) \, xv = x \dfrac{1}{f(D)} V - f'(D) \dfrac{1}{[f(D)]^2} V} \right]$$

$$\text{P. I.} = x \dfrac{1}{-4-4} \cos 2x - \dfrac{2D}{(-4-4)^2} \cos 2x$$

$$= -\dfrac{1}{8} x \cos 2x - \dfrac{1}{32} D(\cos 2x)$$

$$= -\dfrac{1}{8} x \cos 2x - \dfrac{1}{32} (-2 \sin 2x)$$

$$\text{P. I.} = -\dfrac{1}{8} x \cos 2x + \dfrac{1}{16} \sin 2x$$

The general solution is

$$y = \text{C. F.} + \text{P. I.}$$

$$y = c_1 e^{2x} + c_2 e^{-2x} - \dfrac{1}{8} x \cos(2x) + \dfrac{1}{16} \sin(2x) \qquad ...(4)$$

EXERCISE 2.10

I. Theory questions :

1. If $f(D) y = X$ where $X = xV$, and V is a function of x then prove that, $\dfrac{1}{f(D)} xV = x \dfrac{1}{f(D)} V - \dfrac{f'(D)}{[f(D)]^2} V$. $\qquad$ OR [S. U. May 2011]

2. Obtain the particular integral of $f(D) y = xV$, where V is a function of x.

II. Problem :

Solve the following differential equations :

1. $\dfrac{d^2y}{dx^2} + 4y = \cos x$

2. $\dfrac{d^2y}{dx^2} - y = x^2 \cos x$

3. $\dfrac{d^2y}{dx^2} + 2\dfrac{dy}{dx} + y = x \sin x$

4. $(D^3 - 3D^2 + 3D)\, y = xe^x$

5. $(D^2 - 1)\, y = x^2 \sin x$

ANSWERS 2.10

1. $y = c_1 \cos 2x + c_2 \sin 2x + \dfrac{1}{3} x \cos x + \dfrac{2}{9} \sin x$

2. $y = c_1 e^x + c_2 e^{-x} - \dfrac{1}{2}(1 - x^2)\cos x + x \sin x$

3. $y = (c_1 + c_2 x) e^{-x} + \dfrac{1}{2}[x \sin x - (x - 1)\cos x]$

4. $y = [c_1 + c_2 x + c_3 x^2]e^x + \dfrac{1}{24} e^x x^4$

5. $y = c_1 e^x + c_2 e^{-x} - \dfrac{1}{2}(x^2 - 1)\sin x - x \cos x$

UNIVERSITY QUESTIONS

1. If $f(D)\, y = X$ where $X = e^{ax} \cdot V$ and V is a function of x then prove that $\dfrac{1}{f(D)}\, e^{ax}\, V = e^{ax} \dfrac{1}{f(D + a)}\, V$. **[10 M]**

   Also solve $(D^2 - 4D + 4)\, y = x^2 e^{2x}$

2. In usual notations, prove that $\dfrac{1}{f(D^2)}\cos(ax) = \dfrac{1}{f(-a^2)}\cos(ax) \dots$

   if $f(-a^2) \neq 0$ and hence solve $(D^2 - 5D + 6)y = \cos(3x)$. **[10 M]**

3. Solve $\dfrac{d^3y}{dx^3} - 3\dfrac{dy}{dx} + 2y = x$. **[5M]**

4. Solve $(D^2 + 1)\, y = x \sin(2x)$ **[5M]**

April 2013

1. With usual notations prove that,

   $\dfrac{1}{f(D)^2}\sin(ax) = \dfrac{1}{f(-a^2)}\sin(ax)$ where $f(-a^2) \neq 0$.   [8M]

2. Solve : $\dfrac{d^2y}{dx^2} - 5\dfrac{dy}{dx} + 6y = 2e^{3x}$ [4M]

3. Solve : $\dfrac{d^2y}{dx^2} + 4y = \cos(3x)$ [4M]

Nov. 2012

1. Show that, $\dfrac{1}{f(D^2)}\sin(ax) = \dfrac{1}{f(-a^2)}\sin(ax)$. If $f(-a^2) \neq 0$ [8M]

2. If $f(D)y = x$ where $X = e^{ax}V$ and V is a function of x then prove

   that $\dfrac{1}{f(D)}e^{ax}V = e^{ax}\dfrac{1}{f(D+a)}V$.   [8M]

3. Solve $\dfrac{d^2y}{dx^2} + \dfrac{dy}{dx} - 6y = x$.   [4M]

4. Solve : $(D^3 + 2D^2 + D)y = 0$ [4M]

April 2012

1. If $f(D)y = X$, where $X = e^{ax}V$ and V is a function of x then prove

   that $\dfrac{1}{f(D)}e^{ax}V = e^{ax}\dfrac{1}{f(D+a)}V$.   [8M]

2. In usual notations, prove that $\dfrac{1}{f(D)}e^{ax} = \dfrac{1}{f(a)}e^{ax}$. If $f(a) \neq 0$. [8M]

3. Solve : $\dfrac{d^2y}{dx^2} - 4y = \cos(2x)$ [4M]

4. Solve : $(D^2 - 2D + 5)y = 0$ given that $y = 0$ and $\dfrac{dy}{dx} = 4$ when

   $x = 0$.   [4M]

Oct. 2011

1. If $D \equiv \dfrac{d}{dx}$ and $f(D)$ is a polynomial is D with constant

   coefficients, then show that,

   $\dfrac{1}{f(D^2)}\cos(ax) = \dfrac{1}{f(-a^2)}\cos(ax)$. If $f(-a^2) \neq 0$

   and hence solve $(D^2 - 1)y = \cos(2x)$ [8M]

2. Solve : $\dfrac{d^2y}{dx^2} + \dfrac{dy}{dx} - 6y = x$ [4M]

3. Solve : $(D^4 + 2D^3 + D^2)y = 0$ [4M]

May 2011

1. If $f(D) y = X$ where $X = xV$ and V is a function of x then prove that

$$\frac{1}{f(D)} xV = \left\{ x - \frac{1}{f(D)} f'(D) \right\} \frac{1}{f(D)} V$$ [8M]

2. Solve : $\dfrac{d^2y}{dx^2} + 4 \dfrac{dy}{dx} + 4y = 2 \cos(2x)$ [4M]

3. Solve : $(D^2 + 1)^2 (D^2 + D + 1) y = 0$ [4M]

MULTIPLE CHOICE QUESTIONS

Select the Correct alternative for the following :

1. The value of $\dfrac{1}{(D + a)} f(x) = $ ....

   (a) $e^{-ax} \displaystyle\int f(x) e^{ax} dx$ (b) $e^{-ax} \displaystyle\int f(x) e^{-ax} dx$

   (c) $e^{ax} \displaystyle\int f(x) e^{ax} dx$ (d) $e^{ax} \displaystyle\int f(x) x e^{-ax} dx$

2. The value of $\dfrac{1}{(D - 2)^2} e^{2x} = $ ....

   (a) 0 (b) $\dfrac{x^2}{4} e^{2x}$

   (c) $\dfrac{x^2}{2!} e^{2x}$ (d) $x^2 e^{2x}$

3. The complete solution of the differential equation $(D^2 + 6D + 5)$ $y = 0$ is ....
   (a) $y = c_1 e^{-x} + c_2 e^{-5x}$ (b) $y = c_1 e^x + c_2 e^{-5x}$
   (c) $y = c_1 e^x + c_2 e^{5x}$ (d) $y = c_1 e^{-x} + c_2 e^{5x}$

4. $\dfrac{1}{D^2 + 4} \sin x = $ ....

   (a) $\dfrac{1}{3} \sin x$ (b) $\dfrac{1}{5} \sin x$

   (c) $\dfrac{1}{3} \cos x$ (d) $\dfrac{1}{5} \cos x$

5. $D^{-2} (x^2) = $ ....

   (a) $2x$ (b) $\dfrac{x^3}{3}$ (c) $\dfrac{x^3}{12}$ (d) $\dfrac{x^4}{12}$

6. Which of the following form of the equation is of the type homogeneous differential equations.
    (a) $f(D) = 0$ (b) $f(D)y = 0$
    (c) $f(D) = X$ (d) $f(D)y = X$

7. $\dfrac{1}{D-a} X = $ ....
    (a) $e^{ax} \int X e^{-ax} dx$ (b) $e^{-ax} \int X e^{ax} dx$

    (c) $e^{ax} \int X dx$ (d) $e^{-ax} \int X^2 dx$

8. The complete solution of the differential equation
    $(D^2 - 4D + 4)$ $y = 0$ is ....
    (a) $y = (c_1 + c_2 x) e^{2x}$
    (b) $y = c_1 e^{2x} + c_2 e^{-2x}$
    (c) $y = c_1 \cos(2x) + c_2 \sin(2x)$
    (d) $y = $ None of these

9. The particular Integral of the differential equation
    $(D^2 - 5D + 6) y = 12$ is ....
    (a) 2   (b) 27   (c) e^{2x} (d) -2

10. The general solution of the differential equation $\dfrac{d^2y}{dx^2} + B \dfrac{dy}{dx}$
    $+ C = D$ is .... If its auxiliary equation has two roots m_1 and m_2 such that m_1 and m_2 are both real and distinct.
    (a) $y = c_1 e^{m_1} + c_2 e^{m_2}$ (b) $y = c_1 e^{m_1 x} + c_2 e^{m_2 x}$
    (c) $y = (c_1 + c_2) e^{m_1 x}$ (d) $y = (c_1 + c_2) e^{m_2 x}$

11. $\dfrac{1}{D^2} e^{2x} = $ ....
    (a) $\dfrac{e^{2x}}{4}$ (b) $\dfrac{e^{2x}}{2}$ (c) e^{2x} (d) $4e^{2x}$

12. The meaning of $\dfrac{1}{D+a} X = $ ....
    (a) $e^{ax} \int X e^{-ax} dx$ (b) $e^{-ax} \int X e^{ax} dx$

    (c) $e^{ax} \int X dx$ (d) $\int X dx$

13. The particular Integral of the differential equation
    $(D^2 - 9D + 18) y = -18$ is ....
    (a) e^{2x} (b) 18   (c) 1   (d) -1

14. $\frac{1}{D^2 + 9} \sin (2x) = \ldots\ldots\ldots\ldots$

(a) $\frac{\sin (2x)}{13}$ (b) $\frac{\sin (2x)}{5}$ (c) $\frac{\sin (2x)}{7}$ (d) $\frac{\sin (2x)}{11}$

15. The complete solution of the differential equation $(D^2 - 9D + 18)\, y = 0$ is ....

(a) $y = c_1 e^{3x} + c_2 e^{6x}$ (b) $y = c_1 e^{-3x} + c_2 e^{6x}$

(c) $y = c_1 e^{3x} + c_2 e^{-6x}$ (d) none of these

16. The solution of the differential equation $\frac{d^2y}{dx^2} + B \frac{dy}{dx} + C = 0$ is .... if it's auxiliary equation has two roots say m_1 and m_2 such that m_1 and m_2 are real and $m_1 = m_2$.

(a) $y = c_1 e^{m_1} + c_2 e^{m_2}$ (b) $y = c_1 e^{m_1 x} + c_2 e^{m_2 x}$

(c) $y = (c_1 + c_2 x)\, e^{m_1 x}$ (d) $y = (c_1 \cos x + c_2 \sin x)\, e^{m_2 x}$

17. The complete solution of the differential equation $(D^2 + D + 1)\, y = 0$ is ....

(a) $y = e^{-x/2} \left[c_1 \cos \frac{\sqrt{3}}{2} x + c_2 \sin \frac{\sqrt{3}}{2} x \right]$

(b) $y = (c_1 + c_2 x)\, e^{x}$

(c) $y = e^{x/2} \left[c_1 \cos \frac{\sqrt{3}}{2} x + c_2 \sin \frac{\sqrt{3}}{2} x \right]$

(d) $y = (c_1 + c_2 x)\, e^{-x}$

18. The general solution of the differential equation $\frac{d^2y}{dx^2} + B \frac{dy}{dx} + C = 0$ is .... if its auxiliary equation has two roots $\alpha + i\beta$ and $\alpha - i\beta$.

(a) $y = [c_1 \cos \alpha x + c_2 \sin \alpha x]$

(b) $y = [c_1 \cos \beta x + c_2 \sin \beta x]$

(c) $y = [c_1 \cos \alpha x + c_2 \sin \alpha x]\, e^{\beta x}$

(d) $y = [c_1 \cos \beta x + c_2 \sin \beta x]\, e^{\alpha x}$

ANSWERS

1.	(a)	2.	(c)	3.	(a)	4.	(a)	5.	(d)
6.	(b)	7.	(a)	8.	(a)	9.	(a)	10.	(b)
11.	(a)	12.	(b)	13.	(d)	14.	(b)	15.	(a)
16.	(c)	17.	(a)	18.	(d)				

❋ ❋ ❋

EQUATION OF FIRST ORDER BUT NOT OF FIRST DEGREE

3.1 INTRODUCTION

In this unit we shall study various methods of solving the differential equation of first order and degree higher than 1.

The general form of differential equation of first order and n^{th} degree is

$$P_0\left(\frac{dy}{dx}\right)^n + P_1\left(\frac{dy}{dx}\right)^{n-1} + P_2\left(\frac{dy}{dx}\right)^{n-2} + \ldots\ldots + P_n\left(\frac{dy}{dx}\right) + P_n = 0. \ldots(1)$$

where, $P_0, P_1, P_2, P_3, \ldots.. P_n$ are all functions of x and y.

Let us denote $\frac{dy}{dx}$ by p. So the above equation (1) becomes

$$P_0.\,P^n + P_1.\,P^{n-1} + P_2.\,P^{n-2} + \ldots + P_{n-1}\,p + P_n = 0$$

Here we shall discuss three methods of solving the above type of equations in different cases.

Two cases appear for consideration viz :

(a) Equations that can be factorized.

(b) Equations that can not be factorized.

(a) Equations that can be factorized

When the equation

$$P_0.\,P^n + P_1.\,P^{n-1} + P_2.\,P^{n-2} + \ldots + P_{n-1}\,p + P_n = 0$$

can be factorized then it can be solved for p.

3.2 EQUATIONS SOLVABLE FOR P

Let $\quad P^n + P_1 . P^{n-1} + P_2 . P^{n-2} + \ldots + P_{n-1}\, p + P_n = 0 \qquad$ .... (1)

Where $P = \dfrac{dy}{dx}$ and $P_0, P_1, P_2, P_3, \ldots P_n$ are all functions of x any y be a differential equation of first order and n^{th} degree ($n \geq 2, n \in N$).

If equation (1) is solvable for p, then resolve it into linear factors of the type

$(p - f_1(x, y)).(p - f_2(x, y)). (p - f_3(x, y)). \ldots\ldots (p - f_n(x, y)) = 0 \qquad$ ..... (2)

Equating each factor equal to zero, we get n equations of first order and first degree viz.

$p - f_1(x, y) = 0, p - f_2(x, y) = 0, p - f_3(x, y) = 0, \ldots p - f_n(x, y)) = 0$ ...(3)

Replace p by $\dfrac{dy}{dx}$ and solve these equations whose solution will be of the type

$F_1 (x, y, c_1) = 0, F_2(x, y, c_2) = 0, F_3(x, y, c_3) = 0, \ldots F_n(x, y, c_n) = 0 \quad$ .... (4)

Where $c_1, c_2, c_3, \ldots c_n$ are the arbitrary constants of integration.

Since the given equation is of the first order, its general solution will contain only one arbitrary constant. So without loss of generality if we take $c_1 = c_2 = \ldots\ldots = c_n = c$ The general solution of equation (1) is

$F_1 (x, y, c). F_2(x, y, c). F_3(x, y, c) = 0, \ldots F_n(x, y, c) = 0 \qquad$ .... (5)

SOLVED EXAMPLES

Example 3.1 : Solve $p^2 - 5p + 6 = 0$. **(April 2013)**

Solution : The given equation is $p^2 - 5p + 6 = 0$

$\Rightarrow \qquad\qquad\qquad (p - 3)\,(p - 2) = 0$

$\Rightarrow \qquad\qquad p - 3 = 0 \text{ and } p - 2 = 0$

$\Rightarrow \qquad\qquad\quad p = 3 \text{ and } p = 1$

$\Rightarrow \qquad\qquad \dfrac{dy}{dx} = 3 \text{ and } \dfrac{dy}{dx} = 1$

$\Rightarrow \qquad\qquad dy = 3\, dx \text{ and } dy = 1\, dx$

Integrating we get, $y = 3x + c$, $y = x + c$, where c is arbitrary constant.

Hence the solutions are $(y - 3x - c) = 0$ and $(y - x - c) = 0$

The combined solution is $(y - 3x - c) \cdot (y - x - c) = 0$, which is required general solution of given equation.

Example 3.2 : Solve $x^2 p^2 + xyp - 6y^2 = 0$.   (Oct., 2011; April 2012)

Solution : The given equation $x^2 p^2 + xyp - 6y^2 = 0$

$\Rightarrow \qquad x^2 p^2 + 3xy\, p - 2xy\, p - 6y^2 \ = \ 0$

$\Rightarrow \qquad xp\,(xp + 3y) - 2y\,(xp + 3y) \ = \ 0$

$\Rightarrow \qquad\qquad (xp + 3y)\,(xp - 2y) \ = \ 0$

$\Rightarrow \qquad\qquad\qquad xp + 3y \ = \ 0 \text{ and } xp - 2y = 0$

$\Rightarrow \qquad\qquad\qquad x\dfrac{dy}{dx} + 3y \ = \ 0 \text{ and } x\dfrac{dy}{dx} - 2y = 0$

$\Rightarrow \qquad\qquad\qquad \dfrac{dy}{y} \ = \ -3\dfrac{dx}{x} \text{ and } \dfrac{dy}{y} = 2\dfrac{dx}{x}$

Integrating we get

$\log y = -3\log x + \log c$ and $\log y \ = 2\log x + \log c$, where c is arbitrary constant

$\Rightarrow \qquad\qquad\qquad x^3\, y + c \ = \ 0 \text{ and } y - c\, x^2 = 0$

The combined solution is $(x^3\, y + c).\,(y - c\, x^2) = 0$, which is required general solution of given equation.

Example 3.3 : Solve $p^2 + px - xy - y^2 = 0$

Solution : The given equation is $p^2 + px - xy - y^2 = 0$

$\Rightarrow \qquad\qquad (p^2 - y^2) + x\,(p - y) \ = \ 0$

$\Rightarrow \qquad\qquad (p + y + x)\,(p - y) \ = \ 0$

$\Rightarrow \qquad\qquad p + y + x = 0,\, p - y \ = \ 0$

Consider $p + y + x = 0 \Rightarrow \dfrac{dy}{dx} + y = -x$, which is linear differential equation of 1st order. $\therefore$ I.F. $= e^x$ and its solution is

$$ye^x \ = \ \int - xe^x\, dx + c = -e^x\,[x - 1] + c$$

$\Rightarrow \qquad\qquad\qquad y \ = \ -(x - 1) + ce^{-x} \text{ or } y + x - 1 - ce^{-x} = 0$

Now, $\qquad\qquad\qquad \dfrac{dy}{dx} \ = \ y \quad \Rightarrow \dfrac{dy}{y} = 1\, dx$

Integrating we get, $\log y = x + \log c$ or $y - ce^x = 0$

Hence the solutions are $(y + x - 1 - ce^{-x}) = 0$ and $(y - ce^x) = 0$

The combined solution is $(y + x - 1 - ce^{-x}).\,(y - ce^x) = 0$

Example 3.4 : Solve $p^2 - 2p - 3 = 0$

Solution : The given equation is $p^2 - 2p - 3 = 0$

$\Rightarrow \qquad\qquad (p - 3)(p + 1) = 0$

$\Rightarrow \qquad\qquad (p - 3) \text{ or } (p + 1) = 0$

$\Rightarrow \qquad\qquad p = 3 \text{ or } p = 1$

$\Rightarrow \qquad\qquad \dfrac{dy}{dx} = 3 \quad \text{or} \quad \dfrac{dy}{dx} = 1$

$\Rightarrow \qquad\qquad dy = 3\,dx \text{ or } dy = 1\,dx$

Integrating we get, $y = 3x + c,\ y = x + c$

Hence the solutions are $(y - 3x - c) = 0$ and $(y - x - c) = 0$

The combined solution is $(y - 3x - c).(y - x - c) = 0$.

Example 3.5 : Solve $p^3(x + 2y) + 3p^2(x + y) + p(y + 2x) = 0$

Solution : The given equation is

$\qquad\qquad p^3(x + 2y) + 3p^2(x + y) + p(y + 2x) = 0$

$\Rightarrow \qquad p^3x + 2p^3y + 3p^2x + 3p^2y + py + 2px = 0$

$\Rightarrow \qquad p^3x + 3p^2x + 2p^3y + 3p^2y + py + 2px = 0$

$\Rightarrow \qquad p^3x + p^2x + 2p^2x + 2p^3y + 2p^2y + p^2y + py + 2px = 0$

$\Rightarrow \qquad p^3x + p^2x + 2p^3y + 2p^2y + 2p^2x + 2px + p^2y + py = 0$

$\Rightarrow \qquad p^2x(p + 1) + 2p^2y(p + 1) + 2px(p + 1) + py(p + 1) = 0$

$\Rightarrow \qquad\qquad (p + 1)[p^2x + 2p^2y + 2px + py] = 0$

$\Rightarrow \qquad\qquad (p + 1)[p^2(x + 2y) + p(2x + y)] = 0$

$\Rightarrow \qquad\qquad p.(p + 1)[p(x + 2y) + (2x + y] = 0$

$\Rightarrow \qquad p = 0 \text{ and } (p + 1) = 0 \text{ and } p(x + 2y) + (2x + y) = 0$

$\Rightarrow \quad \dfrac{dy}{dx} = 0 \text{ and } \dfrac{dy}{dx} + 1 = 0 \text{ and } \dfrac{dy}{dx}(x + 2y) + (2x + y) = 0$

$\Rightarrow \quad \dfrac{dy}{dx} = 0 \text{ and } dy + dx = 0 \text{ and } (2x + y)\,dx + (x + 2y)\,dy = 0$

Now, $\quad \dfrac{dy}{dx} = 0 \qquad \Rightarrow \quad y = c \text{ or } y - c = 0$

$\qquad\quad dy + dx = 0 \Rightarrow \quad y + x = c \text{ or } y + x - c = 0$

Consider $(2x + y)\,dx + (x + 2y)\,dy = 0$, which is Exact differential equation of the form $Mdx + Ndy = 0$, where $\dfrac{\partial M}{\partial y} = 1 = \dfrac{\partial N}{\partial x}$ and its solution is

$$\int (2x + y)\,dx + \int 2y\,dy = c \Rightarrow x^2 + xy + y^2 = c$$

Hence the solutions are

$(y - c) = 0$ and $(y + x - c) = 0$ and $(x^2 + xy + y^2 - c) = 0$

The combined solution is $(y - c) . (y + x - c) . (x^2 + xy + y^2 - c) = 0$

Example 3.6 : Solve $(x^2 + x) p^2 + (x^2 + x - 2xy - y)p + y^2 - xy = 0$

Solution : The given equation is

$$(x^2 + x) p^2 + (x^2 + x - 2xy - y)p + y^2 - xy = 0$$

$\Rightarrow \qquad x^2p^2 + xp^2 + x^2p + x\,p - 2xyp - py + y^2 - xy = 0$

$\Rightarrow \qquad x^2p^2 + xp^2 + x^2p + x\,p - xyp - xyp - yp + y^2 - xy = 0$

$\Rightarrow \qquad x^2p^2 + x^2p - xyp + x\,p^2 + xp - yp - xyp - xy + y^2 = 0$

$\Rightarrow \qquad xp\,(xp + x - y) + p\,(xp + x - y) - y\,(xp + x - y) = 0$

$\Rightarrow \qquad\qquad (xp + x - y)\,(xp + p - y) = 0$

$\Rightarrow \qquad\qquad (xp + x - y)\,[p(x + 1) - y] = 0$

$\Rightarrow \qquad xp + x - y = 0$ and $p\,(x + 1) - y = 0$

$\Rightarrow \qquad x \dfrac{dy}{dx} + x - y = 0$ and $(x + 1)\dfrac{dy}{dx} - y = 0$

$\Rightarrow \quad (x\,dy - y\,dx) + x\,dx = 0$ and $\dfrac{dy}{y} - \dfrac{dx}{(x + 1)} = 0$

$\Rightarrow \quad \dfrac{(x\,dy - y\,dx) + x\,dx}{x^2} = 0$ and $\dfrac{dy}{y} - \dfrac{dx}{(x + 1)} = 0$

$\Rightarrow \quad \dfrac{(x\,dy - y\,dx)}{x^2} + \dfrac{1}{x}\,dx = 0$ and $\dfrac{dy}{y} - \dfrac{dx}{(x + 1)} = 0$

Integrating, we get

$\left(\dfrac{y}{x}\right) + \log x + \log c = 0$ and $\qquad\qquad \log y - \log (x + 1) = \log c$

or $\quad y + x \log x + x \log c = 0$ and $\log y = \log (x + 1) + \log c$

or $\qquad\qquad y + x \log cx = 0$ and $\qquad y = c\,(x + 1)$

The combined solution is $(\,y + x \log cx).\,(c(x - 1) - y\,) = 0$

Example 3.7 : Solve $p^2 - 2p \cosh x + 1 = 0$

Solution : The given equation is $p^2 - 2p \cosh x + 1 = 0$

$\Rightarrow \qquad p = \dfrac{2 \cosh x \pm \sqrt{4p^2 \cosh^2 x - 4}}{2} = \dfrac{2 \cosh x \pm 2 \sinh x}{2}$

$\Rightarrow \qquad p = \cosh x \pm \sinh x$

$\Rightarrow$ $p = \cosh x + \sinh x$ and $p = \cosh x - \sinh x$

$\Rightarrow$ $\dfrac{dy}{dx} = \cosh x + \sinh x$ and $\dfrac{dy}{dx} = \cosh x - \sinh x$

$\Rightarrow$ $\dfrac{dy}{dx} = \left(\dfrac{e^x + e^{-x}}{2} + \dfrac{e^x - e^{-x}}{2} \right)$ and $\dfrac{dy}{dx} = \left(\dfrac{e^x + e^{-x}}{2} + \dfrac{e^x - e^{-x}}{2} \right) \Rightarrow$

$\Rightarrow$ $\dfrac{dy}{dx} = e^x$ and $\dfrac{dy}{dx} = e^{-x}$

Integrating, we get, $y + c = e^x$, $y + c = -e^{-x}$

Hence the solutions are $(y - e^x + c) = 0$ and $(y + e^{-x} + c) = 0$

The combined solution is $(y - e^x + c) . (y + e^{-x} + c) = 0$

Example 3.8 : Solve $xy \left(\dfrac{dy}{dx} \right)^2 + (3x^2 - 2y^2) \dfrac{dy}{dx} - 6xy = 0$

Solution : The given equation is $xy\, p^2 + (3x^2 - 2y^2)\, p - 6xy = 0$

$\Rightarrow$ $x\, y p^2 + 3x^2 p - 2y^2 p - 6xy = 0$

$\Rightarrow$ $xy p^2 - 2y^2 p + 3x^2 p - 6xy = 0$

$\Rightarrow$ $yp\,(xp - 2y) + 3x\,(xp - 2y) = 0$

$\Rightarrow$ $(xp - 2y)\,(yp + 3x) = 0$

$\Rightarrow$ $xp - 2y = 0$ and $yp + 3x = 0$

$\Rightarrow$ $x\dfrac{dy}{dx} - 2y = 0$ and $y\dfrac{dy}{dx} + 3x = 0$

$\Rightarrow$ $\dfrac{dy}{y} = 2\dfrac{dx}{x}$ and $y\,dy = -3dx$

Integrating, we get

$$\log y + \log c = 2\log x \text{ and } \dfrac{y^2}{2} = \dfrac{-3\,x^2}{2} + \dfrac{c}{2}$$

$\Rightarrow$ $x^2 y + c = 0$ and $y^2 + 3x^2 - c = 0$

The combined solution is $(x^2\, y + c) . (y^2 + 3x^2 - c) = 0$

Example 3.9 : Solve $\left(\dfrac{dy}{dx} \right)^2 = ax^3$

Solution : The given equation is $p^2 = ax^3$

$\Rightarrow$ $p = \pm\sqrt{ax^3}$

$\Rightarrow$ $p = \sqrt{ax^3}$ and $p = -\sqrt{ax^3}$

$\Rightarrow$ $\dfrac{dy}{dx} = \sqrt{ax^3}$ and $\dfrac{dy}{dx} = -\sqrt{ax^3}$

$\Rightarrow$ $dy = \sqrt{ax^3}\, dx$ and $dy = -\sqrt{ax^3}\, dx$

Integrating, we get

$$y + c = \sqrt{a}\,\frac{2}{5}\,x^{5/2} \text{ and } \qquad y + c = -\sqrt{a}\,\frac{2}{5}\,x^{5/2}$$

$$\Rightarrow \qquad 5(y + c) = 2\sqrt{a}\,x^{5/2} \text{ and } \qquad 5(y + c) = -2\sqrt{a}\,x^{5/2}$$

Squaring on both sides, we get

$$25(y + c)^2 = 4ax^5 \qquad \text{and} \quad 25(y + c)^2 = 4ax^5$$

The required solution is $\qquad 25(y + c)^2 - 4ax^5 = 0.$

Example 3.10 : Solve $(p + y + x)(xp + y + x)(p + 2x) = 0$

Solution : The given equation is $(p + y + x)(xp + y + x)(p + 2x) = 0$

$\Rightarrow p + y + x = 0$ and $xp + y + x = 0$ and $p + 2x = 0$

$\Rightarrow \dfrac{dy}{dx} + y + x = 0$ and $x\dfrac{dy}{dx} + y + x + 0$ and $= \dfrac{dy}{dx} + 2x = 0$

$\Rightarrow \dfrac{dy}{dx} + y = -x$ and $(x\,dy - y\,dx) + x\,dx = 0$ and $dy + 2x\,dx = 0$

Consider $\dfrac{dy}{dx} + y = -x$, which is linear differential equation of 1st order.

$\therefore \qquad$ I.F. $= e^x$ and its solution is

$\qquad ye^x = \int -xe^x\,dx + c = -e^x[x - 1] + c$

$\Rightarrow \qquad y = -(x - 1) + ce^{-x}$ or $y + x - 1 - ce^{-x} = 0$

Now, $(x\,dy + y\,dx) + x\,dx = 0$

This on integration gives $(xy) + \dfrac{x^2}{2} = \dfrac{c}{2}$

and $dy + 2x\,dx = 0$, on integration gives $y + x^2 = c$

Hence the solutions are $y + x - 1 - ce^{-x} = 0$, $2xy + x^2 - c = 0$, $y + x^2 - c = 0$

The combined solution is

$(y + x - 1 - ce^{-x}).(2xy + x^2 - c).(y + x^2 - c) = 0$

Example 3.11 : Solve $p^2 + 2px - 3x^2 = 0$

Solution : The given equation is $p^2 + 2px - 3x^2 = 0$

$\Rightarrow \qquad p^2 - px + 3px - 3x^2 = 0$

$\Rightarrow \qquad p(p - x) + 3x(p - x) = 0$

$\Rightarrow \qquad (p - x).(p + 3x) = 0$

$\qquad p - x = 0$ and $p + 3x = 0$

$\Rightarrow \qquad \dfrac{dy}{dx} - x = 0$ and $\dfrac{dy}{dx} + 3x = 0$

$\Rightarrow \qquad dy - x\,dx = 0$ and $dy + 3x\,dx = 0$

Integrating, we get

$$y - \frac{x^2}{2} + \frac{c}{2} = 0 \text{ and } y + \frac{3x^2}{2} + \frac{c}{2} = 0$$

Hence the solutions are $2y - x^2 + c = 0, 2y + 3x^2 + c = 0$

The combined solution is $(2y - x^2 + c). (2y + 3x^2 + c) = 0$

Example 3.12 : Solve $p^3 + 2p^2x - y^2p^2 - 2xy^2p = 0$.

Solution : The given equation is $p^3 + 2p^2x - y^2p^2 - 2xy^2p = 0$.

$\Rightarrow$ $p(p^2 + 2px - y^2p - 2xy^2) = 0$

$\Rightarrow$ $p [p(p + 2x) - y^2 (p + 2x)] = 0$

$\Rightarrow$ $p (p + 2x) (p - y^2) = 0$

$\Rightarrow$ $p = 0$ and $p + 2x = 0$ and $p - y^2 = 0$

$\Rightarrow$ $\frac{dy}{dx} = 0$ and $\frac{dy}{dx} + 2x = 0$ and $\frac{dy}{dx} - y^2 = 0$

$\Rightarrow$ $\frac{dy}{dx} = 0$ and $dy + 2x \, dx = 0$ and $\frac{dy}{y^2} = dx$

Integrating, we get

$$y = c \text{ and } y + x^2 = c \text{ and } x + c = \frac{-1}{y}$$

Hence the solutions are $y - c = 0, y + x^2 - c = 0, xy + cy + 1 = 0$

The combined solution is $(y - c). (y + x^2 - c). (xy + cy + 1) = 0$

EXERCISE 3.1

Solve :

1. $p^2 - 4p + 3 = 0$

2. $p^2 + p - 6 = 0.$

3. $p^2 - 7p + 12 = 0.$

4. $p^3 + 3xp^2 - y^3p^2 - 3xy^3p = 0.$

5. $x^2 \left(\frac{dy}{dx}\right)^2 + 3xy \frac{dy}{dx} + 2y^2 = 0.$

6. $x^2p^2 + xyp - 6y^2 = 0.$

7. $xp^2 + (y - x) p - y = 0.$

8. $yp^2 + (x - y)p - x = 0.$

9. $p^2 + 2py \cot x - y^2 = 0.$

10. $p(p - y) = x (x + y)$

11. $p^2 = x^5$

12. $4y^3p^2 + 2pxy(3x+1) + 3x^2 = 0.$

13. $p^2 + x^3y - x^3p - yp = 0.$

14. $(p - xy)(p - x^2)(p - y^2) = 0.$

15. $p^2x^2 - 2xyp + y^2 = 0.$

ANSWERS 3.1

1. $(y - x - c)(y - 3x - c) = 0.$

2. $(y + 3x - c)(y - 2x - c) = 0.$

3. $(y - 4x - c)(y - 3x - c) = 0.$

4. $(y - c)(x + \dfrac{1}{2y^2} + c)(y + \dfrac{3x^2}{2} - c) = 0.$

5. $(xy - c)(yx^2 - c) = 0.$

6. $(yx^3 - c)(y - cx^2) = 0.$

7. $(y - x - c)(xy - c) = 0.$

8. $(y - x - c)(y^2 + x^2 - c) = 0.$

9. $[y(1 + \cos x - c][y(1 - \cos x) - c] = 0.$

10. $(2y + x^2 + c)(y + x + 1 - ce^x) = 0.$

11. $49(y + c)^2 - 4x^7 = 0.$

12. $(x^2 + 2y^2 - c)(x^3 + y^2 - c) = 0.$

13. $(y - ce^x)(4y - x^4 + c) = 0.$

14. $(x^3 - 3y + c)(e^{x^2/2} + cy)(xy + cy + 1) = 0.$

15. $(y - cx)^2 = 0.$

(b) Equations that can not be factorized

When the equation
$$P_0. P^n + P_1. P^{n-1} + P_2. P^{n-2} + ... + P_{n-1}p + P_n = 0$$
can not be factorized into linear factors. That equation may be expressed in the form
$$f(x, y, p) = 0$$
Which can be solved by one of the following method

1. Equations solvable for y.

2. Equations solvable for x.

3.3 EQUATIONS SOLVABLE FOR Y

Let $$f(x, y, p) = 0 \qquad \text{... (1)}$$

Where, $P = \dfrac{dy}{dx}$

If equation (1) is solvable for y, then it can be put in the form

$$y = f(x, p) \qquad \text{... (2)}$$

Differentiating (2) w. r. t. x and denote $\dfrac{dp}{dx}$ by p, we get

$$p = F\left(x, p, \dfrac{dp}{dx}\right) \qquad \text{... (3)}$$

Which is an equation in two variables x and p. This equation when solved will give us a relation of the from $\psi(x, p, c) = 0$ .... (4)

where c is an arbitrary constant of integration.

Now, by eliminating p between (2) and (4) gives the required solution.

Note : (1) It the elimination of p between (2) and (4) is not possible, then we solve the equations (2) and (4) for x and y in terms of p. Then the two parametric equations $x = \phi_1(p, c)$ and $y = \phi_1(p, c)$ being a parameter.

These two relations together constitute the solution of given equation.

SOLVED EXAMPLES

Example 3.13 : Solve $y = -px + p^2$ (April 2013)

Solution : The given equation is $y = -px + p^2$ ... (1)

Differentiating (1) w.r.t.x, we get

$$\frac{dy}{dx} = -p - x\frac{dp}{dx} + 2p\frac{dp}{dx}$$

$$\Rightarrow \qquad p + p = -x\frac{dp}{dx} + 2p\frac{dp}{dx} = 0$$

$$\Rightarrow \qquad 2p = -(x - 2p)\frac{dp}{dx}$$

$$\Rightarrow \qquad \frac{dx}{dp} = -\left(\frac{x - 2p}{2p}\right)$$

$$\Rightarrow \frac{dx}{dp} + \frac{1}{2p}x = 1, \text{ which is linear differential equation of 1}^{st} \text{ order.}$$

$\therefore$ I.F. $= e^{\int \frac{1}{2p} dp} = e^{\frac{1}{2} \log p} = \sqrt{p}$ and its

solution is

$$x \sqrt{p} = \int 1 . \sqrt{p} \, dp + c = \frac{2}{3} p^{3/2} + c$$

or $$x = \frac{2}{3} p + \frac{c}{\sqrt{p}} \qquad \dots (2)$$

putting for x in the equation (1), we get

$$y = -\frac{2}{3} p^2 - c\sqrt{p} + p^2 \qquad \dots (3)$$

Eliminating p between (2) and (3), we get the required general solution of given equation (1).

Example 3.14 : Solve $y = 2px + p^4 x^2$ (Nov. 2012)

Solution : The given equation is $y = 2px + p^4 x^2$ ...... (1)

Differentiating (1) w. r. t. x, we get

$$\frac{dy}{dx} = 2p + 2x \frac{dp}{dx} + 2 \, x \, p^4 + 4 \, x^2 p^3 \frac{dp}{dx}$$

$\Rightarrow \qquad 2p - p + 2x \frac{dp}{dx} + 2 \, xp^4 + 4 \, x^2 p^3 \frac{dp}{dx} = 0$

$\Rightarrow \qquad \left(p + 2 \, x \frac{dp}{dx} \right) + 2xp^3 \left(p + 2 \, x \frac{dp}{dx} \right) = 0$

$\Rightarrow \qquad (1 + 2xp^3) \left(p + 2 \, x \frac{dp}{dx} \right) = 0$

$\Rightarrow \qquad \left(p + 2 \, x \frac{dp}{dx} \right) = 0$

$\Rightarrow \qquad \frac{dx}{x} + 2 \frac{dp}{p} = 0$

Integrating, we get

$$\log x + 2 \log p = \log c$$

$\Rightarrow \qquad p^2 x = c$

or $$p^2 = \frac{c}{x}$$

putting for p^2 in the given equation (1), we get $y = 2px + \left(\frac{c}{x} \right)^2 x^2$

or $$y = 2px + c^2$$

or $$y - c^2 = 2px$$

or
$$(y - c^2)^2 = 4p^2x^2$$
$$(y - c^2)^2 = 4\left(\frac{c}{x}\right)x^2$$
$$\Rightarrow \quad (y - c^2)^2 = 4cx$$

which is general solution of given differential equation (1)

Example 3.15 : Solve y = 3x + log p

Solution : The given equation is $y = 3x + \log p$ ...... (1)

Differentiation (1) w. r. t. x, we get

$$\frac{dy}{dx} = 3 + \frac{1}{p}\frac{dp}{dx}$$

$$\Rightarrow \quad p = 3 + \frac{1}{p}\frac{dp}{dx}$$

$$\Rightarrow \quad p - 3 = \frac{1}{p}\frac{dp}{dx}$$

$$\Rightarrow \quad p(p - 3) = \frac{dp}{dx}$$

$$\Rightarrow \quad dx = \frac{dp}{p(p - 3)}$$

$$\Rightarrow \quad dx = \frac{1}{3}\left(\frac{1}{p - 3} - \frac{1}{p}\right)dp$$

Integrating, we get

$$x + \frac{1}{3}\log c = \frac{1}{3}[\log(p - 3) - \log p]$$

$$\Rightarrow \quad x + \frac{1}{3}\log c = \frac{1}{3}\left[\log e \frac{p - 3}{p}\right]$$

$$\Rightarrow \quad 3x + \log c = \log \frac{p - 3}{p}$$

or
$$c\, e^{3x} = \frac{p - 3}{p} = 1 - \frac{3}{p}$$

$$\Rightarrow \quad \frac{3}{P} = 1 - c\, e^{3x} \text{ or } p = \frac{3}{1 - c\, e^{3x}}$$

putting for p in the given equation (1), we get $y = 3x + \log \dfrac{3}{1 - ce^{3x}}$

which is general solution of given differential equation (1)

Example 3.16 : Solve $y - 2px + p^2 = 0$

Solution : The given equation is $y - 2px + p^2 = 0$ ...... (1)

Differentiation (1) w. r. t. x, we get

$$\frac{dy}{dx} - 2p - 2x\frac{dp}{dx} + 2p\frac{dp}{dx} = 0$$

$$\Rightarrow \qquad p - 2p - 2x\frac{dp}{dx} + 2p\frac{dp}{dx} = 0$$

$$\Rightarrow \qquad -p - (2x - 2p)\frac{dp}{dx} = 0$$

$$\Rightarrow \qquad p\frac{dx}{dp} + 2x - 2p = 0$$

$$\Rightarrow \qquad \frac{dx}{dp} + 2\frac{x}{p} = 2,$$

which is linear differential equation of 1st order.

$\therefore$ \qquad I.F. $= e^{2\log p} = p^2$ and its solution is

$$xp^2 = \int 2.p^2 dp + c = \frac{2}{3}p^3 + c$$

or \qquad $x = \frac{2}{3}p + c\,p^{-2}$ ...... (2)

putting for x in the equation (1), we get

$$y = 2\,c\,p^{-1}x + \frac{1}{3}p^2$$ ...... (3)

Eliminating p between (2) and (3), we get the required general solution of given equation. (1).

Example 3.17 : Solve $xp^2 - 2yp + x = 0$

Solution : The given equation is $xp^2 - 2yp + x = 0$ ...... (1)

$$\Rightarrow \qquad 2yp = x(p^2 + 1)$$

or \qquad $2y = x\left(p + \frac{1}{p}\right)$

Differentiating this w. r. t. x, we get

$$2\frac{dy}{dx} = 1.\left(p + \frac{1}{p}\right) + x\left(1 - \frac{1}{p^2}\right)\frac{dp}{dx}$$

$$\Rightarrow \qquad 2p - \left(p + \frac{1}{p}\right) = x\left(1 - \frac{1}{p^2}\right)\frac{dp}{dx}$$

or \qquad $\left(p - \frac{1}{p}\right) = x\left(1 - \frac{1}{p^2}\right)\frac{dp}{dx}$

or
$$p = x\frac{dp}{dx}$$

$$\therefore \qquad \frac{dp}{p} = \frac{dx}{x}$$

Integrating, we get

$$\log p = \log x + \log c$$

or
$$p = xc$$

putting for p in the given equation (1), we get $x (xc)^2 - 2y (xc) + x = 0$

or
$$x^3c^2 - 2xyc + x = 0$$

or
$$2cy = x^2c^2 + 1$$

Which is the general solution of the given differential equation (1).

Example 3.18 : Solve $p^2 - py + x = 0$

Solution : The given equation is $p^2 - py + x = 0$

$$\therefore \qquad py = p^2 + x$$

$$\therefore \qquad y = p + \frac{x}{p} \qquad \qquad \text{.... (1)}$$

Differentiating (1) w. r. t. x, we get

$$\frac{dy}{dx} = \frac{dp}{dx} + \frac{1}{p} - \frac{x}{p^2}\frac{dp}{dx}$$

$$p - \frac{1}{p} = \left(1 - \frac{x}{p^2}\right)\frac{dp}{dx}$$

$$\Rightarrow \qquad p - \frac{1}{p} = \left(\frac{p^2 - x}{p^2}\right)\frac{dp}{dx}$$

$$\Rightarrow \qquad \left(\frac{p^2 - 1}{p}\right) = \left(\frac{p^2 - x}{p^2}\right)\frac{dp}{dx}$$

$$\Rightarrow \qquad (p^2 - p) = \left(\frac{p^2 - x}{p^2}\right)\frac{dp}{dx}$$

$$\Rightarrow \qquad p(p^2 - p) = (p^2 - x)\frac{dp}{dx}$$

$$\Rightarrow \qquad \frac{dx}{dp} = \frac{(p^2 - x)}{p(p^2 - p)} = \frac{p}{p^2 - 1} - \frac{x}{p(p^2 - 1)}$$

$$\Rightarrow \qquad \frac{dx}{dp} + \frac{x}{p(p^2 - 1)} = \frac{p}{p^2 - 1}$$

$$\Rightarrow \qquad \frac{dx}{dp} + \left(\frac{p}{p^2 - 1} - \frac{1}{p}\right)x = \frac{p}{p^2 - 1},$$

which is linear differential equation 1st order.

$$\therefore \quad \text{I.F.} = e^{\int \left[\frac{p}{p^2-1} - \frac{1}{p}\right] dp} = e^{\int \left(\frac{1}{2} \log (p^2 - 1)\right)} \cdot e^{-\log p} = \frac{\sqrt{p^2 - 1}}{p}$$

and its solution is

$$x \frac{\sqrt{p^2 - 1}}{p} = \int \frac{p}{p^2 - 1} \frac{\sqrt{p^2 - 1}}{p} dp + c$$

or

$$x \frac{\sqrt{p^2 - 1}}{p} = \int \frac{1}{\sqrt{p^2 - 1}} dp + c = \sin^{-1} p + c$$

or

$$x = \frac{1}{\sqrt{p^2 - 1}} (\sin^{-1} p + c) \qquad \cdots \text{(2)}$$

putting for x in the equation (1), we get

$$y = p + \frac{1}{p} \frac{p}{\sqrt{p^2 - 1}} (\sin^{-1} p + c)$$

or

$$y = p + \frac{p}{\sqrt{p^2 - 1}} (\sin^{-1} p + c) \qquad \cdots \text{(3)}$$

The equations (2) and (3) taken together, p being a parameter, represent the general solution of given differential equation.

Example 3.19 : Solve $y - 2px = f(xp^2)$

Solution : The given equation is $y - 2px = f(xp^2)$ $\qquad \cdots \text{(1)}$

$$\therefore \qquad y = 2px + f(xp^2)$$

which is solvable for y.

$\therefore$ Differentiating (1) w. r. t. x, we get

$$\frac{dy}{dx} = 2p + 2x\frac{dp}{dx} + f'(xp^2) \cdot \left[p^2 + 2px\frac{dp}{dx}\right]$$

$$\Rightarrow \qquad p = 2p + 2x\frac{dp}{dx} + p f'(xp^2) \cdot \left[p + 2x\frac{dp}{dx}\right]$$

$$\Rightarrow \qquad 0 = [p + 2x\frac{dp}{dx}] + p f'(xp^2) \cdot \left[p + 2x\frac{dp}{dx}\right]$$

or

$$0 = [1 + p f'(xp^2)]) \cdot \left[p + 2x\frac{dp}{dx}\right]$$

$\therefore \qquad$

$$p + 2x\frac{dp}{dx} = 0$$

$$\Rightarrow \qquad \frac{dx}{x} + 2\frac{dp}{p} = 0$$

Integrating, we get

$$\log x + 2 \log p = 2 \log c$$

$$\Rightarrow \qquad p^2x = c^2$$

$$\Rightarrow \qquad p^2 = \frac{c^2}{x} \text{ or } p = \frac{c}{\sqrt{x}}$$

putting for p in the given equation (1), we get $y - 2\frac{c}{\sqrt{x}}x = f\left(x.\frac{c^2}{x}\right)$

or $\qquad\qquad y = 2c\sqrt{x} + f(c^2)$

which is general solution of given differential equation (1)

Example 3.20 : Solve $x^3 p^2 + x^2 py + a^3 = 0$

Solution : The given equation is $x^3 p^2 + x^2 py + a^3 = 0$ ..... (1)

$$\Rightarrow \qquad x^2 py = -x^3 p^2 - a^3$$

$$\Rightarrow \qquad y = -xp - \frac{a^3}{x^2 p}$$

which is solvable for y.

Differentiating (1) w. r. t. x, we get

$$\frac{dy}{dx} = -p - x\frac{dp}{dx} - a^3\left(\frac{-2}{x^3}.\frac{1}{p} - \frac{1}{x^2}.\frac{1}{p^2}\frac{dp}{dx}\right)$$

$$\Rightarrow \qquad p + p = -x\frac{dp}{dx} + a^3\left(\frac{2}{x^3}.\frac{1}{p} + \frac{1}{x^2}.\frac{1}{p^2}\frac{dp}{dx}\right)$$

$$\Rightarrow \qquad 2p = -x\frac{dp}{dx} + \frac{2a^3}{px^3} + \frac{a^3}{p^2x^2}\frac{dp}{dx}$$

$$\Rightarrow \qquad \left(2p + x\frac{dp}{dx}\right) = \frac{a^3}{x^3p^2}\left(2p + x\frac{dp}{dx}\right)$$

$$\Rightarrow \qquad \left(1 + \frac{a^3}{x^3p^2}\right)\left(2p + x\frac{dp}{dx}\right) = 0$$

$$\Rightarrow \qquad \left(2p + x\frac{dp}{dx}\right) = 0$$

$$\Rightarrow \qquad 2\frac{dx}{x} + \frac{dp}{p} = 0$$

Integrating, we get

$$2\log x + \log p = \log c$$

$$\Rightarrow \qquad px^2 = c$$

$$\Rightarrow \qquad p = \frac{c}{x^2}$$

putting for p in the given equation (1), we get

$$x^3\left(\frac{c}{x^2}\right)^2 + x^2\left(\frac{c}{x^2}\right)y + a^3 = 0$$

or $\qquad x^3\left(\dfrac{c}{x^4}\right)^2 + x^2\left(\dfrac{c}{x^2}\right)y + a^3 = 0 \qquad$ or $\quad \left(\dfrac{c^2}{x}\right) + c\ y + a^3 = 0$

or $\qquad\qquad\qquad c^2 + cx\,y + a^3\,x = 0$

which is general solution of given differential equation (1)

Example 3.21 : Solve xp² – 2yp + 4x = 0

Solution : The given equation is $xp^2 - 2yp + 4x = 0$ $\qquad\qquad$ ... (1)

$\Rightarrow \qquad\qquad\qquad 2yp = x\,(p^2 + 4)$

or $\qquad\qquad\qquad 2y = x\left(p + \dfrac{4}{p}\right)$

Differentiating this w.r.t.x, we get

$$2\dfrac{dy}{dx} = 1\cdot\left(p + \dfrac{4}{p}\right) + x\left(\dfrac{dp}{dx} - \dfrac{4}{p^2}\dfrac{dp}{dx}\right)$$

$$2\dfrac{dy}{dx} = 1\cdot\left(p + \dfrac{4}{p}\right) + x\left(1 - \dfrac{4}{p^2}\right)\dfrac{dp}{dx}$$

$\Rightarrow \qquad 2p - \left(p + \dfrac{4}{p}\right) = x\left(1 - \dfrac{4}{p^2}\right)\dfrac{dp}{dx}$

or $\qquad \left(p - \dfrac{4}{p}\right) = x\left(1 - \dfrac{4}{p^2}\right)\dfrac{dp}{dx}$

or $\qquad \left(p - \dfrac{4}{p}\right) = \dfrac{x}{p}\left(p - \dfrac{4}{p}\right)\dfrac{dp}{dx}$

$\Rightarrow \qquad \left(p - \dfrac{4}{p}\right)\left(1 - \dfrac{x}{p}\dfrac{dp}{dx}\right) = 0$

$\Rightarrow \qquad\qquad \left(1 - \dfrac{x}{p}\dfrac{dp}{dx}\right) = 0$

$\Rightarrow \qquad\qquad \dfrac{dx}{x} - \dfrac{dp}{p} = 0$

$\Rightarrow \qquad\qquad \dfrac{dx}{x} = \dfrac{dp}{p}$

Integrating, we get

$$\log x + \log c = \log p$$

$\Rightarrow \qquad\qquad p = cx$

putting for p in the given equation (1), we get $c^2x^3 - 2cxy + 4x = 0$

which is general solution of given differential equation (1)

$$\boxed{\textbf{EXERCISE 3.2}}$$

Solve the following differential equation.

1. $x - yp = ap^2$.
2. $y + px = x^4 p^2$.
3. $y = p^2 x + p^4$.
4. $x^2 + p^2 x = yp$.
5. $y - 2px = y^2 p^3$.
6. $2y = \dfrac{ax}{p} + px$.
7. $y - x = xp + p^2$.
8. $y = \sin p - p \cos p$.
9. $(2x - b) p = y - ayp^2$.

$$\boxed{\textbf{ANSWERS 3.2}}$$

1. $x = \dfrac{p}{\sqrt{1 - p^2}} (a \sin^{-1} p + c), \; y = \dfrac{1}{\sqrt{1 - p^2}} (a \sin^{-1} p + c) - ap$.
2. $xy = -c + c^2 x$.
3. $x = \dfrac{1}{(1 - p)^2} \left(\dfrac{4}{3} p^3 - p^4 + c \right)$ and the given relation.
4. $x = \left[-\dfrac{1}{3} p^2 + c\sqrt{p} \right], \; y = \dfrac{\left(c\sqrt{p - \dfrac{1}{3} p^2} \right)^2}{p} + p \left(c\sqrt{p - \dfrac{1}{3} p^2} \right)$.
5. $y^3 = 2cx + c^3$.
6. $x^2 - 2cy + ac^2$.
7. $x = -2 (p - 1) + ce^{-p}, \; y = c (1 + p) e^{-p} + (2 - p^2)$.
8. $x = c - \cos p$.
9. $c (2x - b) = y^2 - ac^2$.

3.4 EQUATIONS SOLVABLE FOR x

Let the differential equation be

$$f (x, y, p) = 0 \qquad \qquad \dots (1)$$

where,

$$p = \dfrac{dy}{dx}$$

If equation (1) is solvable for x, then it can be put in the form

$$x = f (y, p) \qquad \qquad \dots (2)$$

Differentiating (2) w.r.t. y and denote $\dfrac{dx}{dy}$ by $\dfrac{1}{p}$, we get

$$\frac{1}{p} = F\left(y, p, \frac{dp}{dy}\right) \qquad \text{... (3)}$$

which is an equation in two variables y and p. This equation when solved will give us a relation of the form $\psi\,(y, p, c) = 0$ ... (4)

where, c is an arbitrary constant of integration.

Now, by eliminating p between (2) and (4) gives the required solution.

Note : (1) If the elimination of p between (2) and (4) is not possible, then we solve equations $x = \phi_1\,(p,\ c)$ and $y = \phi_1\,(p,\ c)$, p being a parameter.

These two relations together constitute the solution of given equation.

SOLVED EXAMPLES

Example 3.22 : Solve $p = \tan\left(x - \dfrac{p}{1 + p^2}\right)$ **... (April 2013)**

Solution : The given equation is $p = \tan\left(x - \dfrac{p}{1 + p^2}\right)$

$\therefore \qquad\qquad x = \tan^{-1} p + \dfrac{p}{1 + p^2}$ ... (1)

Differentiating this w. r. t. y, we get

$$\frac{dx}{dy} = \frac{1}{1 + p^2}\frac{dp}{dy} + \frac{1}{1 + p^2}\frac{dp}{dy} - \frac{2p^2}{(1 + p^2)^2}\frac{dp}{dy}$$

$$\Rightarrow \qquad \frac{1}{p} = \left[\frac{1}{1 + p^2} + \frac{1}{1 + p^2} - \frac{2p^2}{(1 + p^2)^2}\right]\frac{dp}{dy}$$

$$\Rightarrow \qquad \frac{1}{p} = \left[\frac{1 + p^2 + 1 + p^2 - 2p^2}{(1 + p^2)^2}\right]\frac{dp}{dy} = \left[\frac{2}{(1 + p^2)^2}\right]\frac{dp}{dy}$$

$$\Rightarrow \qquad dy = \left[\frac{2p}{(1 + p^2)^2}\right]dp$$

This on integration gives

$$y = -\frac{1}{1 + p^2} + c \qquad \text{... (2)}$$

Equations (1) and (2) which represents values of x and y in terms of parameter p, together give the required general solution of given equation.

Example 3.23 : Solve $y - 2px = y^2 p^3$ **(May 2011)**

Solution : The given equation is $y - 2px = y^2 p^3$ ... (1)

$\therefore \qquad 2px = y - y^2 p^3$

$\therefore \qquad 2x = \dfrac{y}{p} - y^2 p^2$

which is solvable for x.

Differentiating this w. r. t. y, we get

$$2\frac{dx}{dy} = \frac{1}{p} - \frac{y}{p^2}\frac{dp}{dy} - 2y\, p^2 - 2y^2\, p\frac{dp}{dy}$$

$$\Rightarrow \qquad \frac{2}{p} - \frac{1}{p} = -\frac{y}{p^2}\frac{dp}{dy} - 2y\, p^2 - 2\, y^2\, p\frac{dp}{dy}$$

$$\Rightarrow \qquad \frac{1}{p} + 2y\, p^2 = \left(-\frac{y}{p^2} - 2y^2\, p\right)\frac{dp}{dy}$$

$$\Rightarrow \qquad \left(\frac{1}{p} + 2y\, p^2\right) = -\frac{y}{p}\left(\frac{1}{p} + 2y\, p^2\right)\frac{dp}{dy}$$

$$\Rightarrow \qquad 1 = -\frac{y}{p}\frac{dp}{dy}$$

$$\Rightarrow \qquad \frac{dy}{y} + \frac{dp}{p} = 0$$

This on integration gives

$$\log y + \log p = \log c$$

$$\Rightarrow \qquad py = c$$

or $\qquad p = \dfrac{c}{y}$

Putting for p in the equation (1), we get

$$y - 2\frac{c}{y}\, x = \frac{c^3}{y^3}\, y^2 = 0$$

or $\qquad y^2 - 2\, cx - c^2 = 0$

or $\qquad y^2 = 2cx + c^2$

which is general solution of given differential equation (1)

Example 3.24 : Solve $x = y + p^2$

Solution : The given equation is $x = y + p^2$ ... (1)

Differentiating this w.r.t. y, we get

$$\frac{dx}{dy} = 1 + 2p\frac{dp}{dy}$$

$$\Rightarrow \qquad \frac{1}{p} = 1 + 2p\frac{dp}{dy}$$

$$\Rightarrow \qquad 0 = 1 - \frac{1}{p} + 2p\frac{dp}{dy} \Rightarrow \frac{p-1}{p} + 2p\frac{dp}{dy} = 0$$

$$\Rightarrow \qquad (p - 1) + 2p^2 \frac{dp}{dy} = 0$$

$$\Rightarrow \qquad dy + \frac{2p^2}{p-1}\, dp = 0$$

$$\Rightarrow \quad dy + 2\left[p + 1 + \frac{1}{p-1}\right] dp = 0$$

This on integration gives

$$y + 2\left[\frac{P^2}{2} + P + \log(p-1)]\right] = c$$

or $\quad y = -p^2 - 2p - 2\log(p-1) + c \qquad$ ... (2)

putting for y in the equation (1), we get

$$x = -p^2 - 2p - 2\log(p-1) + c + p^2$$

$$x = c - 2p - 2\log(p-1) \qquad \text{... (3)}$$

Eliminating p between (2) and (3), we get the required general solution of given equation (1).

Example 3.25 : Solve x = y + a log p

Solution : The given equation is x = y + a log p $\qquad$ ... (1)

which is solvable for x.

Differentiating this w. r. t. y, we get

$$\frac{dx}{dy} = 1 + \frac{a}{p}\frac{dp}{dy}$$

$$\Rightarrow \qquad \frac{1}{p} = 1 + \frac{a}{p}\frac{dp}{dy}$$

$$\Rightarrow \qquad 0 = 1 - \frac{1}{p} + \frac{a}{p}\frac{dp}{dy}$$

$$\Rightarrow \qquad \frac{p-1}{p} + \frac{a}{p}\frac{dp}{dy} = 0$$

$$\Rightarrow \qquad (p - 1) = -a\frac{dp}{dy}$$

$$\Rightarrow \qquad dy = -\frac{a}{p-1}\, dp$$

This on integration gives

$$y = -a\log(p-1) + c \qquad \text{... (2)}$$

putting for y in the equation (1), we get

$$x = -a \log (p - 1) + c + a \log p$$

$$x = c + a \log \frac{p}{p - 1} \qquad \text{... (3)}$$

Equations (2) and (3) which represents values of x and y in terms of parameter p, together give the required general solution of given equation (1).

Example 3.26 : Solve x − py = ap²

Solution : The given equation is $x = py + ap^2$ ... (1)

which is solvable for x.

Differentiating this w. r. t. y, we get

$$\frac{dx}{dy} = p + y \frac{dp}{dy} + 2ap \frac{dp}{dy}$$

$$\Rightarrow \qquad \frac{1}{p} = p + y \frac{dp}{dy} + 2ap \frac{dp}{dy}$$

$$\Rightarrow \qquad \frac{1}{p} - p = y \frac{dp}{dy} + 2ap \frac{dp}{dy}$$

$$\Rightarrow \qquad \frac{1 - p^2}{p} = y \frac{dp}{dy} + 2ap \frac{dp}{dy}$$

$$\Rightarrow \qquad (p - 1) = -a \frac{dp}{dy}$$

$$\Rightarrow \qquad dy = -\frac{a}{p - 1} \, dp$$

This on integration gives

$$y = -a \log (p - 1) + c \qquad \text{... (2)}$$

putting for y in the equation (1), we get

$$x = -a \log (p - 1) + c + a \log p$$

$$x = c + a \log \frac{p}{p - 1} \qquad \text{... (3)}$$

Equations (2) and (3) which represents values of x and y in terms of parameter p, together give the required general solution of given equation (1).

Example 3.27 : Solve y − 2px + ap² y = 0

Solution : The given equation is $y - 2px + ap^2y = 0$ ... (1)

$$\therefore \qquad 2px = y + ap^2y$$

$$\therefore \qquad 2x = \frac{y}{p} + apy$$

which is solvable for x.

Differentiating this w. r. t. y, we get

$$2\frac{dx}{dy} = \frac{1}{p} - \frac{y}{p^2}\frac{dp}{dy} + ap + ay\frac{dp}{dy}$$

$$\Rightarrow \quad \frac{2}{p} - \frac{1}{p} = -\frac{y}{p^2}\frac{dp}{dy} + ap + ay\frac{dp}{dy}$$

$$\Rightarrow \quad \frac{1}{p} - ap = \left(-\frac{y}{p^2} + ay\right)\frac{dp}{dy}$$

$$\Rightarrow \quad \left(\frac{1}{p} - ap\right) = -\frac{y}{p}\left(\frac{1}{p} - ap\right)\frac{dp}{dy}$$

$$\Rightarrow \quad 1 = -\frac{y}{p}\frac{dp}{dy}$$

$$\Rightarrow \quad \frac{dy}{y} + \frac{dp}{p} = 0$$

This on integration gives

$$\log y + \log p = \log c$$

$$\Rightarrow \quad py = c$$

or

$$p = \frac{c}{y}$$

putting for p in the equation (1), we get

$$y - 2\frac{c}{y}x + a\frac{c^2}{y^2}y = 0$$

or

$$y^2 - 2cx + ac^2 = 0$$

which is general solution of given differential equation (1)

Example 3.28 : Solve $y^2 \log y = xyp + p^2$.

Solution : The given equation is $y^2 \log y = xyp + p^2$ ... (1)

$$\therefore \qquad xyp = y^2 \log y - p^2$$

$$\therefore \qquad x = \frac{y \log y}{p} - \frac{p}{y}$$

which is solvable for x.

Differentiating this w.r.t. y, we get

$$\frac{dx}{dy} = \frac{p\left[y\cdot\frac{1}{y} + \log y\right] - y\log y\frac{dp}{dy}}{p^2} - \frac{y\frac{dp}{dy} - p}{y^2}$$

$$\Rightarrow \quad \frac{1}{p} = \frac{1}{p} + \frac{1}{p}\log y - \frac{y\log y}{p^2}\frac{dp}{dy} - \frac{1}{y}\frac{dp}{dy} + \frac{p}{y^2}$$

$$\Rightarrow \quad \left(\frac{1}{p} - \frac{1}{p}\right) = \frac{1}{p}\log y - \frac{y\log y}{p^2}\frac{dp}{dy} - \frac{1}{y}\frac{dp}{dy} + \frac{p}{y^2}$$

$$\Rightarrow \quad 0 = \left(\frac{1}{p}\log y + \frac{p}{y^2}\right) - \left(\frac{y\log y}{p^2} + \frac{1}{y}\right)\frac{dp}{dy}$$

$$\Rightarrow \quad 0 = \left(\frac{1}{p}\log y + \frac{p}{y^2}\right) - \frac{y}{p}\left(\frac{1}{p}\log y + \frac{p}{y^2}\right)\frac{dp}{dy}$$

$$\Rightarrow \quad \left(1 - \frac{y}{p}\right)\frac{dp}{dy} = 0$$

$$\Rightarrow \quad \frac{dy}{y} - \frac{dp}{p} = 0$$

$$\text{or} \quad \frac{dy}{y} = \frac{dp}{p}$$

This on integration gives

$$\log y + \log c = \log p$$

$$\Rightarrow \quad cy = p$$

or

$$p = cy$$

putting for p in the equation (1), we get

$$y^2 \log y = xy^2 c + c^2 y^2 \qquad\qquad \text{or}$$

$$\log y = c(x + c)$$

which is general solution of given differential equation (1)

Example 3.29 : Solve $p^3 - 4xyp + 8y^2 = 0$

Solution : The given equation is $p^3 - 4xyp + 8y^2 = 0$ ...(1)

$$\therefore \quad 4xyp = p^3 + 8y^2$$

$$\therefore \quad x = \frac{p^2}{4y} + \frac{2y}{p}$$

$$\text{or} \quad x = \frac{2y}{p} + \frac{p^2}{4y}$$

which is solvable for x.

Differentiating this w.r.t. y, we get

$$\frac{dx}{dy} = \frac{2}{p} - \frac{2y}{p^2}\frac{dp}{dy} + \frac{p}{2y}\frac{dp}{dy} - \frac{p^2}{4y^2}$$

$$\Rightarrow \quad \frac{1}{p} - \frac{2}{p} = \left(-\frac{2y}{p^2} + \frac{p}{2y}\right)\frac{dp}{dy} - \frac{p^2}{4y^2}$$

$$\Rightarrow \quad \left(\frac{p^2}{4y^2} - \frac{1}{p}\right) = \frac{2y}{p}\left(\frac{p^2}{4y^2} - \frac{1}{p}\right)\frac{dp}{dy}$$

$$\Rightarrow \quad 1 = \frac{2y}{p}\frac{dp}{dy}$$

$$\Rightarrow \quad \frac{dy}{y} = \frac{2\,dp}{p} = 0$$

Thus on integration gives

$$\log y + \log c = 2 \log p$$

$$\Rightarrow \qquad cy = p^2$$

or $\qquad p^2 = cy \ \text{ or } p = \sqrt{cy} = \sqrt{c} \ \sqrt{y}$

putting for p in the equation (1), we get

$$(cy) \sqrt{c} \ \sqrt{y} - 4xy \sqrt{c} \ \sqrt{y} + 8y^2 = 0$$

or $\qquad c^{3/2} y^{3/2} - 4x \ c^{1/2} \cdot y^{3/2} + 8y^2 = 0$

or $\qquad c^{3/2} - 4x \ c^{1/2} + 8y^{1/2} = 0$

$$\Rightarrow \qquad c^{1/2} \left(\frac{c}{4} - x \right) = -2y^{1/2}$$

or $\qquad \dfrac{1}{2} \ c^{1/2} \left(\dfrac{c}{4} - x \right) = -y^{1/2}$

squaring we get,

$$\frac{c}{4} \left(\frac{c}{4} - x \right)^2 = y$$

or $\qquad \dfrac{c}{4} \ \dfrac{(c - 4x)^2}{16} = y$

or $\qquad c \, (c - 4x)^2 = 64y$

which is general solution of given differential equation (1)

Example 3.30 : Solve $ayp^2 + (2x - b)p - y = 0$

Solution : The given equation is $ayp^2 + (2x - b)p - y = 0$ $\qquad$ ... (1)

$\therefore \qquad ayp^2 + 2xp - bp - y = 0$

$\therefore \qquad 2xp = y + bp - ayp^2$

or $\qquad 2x = \dfrac{y}{p} + b - ayp$

which is solvable for x.

Differentiating this w. r. t. y, we get

$$2 \frac{dx}{dy} = \frac{1}{p} - \frac{y}{p^2} \frac{dp}{dy} - ap - ay \frac{dp}{dy}$$

$$\Rightarrow \qquad \frac{2}{p} - \frac{1}{p} + ap = - \left(\frac{y}{p^2} + ay \right) \frac{dp}{dy}$$

$$\Rightarrow \qquad \left(\frac{1}{p} + ap \right) = - \frac{y}{p} \left(\frac{1}{p} + ap \right) \frac{dp}{dy}$$

$$\Rightarrow \qquad 1 = - \frac{y}{p} \frac{dp}{dy}$$

$$\Rightarrow \qquad \frac{dy}{y} + \frac{dp}{p} = 0$$

This on integration gives

$$\log y + \log p = \log c$$

$$\Rightarrow \qquad py = c$$

or

$$p = \frac{c}{y}$$

Putting for p in the equation (1), we get

$$ay\,\frac{c^2}{y^2} + (2x - b)\frac{c}{y} - y = 0$$

or

$$ac^2 + (2x - b)\,c - y^2 = 0$$

which is general solution of given differential equation (1)

Example 3.31 : Solve $yp^2 - 2xp + y = 0$

Solution : The given equation is $yp^2 - 2xp + y = 0$ ... (1)

$$\therefore \qquad 2px = y + yp^2$$

$$\therefore \qquad 2x = \frac{y}{p} + yp$$

which is solvable for x.

$\therefore$ Differentiating this w.r.t. y, we get

$$2\,\frac{dx}{dy} = \frac{1}{p} - \frac{y}{p^2}\frac{dp}{dy} + p + y\frac{dp}{dy}$$

$$\Rightarrow \qquad \frac{2}{p} - \frac{1}{p} = -\frac{y}{p^2}\frac{dp}{dy} + p + y\frac{dp}{dy}$$

$$\Rightarrow \qquad \frac{1}{p} - p = \left(-\frac{y}{p^2} + y\right)\frac{dp}{dy}$$

$$\Rightarrow \qquad \left(\frac{1}{p} - p\right) = -\frac{y}{p}\left(\frac{1}{p} - p\right)\frac{dp}{dy}$$

$$\Rightarrow \qquad 1 = -\frac{y}{p}\frac{dp}{dy}$$

$$\Rightarrow \qquad \frac{dy}{y} + \frac{dp}{p} = 0$$

Thus on integration gives

$$\log y + \log p = \log c$$

$$\Rightarrow \qquad py = c$$

or

$$p = \frac{c}{y}$$

putting for p in the equation (1), we get

$$y\,\frac{c^2}{y^2} - 2\frac{c}{y}\,x + y = 0$$

or

$$c^2 - 2cx + y^2 = 0$$

or

$$y^2 = 2\,cx - c^2$$

which is general solution of given differential equation (1)

EXERCISE 3.3

Solve the following differential Equations :

1. $x - yp = ap^2$
2. $y + px = x^4 p^2$
3. $y = p^2 x + p^4$
4. $x^2 + p^2 x = yp.$
5. $y - 2px = y^2 p^3$
6. $p^3 - xy^4 p - y^5 = 0$
7. $y = 2px + yp^2$
8. $y = 3px + 6p^2 y^2$
9. $x + py = p^3$

ANSWERS 3.3

1. $x = \dfrac{p}{\sqrt{1 - p^2}} (a \sin^{-1} p + c), \ y = \dfrac{1}{\sqrt{1 - p^2}} (a \sin^{-1} p + c) - ap.$

2. $xy = -c + c^2 x.$

3. $x = \dfrac{1}{(1 - p)^2} \left(\dfrac{4}{3} p^3 - p^4 + c \right)$ and the given relation.

4. $x = \left[-\dfrac{1}{3} p^2 + c\sqrt{p} \right], \ y = \dfrac{\left(c\sqrt{p - \dfrac{1}{3} p^2} \right)^2}{p} + p \left(c\sqrt{p - \dfrac{1}{3} p^2} \right).$

5. $y^3 = 2cx + c^3.$

6. $xy = c^2 y - \dfrac{1}{c}.$

7. $y^2 = 2cx + c^2.$

8. $y^2 = 3yc + 3c^2.$

9. $x = \dfrac{p}{1 + p^2} \tan^{-1} p + c_1 \ \ y = \dfrac{p}{1 + p^2} + c.$

MULTIPLE CHOICE QUESTIONS

Select the Correct alternative for the following :

1. The solution of p. $(p - 1) = 0$ is ....
    (a) $(y - c)(y + x + c) = 0$ (b) $(y - c)(y + x - c) = 0$
    (c) $(y - c)(y - x - c) = 0$ (d) $(y + c)(x + c) = 0$

2. The solution of differential equation $p^2 - 3p - 10 = 0$ is
    ....
    (a) $(y + 2x - c)(y + 5x - c) = 0$
    (b) $(y + 2x + c)(5x + x + c) = 0$
    (c) $(y - 2x - c)(y + 5x - c) = 0$
    (d) $(y + 2x - c)(y - 5x - c) = 0$

3. The solution of p. $(p + 5) = 0$ is ....
    (a) $(y + c)(5x + c) = 0$ (b) $(y - c)(y - 5x - c) = 0$
    (c) $(y - c)(y + 5x - c) = 0$ (d) $(y - c)(y + 5x + c) = 0$

4. The solution of $p^2 + 3p - 10 = 0$ is ....
    (a) $(y + 2x - c)(y + 5x - c) = 0$
    (b) $(y - 2x - c)(y + 5x - c) = 0$
    (c) $(y - 2x - c)(y + 5x - c) = 0$
    (d) $(y + 2x + c)(5y + x + c) = 0$

5. The solution of differential equation $p^2 - 6p + 8 = 0$ is
    ....
    (a) $(y + 4x - c)(y + 2x - c) = 0$
    (b) $(y + 4x - c)(y - 2x - c) = 0$
    (c) $(y - 4x - c)(y - 2x - c) = 0$
    (d) $(y - 4x - c)(y + 2x - c) = 0$

6. The differential equation $p^3 - xyp + 2y^2 = 0$ is of the type
    ....
    (a) Solvable for x   (b) Solvable for p
    (c) Solvable for y   (d) Solvable for x and y

7. The differential equation $p^4 - 2xyp + 8x^2 = 0$ is of the type
    ....
    (a) Solvable for x   (b) Solvable for p
    (c) Solvable for y   (d) Solvable for x and y

ANSWERS

1.	(c)	2.	(d)	3.	(c)	4.	(b)	5.	(c)
6.	(a)	7.	(c)						

✳ ✳ ✳

CLAIRAUT'S EQUATION

4.1 CLAIRAUT'S FORM

If the equation of the type $f(x, y, p) = 0$ is of first degree in x and y, then it being solvable for x, and for y. However, there is one particular form of these equations of the first degree in x and y that is of special importance, namely $y = px + f(p)$, which is known as Clairaut's equation.

Definition : An equation of the form $y = px + f(p)$, where $p = \dfrac{dy}{dx}$ and $f(p)$ is a function of p is known as Clairaut's equation.

4.2 METHOD OF SOLUTION

To solve the Clairaut's equation $y = px + f(p)$ ... (1)

Differentiating equation (1) w.r.t. x, we get

$$\frac{dy}{dx} = p + x\frac{dp}{dx} + f'(p).\frac{dp}{dx}$$

Denoting $\dfrac{dy}{dx} = p$, we get

$$\therefore \qquad p = p + x\frac{dp}{dx} + f'(p).\frac{dp}{dx}$$

$$\therefore \qquad x\frac{dp}{dx} + f'(p).\frac{dp}{dx} = 0$$

$$\therefore \qquad \{x + f'(p)\}\frac{dp}{dx} = 0$$

$$\therefore \qquad \{x + f'(p)\} = 0 \text{ or } \frac{dp}{dx} = 0$$

Rejection factor $x + f'(p) = 0$, since it does not contain $\dfrac{dp}{dx}$ we have

$$\therefore \qquad \frac{dp}{dx} = 0$$

These equation on Integration gives

$$p = c \qquad \qquad \dots (2)$$

Eliminating p between (1) and (2), we get the required general solution of the given differential equation (1) as

$$y = cx + f(c)$$

Note : (1) The general solution of Clairaut's equation $y = px + f(p)$ is obtained by replacing p by c, where c is arbitrary constant.

(2) If we eliminate p between $x + f'(p) = 0$ and the equation $y = px + f(p)$, we get another solution which does not contain any arbitrary constant and is called singular solution.

SOLVED EXAMPLES

Example 4.1 : Solve $(y - px)^2 = a^2 (1 + p^2)$.   (Nov. 2012; April 2013)

Solution : The given equation is $(y - px)^2 = a^2 (1 + p^2)$ $\dots (1)$

$$\therefore \qquad (y - px)^2 = 1 + a^2 p^2$$

$$\therefore \qquad y - px = \pm\sqrt{1 + a^2 p^2}$$

$$\therefore \qquad y = px \pm \sqrt{1 + a^2 p^2} \qquad \dots (2)$$

(2) is a Clairaut's equation. Hence its solution is

$$y = cx \pm \sqrt{1 + a^2 c^2}, \text{ where c is an arbitrary constant of}$$

integration.

$$\Rightarrow \qquad y - cx = \pm\sqrt{1 + a^2 c^2}$$

$$\Rightarrow \qquad (y - cx)^2 = 1 + a^2 c^2$$

or $\qquad (y - cx)^2 = a^2 (1 + c^2)$

Example 4.2 : Solve $xp^2 - yp + 2 = 0$

Solution : The given equation is $xp^2 - yp + 2 = 0$ $\dots (1)$

$$\therefore \qquad yp = xp^2 + 2$$

$$\therefore \qquad y = xp + \frac{2}{p} \qquad \dots (2)$$

(2) is a Clairaut's equation. Hence its solution is

$$y = xc + \frac{2}{c}, \text{ where c is an arbitrary}$$

constant of integration.

$$\Rightarrow \qquad yc = xc^2 + 2$$

$$\Rightarrow \qquad xc^2 - yc + 2 = 0$$

Example 4.3 : Solve $(x - a) p^2 + (x - y) p - y = 0$

Solution : The given equation is $(x - a) p^2 + (x - y) p - y = 0$ ... (1)

$\therefore \qquad p^2 x - ap^2 + xp - yp - y = 0$

$\therefore \qquad p^2 x + xp - yp - y - ap^2 = 0$

$\therefore \qquad p x (p + 1) - y (p + 1) - ap^2 = 0$

$\therefore \qquad y (p + 1) = p x (p + 1) - ap^2$

$\Rightarrow \qquad y = px - \dfrac{ap^2}{p + 1}$ ... (2)

(2) is a Clairaut's equation. Hence its solution is

$y = cx - \dfrac{ac^2}{c + 1}$, where c is an arbitrary constant of integration

---

Example 4.4 : Solve $\sin (px - y) = p$.

Solution : The given equation is $\sin (px - y) = p$ ... (1)

$\therefore \qquad px - y = \sin^{-1} p$

$\therefore \qquad y = px - \sin^{-1} p$ ... (2)

(2) is a Clairaut's equation. Hence its solution is

$y = cx - \sin^{-1} c$, where c is an arbitrary constant of integration.

$\Rightarrow \qquad cx - y = \sin^{-1} c$

$\Rightarrow \qquad \sin (cx - y) = c$

Example 4.5 : Solve $\dfrac{(y - px)^2}{(1 + p^2)} = a^2$

Solution : The given equation is $\dfrac{(y - px)^2}{(1 + p^2)} = a^2$ ... (1)

$\therefore \qquad (y - px)^2 = (1 + p^2) a^2$

$\therefore \qquad y - px = \left(\sqrt{1 + p^2}\right) a$

$\therefore \qquad y = px + \left(\sqrt{1 + p^2}\right) a$ ... (2)

(2) is a Clairaut's equation. Hence its solution is

$y = cx + \left(\sqrt{1 + c^2}\right) a$, where c is an arbitrary constant of integration.

$\Rightarrow \qquad y - px = \left(\sqrt{1 + c^2}\right) a$

$\Rightarrow \qquad (y - px)^2 = (1 + c^2) a^2$

$\Rightarrow \qquad \dfrac{(y - cx)^2}{(1 + c^2)} = a^2$

Example 4.6 : Solve $y^2 + x^2 \left(\dfrac{dy}{dx}\right)^2 - 2xy\dfrac{dy}{dx} = 4\left(\dfrac{dx}{dy}\right)^2$

Solution : The given equation can be written as

$$y^2 + x^2 p^2 - 2xy\,p \;=\; \dfrac{4}{p^2}$$

where, $p = \dfrac{dy}{dx}$

$\therefore$ $$(y - px)^2 \;=\; \dfrac{4}{p^2}$$

$\therefore$ $$y \;=\; px \pm \dfrac{2}{p} \qquad\qquad \ldots (2)$$

(2) is a Clairaut's equation. Hence its solution is

$$y \;=\; cx \pm \dfrac{2}{c}, \text{ where } c \text{ is an arbitrary}$$

constant of integration.

or $$(y - cx)^2 \;=\; \dfrac{4}{c^2}$$

Example 4.7 : Solve $p^2 x = py - 1$

Solution : The given equation is $p^2 x = py - 1$ $\qquad\qquad \ldots (1)$

$\therefore$ $$py \;=\; p^2 x + 1$$

$\therefore$ $$y \;=\; px + \dfrac{1}{p} \qquad\qquad \ldots (2)$$

(2) is a Clairaut's equation. Hence its solution is

$$Y = cx + \dfrac{1}{c}, \text{ where } c \text{ is an arbitrary constant of integration.}$$

$\Rightarrow$ $$yc \;=\; c^2 x + 1$$

$\Rightarrow$ $$c^2 x \;=\; cy - 1$$

Example 4.8 : Solve $\sin px.\cos y = \cos px.\sin y + p$

Solution : The given equation is $\sin px.\cos y = \cos px.\sin y + p$ $\ldots (1)$

$\therefore$ $$\sin px.\cos y - \cos px.\sin y \;=\; p$$

$\therefore$ $$\sin(px - y) \;=\; p$$

$$px - y \;=\; \sin^{-1} p$$

$\therefore$ $$y \;=\; px - \sin^{-1} p \qquad\qquad \ldots (2)$$

(2) is a Clairaut's equation. Hence its solution is

$$y = cx - \sin^{-1} c, \text{ where } c \text{ is an arbitrary constant of integration.}$$

Example 4.9 : Solve $(y - px)^2 = a^2 p^2 + b^2$

Solution : The given equation is $(y - px)^2 = a^2 p^2 + b^2$ ... (1)

$\therefore \qquad\qquad\qquad y - px = \pm\sqrt{a^2 p^2 + b^2}$

$\therefore \qquad\qquad\qquad\qquad y = px \pm \sqrt{a^2 p^2 + b^2}$ ... (2)

(2) is a Clairaut's equation. Hence its solution is

$\qquad y = cx \pm \sqrt{a^2 c^2 + b^2}$, where c is an arbitrary constant of integration.

$\Rightarrow \qquad\qquad\qquad y - cx = \pm\sqrt{a^2 c^2 + b^2}$

$\Rightarrow \qquad\qquad\qquad (y - cx)^2 = a^2 c^2 + b^2$

Example 4.10 : Solve $y - 1 = p(x + p)$.

Solution : The given equation is $y - 1 = p(x + p)$ ... (1)

$\therefore \qquad\qquad\qquad y - 1 = px + p^2$

$\therefore \qquad\qquad\qquad\quad y = px + (1 + p)$ ... (2)

(2) is a Clairaut's equation. Hence it's solution is

$\qquad y = cx + (1 + c)$, where c is an arbitrary constant of integration.

or $\qquad\qquad\qquad y - 1 = cx + c^2$

or $\qquad\qquad\qquad y - 1 = c(x + c)$

Example 4.11 : Solve $p = \log(px - y)$.   (Oct. 2011)

Solution : The given equation is $p = \log(px - y)$ ... (1)

$\therefore \qquad\qquad\qquad e^p = px - y$

$\therefore \qquad\qquad\qquad\quad y = px - e^p$ ... (2)

(2) is a Clairaut's equation. Hence its solution is

$\qquad y = cx - e^c$, where c is an arbitrary constant of integration.

or $\qquad\qquad\qquad cx - y = e^c$

or $\qquad\qquad\qquad\quad c = \log(cx - y)$.

$$\boxed{\textbf{EXERCISE 4.1}}$$

Solve

1. $x - yp = ap^2$
2. $y + px = x^4 p^2$
3. $y = p^2 x + p^4$
4. $x^2 + p^2 x = yp.$
5. $y - 2px = y^2 p^3$
6. $y^2 - 2pxy = m^2 + (1 - x^2) p^2.$

7. $\tan^{-1} p (1 + p + p^2) = p (y - px)$.

8. $p (y - px) = a$.

9. $y = x \dfrac{dy}{dx} + \left(\dfrac{dy}{dx}\right)^2$.

10. $p = \log (px - y)$.

11. $xp^3 - (y + 3) p^2 + 4 = 0$.

$$\boxed{\textbf{ANSWERS 4.1}}$$

1. $x = \dfrac{p}{\sqrt{1 - p^2}} (a \sin^{-1} p + c),\ y = \dfrac{1}{\sqrt{1 - p^2}} (a \sin^{-1} p + c) - ap$.

2. $xy = - c + c^2 x$

3. $x = \dfrac{1}{(1 - p)^2} \left(\dfrac{4}{3} p^3 - p^4 + c\right)$ and the given relation.

4. $x = \left[-\dfrac{1}{3} p^2 + c\sqrt{p}\right],\ y = \dfrac{\left(c\sqrt{p - \dfrac{1}{3} p^2}\right)^2}{p} + p\left(c\sqrt{p - \dfrac{1}{3} p^2}\right)$.

5. $y^3 = 2cx + c^3$

6. $y^2 - 2cxy = m^2 + (1 - x^2) c^2$.

7. $y = cx + \tan^{-1}\left(\dfrac{1}{c} + 1 + c\right)$.

8. $y = cx + \dfrac{a}{c}$.

9. $y = xc + c^2$.

10. $y = cx - e^c$.

11. $y = cx + \dfrac{4}{c^2} - 3$.

4.3   EQUATIONS REDUCIBLE TO CLAIRAUT'S FORM

Sometimes the given equation is not in the Clairaut's form but can be reduced to the Clairaut's form by proper substitution (by change of variables in a suitable manner).

There is no general method of deciding about the proper substitution in certain problem.

SOLVED EXAMPLES

Example 4.12 : Solve $(px - y) (x - py) = p$.   (April 2013)

Solution : The given equation is $(px - y) (x - py) = p$ ... (1)

Put $x^2 = u$ and $y^2 = v$

∴ 2x dx = du and   2y dy = dv

⇒ $$\frac{dy}{dx} = \frac{x}{y}\frac{dv}{du}$$

or $p = \dfrac{x}{y}\,P,$ where, $p = \dfrac{dy}{dx}$ and $P = \dfrac{dv}{du}$

∴ The given equation (1) reduces to

$$\left(\frac{x}{y}px - y\right)\left(x - \frac{x}{y}Py\right) = \frac{x}{y}P$$

⇒ $$(x^2 P - y^2)(x - px)\frac{1}{y} = \frac{x}{y}P$$

or $$(x^2 P - y^2)(1 - p)\frac{x}{y} = \frac{x}{y}P$$

or $$(x^2 P - y^2)(1 - p) = P$$

or $$(x^2 P - y^2) = \frac{P}{1-P}$$

⇒ $$(u P - v) = \frac{P}{1-P}$$

or $v = u\,P - \dfrac{P}{1-P}$, which is in Clairaut's form and its solution

is

$$v = uc - \frac{c}{1-c}$$

∴ The solution of given equation (1) is $y^2 = cx^2 - \dfrac{c}{1-c}$

Example 4.13 : Solve $(y - p.x).\,x^2 = p^2 y$.   **(April 2012)**

Solution : The given equation is $(y - p.x)).\,x^2 = p^2 y$ ... (1)

Put $x^2 = u$ and $y^2 = v$

∴ 2x dx = du and   2y dy = dv

⇒ $$\frac{dy}{dx} = \frac{x}{y}\frac{dv}{du}$$

or $p = \dfrac{x}{y}\,P,$ where, $p = \dfrac{dy}{dx}$ and $P = \dfrac{dv}{du}$

∴ The given equation (1) reduces to

$$\left(y - \frac{x}{y}P.\,x\right).\,x^2 = \frac{x^2}{y^2}P^2 y$$

or $$(y^2 - x^2.\,P) = P^2$$

or $$y^2 = x^2 . P + P^2$$

$\therefore$ $v = up + P^2$, which is in Clairaut's form and its solution is

$$v = u c + c^2$$

$\therefore$ The solution of given equation (1) is $y^2 = c.x^2 + c^2$.

Example 4.14 : Solve xy (y − px) = x + py.   (Nov. 2012)

Solution : The given equation is $xy (y - px) = x + py$ ... (1)

Put $x^2 = u$ and $y^2 = v$

$\therefore$ $2x\, dx = du$ and $2y\, dy = dv$

$\Rightarrow$ $\dfrac{dy}{dx} = \dfrac{x}{y} \dfrac{dv}{du}$

or $p = \dfrac{x}{y} P,$ where, $p = \dfrac{dy}{dx}$ and $P = \dfrac{dv}{du}$

$\therefore$ The given equation (1) reduces to

$$xy \left(y - \frac{x}{y} P. x \right) = x + \frac{x}{y} P y$$

or $x (y^2 - x^2 . P) = x (1 + P)$

or $(y^2 - x^2 . P) = (1 + P)$

or $y^2 = x^2 . P + (1 + P)$

$\therefore$ $v = uP + (1 + P)$, which is in Clairaut's form and its solution is

$v = u c + (1 + c)$

$\therefore$ The solution of given equation (1) is $y^2 = c . x^2 + (1 + c)$

Example 4.15 : Solve y = 2px + y² p³.

Solution : The given equation is $y = 2px + y^2 p^3$ ... (1)

Put $y^2 = v$

$\therefore$ $2y\dfrac{dy}{dx} = \dfrac{dv}{dx}$

$\Rightarrow$ $\dfrac{dy}{dx} = \dfrac{1}{2y} \dfrac{dv}{dx}$

or $p = \dfrac{1}{2y} P,$ where, $p = \dfrac{dy}{dx}$ and $P = \dfrac{dv}{dx}$

$\therefore$ The given equation (1) reduces to

$$y = 2\frac{1}{2y} P x + y^2 \left(\frac{1}{2y} P \right)^3 P$$

$\Rightarrow$ $y = \dfrac{1}{y} P x + y^2 \dfrac{P^3}{8y^3}$ or $y = \dfrac{1}{y} P x + \dfrac{P^3}{8y}$

$$\Rightarrow \qquad y^2 = Px + \frac{P^3}{8}$$

or $\qquad v = Px + \frac{P^3}{8}$, which is in Clairaut's form

and its solution is

$$v = cx + \frac{c^3}{8}$$

$\therefore$ The solution of given equation (1) is $y^2 = cx + \frac{c^3}{8}$

Example 4.16 : Solve $4yp^2 + 2xp - y = 0$.

Solution : The given equation is $4yp^2 + 2xp - y = 0$ ... (1)

$$\text{Put } y^2 = v$$

$\therefore \qquad 2y \dfrac{dy}{dx} = \dfrac{dv}{dx}$

$\Rightarrow \qquad \dfrac{dy}{dx} = \dfrac{1}{2y}\dfrac{dv}{dx}$

or $\qquad p = \dfrac{1}{2y}P,$ where, $p = \dfrac{dy}{dx}$ and $P = \dfrac{dv}{dx}$

$\therefore$ The given equation (1) reduces to

$$4y\left(\frac{1}{2y}P\right)^2 + 2x\frac{1}{2y}P - y = 0$$

$\Rightarrow \qquad 4y\dfrac{P^2}{4y^2} + x\dfrac{1}{y}P - y = 0$ or, $\dfrac{P^2}{y} + \dfrac{1}{y}px - y = 0$

$\Rightarrow \qquad y^2 = Px + P^2$

or $\qquad v = Px + P^2$, which is in Clairaut's form and its solution is

$\qquad\qquad v = cx + c^2$

$\therefore$ The solution of given equation (1) is $y^2 = cx + c^2$

Example 4.17 : Solve $(px - y)(x - py) = 2p$.

Solution : The given equation is $(px - y)(x - py) = 2p$ ... (1)

$$\text{Put } x^2 = u \text{ and } y^2 = v$$

$\therefore \qquad 2x\,dx = du \text{ and } 2y\,dy = dv$

$\Rightarrow \qquad \dfrac{dy}{dx} = \dfrac{x}{y}\dfrac{dv}{du}$

or $\qquad p = \dfrac{x}{y}P,$ where $p = \dfrac{dy}{dx}$ and $P = \dfrac{dv}{du}$

$\therefore$ The given equation (1) reduces to

$$\left(\frac{x}{y}Px - y\right)\left(x - \frac{x}{y}Py\right) = 2\frac{x}{y}P$$

$\Rightarrow$ $\qquad$ $(x^2 P - y^2)(x - px)\dfrac{1}{y} = 2\dfrac{x}{y} P$

or $\qquad$ $(x^2 P - y^2)(1 - p)\dfrac{x}{y} = 2\dfrac{x}{y} P$

or $\qquad$ $(x^2 P - y^2)(1 - p) = 2P$

or $\qquad$ $(x^2 P - y^2) = \dfrac{2P}{1 - P}$

$\Rightarrow$ $\qquad$ $(u P - v) = \dfrac{2P}{1 - P}$

or $\quad$ $v = u P - \dfrac{2P}{1 - P}$, which is in Clairaut's form and its solution is

$\qquad v = uc - \dfrac{2c}{1 - c}$

$\therefore$ The solution of given equation (1) is $y^2 = c\,x^2 - \dfrac{2c}{1 - c}$

Example 4.18 : Solve axyp^2 + (x^2 – ay^2 – b) p – xy = 0 $\qquad$ ... (1)

$\qquad$ Put $x^2 = u$ and $y^2 = v$

$\therefore$ $\qquad$ $2x\,dx = du$ and $2y\,dy = dv$

$\Rightarrow$ $\qquad$ $\dfrac{dy}{dx} = \dfrac{x}{y}\dfrac{dv}{du}$

or $\quad p = \dfrac{x}{y} P,$ $\qquad\qquad$ where, $p = \dfrac{dy}{dx}$ and $P = \dfrac{dv}{du}$

$\therefore$ The given equation (1) reduces to

$\qquad axy\left(\dfrac{x}{y}P\right)^2 + (x^2 - ay^2 - b)\dfrac{x}{y} P - xy = 0$

$\Rightarrow$ $\qquad a\dfrac{x^3}{y} P^2 + (x^2 - ay^2 - b)\dfrac{x}{y} P - xy = 0$

$\Rightarrow$ $\qquad a\,x^2 P^2 + (x^2 - ay^2 - b) P - y^2 = 0$

$\Rightarrow$ $\qquad a\,u\,P^2 + (u - av - b) P - v = 0$

or $\qquad au\,P^2 + uP - avP - bP - v = 0$

$\therefore$ $\qquad (1 + aP)v = (aP + 1)uP - bP$

$\Rightarrow$ $v = uP - \dfrac{bP}{1 + aP}$, which is in Clairaut's form and its solution is

$\qquad v = uc - \dfrac{bc}{1 + ac}$

$\therefore$ The solution of given equation (1) is $y^2 = cx^2 - \dfrac{bc}{1 + ac}$

Example 4.19 : Solve $(y + p.x)^2 = x^2p$.

Solution : The given equation is $(y + p.x)^2 = x^2p$ ... (1)

$$\text{Put } xy = v$$

$\therefore \qquad\qquad y + x\dfrac{dy}{dx} = \dfrac{dv}{dx}$

$\Rightarrow \qquad\qquad y + xp = P, \qquad \text{where } p = \dfrac{dy}{dx} \text{ and } P = \dfrac{dv}{dx}$

$\therefore$ The given equation (1) reduces to

$$P^2 = x^2p \text{ or } P^2 = x.x.p$$

or $\qquad\qquad P^2 = x\,(P - y) \qquad\qquad \because y + xp = P$

or $\qquad\qquad P^2 = Px - xy$

or $\qquad\qquad P^2 = Px - v$

$\therefore \qquad\qquad v = Px - P^2$, which is in Clairaut's form

and its solution is

$$v = c\,x - c^2$$

$\therefore$ The solution of given equation (1) is $xy = cx - c^2$

Example 4.20 : Solve $y^2\,(y - p \cdot x) = x^4p^2$ by using substitution $\dfrac{1}{x}$ $= u, \dfrac{1}{y} = v$.

Solution : The given equation is $y^2\,(y - p.x) = x^4\,p^2$.

$\therefore \qquad\qquad (y^3 - p.x\,y^2) = x^4\,p^2$

Dividing the given equation by y^4, we get

$$\dfrac{1}{y} - \dfrac{px}{y^2} = \dfrac{x^4\,p^2}{y^4}$$

$\Rightarrow \qquad\qquad \dfrac{1}{y} = \dfrac{px}{y^2} + \dfrac{x^4\,p^2}{y^4}$

or $\qquad\qquad \dfrac{1}{y} = \dfrac{1}{x} \cdot \dfrac{px^2}{y^2} + \left(\dfrac{x^2\,p}{y}\right)^2 \qquad$ ... (1)

Put $\qquad\qquad \dfrac{1}{x} = u \text{ and } \dfrac{1}{y} = v$

$\therefore \qquad\qquad \dfrac{-1}{x^2}\,dx = du \text{ and } \dfrac{-1}{y^2}\,dy = dv$

$\Rightarrow \qquad\qquad \dfrac{dv}{du} = \dfrac{x^2}{y^2}\dfrac{dy}{dx}$

$\Rightarrow \qquad\qquad P = \dfrac{x^2}{y^2}\,p, \qquad \text{where, } p = \dfrac{dy}{dx} \text{ and } P = \dfrac{dv}{du}$

∴ The equation (1) reduces to

$v = u P + P^2$, which is in Clairaut's form and its solution is

$v = uc + c^2$

∴ The solution of given equation is $\dfrac{1}{y} = \dfrac{1}{x} c + c^2$

Or $c^2xy + cy - x = 0$.

Example 4.21 : Solve $(px^2 + y^2)(px + y) = (p + 1)^2$ by using substitution $x + y = u$, $xy = v$.

Solution : The given equation is $(px^2 + y^2)(px + y) = (p + 1)^2$

Now $px^2 + y^2 = (Px + y)(x + y) - xy(p + 1)$

∴ The given equation can be re-written as

$$[(Px + y)(x + y) - xy(p + 1)](px + y) = (p + 1)^2$$

$$\Rightarrow \quad [(Px + y)^2(x + y) - xy(px + y)(p + 1)] = (p + 1)^2$$

$$\Rightarrow \quad \frac{[(Px + y)^2(x + y) - xy(px + y)(p + 1)]}{(p + 1)^2} = 1$$

$$\Rightarrow \quad \left[\frac{(Px + y)}{(p + 1)}\right]^2 (x + y) - xy\frac{(Px + y)}{(p + 1)} = 1 \qquad \dots (1)$$

Put $x + y = u$ and $xy = v$

∴ $\qquad 1 + \dfrac{dy}{dx} = \dfrac{du}{dx}$ and $y + x\dfrac{dy}{dx} = \dfrac{dv}{dx}$

$$\Rightarrow \qquad \frac{dv}{du} = \frac{y + x\dfrac{dy}{dx}}{1 + \dfrac{dy}{dx}}$$

$$\Rightarrow \qquad P = \frac{y + xp}{1 + p}, \quad \text{where } p = \frac{dy}{dx} \text{ and } P = \frac{dv}{du}$$

∴ The equation (1) reduces to

$$P^2u - vP = 1$$

or $\qquad v = Pu - \dfrac{1}{p}$, which is in Clairaut's form

and its solution is

$$v = cu - \frac{1}{c}$$

∴ The solution of given equation is $xy = c(x + y) - \dfrac{1}{c}$

or $c^2(x + y) - cxy - 1 = 0$.

Example 4.22 : Solve $xp^2 - 2yp + x + 2y = 0$ by using substitution $y - x = v, x^2 = u.$

Solution : The given equation is $xp^2 - 2yp + x + 2y = 0$ ... (1)

Put $y - x = v$ and $x^2 = u$

$\therefore \qquad \dfrac{dy}{dx} - 1 = \dfrac{dv}{dx}$ and $2x = \dfrac{du}{dx}$

$\Rightarrow \qquad \dfrac{dv}{du} = \dfrac{\dfrac{dy}{dx} - 1}{2x}$

$\Rightarrow \qquad P = \dfrac{p-1}{2x}$, where, $p = \dfrac{dy}{dx}$ and $P = \dfrac{dv}{du}$

$\Rightarrow \qquad p = 2x. + 1$

$\therefore$ The equation (1) reduces to

$\qquad x(2x.\,P + 1)^2 - 2y(2x.\,P + 1) + x + 2y = 0$

$\Rightarrow \qquad 4x^3 P^2 + 4x^2 P + x - 4xy\,P - 2y + x + 2y = 0$

$\Rightarrow \qquad 4x^3 P^2 + 4x^2 P - 4xy\,P + 2x = 0$

$\Rightarrow \qquad 4x^2 P^2 + 4xP - 4yP + 2 = 0$

$\Rightarrow \qquad 4x^2 P^2 + 4P(x - y) + 2 = 0$

$\Rightarrow \qquad 4u.P^2 + 4P(-v) + 2 = 0$

$\Rightarrow \qquad 4u.P^2 - 4P.v + 2 = 0$

$\Rightarrow \qquad v = uP + \dfrac{1}{2P}$, which is in Clairaut's form and its solution is

$\qquad v = uc + \dfrac{1}{2c}$

$\therefore$ The solution of given equation is $(y - x) = x^2 c + \dfrac{1}{2c}$

or $\qquad\qquad 2c(y - x) = 2x^2 c^2 + 1$

or $\qquad 2x^2 c^2 - 2c(y - x) + 1 = 0$

$$\boxed{\textbf{EXERCISE 4.2}}$$

Solve

1. $(px - y)(py + x) = h^2 p.$
2. $xyp^2 - (x^2 - y^2 - 1)p + xy = 0.$
3. $y = px + \dfrac{p}{x}.$
4. $xy(y - px) = x + py.$

5. $x^2 (y - px) = p^2 y.$

6. Using the transformation $x^2 = u$ and $y^2 = v$, solve the equation $(y - px) x^2 = p^2 y.$

7. Using the transformation $x^2 = u$ and $y^2 = v$, solve the equation $xy (y - px) = x + py.$

8. Using the transformation $x^2 = u$ and $y^2 = v$, solve the equation $(x - py) (px - y) = 2p.$

9. Using the transformation $x^2 + y^2 = v$ and $x + y = u$, solve the equation $(x^2 + y^2) (1 + p)^2 - 2 (x + y) (1 + p) (x + y p).$

10. Using the transformation $y = u$ and $x \cdot y = v$, solve the equation $x^2 p^2 + y (2x + y) p + y^2 = 0.$

11. Using the transformation $y - x = v$ and $x^2 = u$, solve the equation $x^2 p^2 - 2yp + x + 2y = 0.$

$$\boxed{\textbf{ANSWERS}}$$

1. $y^2 = cx^2 - \dfrac{c}{c + 1} h^2.$ (Use $u = x^2$, $v = y^2$)

2. $y^2 = cx^2 - \dfrac{c}{c - 1}.$ (Use $u = x^2$, $v = y^2$)

3. $y^2 = cx^3 + c.$ (Use $u = x^2$, $v = y^2$)

4. $y^2 = cx^2 + (1 + c).$ (Use $u = x^2$, $v = y^2$)

5. $y^2 = cx^2 + c^2.$ (Use $u = x^2$, $v = y^2$)

6. $y^2 = cx^2 + c^2.$

7. $y^2 = cx^2 + (1 + c).$

8. $y^2 = cx^2 - \dfrac{2c}{1 - c}$

9. $x^2 + y^2 = c (x + y) - \dfrac{1}{4} c^2.$

10. $xy = cy + c^2.$

11. $2c^2 x^2 - 2c (y - x) + 1 = 0.$

4.4 SPECIAL FORMS REDUCIBLE TO CLAIRAUT'S FORM

We consider three special forms of the differential equations which can be reduced to then Clairaut's form by standard substitutions.

(I) The Form : $y = 2px + f(p^2 x)$

If the equation is of the form $y = 2px + f(p^2 x)$, then to reduce it in Clairaut's form, we put

$x = u^2$ and $y = v$, we get $dx = 2u \, du$, $dy = dv$

$\therefore \qquad\qquad\qquad\qquad \dfrac{dy}{dx} = \dfrac{dv}{2udu}$

$\Rightarrow \qquad\qquad\qquad\qquad p = \dfrac{P}{2u}, \qquad$ where $p = \dfrac{dy}{dx}$ and $P = \dfrac{dv}{du}$

The given equation then reduces to

$$y = \dfrac{2Px}{2u} + f\left(\dfrac{P^2 x}{4u^2}\right)$$

$\therefore \qquad\qquad\qquad\qquad v = \dfrac{2Pu^2}{2u} + f\left(\dfrac{P^2 u^2}{4u^2}\right)$

Thus $\qquad\qquad\qquad\qquad v = uP + f\left(\dfrac{P^2}{4}\right)$

Which is in Clairaut's form. Its solution is $v = cu + f\left(\dfrac{c^2}{4}\right)$

i.e. $\qquad\qquad\qquad\qquad y = c\sqrt{x} + f\left(\dfrac{c^2}{4}\right)$

SOLVED EXAMPLES

Example 4.23 : Solve $y = 2px + \sin^{-1}(p^2 x)$.

Solution : The given equation is $y = 2px + \sin^{-1}(p^2 x)$ $\qquad$ ... (1)

It is of the form $y = 2px + f(p^2 x)$

$\therefore \qquad\qquad$ Put $x = u^2 \qquad$ and $\qquad\qquad\qquad y = v$

$\therefore \qquad\qquad\qquad dx = 2u.du \qquad$ and $\qquad\qquad dy = dv$

$\Rightarrow \qquad\qquad\qquad \dfrac{dy}{dx} = \dfrac{1}{2u}\dfrac{dv}{du}$

or $\qquad\qquad\qquad p = \dfrac{1}{2u}P, \qquad$ where, $p = \dfrac{dy}{dx}$ and $P = \dfrac{dv}{du}$

$\therefore$ The given equation (1) reduces to

$$v = 2\dfrac{1}{2u}Pu^2 + \sin^{-1}\left(\dfrac{1}{4u^2}P^2 u^2\right)$$

$\Rightarrow \qquad\qquad\qquad v = Pu + \sin^{-1}\left(\dfrac{1}{4}P^2\right),$

which is in Clairaut's form and its solution is

$$v = cu + \sin^{-1}\left(\dfrac{1}{4}c^2\right)$$

$\therefore$ The solution of given equation (1) is $y = c\sqrt{x} + \sin^{-1}\left(\dfrac{1}{4}c^2\right)$

Example 4.24 : Solve y − 2px + p² x = 0.

Solution : The given equation is $y - 2px + p^2x = 0$ ... (1)

$$\therefore \qquad y = 2px - p^2x$$

It is of the form $y = 2px + f(p^2x)$

$\therefore$ Put $x = u^2$ and $y = v$

$\therefore$ $dx = 2u.du$ and $dy = dv$

$\Rightarrow$ $\dfrac{dy}{dx} = \dfrac{1}{2u}\dfrac{dv}{du}$

or $p = \dfrac{1}{2u}P,$ where $p = \dfrac{dy}{dx}$ and $P = \dfrac{dv}{du}$

$\therefore$ The given equation (1) reduces to

$$v = 2\frac{1}{2u}\,P\,u^2 - \frac{1}{4u^2}\,P^2\,u^2$$

$\Rightarrow$ $v = P\,u - \dfrac{1}{4}\,P^2$, which is in Clairaut's form and its solution is

$$v = c\,u - \frac{1}{4}\,c^2$$

$\therefore$ The solution of given equation (1) is $y = c\sqrt{x} - \dfrac{1}{4}\,c^2$

Example 4.25 : Solve y − 2px + log (p²x) = 0.

Solution : The given equation is $y - 2px + \log(p^2x) = 0$ ... (1)

$$\therefore \qquad y = 2px - \log(p^2\,x)$$

It is of the form $y = 2px + f(p^2x)$

$\therefore$ Put $x = u^2$ and $y = v$

$\therefore$ $dx = 2u.du$ and $dy = dv$

$\Rightarrow$ $\dfrac{dy}{dx} = \dfrac{1}{2u}\dfrac{dv}{du}$

or $p = \dfrac{1}{2u}P,$ where, $p = \dfrac{dy}{dx}$ and $P = \dfrac{dv}{du}$

$\therefore$ The given equation (1) reduces to

$$v = 2\frac{1}{2u}\,P\,u^2 - \log\left(\frac{1}{4u^2}P^2\,u^2\right)$$

$\Rightarrow$ $v = P\,u - \log\left(\dfrac{1}{4}P^2\right),$

which is in Clairaut's form and its solution is

$$v = cu - \log\left(\frac{1}{4}c^2\right)$$

∴ The solution of given equation (1) is $y = c\sqrt{x} - \log\left(\frac{1}{4}c^2\right)$

Example 4.26 : Solve $y = 2px - \tan(p^2 x)$.

Solution : The given equation is $y = 2px - \tan(p^2 x)$ ... (1)

It is of the form $y = 2px + f(p^2 x)$

∴ Put $x = u^2$ and $y = v$

∴ $dx = 2u.\,du$ and $dy = dv$

$$\Rightarrow \frac{dy}{dx} = \frac{1}{2u}\frac{dv}{du}$$

or $p = \frac{1}{2u}P,$ where, $p = \frac{dy}{dx}$ and $P = \frac{dv}{du}$

∴ The given equation (1) reduces to

$$v = 2\frac{1}{2u}Pu^2 - \tan\left(\frac{1}{4u^2}P^2 u^2\right)$$

$\Rightarrow v = Pu - \tan\left(\frac{1}{4}P^2\right)$, which is in Clairaut's form and its solution is

$$v = cu - \tan\left(\frac{1}{4}c^2\right)$$

∴ The solution of given equation (1) is $y = c\sqrt{x} - \log\left(\frac{1}{4}c^2\right)$

Example 4.27 : Solve $y - 2px + 1 = 0$.

Solution : The given equation is $y - 2px + 1 = 0$ ... (1)

∴ $y = 2px - 1$

It is of the form $y = 2px + f(p^2 x)$

∴ Put $x = u^2$ and $y = v$

∴ $dx = 2u.du$ and $dy = dv$

$$\Rightarrow \frac{dy}{dx} = \frac{1}{2u}\frac{dv}{du}$$

or $p = \frac{1}{2u}P,$ where, $p = \frac{dy}{dx}$ and $P = \frac{dv}{du}$

∴ The given equation (1) reduces to

$$v = 2\frac{1}{2u} P u^2 - 1$$

⇒ $v = P u - 1$, which is in Clairaut's form and its solution is

$$v = c u - 1$$

∴ The solution of given equation (1) is $y = c\sqrt{x} - 1$

(II) The Form : $y^2 = pxy + f\left(\dfrac{p\,y}{x}\right)$

If given equation is of the form $y^2 = pxy + f\left(\dfrac{py}{x}\right)$, then to reduce it in, clairaut's form

we put $x^2 = u$ and $y^2 = v$, we get $2x\,dx = du$, $2y\,dy = dv$

∴ $$\frac{dy}{dx} = \frac{x\,dv}{y\,du}$$

⇒ $p = \dfrac{x}{y} P$,   where, $p = \dfrac{dy}{dx}$ and $P = \dfrac{dv}{du}$

The given equation then reduces to

$$y^2 = \frac{x}{y} P xy + f\left(\frac{x\,Py}{yx}\right)$$

$$y^2 = x^2 P + f(P)$$

Thus $v = uP + f(P)$

Which is in Clairaut's form. Its solution is $v = cu + f(c)$

i.e. $y = c x^2 + f(c)$

SOLVED EXAMPLES

Example 4.28 : Solve $y^2 - pxy + \dfrac{py}{x} = 0$.

Solution : The given equation is $y^2 - pxy + \dfrac{py}{x} = 0$ ... (1)

∴ $$y^2 = pxy - \frac{py}{x}$$

It is of the form $y^2 = pxy + f\left(\dfrac{p\,y}{x}\right)$

∴   Put $x^2 = u$ and $y^2 = v$, we get $2x\,dx = du$, $2y\,dy = dv$

∴ $$\frac{dy}{dx} = \frac{x\,dv}{y\,du}$$

⇒ $$p = \frac{x}{y}\,P, \quad \text{where, } p = \frac{dy}{dx} \text{ and } P = \frac{dv}{du}$$

∴   The given equation (1) reduces to

$$v = \frac{x}{y}\,P\,xy - \frac{x}{y}\,P\frac{y}{x}$$

⇒ $$v = P\,x^2 - P$$

⇒ $v = P\,u - P$, which is in Clairaut's form and its

solution is

∴ $$v = cu - c$$

∴   The solution of given equation (1) is $y^2 = c\,x^2 - c$

Example 4.29 : Solve $y^2 - pxy - \dfrac{p^2\,y^2}{x^2} = 0.$

Solution : The given equation is $y^2 - pxy - \dfrac{p^2\,y^2}{x^2} = 0$ ... (1)

∴ $$y^2 = pxy + \frac{p^{2z}y^2}{x^2}$$

It is of the form $y^2 = pxy + f\left(\dfrac{p\,y}{x}\right)$

∴   Put $x^2 = u$ and $y^2 = v$, we get $2x\,dx = du$, $2y\,dy = dv$

∴ $$\frac{dy}{dx} = \frac{x\,dv}{y\,du}$$

⇒ $$p = \frac{x}{y}\,P, \quad \text{where, } p = \frac{dy}{dx} \text{ and } P = \frac{dv}{du}$$

∴   The given equation (1) reduces to

$$v = \frac{x}{y}\,P\,xy + \frac{x^2}{y^2}\,P^2\frac{v}{u}$$

⇒ $$v = P\,x^2 + \frac{u}{v}\,P^2\frac{v}{u}$$

⇒ $v = P\,u + P^2$, which is in Clairaut's form and its

solution is

$$v = cu + c^2$$

∴   The solution of given equation (1) is $y^2 = c\,x^2 + c^2$

Example 4.30 : Solve xy (y − px) − x − py = 0.

Solution : The given equation is $x y (y - px) - x - py = 0$ ... (1)

$\therefore \qquad xy^2 - x^2 py - x - py = 0$

$\therefore \qquad y^2 = pxy + (1 + \dfrac{py}{x})$

It is of the form $\quad y^2 = pxy + f\left(\dfrac{p\,y}{x}\right)$

$\therefore$ Put $x^2 = u$ and $y^2 = v$, we get $2x\,dx = du$, $2y\,dy = dv$

$\therefore \qquad \dfrac{dy}{dx} = \dfrac{x\,dv}{y\,du}$

$\Rightarrow \qquad p = \dfrac{x}{y}\,P,$ where, $p = \dfrac{dy}{dx}$ and $P = \dfrac{dv}{du}$

$\therefore$ The given equation (1) reduces to

$$v = \dfrac{x}{y}\,P\,xy + \left(1 + \dfrac{x}{y}\,P\,\dfrac{y}{x}\right)$$

$\Rightarrow \qquad v = P\,x^2 + (1 + P)$

$\Rightarrow \qquad v = P\,u + (1 + P)$, which is in Clairaut's form and its solution is

$$v = cu + (1 + c)$$

$\therefore$ The solution of given equation (1) is $y^2 = cx^2 + (1 + c)$

Example 4.31 : Solve $x^2 y^2 - px^3 y + p^2 y^2 = 0$.

Solution : The given equation is $x^2 y^2 - px^3 y + p^2 y^2 = 0$ ... (1)

$\therefore \qquad y^2 - pxy + \dfrac{p^2 y^2}{x^2} = 0$

$\therefore \qquad y^2 = pxy - \dfrac{p^2 y^2}{x^2}$

It is of the form $y^2 = pxy + f\left(\dfrac{p\,y}{x}\right)$

$\therefore$ Put $x^2 = u$ and $y^2 = v$, we get $2x\,dx = du$, $2y\,dy = dv$

$\therefore \qquad \dfrac{dy}{dx} = \dfrac{x\,dv}{y\,du}$

$\Rightarrow \qquad p = \dfrac{x}{y}\,P,$ where $p = \dfrac{dy}{dx}$ and $P = \dfrac{dv}{du}$

$\therefore$ The given equation (1) reduces to

$$v = \dfrac{x}{y}\,P\,xy - \dfrac{x^2}{y^2}\,P^2\,\dfrac{v}{u}$$

$\Rightarrow \qquad v = P\,x^2 - \dfrac{u}{v}\,P^2\,\dfrac{v}{u}$

$\Rightarrow$ $\qquad\qquad\qquad$ v $=$ P u $-$ P², which is in Clairaut's form and its solution is

$$v = cu - c^2$$

$\therefore$ $\quad$ The solution of given equation (1) is $y^2 = c\,x^2 - c^2$

(III)   The Form : $e^{by}\,(a - bp) = f\,(pe^{by\,-\,ax})$

If given equation is of the form $e^{by}\,(a - bp) = f\,(pe^{by\,-\,ax})$, then to reduce it in Clairaut's form, we put

Putting $e^{ax} = u$ and $e^{by} = v$, we get $ae^{ax}\,dx = du,\ be^{by}\,dy = dv$

$\therefore$ $\qquad\qquad\qquad$ $\dfrac{dy}{dx} = \dfrac{a.e^{ax}}{b.e^{by}}\dfrac{dv}{du}$

$\Rightarrow$ $\qquad$ $p = \dfrac{a.e^{ax}}{b.e^{by}}\,P$ or $p = \dfrac{a.u}{b.v}\,P$, where $p = \dfrac{dy}{dx}$ and $P = \dfrac{dv}{du}$

The given equation then reduces to

$$v\left(a - b\dfrac{a.u}{b.v}\,P\right) = f\left(\dfrac{a.u}{b.v}\,P\dfrac{v}{u}\right)$$

$\Rightarrow$ $\qquad\qquad$ $(av - auP) = f\left(\dfrac{a}{b}P\right)$

$\Rightarrow$ $\qquad\qquad\qquad$ $av = auP + f\left(\dfrac{a}{b}P\right)$

Thus $\qquad\qquad\qquad\qquad$ $v = uP + \dfrac{1}{a}\,f\left(\dfrac{a}{b}P\right)$

Which is in Clairaut's form. Its solution is $v = cu + \dfrac{1}{a}\,f\left(\dfrac{a}{b}\cdot c\right)$

i.e. $\qquad\qquad\qquad\qquad$ $e^{by} = c\,e^{ax} + \dfrac{1}{a}\,f\left(\dfrac{a}{b}\cdot c\right)$

SOLVED EXAMPLES

Example 4.32 : Solve $e^{3x}\,(p - 1) + p^3\,e^{2y} = 0$.

Solution : The given equation is $e^{3x}\,(p - 1) + p^3\,e^{2y} = 0$ $\qquad$ ... (1)

$$e^{3x}\,(p - 1) = -p^3\,e^{2y}$$

It is of the form $e^{by}\,(a - bp) = f\,(pe^{by-ax})$

$\therefore$ $\quad$ Put $e^x = u$ and $e^y = v$, we get $e^x\,dx = du,\ e^y\,dy = dv$

$\therefore$ $\qquad\qquad\qquad$ $\dfrac{dy}{dx} = \dfrac{e^x}{e^y}\dfrac{dv}{du}$

$\Rightarrow$ $\ p = \dfrac{e^x}{e^y}\,P$ or $p = \dfrac{u}{v}\,P,$ $\qquad\qquad$ where, $p = \dfrac{dy}{dx}$ and $P = \dfrac{dv}{du}$

$\therefore$ $\quad$ The given equation (1) reduces to

$$u^3 \left(\frac{u}{v} P - 1\right) + \frac{u^3}{v^3} P^3 \cdot v^2 = 0$$

$\Rightarrow \qquad\qquad uP - v + P^3 = 0$

$\Rightarrow \qquad v = uP + P^3$, which is in Clairaut's form and its solution is

$\qquad\qquad v = uc + c^3$

$\therefore$ The solution of given equation (1) is $e^y = e^x c + c^3$

Example 4.33 : Solve $p^3 e^{2y} + (e^{2x} + e^{3x}) p - e^{3x} = 0$.

Solution : The given equation is $p^3 e^{2y} + (e^{2x} + e^{3x}) p - e^{3x} = 0$ ... (1)

$\therefore \qquad\qquad p^3 e^{2y} + pe^{2x} + p e^{3x} - e^{3x} = 0$

$\therefore \qquad\qquad e^{3x} (p - 1) + p^3 e^{2y} + p e^{2x} = 0$

$\therefore \qquad e^y (p - 1) + p^3 e^{3y - 3x} + p e^{y - x} = 0$

$\therefore \qquad\qquad\qquad e^y (p - 1) = - p^3 e^{3y - 3x} - p e^{y - x} = 0$

It is of the form $e^{by} (a - bp) = f (pe^{by - ax})$

$\therefore$ Put $e^x = u$ and $e^y = v$, we get $e^x dx = du$, $e^y dy = dv$

$\therefore \qquad\qquad\qquad \dfrac{dy}{dx} = \dfrac{e^{ax}}{e^{by}} \dfrac{dv}{du}$

$\Rightarrow \; p = \dfrac{e^{ax}}{e^{by}} P$ or $p = \dfrac{u}{v} P$, where, $p = \dfrac{dy}{dx}$ and $P = \dfrac{dv}{du}$

$\therefore$ The given equation (1) reduces to $p^3 e^{2y} + (e^{2x} + e^{3x}) p - e^{3x} = 0$

$$v^2 \frac{u^3}{v^3} P^3 + u^2 \frac{u}{v} P + u^3 \frac{u}{v} P - u^3 = 0$$

$\Rightarrow \qquad\qquad \dfrac{u^3}{v} P^3 + \dfrac{u^3}{v} P + \dfrac{u^4}{v} P - u^3 = 0$

$\Rightarrow \qquad\qquad P^3 + P + Pu - v = 0$

$\Rightarrow \; v = uP + P + P^3$, which is in Clairaut's form and its solution is

$\qquad v = uc + c + c^3$

$\therefore$ The solution of given equation (1) is $e^y = e^x c + c + c^3$

Example 4.34 : Solve $e^{4x} (p - 1) + e^{2y} p^2 = 0$.

Solution : The given equation is $e^{4x} (p - 1) + e^{2y} p^2 = 0$ ... (1)

$$e^{4x} (p - 1) = - p^2 e^{2y}$$

It is of the form $e^{by} (a - bp) = f (pe^{by - ax})$

$\therefore$ Put $e^{2x} = u$ and $e^{2y} = v$, we get $2e^x dx = du$, $2e^y dy = dv$

$\therefore \qquad\qquad \dfrac{dy}{dx} = \dfrac{e^{2x}}{e^{2y}} \dfrac{dv}{du}$

$\Rightarrow \; p = \dfrac{e^{2x}}{e^{2y}} P$ or $p = \dfrac{u}{v} P$, where $p = \dfrac{dy}{dx}$ and $P = \dfrac{dv}{du}$

∴   The given equation (1) reduces to

$$u^2 \left(\frac{u}{v}P - 1\right) + \frac{u^2}{v^2} P^2 . v = 0$$

⇒ $uP - v + P^2 = 0$

⇒ $v = uP + P^2$, which is in Clairaut's form and its solution is

        $v = uc + c^2$

∴   The solution of given equation (1) is $e^{2y} = e^{2x} c + c^2$

Theory Questions :

1. Define Clairaut's equation and obtain its general solution.
2. Show how to solve the differential equation $y = px + f(p)$, where, $p = \frac{dy}{dx}$.

MULTIPLE CHOICE QUESTIONS

Select the Correct alternative for the following :

1. The solution of the differential equation $\sin^{-1}(y - px) = p$ is
    ....
    (a) $y = cx - \sin c$ (b) $y = cx + \sin c$
    (c) $y = cx + \sin^{-1} c$ (d) $y = cx - \sin^{-1} c$

2. The solution of $(y - px)(p - 1) = p$ is ....
    (a) $y = cx - \dfrac{c}{c + 1}$ (b) $y = cx + \dfrac{c}{c + 1}$
    (c) $y = cx + (c - 1)$ (d) $y = cx + c.(c - 1)$

3. The solution of $\sin(y - px) = p$ is ....
    (a) $y = \sin c - cx$ (b) $y = cx - \sin c$
    (c) $y = cx - \sin^{-1} c$ (d) $y = cx + \sin^{-1} c$

4. The solution of $\log(px - y) = p$ is ....
    (a) $y = cx + \log c$ (b) $y = cx + e^c$
    (c) $y = cx - e^c$ (d) $p = \log(x - y)$

5. The solution of $\cos^{-1}(px - y) = p$ is ....
    (a) $y = \cos c - cx$ (b) $y = cx - \cos^{-1} c$
    (c) $y = cx - \cos c$ (d) $y = cx + \cos^{-1} c$

6. The solution of $\tan(px - y) = p$ is ....
    (a) $y = cx + \tan^{-1} c$ (b) $y = cx + \tan c$
    (c) $y = cx - \tan^{-1} c$ (d) $y = \tan^{-1} c - xc$

7. General solution of differential equation $y = xp + p$ is
....

(a) $y = cx + c$

(b) $y = x + c$

(c) $y = x + 2$

(d) $y = cx + 2$

8. The solution of the differential equation $(y - px)(p + 2) = p$ is
....

(a) $y = px + \dfrac{c}{c + 2}$

(b) $y = cx + \dfrac{c}{c + 2}$

(c) $y = cx - \dfrac{c}{c + 2}$

(d) $y = cx + c.(c + 2)$

9. If $y = px + e^p$, then its solution is ....

(a) $y = cx + e^p$

(b) $y = cx + p^c$

(c) $y = cx + e^c$

(d) $y = cx + c^p$

10. The solution of the differential equation $(y - px)(p + 1) = p$ is
....

(a) $y = px + \dfrac{p}{p + 1}$

(b) $y = px - \dfrac{c}{c + 1}$

(c) $y = cx + \dfrac{p}{p + 1}$

(d) $y = cx + \dfrac{c}{c + 1}$

11. The solution of $y = px + \log p$ is $y = $ ....

(a) $cx + e^c$

(b) $y = cx + x^2$

(c) $y = cx + \log c$

(d) $y = cx + e^x$

12. The solution of $y = px - \sin^{-1} p$ is ....

(a) $x = cy - \sin^{-1} c$

(b) $y = cx - \sin^{-1} c$

(c) $y = px - \sin^{-1} c$

(d) none of these

13. General solution of the differential equation $\sqrt{y - px} = p$ is
....

(a) $y = cx + c$

(b) $y = cx - c^2$

(c) $y = cx + 1$

(d) $y = cx + c^2$

14. General solution of the differential equation $(y - px)^{\frac{1}{3}} = p$ is
....

(a) $y = cx + c^3$

(b) $y = cx - c^3$

(c) $y = cx + c$

(d) $y = cx + c^2$

15. The differential equation of the form $y = 2px + f(p^2x)$ can be reduced to Clairaut's form by using standard substitution ....

　(a) $x = u^2$ and $y = v^2$　　　　(b) $x = u^2$ and $y = v$

　(c) $x = u$ and $y = v^2$　　　　(d) none of these

16. The differential equation of the form $y^2 = pxy + f\left(\dfrac{p\,y}{x}\right)$ can be reduced to Clairaut's form by using standard substitution ....

　(a) $x^2 = u$ and $y^2 = v$　　　　(b) $x = u$ and $y^2 = v$

　(c) $x^2 = u$ and $y = v$　　　　(d) none of these

17. The differential equation of the form $e^{by}(a - bp) = f(pe^{by - ax})$ can be reduced to Clairaut's form by using standard substitution ....

　(a) $e^{ax} = u^2$ and $e^{by} = v$

　(b) $e^{ax} = u$ and $e^{by} = v^2$

　(c) $e^{ax} = u$ and $e^{by} = v$

　(d) $e^{ax} = u^2$ and $e^{by} = v^2$

ANSWERS

1.	(b)	2.	(b)	3.	(c)	4.	(c)	5.	(c)
6.	(c)	7.	(a)	8.	(b)	9.	(c)	10.	(d)
11.	(c)	12.	(b)	13.	(d)	14.	(a)	15.	(b)
16.	(a)	17.	(c)						

✳ ✳ ✳

MODEL QUESTION PAPER

B. Sc. (Part - I) (Semester - II) Examination
MATHEMATICS (Paper - IV)

Time : 2 Hours   Total Marks: 50

Instructions :
1. All questions are compulsory.
2. Figures to the right indicate full marks.

1. Select the correct alternative for each of the following and rewrite the statement. **(10)**

(i) The degree of the differential equation is

$$\left(\frac{d^2y}{dx^2}\right)^5 + \left(\frac{dy}{dx}\right)^7 + x^3 y = 0 \text{ is } _____.$$

    (a) 7   (b) 5   (c) 2   (d) 3

(ii) In the differential equation $Mdx + Ndy = 0$, if $\frac{1}{N}\left(\frac{\partial M}{\partial y} - \frac{\partial N}{\partial x}\right)$ is a function of x alone then I. F. = _____.

    (a) $\frac{1}{Mx + Ny}$, provided $Mdx + Ndy \neq 0$

    (b) $\frac{1}{Mx - Ny}$, provided $Mdx - Ndy \neq 0$

    (c) $e^{\int f(y)\, dy}$

    (d) $e^{\int f(x)\, dx}$

(iii) The solution of the differential equation $\frac{ydx - xdy}{y^2} = 0$ is _____.

    (a) $\frac{y}{x} = c$ (b) $\frac{x - y}{y} = c$

    (c) $xy = c$ (d) $\frac{x}{y} = c$

(iv) If the auxiliary equation has a root $a \pm ib$, repeated thrice then the part of solution reference to these roots will be _____.
    (a) $e^{ax}[(c_1 + c_2x + c_3x^2)\cos bx + (c_4 + c_5x + c_6x^2)\sin bx]$,
    (b) $e^{ax}[(c_1 + c_2x)\cos bx + (c_3 + c_4x)\sin bx]$,
    (c) $e^{bx}[(c_1 + c_2x + c_3x^2)\cos ax + (c_4 + c_5x + c_6x^2)\sin ax]$,
    (d) $e^{ax}[(c_1\cos ax + c_2\sin ax)]$

(v) $\dfrac{1}{D^2 + 4} \sin x = $ _____.

(a) $\dfrac{-x}{3} \sin x$

(b) $\dfrac{x}{3} \cos x$

(c) $\dfrac{x}{3} \sin x$

(d) $\dfrac{x}{5} \sin x$

(vi) The complete solution of differential equation

$(D^2 - 5D + 6) y = 0$ is _____.

(a) $y = c_1 e^{3x} + c_2 e^{-2x}$

(b) $y = c_1 e^{3x} + c_2 e^{2x}$

(c) $y = c_1 e^{-3x} + c_2 e^{-2x}$

(d) none of these

(vii) The differential equation of the form $y^2 = pxy + f\left(\dfrac{p\,y}{x}\right)$ can be reduced to Clairaut's form by using standard substitution _____.

(a) $x^2 = u$ and $y^2 = v$

(b) $x = u$ and $y^2 = v$

(c) $x^2 = u$ and $y = v$

(d) none of these

(viii) The solution of $\cos^{-1}(px - y) = p$ is _____.

(a) $y = \cos c - cx$

(b) $y = cx - \cos^{-1} c$

(c) $y = cx - \cos c$

(d) $y = cx + \cos^{-1} c$

(ix) $\dfrac{1}{f(D)} xV = $ _____.

(a) $\left\{ x - \dfrac{1}{f(D)} \cdot f'(D) \right\} \cdot \dfrac{1}{f(D)} V$

(b) $\left\{ x + \dfrac{1}{f(D)} \cdot f'(D) \right\} \cdot \dfrac{1}{f(D)} V$

(c) $\left\{ V - \dfrac{1}{f(D)} \cdot f'(D) \right\} \cdot \dfrac{1}{f(D)} x$

(d) none of these

(x) The solution of differential equation $p^2 - 6p + 8 = 0$ is _____.

(a) $(y + 4x - c)(y + 2x - c) = 0$

(b) $(y + 4x - c)(y - 2x - c) = 0$

(c) $(y - 4x - c)(y - 2x - c) = 0$

(d) $(y - 4x - c)(y + 2x - c) = 0$

2. Attempt any two of the following :   20

(i) Define Bernoulli 's equation and explain the method of solving it. Hence solve

$$\frac{dy}{dx} + xy = x^2 y^3.$$

(ii) If $D \equiv \frac{d}{dx}$ and f(D) is a polynomial in D with constant coefficients, then show that $\frac{1}{f(D^2)} \cos x = \frac{1}{f(-a^2)} \cos x$, if $f(-a^2) \neq 0$. Hence solve $(D^2 - D - 2) y = \cos 3x$.

(iii) If $f(D) y = X$, where $X = e^{ax} V$ and V is a function of x, then prove that $\frac{1}{f(D)} e^{ax} V = e^{ax} \frac{1}{f(D + a)} V$ and hence solve $(D^2 - 4D + 4) y = e^{2x} \sin 2x$.

3. Attempt any four of the following :   20

(i) Solve : $\frac{dy}{dx} + \frac{y}{x} = \frac{y^2}{x^2}$.

(ii) Using the transformation $x^2 = u$ and $y^2 = v$, solve the equation $(x - py)(px - y) = 2p$.

(iii) Solve : $(x^2 - 2xy - y^2) dx = (x^2 + y^2) dy$.

(iv) Define Clairaut's equation and explain the method of solving it.

(v) Solve $\frac{d^2 y}{dx^2} + \frac{dy}{dx} - 2y = x + \sin x$.

(vi) Solve : $\frac{d^2 y}{dx^2} + 4\frac{dy}{dx} + 4y = 2 \cosh 2x$.

www.ingramcontent.com/pod-product-compliance
Lightning Source LLC
Chambersburg PA
CBHW080012040726
47505CB00016B/2221